Praise for CHILDREN OF APOLLO

"…Haviaras handles it all with smooth skill. The world of third-century Rome—both the city and its African outposts—is colorfully vivid here, and Haviaras manages to invest even his secondary and tertiary characters with believable, three-dimensional humanity." *Historic Novel Society*

"Well written historical drama with an eye for detail... I can't wait for the next book… Killing the Hydra. There is so much more misery and mischief to puzzle and vex our worthy Metellus." *Epinions*

"… a very entertaining read; Haviaras has both a fluid writing style, and a good eye for historical detail, and explores in far more detail the faith of the average Roman than do most authors." *Goodreads*

"Historical fiction at its best! … if you like your historical fiction to be an education as well as a fun read, this is the book for you!" *Amazon reader*

"An outstanding and compelling novel!" *Amazon reader*

Join the Legions!

Sign-up for the Eagles and Dragons Publishing
Newsletter and get a FREE BOOK today.

Subscribers get first access to new releases, special
offers, and much more.

Go to:
www.eaglesanddragonspublishing.com

For Angelina,

My inspiration in all things.

Για την Αγγελίνα.

Έμπνευσή μου σε όλα τα πράγματα.

CHILDREN
OF
APOLLO

EAGLES AND DRAGONS

BOOK I

ADAM ALEXANDER HAVIARAS

PROLOGUS

202 B.C.

She was like a weathered sack of bones, possessed bones. The seeress rocked back and forth, inhaling the pungent smoke of the fire. Her body creaked and a childlike whining emanated from deep within her throat.

What am I doing here? the Roman thought as he knelt uncomfortably on the other side of the flames. *I'm a soldier, a man of reason.*

The woman was Punic, of Carthage. His first thought was to have her flogged out of camp but he could not, not after seeing the look in her eyes when she clutched his forearm with her gnarled fingers.

"The Gods send me to you with a message," she had whispered. "You *must* hear it!"

Reason or not, Punic or not, he could not afford to offend the Gods.

"Come inside," he remembered saying before she shuffled past his personal guard. And now he sat there, dizzy with smoke on the morning of battle, audience to the ramblings of a decrepit hag.

The wind on the plain was up. It lashed the tent walls, pulled the roof skyward. There was a loud bang, not like thunder or angry gales, but like a distant call or announcement. The Roman clutched his knees, tried to hold back the bile that rose up in his throat.

Pieces of papyrus flew about the tent, a lamp fell over and went out in the sand. The fire was suddenly still. The crone threw her head back as if slapped, gurgled some words in a tongue he did not know. Her eyes rolled and she nodded. The Roman looked around but they were alone. He felt cold, began to sweat where the hair on the back of his neck stood on end.

The seeress collapsed and the flames began to move again. The Roman got to his feet and moved to her side. She was breathing. He nudged her gently.

"Woman. Are you all right?" He tried not to let his fear or disgust show.

The bones suddenly jerked to life and her arms clawed at his, pulling him down as she crawled up, something out of the underworld. She was strong.

"I have words…I have words…" Her voice was raspish, her breath fowl. But, he had to listen. It was as though someone were pushing him downward to her, from behind. "It will be a mark of greatness in your line."

"What will?" His voice shuddered, fear beginning to show as his courage waned. "My line is already great." He tried to sound defiant but she shook her head, her eyes now open.

"For blood and butchery, maybe. The God has given you this symbol of wisdom and strength. You are chosen to carry it."

"Which god? What symbol? I don't understand. Chosen for what? Tell me!" He held her tightly by the shoulders, bones lost in his grip.

Then, her appearance, her features, softened so that she resembled a kindly grandmother. She spoke soothingly to him.

"You are blessed, Metellus." She reached for the filthy satchel she had brought with her, rooted around inside. "I had a dream…" she muttered, "…in it…I saw this." She drew something out, something no larger than the palm of her wrinkled hand.

"What is it?" he asked.

She held it up to the firelight, turned it around reverently. It was a flat, clay image of a dragon.

"This is the symbol of your line to come." She handed it to him. He accepted it, still unsure as to the meaning. "It is a symbol of wisdom, of strength."

"Yes, you said that already," he responded, impatient.

She raised her arms as if to the heavenly stars. "He has honoured you with it."

"Who?"

"The God."

"Which one?"

"You will know when you are ready. He will come to you as he always comes to the chosen."

The Roman shuddered at the thought. "Visited by a god?" Out in the camp, horns roused the army.

"I must go," she said abruptly, packing up her things and standing.

"Wait! I have many questions."

"Men always do." She turned back to him. "They will be answered in time. For now, keep this symbol with you always." She closed his hand around it. "Pass it on to the worthiest of your line only."

"Why?"

She became impatient, as one does with a child who questions without end. "It is sacred, powerful, meant only for those strong enough to bear the burden." She paused, peered into his eyes one last time. "Remember. You fight for more than yourself this day at Zama, more than Rome's glory. I must go."

"Wait, I'll call you an escort out of camp…"

She was gone.

Part I

THE SANDS OF
AFRICA

A.D. 202

I

TRIBUNUS

'The Tribune'

It was a forgotten place, an ancient wasteland that must once have been privy to the great maw of battle between Gods and Titans. All was emptiness and heat, bleached bone and boredom. That such a place existed was beyond reason. In fact, it was beyond sanity itself that men would even cross the sandy seas, the desert.

Lucius Metellus Anguis sat atop his black stallion, a dusty hand shielding his eyes from the burning whiteness enveloping him and his men. He thought that he would be able to see more from the top of the dune, better observe the plodding troops as their column struggled up and down the shifting sand. They had lost the road, covered over the previous night by some god's howling breath. The Romans longed for that wind now, for some relief from the burning world. But it was not to be, for the heavenly orb beat down on them so that not even their sandalled feet were immune to the ashen earth.

The situation was desperate. The men were grumbling and, it seemed to their young officer, waiting for him to make a mistake. His recent promotion to the rank of Tribune had at first excited him; to be given command of four hundred and eighty men as well as a cavalry unit was a huge responsibility, a challenge he welcomed. His ancestors had commanded Rome's Legions, been conquerors of Crete, Numidia and Macedonia. Hundreds of years later, Lucius Metellus Anguis, descendant of the Equestrian class, now led a routine patrol to 'discourage nomad activity along the empire's southern frontier', from Alexandria in Aegyptus to the legionary base of Lambaesis in Numidia. Questions rang loud in his head. Was he capable of command? Could he live up to the expectations that weighed so heavily upon him? The Metelli were staring at him from across Death's black river, and he could feel their gaze.

Lucius looked down at the sleeves of his tunic where they protruded from beneath his leather and bronze cuirass; it was no longer soft and white, but torn and sweat-stained. The thin purple stripe around the hem, a sign of his rank and class, was faint and grimy. His body was caked with salt and sand, he could feel its coarseness everywhere under his clothing, taste it at the back of his throat. Lucius shifted in the saddle and felt his muscles complain. He swung a leg over the stallion's black neck and a scorpion skittered away from where his boots disturbed the flour-like sand. He removed his helmet, hung it on one of the four saddle horns and drank from a leather water skin, choked by the wetting of his parched throat. When he recovered, he poured some in the palm of his hand and held it up to the stallion.

"Here, Pegasus. It's not much but it'll do until we reach the oasis." The stallion lapped the liquid up quickly and nudged Lucius with his snout. "All right, here's some more." Lucius could not help smiling. His horse was in a better mood than any of the men. That was a problem. He pat the muscular neck as the last of the men passed below. "Time to go." Lucius swung up into the saddle. Several miles to the south, he could see a dust cloud running parallel to his cohort. He adjusted his crimson cloak, gladius and pugio. His eyes searched through the thick, scentless air. "They're following us," he muttered. Pegasus stomped a hoof in the sand and Lucius kicked him down the dune's steep slope to the front of the marching column.

The first time Lucius saw the desert he was in awe of its simplicity, its beauty. A man could think out in the emptiness, sort through the memories of his past. The senses were heightened too, especially one's hearing, though some said that in the desert, the keenest sense was one that was inexplicable.

Strange things happened among the dunes, beneath the sea-blue sky or on nights when the full moon cast its cool blanket over the land. However, as he rode beneath the fiery sun, Lucius could only think of arriving at the next oasis, of cool water and a campaign cot.

He turned in the saddle to see his men; they were exhausted. It was a dangerous time of day, when strength has been sucked from the limbs and minds wander. To be lulled into a false sense of security could get them killed. Lucius looked again to the south, the cloud was still shadowing them. He turned to his first centurion, Alerio Cornelius Kasen. The centurion nodded, having seen it too. Two weeks into a three-month, two-thousand mile patrol, and already they were being followed. But why were they not attacking? Lucius told himself that his men would be ready when it happened. If only they were on solid ground and not the giving sands of Cyrenaica Province.

When the oasis finally came into view, a wave of elation swept through the ranks of legionaries as though to wash away the day's misery. No matter that it was a mere scattering of trees or that they had yet to make a fortified camp; the sight of that still pool of water was enough reward, the shade that would be offered by the rustling palms, perfect. Lucius was relieved that the old maps he had been given at the outset of his assignment were correct about the location of each oasis thus far.

"Make camp!" Lucius ordered, his six centurions echoing the command to each of their units. A roar of approval went up and the favourite bawdy songs emerged from the men's mouths. They shifted heaps of sand and drove their wooden stakes to form the fortifications of their camp around planned avenues which the engineers had quickly laid out. It was routine, and within two hours the fortifications were set. The sand was not ideal terrain for a marching camp but it was essential, especially with their distant travelling companions.

Lucius finished tying off the last peg of his command tent at the centre of camp. The tanned leather was thin and needed stitching in places, but it was his. He unloaded the two chests from the pack horse that carried his things and placed them inside. The first room was for meeting with his officers and beyond that, behind a small partition, was his private area. The first thing he unpacked was always the small stone altar which he placed on a mound of packed sand next to his cot. Next to the altar, he placed a miniature statue of Apollo, his family's patron god for hundreds of years.

"Tribune?" The voice startled Lucius momentarily but he quickly recognized the hesitant manner of one of his centurions.

"Antanelis. How goes it?"

The young man saluted, then relaxed. "Just wanted to let you know that the sentries have been posted every ten paces and the cavalry auxiliaries sent out on patrol, as you ordered. The rest of the men are eating now."

"Good. They need the rest."

"I've also brushed down and fed Pegasus for you. He's just outside your tent."

"You know, Antanelis, you don't need to do that for me." One of the reasons Lucius did not have a slave with him, as was his right as a tribune, was because he did not want someone fussing over him all the time. He preferred to enjoy what few quiet moments he had for himself.

"I know. I just enjoy it...makes me feel normal." The scar across his forehead reddened and creased in thought as he looked down; it had healed well since Parthia. Lucius thought that if only he had been quicker to pull Antanelis out of the way of that Parthian battle axe, his face would still be youthful, flawless. On the other hand, his friend was alive, and scars suited soldiers, especially silent, tough ones like Antanelis. Ever since that day, the young man had gone out of his way to pay Lucius back for saving his life.

"You're right. We all need some measure of normalcy in our lives." Lucius looked at a small cedar box that contained his precious scrolls. "Those are what keep *me* sane." He put his hand on the centurion's shoulder. "Go. Get yourself something to eat. I want all six of you here in three hours."

"Yes, Tribune!" Antanelis saluted again before leaving.

When he was alone again and had eaten a small meal of dried meat, cheese and dates, Lucius took a piece of incense from a small pouch among his things and lit it on the altar. The camp was quieting down as men washed and drank and nodded into restful oblivion beneath a sleepy pink and orange sky.

Lucius set about his own ritual, removed his armour and weapons, brushed away the dust, polished them. With a folded piece of doeskin dipped in oil, he revived his breastplate, crimson-crested helmet and greaves, paying special attention to the images of embossed dragons on the chest and cheek guards.

"Anguis," he whispered the word in reverence, *dragon*. This armour was a Metellus family heirloom, his charge. The images upon it had haunted and mystified him from the day they were placed in his care. The name he bore, signifying his vague branch of the Metelli, had weighed on him from a young age when he and his tutor, Diodorus, had walked the streets of Rome in lesson, until now, in his twenty-fourth year, when battle-hardened veterans spoke the name with superstitious caution or avoided saying that part of his name altogether. By caring for this armour nightly, he was reminded of who he was, and it brought him a sense of pride but also dread.

When the treasured pieces were gleaming, he hung them on a wooden stand in the corner of his tent and began to sharpen and oil his gladius, pugio and spatha, the two former also having seen service in the hands of Metelli warriors. They never left his side.

A bowl of cool water and a sponge had been brought in for him. Lucius removed his tunic and breeches and began to wash the filth from his body. He hated the way he smelled, how his dark hair matted around his scalp, stiff and itchy. They were a long way from the baths of Alexandria.

Alexandria... He passed the sponge over the scars on his arm and memories flooded back, of pain. What was supposed to be a civilized polis had proved to be as barbaric and unendurable as the seediest Cilician port. Each scar on his body held a memory, but this was one he pushed away.

When he was clean and had donned a cleaner tunic over his pteruges, the armoured leather skirt that hung to just above his knees, Lucius knelt in the sand before the smoke-engulfed altar.

"Apollo, guide me..."

II

NOX IN DESERTIS

'Night in the Desert'

Lucius was at a stool in the meeting area of his tent, reading a scroll detailing Alexander the Great's campaigns in the East, when the first of the centurions arrived. He had put his breastplate back on for the meeting as well as his gladius and pugio. He stood tall to greet them, golden-eyed Alerio with his horizontally-crested centurion's helmet tucked neatly under his arm, solid Antanelis, and the dark, silent Maren.

"The others are on their way," Alerio offered.

"Good. Have some wine. It's the last of it until we can replenish our supplies in Cyrene."

Maren and Alerio helped themselves. Antanelis declined for the moment. The four of them then moved to face the leather map of the southern empire that hung loosely from the tent frame.

"Don't bother looking at that thing!" a voice cut into the tent from the entrance. It was Garai, followed by his twin brother, Eligius. "We just started this march. If we start looking at how far we have to go we'll just have to turn around and go back to Alexandria."

"Then you'll miss bathing in Cyrene." Lucius replied flatly, pointing to the wine and cups. "Eligius, best keep your brother close or else he'll end up back in the arms of that Alexandrian man he mistook for a woman."

"That wasn't my fault!" Garai cut back. Argus recommended that place." A chuckle went around the group.

"Of course I recommended it! Just for you, Garai." Argus filled the tent's entrance, the torches outside holding him in silhouette. Lucius poured a cup of wine and handed it to his boyhood friend.

"About time you arrived."

"Thanks. Knew you wouldn't start without me. Besides, I was laying a few lashes on one of my men for having a dull blade. Bastard was going to get himself killed if he fought with that thing. When he heals, he'll have the keenest edge around." Argus slapped Lucius on the back and sat on the stool next to the table.

Ever since Argus' parents had been killed and he had come to stay with the Metelli as one of their own, Lucius had always perceived him as gruff, unrefined and indignant of command. He was also tough as nails and a great asset in any battle. Even so, there were times when Lucius wished his adoptive brother had stayed in Rome all those years ago. He grew tired of worrying about Argus, weary of his jealousies. But, he had ever been there when needed and Lucius wanted to return the favour.

They had all risen through the ranks together and thanks to Lucius, the six others were made centurions when he was given permission to choose officers for his cohort. Each had his strengths and weaknesses but Lucius knew that they worked well together. What did not work well for them was their assignment; each questioned the validity of sending their force, young, tough and seasoned from battle on the plains of Parthia, on a simple patrol against a few desert nomads along a frontier that for all the war on the edges of the Roman Empire, was quiet. Whenever questioned about this matter, Lucius reiterated that Emperor Severus was making changes to the army, changes that were meant to strengthen Rome's Legions in the aftermath of the civil war. As a result, his cohort was being sent to joint up with the veteran III Augustan Legion, in Numidia.

As the wine was consumed, conversation deteriorated and the seven friends were soon bellowing with raucous laughter.

"All right, all right," Lucius interrupted another one of Garai's jokes. "Let's get down to business."

"You mean our friendly desert shadow?" Alerio asked.

"Yes." Lucius noticed the others nod in agreement, was pleased that the nomad force had not escaped any of them.

"What are we going to do about it, Lucius?" Argus demanded. "We were hunting those camel turd bastards for days and then all of a sudden, they're following us. We need to engage them!"

"Absolutely," Eligius chimed in. "Before they take us in the rear."

"I thought you liked it in the rear."

"Lucius is trying to tell us something, Argus." Antanelis stepped up, Argus faced him.

"Stop kissing his ass, Antanelis, or I'll slap you like a Babylonian whore."

Lucius jumped in quickly and pushed both men apart. They stepped back; Lucius was taller than both, stronger, but to break up a full-blown fight between them would be no easy thing. The desert was getting to everyone, he could tell.

"Enough!" The tribune pounded his fist on the table and the men fell silent. Argus stood staring, arms crossed. He hated when Lucius pulled rank. "Listen, all of you!" Alerio stood beside Lucius. "I agree we should engage them. But! There are at least a hundred of them on horse. We'll never catch them on foot. We have to make use of the cavalry auxiliaries to round them up and drive them against our shield wall."

"In the open desert, that's suicide."

"Maybe Antanelis, but until we reach the populated plains around Cyrene, we can be picked off anyway." Lucius turned to Alerio. "Has the cavalry reported seeing anything on their patrol?"

"Nothing. Their commander, Brutus, said that they patrolled as far out as ten miles and didn't see a thing. Maybe the nomads have given up and gone south?"

"Maybe. But I don't want us to get comfortable. Keep the sentries fresh and torches lighting the edges of camp."

"So what then? We just sit and wait?"

"That's right, Argus, at least until we can engage them smartly. I'm not going to take these men off into the deep desert, blind and vulnerable."

"But what about-"

"Those are your orders." Lucius turned his back to point to a spot on the map. "We just need to get to Cyrene." He was silent for a moment.

"We'll get there," Alerio said. "And we can replenish supplies, bathe and whore all we want!" He slapped Eligius and Garai on the shoulders. Alerio was always good at lightening the mood when needed.

"Sounds good," Garai said.

"I'll see you all in the morning." Lucius saw them out and each man went back to his century. For a few moments, he stood still in the sand outside his tent, the night sky twinkling fervently; a beautiful night after a day in Hades.

He felt warm breath on the back of his neck where Pegasus had moved to nudge him and Lucius stroked the smooth mane, scratched his ears. He had known he wanted to purchase Pegasus from the first time he saw him in the markets of Alexandria and when he received his promotion and orders, the first thing he did was buy the animal. It cost him much of his savings but, since then, the two of them were inseparable.

Something made Lucius stop for a moment. He stepped onto the main avenue and listened, the glow of dying cooking fires from neighbouring tents lit his face. He could see the dark outline of the oasis palms against the night sky, hear their rustling. But that was all. Still, something ate at him. He spun and went back into his tent. He grabbed a black woollen cloak from a chest and strode out of the tent and down the sandy avenue.

"I'm going on inspection," he notified the nearest sentry before disappearing into the shadows. The guard saluted, wondered why the tribune was not abed.

19

Lucius stopped once he reached the southern edge of camp, stared into the darkness from beneath the hood of his cloak. The two gate sentries had been startled when he appeared from behind them with silent footfalls. They watched now as he strode past the palisade, into the open.

The moon was nearly full, drew him like a heavenly siren humming in the absolute stillness. Lucius felt his breastplate and the image of the dragon, cool to his touch.

"What is it I am supposed to do?" His mouth moved but his voice barely escaped. The desert seemed idyllic in that moment, the peace of it moved Lucius so that his mind sailed through myriad memories, of home, but also of something else, something elusive. "Gods of my ancestors, I will trust your judgment, your guidance."

He bent over to pick up a handful of cool sand, let it spill through his fingers before picking up another handful and releasing it again.

"Are you well, Tribune?" one of the sentries asked from Lucius' left, concern in his voice.

Lucius turned to him. "I'm fine, Otho." The trooper looked surprised that he should remember his name. "Nights like this are rare, aren't they?"

"Not sure I follow, sir." Otho planted his rectangular scutum and his pilum in the sand.

"What are you thinking about while at your post? Besides keeping the watch."

"I suppose I'm thinking of home. Yes, mostly home."

"What about home?" Lucius smiled.

"The smell of my mother's honey cakes...and...bringing in the grape harvest."

"Hmm. Sounds good." Lucius turned to look out again at the desert. "It's strange."

"What's that, sir?"

"Earlier today, I hated the desert, everything about it. But now, it seems perfect."

"I suppose I can see what you mean."

Lucius realised he must have sounded mad to the trooper. "The Gods speak to us out here, Otho. It's as though the peace allows us to hear them more."

"The Gods speak to you?" Otho stiffened.

"No, no. That's not what I meant. What I mean is that you can feel their presence more here, in this place. Does that make sense to you?"

"Can't say that it does, sir. I've never been one to understand the ways of the Gods myself. All's I do is make what offerings I can, whenever I can."

Lucius nodded. "That is enough, I'm sure." He stepped forward. Thought he saw something near one of the tall palms. "Did you see that?"

The sharp hissing was immediately followed by an impact and then gasping. Lucius spun to see Otho clawing where a black arrow had pierced through both sides of his neck. His eyes were wide in horror as he stumbled backward. Two more arrows whizzed by Lucius before he grabbed Otho's shield and spear. Another arrow ricocheted off the shield boss.

"ATTACK! ATTACK!" he yelled back to the camp. A horn began to sound and the other gate sentry was running with two others to where Lucius straddled the fallen man's body, shield up.

The attackers were everywhere, it seemed, their wraith-like shadows flying sporadically like frenzied flies upon a fresh kill. Lucius peered over the rim of the scutum and cursed himself for not having worn his helmet. Black horses sped around the entire camp. He looked back to the three men.

"Shields on me! Form up! Where's the damned cavalry?"

"I sent a man to wake them, sir!" The first man replied as the four men locked shields and backed toward the camp. Then, three horsemen formed up and charged the small group.

"Here they come! Ready pila... Iacite!" Lucius gave the order and all four spears were sent flying. Two of the riders were impaled but the third persisted. "Kneel! Swords up!" As the horseman came to the shield wall, the men crouched behind their shields and sliced upward. The horse screamed as it soared over them and tumbled in the sand. Lucius leaped away from the group and disembowelled the rider before he could get his bearings. "Quickly, back to camp!"

By that time, Argus had formed up his century in front of the gate to which Lucius and the others were driving.

"Lucius!" Argus called. "Who is it?"

"Nomads. Stay here, they're everywhere."

"But-"

"No buts, Centurion! Hold them off here! Don't go out in the open." Argus slammed his vinerod into his hand. Lucius looked about. "Where's the damn cavalry?"

"Right here, Tribune." Brutus, the cavalry captain, appeared at the gate with a squad.

Lucius strode up to him. "I want you to drive them against us and the palisade. Go!" the man hesitated. "That's an order, swine!" Lucius smacked the man's horse's rump and the cavalry disappeared. He looked back to see men lined up between the camp's sharpened stakes, shields up and pila ready between the torches. Lucius stood with Argus at the front of the century.

Arrows continued to fly and hiss in the darkness. A few distant screams could be heard above the neighing of horses on the other side of camp.

"What's going on?" Argus stepped out from the line. The night turned silent again.

"Where'd they go? Damn auxiliaries let them get away!" Lucius peered out into the stillness, beyond where Otho's body lay in the sand. The attackers were gone. "They've bloody vanished."

"Impossible." Argus stood next to him. "We should've gone after them."

"Not now, Argus," Lucius muttered through clenched teeth. "Maybe the cavalry is pursuing them. Stay here, stay alert!"

Lucius ordered before taking two men to retrieve their comrade's body.

There were no other attacks that night. After an hour, the Egyptian cavalry captain named Brutus, returned with his men. Lucius questioned him immediately. Apparently, they had ridden hard in pursuit of the nomad force, deep into the desert.

"And?" Lucius asked. "Where did they go? How many were there? How many did you kill?"

Brutus stared back, his dark round head making no effort to hide the smugness with which he viewed the young tribune and his equally young centurions. He never wanted this assignment in the first place.

"I don't know where they went, Tribune. There weren't that many of them."

"Then it should have been easy for you and your men to round the bastards up," Lucius answered. His anger was evident. He hated being taken by surprise. If they had not built a camp they would have been massacred where they slept. Something inside told him to be wary of the man before him.

Argus stepped up to Brutus. "The Tribune asked you a question, camel fucker."

Lucius put his hand on Argus' shoulder, subtly pulled him back. "Well, Brutus? Where are they?"

"We only captured one, sir."

"Where is he? Bring him in here so we can question him."

Brutus smirked, turned to one of his men, signalled for him to bring the prisoner in. A moment later, two auxiliaries returned carrying a black-robed man between them. They approached Lucius and the centurions and dropped their burden into the sand.

"What's this?" Lucius demanded.

"Your prisoner, sir."

"He's dead. How in Hades can we question him now?"

"That's your decision, sir."

23

Brutus had no time to react as Argus landed a crushing blow into his stomach with his vinerod, winding him to his knees.

"Centurion!" Lucius pushed Argus away. Alerio noted the look of satisfaction on Argus' face. "Get him out of here!" Lucius ordered the two cavalrymen to take Brutus back to his tent, leaving himself and the other centurions staring at the nomad corpse. He looked at the others. "How many men have we lost?"

Antanelis spoke. "Three, Tribune. Otho and two others."

"Could have been worse," Maren added.

Lucius looked at him. "Could have been better." He knelt down to look at the corpse, pull back the black face coverings. "Mars plays with me." For a moment, Lucius hesitated. All the attackers had been dressed the same, true, but for an instant it seemed to him that the wounds on this one were similar to the ones he had inflicted on the horseman who had charged them. He dismissed the thought; sword and kill techniques with a gladius were common to every trooper because of their training. Any man in the cohort might have inflicted a similar wound. He stood up. "We'll hold funeral rites for the three dead men at sun up. Make sure the pyres are set."

The centurions saluted and left to see that order and discipline had been re-established in their units. Few men slept the remainder of the night. Their boring routine patrol had turned nightmarish.

Several days later, when the night attack had faded into the memory of odd and forgotten occurrences of so many army careers, the cohort finally neared civilization and the fertile plains of Cyrene.

They were to camp outside the city for two nights, in which time two centuries at a time were to be given leave to go within the walls to enjoy the pleasures that awaited them, whether bathing, drinking, gambling or whoring. Each man, tired and stinking, had his own idea as to what form his relaxation would take and envisioned it in minute detail from the time those heavenly grain fields and olive groves waved in the distance.

Cyrenaica and Africa Proconsularis were rich, as befits the granaries of an empire. The cohort marched on over the lush flat lands with ease. All that could be seen for miles and miles now were golden fields and row after row of silver-leaved groves. Though the fruit was not yet ready for harvest, some men could not resist plucking plump olives from the branches as they passed to suck on their bitterness. Soon enough, the fruit would be pressed into oil to be sent to all corners of the Roman world.

Lucius closed his eyes for a moment and felt a faint breeze on his face, hinting at the distant sea. Instead of the harsh feeling of dry, gritty air, their lungs now heaved with the familiar, strong scent of the local presses that reached their nostrils. The Gods seemed to be smiling once again.

At Lucius' orders, they made camp on a plateau of over thirty hectares that provided a defensive position and a decent view of the surrounding area. Immediately, the tribune sent out cavalry scouts. He did not want any surprises this time.

When his tent was secured and with a little spare time to himself that afternoon while Garai and Eligius' centuries went into town, Lucius settled to read passages from his scrolls. He sought inspiration to reinforce the commander he knew dwelt within. Whether he read from Virgil, Caesar's diaries, or Arrian's account of Alexander's campaigns, every time he unrolled the papyrus scrolls and considered the words therein, he felt enriched, better-armed to deal with the next day.

It was not until he was at peace, alone, that Lucius Metellus Anguis realized the great responsibility that he now faced. He was not commanding legions, but he was, in a more intimate way, charged with the lives of close to five hundred men. He knew many of them too. Like an eagle with her hatchlings on some far-flung eyrie, it was within his power to either push the men into a dark, craggy void or to rouse their courage to fly into the heavens, uncaring of what lay below. Their lives were in his hands. He hoped, and in some way feared, that they trusted him implicitly. Men were often sent to die on the fields of foreign lands and, only too often, had he seen the actions of arrogant generals and cowards cost lives. For Lucius, when he boarded the black boat for the Otherworld, he did not want throngs of dead and vengeful warriors he had led awaiting him on the sad shore. The thought was too terrifying for any man of arms.

As evening swirled the sky in colours of plum and pomegranate, Lucius found himself walking amid the olive trees at the bottom of the plateau. He had finished his inspection of the camp and took the opportunity to walk alone for a while, away from the camp's noise.

The silvery leaves reminded him of summers at his family's Etrurian estate. As a child he would play among the trees along the stream on hot days, sometimes alone or with Argus, other times with his sister. *Alene...* He had not written to her since Alexandria, forgot how much he missed her. The years had flown.

He stopped abruptly, froze. A serpent was coiling its way around his ankle. It slithered and stopped, as though feeling Lucius' eyes on it. He thought of reaching for his sword but knew that could frighten it into attack. Besides, he was in a land where snakes were highly sacred. Sacrilege was not something he wanted hanging over his head. He breathed calmly and watched as the creature moved on, like quicksilver through hot sand. Lucius smiled to himself.

"Stay still, Lucius!" Argus' blade ripped through the silent air to sever the serpent's body. It shuddered several times and then was still, its blood clotting the dusty ground.

"Why did you do that?" Lucius turned on Argus, his reverie broken.

Argus protested, shocked by his friend's reaction. "What do you mean? I just saved your life!"

"It was moving on." Lucius looked down at the pathetic remnants, ants already crawling on the bloody bits. "Those are sacred here, Argus."

"Oh get over it! You can't believe that! The last thing I want is to watch you spasm and foam at the mouth before I have to carry your dead body the rest of the way to Lambaesis. Good thing I came down here when I did."

Lucius just shook his head, unable to comprehend his friend's actions at times, his disregard. He did not want to argue. "What was it you wanted anyway?"

Argus frowned. He knew that Lucius would not agree with him this time. "Just letting you know that Eligius and Garai are back. I think something happened in the town."

"Perfect." Lucius rubbed his tightening jaw, turned and walked back up the plateau embankment. As he went, he heard several hollow thumps and knew that Argus was cutting up the rest of the mangled serpent in frustration.

When Eligius and Garai entered the command tent, Lucius was standing, arms crossed, staring absently at the map on the wall. The two men stopped and looked at each other before speaking.

"What happened?" Lucius spoke first.

"It wasn't that bad, Lucius, I mean, Tribune." Garai forgot there were others just outside the tent. They were supposed to address Lucius formally around the men.

Eligius continued. "Apparently, two of our men were gambling at one of the taverns. They say that two of the local auxiliaries cheated and when they called them on it a fight broke out. You know how these things work; one man throws a punch and then the whole bloody place is in an uproar."

Lucius' face was stern, thoughtful. "We're trying to keep the honest people of this region warm to us. We're here to help them against the nomads who raid their farms. But how are we going to do this, how are we going to nurture the people's trust in us, in Rome, if we start brawls in their home?"

"We won't." Garai continued. "There were several witnesses who said that the local guys started the brawl. I paid the tavern keeper and made a show of reprimanding our men, even though they are innocent."

"Doesn't matter if they are innocent or not. Discipline them. Put them on latrine duty for the next six days, digging and filling the pits."

"Isn't that a bit harsh?"

"No. Listen to me, both of you. We need to maintain our discipline, that's what makes this army. Do it."

"Fine. Yes Tribune." The two men saluted.

"One more thing," Lucius remembered. "Did you stop by the offices of the city prefect to tell him I would be by tomorrow?"

"Yes we did." Eligius answered. "His name's Cassius Meladoros. Another fat-assed merchant turned frontier administrator. We told him that you would be by after you visited the baths. He's expecting you."

"Good. Thanks to you both." Lucius smiled half-heartedly to them, knew that they thought he was overreacting. He tried not to let it anger him.

By the time the sun had risen over the plains to set alight the new day, Lucius was riding along the road to Cyrene with Argus, Antanelis, their two centuries and a small contingent of cavalry, including Brutus.

The young tribune had been eager to see the city. While Carthage had always been the wealthiest and most prosperous city of Africa Proconsularis, the other large cities of the neighbouring provinces, especially Cyrene, had begun to rival the might of the former Punic capital. To protect their wealthy populace from attacks, the cities were fortified with stone walls. Each city built monuments to display its wealth: bath complexes, theatres, libraries and temples to the Gods. Lucius looked forward to walking the civilized streets and experiencing all of the stimuli that he had missed in the desert.

III

FESTINARE VIA ET THERMARUM

'Bustling Streets and Baths'

Had Lucius known it was market day in Cyrene he might have reconsidered going at all, especially with two hundred men. Not that he doubted Argus and Antanelis' grasp of command, it was the locals he was worried about and how they would react to such a large force of outside troops, especially after the previous night's incident. He hoped that the business his men would bring would help the people to forget.

People gazed absently at the sight of the tribune as he made his way through the press of sweaty flesh, his helmet's crest visible above all else. The sun had risen, it was stifling. This was a far cry from the quiet of the open desert. It was an assault on the senses.

He was pushed and pulled from all sides by men haggling over the price of animals, spices and pots. Old, haggardly women yelled at him as he attempted to make his way through the throng of bodies. Occasionally, merchants would grab Lucius' arm in an attempt to drag him into their stalls where they wished to sell him bits of pilfered armour and weapons. It did not matter that he was a Roman officer or that his weapons were far superior to any the merchants had ever seen. On market day, any passer-by was fair game. Why else would anyone be there?

The variety of people amazed Lucius. There were merchants, both rich and poor, peasants performing menial tasks for anyone who would pay them. Rich ladies paraded themselves in perfumed litters carried by four to eight slaves while well-to-do citizens pushed into the fray with their own slaves in tow, shopping for household items. In the midst of the chaos, local auxiliary troops attempted to maintain some semblance of order as they rubbed along with everyone else. Nubians, Egyptians, Greeks, Massilians, Parthians and countless other peoples were all mixed together in an orgy of buying and selling.

Lucius glanced back in the direction from which he had come, could see the centurion's crests of Antanelis and Argus, caught in the middle of the animal market as a herd of camels swarmed about them. Argus' voice raged above the din of murmuring dromedaries. He smiled to himself at the thought of his friends' progress toward the baths, hindered by both beast and merchant. They would need to bathe after that. Finally, Lucius neared the forum at the centre of town. It was packed to capacity. Local politicians waved their arms about in dramatic arcs, street performers enacted bits of classic comedies, and fortune tellers read what the Fates had in store in scattered bits of bone for those who wanted a little guidance. On the right, Lucius spotted snake charmers playing their magical flutes, their reptilian audience swaying to the lulling music like cradled babes to their mothers' nightly hymns.

Lucius moved along, noticed the slave market to his left. There was a large wooden platform on which the slave trader paraded his goods so that buyers could make their choice. Lucius stood for a moment and watched. To one side of the dais the slaves were bunched together awaiting their turn: children, men and women. Lucius felt his heart seize up at the sight of boys and girls, no more than ten years old, who would be sold as labourers, house slaves or other unthinkable uses.

There were also many stunning women to be auctioned off. No doubt they would fetch the highest prices from rich matrons who needed body servants or rich men who wished to impress their friends by displaying an array of concubines about their homes. One girl of about twenty-two was brought up next. She was stunning in every respect with golden hair, green eyes and a figure to render Venus jealous; she wore only the slightest of coverings, intended to show her off. No doubt

31

she was taken from her home somewhere in the northern provinces, perhaps Germania or Britannia.

"And now!" The auctioneer's voice rose above the bubbling crowd. "Who could resist this young beauty?" He yanked the girl closer. She made a weak attempt to pull away, his hand closed tightly about her wrist. "Any takers for this virgin barbarian?" The man's gaze concentrated upon the row of rich merchants in front. The virginity of the girl in question was unlikely, the pained, tired look in her eyes telling otherwise. She tried to hide behind her long hair.

Lucius, who could see above the heads of the crowd, felt a pang of dread for the young woman when an old, rich-looking Egyptian tossed a heavy pouch of aurea at the trader's feet. The girl's eyes filled with tears as she was handed over to the lecher, half-naked and afraid. Then, at that moment, as if looking into the crowd for help, she held Lucius' eyes and shook her head pleadingly.

The torment of seeing this perfect being dragged away on the end of a rope held by that pig was almost too much. Lucius hated feeling so helpless and angry for there was nothing he could do. He tore himself from the poor creature's gaze, turned abruptly and shoved his way through the crowd toward the other side of the forum and the offices of the prefect. The girl shut her eyes and broke down, the reality of her situation all too harsh and terrifying.

After his sweaty journey through the crowds, Lucius finally arrived at the baths. On the outside, the roof of the basilica bulged out above the surrounding buildings. Lucius admired the strong simplicity of the structure and wondered if it was the same on the inside. It was relatively quiet in that part of the town with everyone on the main street and in the forum for the market. Only a few citizens went in or came out of the bath complex as he approached.

Once inside, he was shown the way to the apodyterium, a changing area reserved for high-ranking military personnel and citizens. The slave who led him into the large room was a young, well-groomed boy, attentive yet silent. There was a guard at the entrance to prevent anyone from coming in and stealing private items that might appeal to them.

Lucius went over to one of the benches along the far wall of the room, above which were cupboards for placing personal belongings. The young boy helped him remove his armour and placed it in a storage area with great care. He did the same with his weapons.

When Lucius finished undressing, the boy handed him a towel and pointed towards an adjacent door that led to the palaestra where a few soldiers and others exercised. Some were wrestling, others lifting blocks of stone to build and strengthen muscles. On either side of the room, rows of columns reached up to the ceiling where windows allowed sunlight to pour in.

As Lucius did not have enough time for exercise, he went straight to the tepidarium. The floor was made of richly coloured mosaic, Greek designs around a massive image of the god Neptune surrounded by sirens as he rode the waves on giant sea horses. The walls of this particular room were painted bright blue with various scenes of sea life, gods and goddesses. His body relaxed in the warm, humid air. Beads of sweat began to trickle down his back.

The slave boy reappeared and handed Lucius a small jar of oil and a strigil before he went into the caldarium where the extreme steam and heat from the hot pool caused a more profuse sweating. The air was so close that Lucius could barely see two paces in front of him. He eased himself into the steamy waters of the pool, the burning sensation travelling up hesitantly, until it reached his neck. He plunged his head underwater, thought it odd how hot water always seemed thicker, slower.

His eyes closed only to be met by the scene at the slave market, catching him up in a tangle of thoughts about the poor girl who had looked to him for help. He felt his heart tighten at the returning image of the look of fear in her young eyes. He had come to the aid of a slave woman once before and it had only caused him grief. *Too much*, he thought.

That look of fear... It rekindled memories, painful memories of his time in Alexandria, of a woman, a friend. In Alexandria he had quit the final vestiges of boyhood. He wanted to forget, but he could not. As he soaked in the steaming waters of the baths, alone, he gave in to the thoughts he had avoided since leaving Aegyptus.

The woman's name was Medea, an upscale prostitute in Alexandria, a city that was rich in gold and far more lax in morals than Rome had ever been. After a hard day of training, the men had decided to go to one of the famous orgies held weekly by a local businessman in a seedier district of the city. It was a place where all tastes were catered to. Lucius had been once before, at Argus' urging, but had left early, unable to stomach the sight of some activities. Instead, he had decided to go to the man named Barbarus, a decent fellow who was rumoured to own some of the most luxuriant women in Alexandria.

Barbarus took one look at the young, toga-clad Roman when he entered his home and knew exactly what to say, "Medea. Yes." That was all it took. The man assured Lucius he would not be disappointed, gave him directions to her home along the river and that was that. "Be there tonight, first hour of darkness."

The steam in the baths thickened and Lucius tried to shut his eyes against further memory. But, he had to go on, remember; up the villa's path, flanked by tall palms and scented jasmine bushes, the lush, private garden where mosaic satyrs and nymphs danced to the sound of splashing water from the fountain. The tall, slender woman, Medea, as she emerged from a cloud of incense, her voice soft and reassuring. He'd been with women, many on campaign, but never like that, never the trance-like state of euphoric

34

forgetfulness he had experienced every time he visited her. He wished for that forgetfulness again.

Lucius' fists clenched under water as the memory of one particular day rushed back. He'd gone to bid farewell to her. *I've been made Tribune and I have to leave on an assignment, a patrol*, he was going to say. But all that met him on that last visit was fear, horror. Men's voices and the bitter sound of muffled weeping. *I* grew up *in Alexandria*, he thought. The look of fear in her eyes. The pain.

He could feel it, even now, the weight of his sword plunging into the belly of that hulking brute as he stood over Medea and her dead girls. He could smell the garlic on the breath of the second man as he lunged for Lucius' throat, their struggle on the bloody mosaic. They had invaded paradise and he wanted to kill them for it. He did. He did not know however, if he had done it out of love or lust for her, or out of anger, rage or even fear. His life was soiled and he wanted to leave that place. *I should have talked to her*, he scolded himself. *I was a coward!* She would have said 'No. You are not. You saved me.' But, when Barbarus arrived, Lucius said nothing. *I am a coward!* he cursed himself as he rode away from that place as fast as he could.

The world could be a cruel place and from then on he questioned himself and what he was doing with his life. He did not have any slaves himself but was that enough? He did not know. Slavery had always been part of life in the empire, his own family had several slaves, for as long as he could remember. When he was young he merely enjoyed having many people about the household. Now, his perceptions were different. Having seen men die in the field, women taken in the sacking of cities, how could he enslave people in his own home? He shook the whirling thoughts from his head. He opened his eyes.

Lucius extricated himself from the sleepy water, picked up the oil and strigil and went over to a pedestal with a large bowl full of fresh water. There were several extra bronze strigils on a nearby table. He rubbed the oil over his whole body, picked up his strigil and began to scrape away the oils and dirt that had risen to the surface of his skin with the heat. Every muscle began to relax as he passed the bronze hook over himself. He then took a slightly longer strigil so that he could reach his back, rinsing after every stroke. He could not see the details of the room due to the steam but had a sense of brilliant blues and greens.

After scrapping himself clean, he then passed through another doorway to the frigidarium where the cool air embraced his sweating limbs on his way to the cold plunge. An old man rubbed his face briskly in a corner of the pink, marble-lined pool. He glanced at Lucius, smiled, made a loud shivering sound and bounced up and down in the water. Lucius kept to himself, quiet on the other side of the pool. The water was a shock at first but it soon began to feel quite refreshing.

The cold had revived Lucius and he headed to the massage room. There, the young slave boy awaited him and handed him another towel, to dry himself before laying down on a table where a large, strong-looking man stood ready with scented oils. As Lucius lay there, the hefty fellow's thick hands dug deep into his muscles, relaxing him completely, any remaining knots hammered away. The oil was perfumed with rose petals and what smelled like cloves. A little too feminine for his own liking but, anything was better than soldier's grunt-sweat.

After his massage, Lucius rose to make his way back to the apodyterium where the young boy had laid out his clothes, armour and weapons. He had even cleaned the armour, swords and daggers of market dust. Lucius was amazed at how hard the boy worked and patted him on the back.

When he was fully dressed, looked the part of a tribune of Rome, he took a small purse containing a few coins and tossed it to the lad whose eyes went wide with excitement. The silent boy bowed and bowed as Lucius turned and went out the door. He noticed the guard at the door, grinning.

Outside, Lucius realized that the guard would probably take the poor boy's hard-earned money and he returned to the changing room. Upon entering, he saw that the guard held the money in one hand, his other hand high in the air, prepared to land a blow on the huddled slave.

"Trooper!" The guard spun around, shocked by the booming voice that came from behind him. He turned to see the tribune's imposing figure standing in the doorway. Lucius held his head high, jaw set as he stared down the trembling guard. "You will hand that back to the boy right now or I swear I'll have you flogged and fed to the lions!"

"Bu...but...Tribune? What does a slave need money for? He'll only waste it." Lucius strode over to the man and stood right in front of him so that he stared into his eyes, breathed in his face.

"It was I who gave him the money and it will remain his, understood?" The man nodded spastically. "Give it to him. Now!" The man handed it back to the boy who grabbed it from him and gave him a kick in the shins. The man winced slightly but did not look away from Lucius' stare. "What's your name, grunt?"

"Pluvius, sir."

"Well Pluvius, I'm going to see the prefect now and I'll inform him of your behaviour towards a superior officer. I will also tell him that if you lay so much as a hand on this small boy, you are to be beaten senseless until your head is cracked open. I'm sure there are a few troops in your garrison who wouldn't mind being appointed such a task. Now, get out of here before I do it myself."

"Yes Tribune!" The man saluted, turned and marched hurriedly out of the building. Lucius looked to the boy who gazed up at him in admiration, the salt from his tears dry now upon his little face.

"Are you hurt little one?" The boy shook his head. Lucius knew that he had been very scared but he was determined not to show it. Lucius reached into the scrip that hung at his waist, pulled out an extra coin and tossed it to him. "Hide that so that no one will find it. In return you can take care of me if I come back to Cyrene, agreed?" The boy saluted and stood at attention, nodding in the affirmative. "Good. Take care my young friend." And with that Lucius spun and headed out the door, his crimson cloak waving in a fluid motion as he turned the corner.

"I need to see the prefect now. He's expecting me and I don't have all day!" Lucius was growing annoyed with the skinny secretary in the waiting room outside the prefect's office. He stood over the little man, his arms crossed as he stared down.

"Marcus! Who's out there? I'm expecting..." A plump looking man walked into the room and suddenly realized what was going on. "Marcus, you idiot!" He slapped him on the back of the head and turned to Lucius. "Forgive me, Tribune. He is slow and dumb. I am Cassius Melodoros, Prefect of Cyrene. Will you join me in the garden?"

Lucius followed the man into a room the walls of which were lined with shelves of scrolls, then through another door that led into an open courtyard. In the centre of a lush garden was a fountain, spouting water from the mouths of four nymphs. Birds sang in the trees above two couches that were placed in the shade. Nearby was a table laden with wine, fruit and nuts.

"Please, sit down and relax Tribune Metellus." Lucius sat on the edge of his couch, adjusting his sword to be more comfortable. The prefect, who was short and very well fed, was dressed in his formal toga. He reclined fully on his couch as a slave offered them both watered wine. Cassius spoke on. "I have never met a Metellus before today. It's quite a family you hail from. You must be related to Caecilia Metella, the Dictator Sulla's wife?"

Lucius sighed. He always wondered why that was the first thing anyone ever remembered about his family. "Only very distantly. I'm not exactly sure of how. That was a long time ago."

"I suppose so. Back in the days of the Republic. Although Sulla's dictatorship was not a pleasant one, according to the histories. Say, that" he pointed at Lucius' breastplate, "is some interesting armour. I've never seen its like before. Are those dragons?" Lucius began to wonder what he was doing there at all. "Please forgive me. My mouth is running away with me again, Tribune. What can I do for you?"

"Well," began Lucius after taking a sip of wine. "As you know we are on patrol from Alexandria to the legionary base at Lambaesis-"

"I know! The whole town is talking about it. They saw some of your troops come in yesterday. There was a bit of a disturbance in a tavern or something?"

"Yes. Between two of my troops and two of your auxiliaries. My men have been disciplined. Even though it appears to have been the fault of the other two."

"That doesn't surprise me. These auxiliaries are an ill-disciplined lot. They are definitely not seasoned legionaries. How many of you are there?"

"A full cohort plus a hundred and twenty cavalry. What I wanted to know is, have there been any attacks or raids lately to the south of here along the frontier?"

Cassius rubbed his chin for a few moments, pondering the question. "No..wait!..Hmmm. No, not lately. There was an attack on one of the forts about six months ago but that's it. Come to think of it, that seems like an awful long time to go without any problems. There should have been a few at least, what with all the rich villas and plantations around here."

"You're sure now?"

"Oh yes. Absolutely. Is there a problem?"

"A nomad force has been shadowing us for some time now. They attacked our camp several nights back." Lucius looked a bit puzzled. "It is surprising that they haven't raided any of the farms hereabouts." Lucius was thinking out loud. "Perhaps, if they haven't attacked lately, they must be preserving their resources for something."

"Well Tribune, I'm afraid that I am an administrative man and not very military-minded. The towns along the coast are wealthy and any one of them would be a rich prize. Especially easy I would think with the only legion around here being the Numidian one?"

"Yes. Unfortunately, many of the legions are either in the east or the north. That is one reason we are patrolling across the southern provinces." Lucius leaned toward the table for a handful of fruit and nuts then leaned back on the couch, breathing in the fresh garden air. The two sat in silence for a few moments.

"Let me give you some advice, Tribune Metellus." Cassius sat up and leaned closer to Lucius who looked at him, wondered what nonsense he might utter this time. "These southern provinces are very different from the rest of the empire. All seems quiet but there are plots and schemes underneath the calm surface. Watch your back and mind who you trust. There are many eager to move up the social scale and make their way to the rich cities of Carthage, Leptis Magna, here, or even Rome. I say this as one who knows how things work and has had first-hand experience. I am Greek by birth but came here from a young age and managed to blend in. They don't like outsiders thwarting their plans. Those whose aspirations are high and greed-driven do not care who they step on to get to where they want."

"I thank you for the warning, Prefect, but we are only going to Lambaesis."

Cassius looked worried and Lucius sensed that he was quite serious. He was also fearful but Lucius could not make out why. "I do but give you some honest, friendly advice. I know it is a rare thing, to get 'honest' advice, but it does exist."

"Again, my thanks." Lucius leaned back once more and then recounted the story of what had happened at the baths with the guard and the slave boy. Cassius was furious.

"Another idiot! I tell you, sometimes these auxiliaries are too much. I'll have him posted elsewhere, don't you worry. That young boy is my favourite too. He takes such good care of me when I go to the baths. I bring him spiced apples from the market and other things to reward him for his work. He'll be protected, I promise you that."

Lucius then noticed that it was nearly midday and he still wanted to pay his respects at the temple of Apollo. "Well, I must be leaving now but thank you for your hospitality, Prefect, and for your advice."

"Not to worry Tribune. I'm glad I could help a little at least." He then rose and led Lucius back through the office and into the front room. "Take care Tribune and may the Gods guide you on your way." Lucius nodded and headed for the forum. Cassius turned to his secretary. "Back to work! Next time write things down or I'll have them burned on your forehead!" He went back into his garden.

As he approached the temple of Apollo, Lucius felt a familiar sense of awe. It was a large temple with long arcades of columns. Carved representations of the Gods decorated the friezes. The steps leading up to the entrance were high and wide. At the top, towering above, was the ornate pediment with statues portraying the birth of Apollo and his sister Artemis under a great palm tree.

As Lucius entered the temple, he bowed his head and walked over to a tripod in which a fire was burning. From another tripod he took a handful of powder and tossed it onto the flames. The powder ignited, created a flash of light and colour that lit the temple for a moment. He made his way to the far end, dwarfed by the huge columns that supported the ceiling. Beneath a colossal effigy of the god, Lucius knelt and looked up at his marble face.

"Great Apollo," Lucius said in a low voice. "Please make me wise and strong. Let me lead my men to victory and safety in all things. I do not know what the Gods have in store for me,

41

but let me stand the test and prove my worth to you, to my men, to my family, and to myself. I place myself in your keeping. Watch over me and guide my sword and my heart." Lucius, deeply moved by the power of the place, bowed his head and let Apollo's presence envelop him. He could feel Him looking over him, His gaze bringing peace and calm like waves of warm summer breeze.

Lucius rose, his breastplate glinting in the flickering flames of the tripod's fire. He backed up slowly looking up into His eyes, turned and went out of the temple, back into the light of day and the world once more.

As he descended the steps, Antanelis hurried to meet him. The forum was emptying out as the vendors began to pack up their things.

The centurion was out of breath. "Tribune! A rider from camp! Alerio sends word that they're under attack!"

"Who in Hades is attacking us? When did the rider arrive?"

"I don't know who. Nomads, I'd guess. The rider arrived less than an hour ago." They began walking briskly across the forum.

"Are the men assembled?"

"Yes. Argus rounded them all up and they're waiting outside the city gates with the cavalry. Your horse is ready and waiting."

"Good work. Let's hope we're not too late. I'll ride on ahead with the cavalry. I want you and Argus to lead your centuries at a fast march to join us as quickly as possible. Understood?"

"Yes Tribune! Whoever it is, they'll wish they never set foot in the province."

IV

DE IMMENSITE

'Out of the Vastness'

Lucius and the cavalry troops rode fast and hard to the camp while Argus, Antanelis and their centuries followed. For all Lucius knew, the fighting could be over by the time they arrived. As they approached the north face of the plateau on which the camp was set, he noticed smoke rising and could hear the faint clanging of weapons in the distance. He halted his group and listened for a moment before giving orders.

"All right! I want twenty men to go east around to the camp's entrance and the other twenty to come with me around the western face. We'll meet up in the middle on the southern side of the plateau. Hopefully our men were able to get some troops out onto the plain below. Now go!"

The attack had been sudden. The enemy consisted of lightly mounted cavalry carrying long broad-headed spears. There were also some archers in their group that kept the men on the plateau's defences pinned down. Alerio had managed to get one century and some cavalry onto the field below, where they now held out against the attackers. The enemy force was small but fast, striking at the ranks and then retreating while another group did the same.

The few cavalrymen that had managed to get their mounts into formation charged in to take out the archers who were hiding behind their own cavalry, the latter wheeling and darting to confuse the surprised Romans.

Lucius rounded the plateau, halted to take stock of the situation. "Let's ride further around and take them from behind!" he yelled to the horsemen. "We can't let them see us until the right time. Go!" The enemy did not notice the Roman cavalry, the full force of their attention concentrated on the plateau and the legionaries coming in from the eastern side. Once he was behind the line of enemy archers, Lucius and his squad attacked, breaking their ranks and running them down. The archers panicked and scattered.

Pegasus pounded the earth beneath his hooves as he flew into the commotion like some winged god; Lucius' spatha flashed left and right, cutting men down. Spears flew by, nearly striking him but he was moving too quickly. He heard the cry of one of his cavalrymen who received an arrow in the pit of his arm and fell to the ground. The man managed to hold onto his sword and take out a couple archers before being despatched himself.

As Lucius' formation came through to the other side of the enemy he heard a cry from the right. "Tribune!" It was the other twenty cavalry, joined with those who had made it down out of the camp. Their attack was swift and just as Lucius had finished his charge on the enemy, this next group began their own from the opposite side. The attackers saw this and began to break up and flee in confusion, knowing that they could not survive another onslaught from the new force of Romans. At the same time the legionaries that Alerio had formed up at the base of the plateau began to move forward, their swords drawn at the side of their large, rectangular shields.

The enemy dispersed into the distant desert as quickly as they had appeared, like a swarm of ghostly bees. Lucius glanced Brutus on the horse next to him. "Brutus! Take fifty of your men and pursue them to make sure they don't regroup and come back. Don't engage them, just make sure they've left and in which direction." Brutus looked at Lucius, half hearing what he had said. His interest was set upon the fleeing enemy. "Brutus! Did you hear me?"

"Yes, Tribune," he responded dully before gathering together some of his auxiliaries. They rode off in pursuit of the remaining attackers.

Lucius dismounted and walked over to a few of the fallen attackers. He flipped one over to look at him. Blood dripped into the sand from a sword slash to his neck. Alerio came up beside him.

"Lucius, you injured?"

"No, I'm fine. What happened?"

"I'm not sure. They just appeared out of nowhere, attacked the south face. Our sentries spotted some movement but it was too late. They moved so fast that they hit us even before the alarm was raised. I sent a rider immediately to find you. Thank the Gods you arrived when you did. We could've had them but it would have taken a lot longer since they had us pinned down up there. I wonder why they weren't spotted by the far outposts?"

"I'm not sure Alerio but something's not right here." Lucius looked puzzled and pointed to the dead attacker at his feet. "This wasn't the average raiding party. Almost all of them had mounts and were well armed. Look at their clothing. They're definitely desert people but their arms suggest supply from elsewhere. Maybe that's what they were trying to gain here? Who knows? At any rate, we'll have to be more cautious. For now, take care of the wounded and get the men organized. I want two columns marching around the perimeter of the plateau and two groups of twenty cavalry patrolling the surrounding area."

"I'll get right on it." Alerio turned to leave but Lucius called to him again.

"Centurion! One more thing. Find two of the fastest riders and send them to that outpost south of here to find out if they saw anything." Alerio saluted and went about it. Lucius mounted up again and rode into the camp.

When Lucius arrived at his tent, the men were busy extinguishing fires that had been ignited by flaming arrows shot from below. The damage was minimal.

His tent had been untouched and at the entrance a trooper stood waiting for him. "Tribune!" The man saluted. "Centurions Argus and Antanelis send word that they have arrived and are aiding in the clean-up."

"Good," Lucius replied. "Tell them and the other centurions to be in my command tent within two hours."

"Yes, Tribune!" The man spun and went straight to deliver the message.

Inside the tent Lucius went to the table, put down his spatha and gladius, removed his helmet and hung it on a hook protruding from a tent post. "So much for bathing," he muttered as he went over to the wash basin. His hands and forearms were spattered with blood. He rinsed them, transforming the water into a bloody pool.

He stood up, dried his hands. They were shaking. The period after a battle always unnerved him. He sighed, rolled his neck. The sunlight peeked through the seams and a few holes in the leather tent, shedding light onto his face. He poured a cup of wine and drank it down in one swallow.

He gathered his senses, knew his command could not allow for weakness of any kind. "Something's not right here." He would know more when news from the southern outpost arrived. He remembered what the prefect had told him: *Watch your back at all times and mind who you trust.* Lucius had been very successful in straight-forward military matters but the round-about ways of scheming in politics was something different. *What did the prefect mean by all that?* He was happy to be a soldier, surrounded by friends to whom he could entrust his life.

Lucius then rose, replaced his helmet and checked his gladius was secure beneath his cloak before going out. The sun was hot and a haze was forming in the distance, above the desert. He made his way up onto one of the south facing embankments and looked into the distance. He could see Brutus and his auxiliaries returning from their pursuit. Lucius turned and made his way back into the camp. A group of men saluted sharply as he passed. Lucius noticed the shocked looks on their faces. Nobody had been expecting this.

Unfortunately, he would have to inform Alerio and Maren that their men would not be able to go into town because of the unexpected attack. They would be given the rest of the day off from duties around the camp, able to relax and yet be close at hand in case the enemy returned.

"Tribune!" Alerio called. "Here's one of the cavalry troopers come to report." The man stepped forward and half saluted.

"Well, trooper? What happened in the pursuit?" Lucius demanded.

"We followed them at a distance for several leagues, Tribune. They moved quickly but we managed to keep up. They headed south-west, into the desert. They won't be coming back this way, not tonight."

Lucius rubbed his chin. "Did you engage them at all?"

"No, Tribune."

He turned to Alerio, "Have the two riders returned from the southern outpost yet?"

"They haven't reported back yet. We're still waiting," Alerio answered.

Lucius thought for a moment, then spoke to the cavalry trooper. "You can go back to your squadron now. Inform your commander that I want two groups of cavalry patrolling the surrounding area throughout the night so we have some advance warning." The man saluted and went down the rows of tents. "Alerio, I want to see you and the others in about one hour. And since yours and Maren's centuries won't be able to go into town, I'm giving them the rest of the day off from duties as soon as everything is back to normal. You and Maren as well."

"That's a good idea. I know the men were looking forward to going. But, they'll enjoy drinking and gaming a little more than usual."

"Good, leave them to it. Just make sure there aren't any brawls. I'll see you and the others shortly."

"Yes, Tribune. One hour." Alerio saluted and went about his orders. Lucius continued his inspection of the camp.

Lucius waited for his centurions. He had removed his cuirass and tunic and wore only a linen shirt. At the command table he went over the route that the cohort was to take, noting how many outposts they would pass and the areas where they would be marching through open desert. As usual, he noted any oases along the way where they could gather water and rest.

Morale would be down with the recent attack, the blood up. They would be vulnerable to further attack from all sides, especially since the outposts were more sparsely scattered. They would have to be very careful, alert. Lucius knew his men, their strengths, their limits; out in the desert anything could happen.

"Tribune? May we enter?"

"Yes, come in," Lucius replied to the voice outside. In came Alerio and the others. "Is the camp secure?"

"Yes," Argus answered. "And the two riders have returned from the outpost with some interesting news. Apparently they didn't see a damn thing! Neither did any of their patrols. It seems strange that the attackers could pass unnoticed."

Lucius stood and motioned for them all to take their seats. "Well my friends. Let's not forget that this is their native land. They know the terrain better than we do. They can probably appear and disappear anywhere they please. That's what makes them so dangerous."

"It would seem we're facing a band of desert shades," Maren added sarcastically.

"It would. However, many of our frontier auxiliaries are natives of this land and might therefore know how these attackers move about. Some of the dunes out in the desert are as much as fifty feet in height and would easily hide a force of men moving quietly, using the dunes as cover. Either the troops at the outposts didn't see anything, as they say, or they neglected to raise the alarm." No one spoke. This had different implications for their so-called 'routine patrol'.

Antanelis asked what everyone was thinking. "Tribune, do you think they're being paid to keep quiet, not notice certain goings on?"

"It's possible. Eligius, after our meeting I want you to send a rider to the Prefect of Cyrene with a message. I'll tell him what's happened and that he should investigate the matter. We certainly don't have the time for it."

Garai, tapping the end of his vinerod on the edge of the table, spoke next. "Lucius, what'll the route be from here on? We'd better move quickly just in case they come back."

"Why would we want to do that Garai? The reason for this patrol is to clear away any enemy forces causing trouble. We need to engage them if they show up again." Garai shrugged.

"Damn right!" Argus smacked the table. "Finish the whores off to the last man! That's what we need to do. March south, past the frontier and hit'em in their own lands. Right, Lucius?"

"That won't do either. We're not here to charge stupidly into a fight in a land where the enemy has all the advantages. We're just here to keep them from causing trouble on Roman territory. We just have to keep constant surveillance of the surrounding areas. The cavalry will ride on patrol on all four sides of the column as we march. I don't like to trust them with so much responsibility but we don't have a choice. As for the route we're going to take, I'll show you." Lucius leaned over the table to trace their route on the map. "We'll set out early tomorrow morning along the main road to Berenice but at that point will head south-west into the desert again, in the direction of the oasis here. There, we'll be able to replenish our water supply and rest before entering Africa Proconsularis. After heading west for a while, we'll turn north-westward to meet up with the road to Sabratha. From there we'll take the road to Nepeta, across the salt desert and then up to

Lambaesis. That's the plan, for now at least. We'll see what happens along the way. I thought we would get to Leptis Magna but it's more important that we patrol the frontier. We'll pick up our supplies in Sabratha and any other small settlements along the way."

The men sat for a moment looking at the map, noting the various oases and outposts along the way. "Water's going to be essential," Alerio said, "and each man will be carrying two water skins in addition to those loaded onto the pack horses."

"The oases are spread out so that we should come to one just as the supply from the previous one will be finished," Maren added.

Lucius calculated the distance. "If we can maintain a constant march we'll be fine."

After discussing more trivial matters and what had happened in Cyrene with the prefect, Lucius dismissed the men. Argus stayed behind to speak with him.

"Lucius, I think we should go after the bastards." He poured himself some wine while Lucius stood up, arms crossed. "You know I'm right," he persisted. "If we just go on our merry way we'll be vulnerable, open to attack at any time, anywhere. But, if we go after *them*, cut'em to pieces before they recover from today, then that'll be the end of it. We'll each be given rewards, the respect we deserve." Argus sat back down, slugged his wine.

"We're not going after them, Argus." Lucius' voice had an odd severity about it. He never liked speaking to Argus that way but found he had to. "If we go after them we'll be disobeying orders, going into an area beyond Roman control and knowledge. There might not even be any water beyond the frontier for all we know."

"Gods, Lucius! It won't be like that. We're the superior fighting force. They're just a bunch of desert rats, nothing more. Or are you afraid?"

"Ever since we were young you'd bait me by calling me a coward. Grow up my friend, we're not children anymore.

50

We're soldiers with duties and responsibilities." Argus kicked back his stool and paced the sandy ground. "Argus, I think you're underestimating this enemy."

"Balls, Lucius! We could stamp them out in one clean fight if you'd get over yourself. They're no match for Romans."

"That's what they said about Hannibal. Look what he did to Rome's armies."

"Yeah, Rome crushed that desert bumpkin, ground his army into the dirt."

"After years of blood."

"I'm right this time. I don't care what you say. You'll see, Lucius. The attack today is just the beginning. That force is going to pop up again and again."

"If they're on Roman lands, we'll engage them as we must. For now let it be, Argus. Don't force me to pull rank. It's my decision. That's it." Lucius put his hand on Argus' shoulder. His friend did not budge. Only stared into Lucius' eyes.

"Fine, Lucius. Have it your way." That was it. As he always had done when they were younger, Argus shut down, was unwilling to speak further. He would go to his tent, pound the sand in anger and then all would be back to normal the next day. It had always been the same.

After Argus had gone, Lucius thought further on the situation. He hoped the raiders were not rejoining a larger force. Luckily, a force that large could not remain in Roman territory without being noticed. He hoped that if Roman troops were being paid to look the other way, that they were few in number. The loyalty of those outposts was essential.

"Let's be alert and hope that the Gods watch over us," he had said to Argus as he was leaving.

Argus had chuckled. "You and your gods. They play with us. The only one who will look out for me is me, not Mars, Jupiter or even your Apollo." He flung back the tent flap and went out into the darkness.

"Argus, a little faith never hurt anyone," Lucius said to his back.

Lucius went over to his cot and, listening to the crackling of campfires and the laughter of the men off duty, he fell asleep. Before long he was lost in a torrent of dreams, one upon the other, images of the recent battle flashing on some obscene canvas of the Gods' making. Then...serenity.

During the night, in that other realm, Lucius walked among the great dunes of the deep desert under a starlit sky. In the distance he saw a tall, strong figure approaching. The man moved with a powerful, mesmerizing grace. He came closer, was dressed in a brilliant silver breastplate and greaves and wore a golden helm with a hair crest of bright blue. Wrapped around him was a cloak that shone of an otherworldly turquoise. It wavered like a calm sea with sun glinting on its water, though it was night. Lucius went down on one knee before his protector.

"Rise, young Metellus," said the God in a calm, deep voice. Apollo was beautifully imposing with his dark hair and piercing grey eyes. He was tall and perfectly proportioned, the epitome of an Olympian. Lucius rose, listened. "You do not yet realize your role in this life but you will find your way. I will look out for you, but you must be strong, wise. Follow the road with care and you will find your destiny."

Lucius managed to muster his voice. "Great God Apollo, how do I know that I lead my men wisely? I have doubts."

"You are mortal. Do not think about it. Feel. Feel it within you, in the depths of your being. Remain true to yourself and your heart and the mind will follow." Apollo held out his hand and with a flash there appeared a sword, gleaming in the moonlight. It was of a metal the likes of which Lucius had never seen. The shape was ancient, looked strong with its strange metal, its golden hilt.

"This sword will lead you to your destiny. One day it will come to you and you will know you have been wise, that you have listened." Then the Olympian held aloft the magnificent sword and hurled it far into the northern night sky. It soared across the heavens like a glinting star. Lucius gazed in amazement. Apollo looked at him with the affection of a father and turned to leave. Then, he turned back and, reaching out to Lucius' chest, touched the dragon emblem on his breastplate.

Lucius felt a welling up inside him, a heat that flowed throughout his body. He fell to his knees again, blinded by the light. "Farewell, young Metellus. Your heart will lead the way." With that, the God disappeared, leaving Lucius alone among the dunes beneath the stars and the moon.

Come morning, the trumpets rang. Once the camp was taken down, Lucius inspected the men before their continued march into the desert. He rode to the head of their formations, looked down at his breastplate; the shape of the dragon was cool beneath his fingertips. The sands seemed different. He raised and lowered his hand and the drum began to beat. "Forward!" he yelled. The cohort lurched reluctantly into motion; the sun was already warming the earth.

As he rode, Lucius remembered the previous night. It was all he could think of. He felt as though he was being watched now. He wondered why, in all the world of gods and men, would the God of Light, of Wisdom, come to him? *Was it just a fanciful dream?* he wondered. *It couldn't have been real. Perhaps I'm just tired?* Then, he remembered Diodorus, his tutor. The old man had once said that it is often during the calmness of night that gods and men meet. He had said that during the day, the Gods speak through their envoys: 'eagles and omens' as the saying went.

This made sense to Lucius. He remembered the blinding light, thought that if he were to see shining Apollo in the full brightness of day, when his sun's rays penetrate all things, he would go blind or even mad. The brilliance would be too much for a mortal man's eyes to bear. For most of that day, Lucius rode farther ahead, silent.

V

ANGUIS

'The Dragon'

The wind blew with a ferocity they had not experienced to that point, great funnels of sand swept up to the heavens by two massive whirlwinds that danced about the cohort. For weeks, it seemed, they had hoped for some form of breeze to ease the march. They regretted that wish. The mouths of distant Titans were now agape, their deafening howl threatening to rupture eardrum and spirit. The men scrambled to find any piece of cloth, no matter how ragged or filthy, to protect themselves from the suffocating wind, the biting sand. It was blinding and the pace of the march had fallen to a virtual standstill.

Lucius could feel the sand gritting against his teeth as he tried to breathe or swallow. He felt blinded and rode with one hand shielding his eyes. Pegasus and the other horses protested and reared up in fear and discomfort. The wind grew stronger and stronger and the whirlwinds attacked and retreated. Lucius and the other riders had covered their horses' eyes and muzzles to protect them but for many of the beasts it only furthered the sense of panic, the sandy ground constantly giving way beneath them.

After a long beating, the wind rested for a brief moment. Lucius caught a glimpse of what looked like large rock formations about half a mile ahead. He hoped it was real, that it would provide some protection until the sandstorm abated.

"ALERIO!" His voice was lost on the wind. He pointed to the rocks. Alerio knew exactly what he was thinking and nodded emphatically, his eyes half shut and irritated. They quickened the pace and after what seemed like four miles instead of half a mile, they reached the protection of the rocky sanctuary where there was just enough room for the men and horses to take cramped shelter.

As soon as they were safe, the men removed the cloths covering their mouths. Dry, gritted lungs heaved and many of the troops coughed up sand and bile, gasped for cleaner air. It hurt Lucius to breathe and he felt as though the sand were grinding away his insides with every breath. The wind was still very strong and the troops collapsed on the ground against the rock outcroppings, their shields in front of their faces. Lucius dismounted, pushed Pegasus down onto the ground and leaned up against the stallion, stroking his neck soothingly.

The sun was just barely visible through the sand-choked air. Lucius removed his helmet, wiped the grimy sweat from his brow before replacing it. He took his water skin, removed the stopper and took a sip. It hurt going down. He could feel the sand swirling around in his mouth.

It had been at least two weeks since they had departed from Cyrene and ever since, the cohort had experienced nothing but problems. In addition to sandstorms, a dried up oasis and a few sick troopers, they had been plagued by the nomads who harried the Romans as they picked their way across Africa.

The enemy seemed to be heading in the same direction. Lucius had lost only a few men in one of the dusk attacks when the strange desert light played tricks on the eyes and danced on the never-ending dunes. They had been hit six times; a quick charge of mounted archers at a safe distance launching volleys into the cohort. By the time the troops had formed up, they were gone again. It was as if they were merely letting the Romans know of their presence, that they were unafraid and were always there.

Why the attacks never came at night when they were most vulnerable Lucius did not know, but he was grateful it was so. The constant uncertainty was a bigger problem than the attacks themselves.

"Tribune? Tribune?" Lucius came back out of his thoughts and turned to see Eligius and Garai. "Tribune," began Eligius.

"The men can't take much more of this. Some of them have nearly choked to death and others are half blinded. Centurion Antanelis' eyes are bleeding too; he rubbed them a bit too much."

"Will he be all right?"

"He'll be fine. Nothing a little clean water and a poultice won't heal. The sun will be going down in a few hours Tribune. We'll need to find a place to camp."

"I know, Centurion. According to the map, there's a large oasis a few miles from here. As soon as the storm eases up we'll move out. It looks as though the wind is dying down already. Pass it on to the men so they have something to look forward to. I'll let you know when to move out."

"Yes, Tribune!" the two brothers replied. They were looking the worse for wear.

Lucius looked down at his cuirass, caked with sand. His cloak was filthy, a billowing cloud of dust whenever he moved. The only thing that identified him was his helmet, though the crimson crest was now as colourless as the rest of his armour. He shrugged off the sand as best he could and tapped his breastplate free of dust, revealing the dragon beneath. He cleared the symbol of sand; he recalled the memory of Apollo's visitation, his dream. *No time to think of that now, Lucius,* he thought to himself. *The men need you.* "All right! Move out!" The men helped up their mates who had need of help. "Not much farther men!" Lucius tried to sound encouraging. "Extra wine rations for everyone tonight!" A muffled cheer went up.

The oasis was heavenly. Elysium on Earth; as peaceful and serene as its golden fields. The evening was as quiet as the inner sanctum of a temple on some far-removed island shore. Lucius allowed the men to rest, get water for themselves and the horses before they had to make camp on the northern edge of the oasis. Guards were posted.

The attack the officers fully expected never came. The gently swaying palm trees shaded them from the sun's dwindling heat as they refreshed themselves in the large pool of water within the natural refuge. There were even date trees; many of the men gathered bunches, a welcome treat to share around the campfires. Those who had suffered severely from the storm were cared for immediately by any troops with medical experience.

Lucius saw to it that Antanelis was allowed to rest and nurse his eyes. The young man protested, said he would appear weak in front of his men, but Lucius ordered him to stand down for a while, he would need to be well enough to travel the following day. Argus took command of both centuries for the evening.

The camp was finally set up, guards patrolling the area. Lucius sat solemnly in his tent, wondered what else lay in store for them. The storm was one thing, but how could the nomads know exactly which way they were headed? Back in Cyrene, Brutus and his cavalry had pursued them far enough to ensure they could not come any closer. He had said that they were headed toward the far south-west.

Lucius asked not to be disturbed that evening, for he wished to retire early and rest. After eating and washing up, he went to his quarters and knelt before the statue of Apollo. His polished armour hung on the central tent pole. His cloak had been washed and was also drying near one of the braziers in the tent.

He gazed at the effigy of Apollo. Confused, Lucius turned to look at his cuirass again, the dragon reflected the flickering firelight. Once more he remembered the strange dream. Ever since, he had been hoping to hear the voice again, a voice like music as he recalled. *Had He smiled? Why did He point to my armour? Why me?* The questions were infinite. He rose immediately to strap on his breastplate, slung his gladius over his shoulder and put on the belt that carried his dagger. He then put on a black cloak that he removed from the trunk near his cot and went out of the tent into the cooling night air.

He made his way through the camp, silently acknowledging those who recognized him, and went into the oasis. Moonlight reflected off of the pool of water. It was as still and perfect as glass. The moon was full that night and the final traces of the sun's red light on the horizon dissolved into the distance. The stars too, shone brightly and twinkled in the night sky as Lucius approached the edge of the tree line.

The troops who were patrolling at that time halted him but as soon as he revealed himself they saluted and stood at attention.

"All's well I trust?" Lucius asked.

"Yes, Tribune! No sign of the enemy or anything else."

"Good. I know it was a hard day and you would rather be in your tents but we can't afford to take chances. When your shift is up then you can relax. Until then stay alert. I'm walking in that direction. If I need you I'll call."

"Yes, Tribune." The two men watched their commander go, then looked at each other.

"Why do you suppose he's walking about alone like that?" asked one as he leaned on his shield.

"Beats me. Maybe he just wants some time alone?" answered the other.

"I heard someone say he heard centurion Argus telling one of the other centurions that the Tribune thinks the Gods talk to him."

"And you believe that? You're a moron if you do. He's not a priest, he's a soldier, and a good one at that. He's a good lad, our tribune. A soldier's beliefs are his own." They stood silent, watched Lucius as his head tilted back, his eyes skyward. He walked farther away.

Lucius looked up at the beautiful star-shrouded sky. "I wish you would speak to me again, Far-Shooting Apollo. I have so many questions and no answers. I honour you, Lord." He hoped that something would happen, but nothing did. The sky was still. He walked back and forth along the edge of the dune, staring up for what seemed like an hour to the two troopers watching him.

He breathed deeply. The air was clean again, scentless.

A faint sound reached his ears. He pulled back the hood of his cloak. Cries for help. Lucius stood still, listening intently, trying to guess which direction the noise was coming from. Someone was being attacked. *Who in Hades could that be out here?* he wondered. He hurried south-east over two rows of small dunes.

"What? Where's he gone to then?"

"Should we follow?" The two men thought about it for a moment.

"Come on! Let's go!" The two troopers hoisted their shields and followed after.

The sand was soft; Lucius was able to approach without making a sound. In a dip between the dunes, next to a small fire, he saw five men surrounding a sixth man who appeared to be a lost traveller.

The man was lying flat on the ground, tied to four stakes, one for each limb. His tormentors were dressed all in black, the style of the desert nomads. They were armed with bows and daggers.

Their victim was cursing at them, challenging them to do their worst, warning them that the Gods would punish them for their blasphemy. He had been stripped of all his clothing which lay in a white pile nearby. The fiends standing over him had cut him in places, beaten him to bruising.

"What's that? You want some more?" said one nomad who spat on the prostrate man. "Cut him again!"

Lucius cringed as a dagger was run along the traveller's leg. He bled into the sand around him, but continued to curse. His muscles tensed in an attempt to pull out the stakes, his wounds gaped painfully.

Then one of the men went over to the fire, took up a red-hot iron. He smiled at their victim, taunted him with a little dance.

The others held his limbs tightly as he made to burn the man's mid section. Lucius felt a rage well up inside at the cruelty being inflicted on the traveller. His dagger was already unsheathed when he leapt from behind the dune's peak and charged. The blade flew from his hand and planted itself in the throat of the man with the hot iron. Blood spurted from his neck, he tripped and fell into the fire.

"What? Get him!" shouted one of the other nomads.

Lucius unsheathed his gladius and was running down the hill at the dead man's companions who stared in shock at their attacker while their comrade writhed on the ground, burning. Before they had realized what was going on, Lucius' sword plunged into the breastbone of another of them. The metal blade gleamed in the moonlight as he plunged it into the hated flesh of yet a third.

The other two managed to draw their long daggers and with frightening war cries they ran at Lucius who crouched, ready for the onslaught. He flung his cloak over the head of one of them and pushed him aside as he spun. At the same time he cleaved the other's dagger hand from his body. The man yelled and turned to jump back for another crazed attack but before he could take a step, Lucius' forearm laid a crushing blow on his throat, knocking him to the ground gasping for air through his crushed windpipe.

Meanwhile, the last man had thrown the cloak to the ground and charged once more. It was too late. The cold, sharp point of the Roman's sword came up under his chin, cutting deep before being withdrawn in a circular motion, to come down directly, cleaving the man's skull in two. His dagger fell to the ground from where it had stabbed harmlessly at Lucius' armoured chest. The body fell limp with a thud onto the blood-soaked sand.

It was quiet again, deathly so with the carnage about his feet. Lucius felt the blood pumping in his ears. It had all happened so quickly, his rage at seeing the man being tortured had taken over and now he returned to the world around him, felt himself once more. The man on the ground stared at Lucius in gratitude and amazement. *He's actually smiling!* Lucius thought, believing it another dream. The blood on his hands said otherwise.

He knelt down, untied the traveller and gave him his clothes.

"Are you all right? Why were they torturing you like that? Gods!" Lucius looked at the man's body. He was badly wounded but it did not seem to bother him. He did not speak. There was something about him. "You're lucky. You should be dead." Still no words, only the traveller's studying gaze. "Don't speak Latin huh? Greek?" Nothing. He helped the man up. "You'd better come to camp with me. We've got medical supplies to bind those wounds. You'll bleed to death otherwise."

The man was shorter than Lucius, but well built. His dark skin contrasted with his white desert garb. He stared at Lucius with his unusual blue eyes and smiled.

"You wear the dragon upon your breast," he said and nodded to Lucius' breastplate, sprinkled with drops of blood. "Beware..." he continued. "There are those in your ranks who would betray you, mighty dragon." Lucius looked at him, as if in a daze.

"What did you say? Who are you? Why didn't you speak before?"

Just then there was a cry from the dunes behind them. "Tribune! Tribune! Are you all right?" The two troopers came running up the dune and Lucius waved, indicating he was fine. When he turned back, the man was gone, vanished, carried away on the desert breeze. For a moment, Lucius believed that he had encountered a shade.

"What in Apollo's name is going on here?" He picked up his sword and pulled his dagger out of the neck of the first corpse. The two troopers came running up. "Did you two see where he went?"

"Who, Tribune?" They looked about the ground.

"The man who was being tortured by these whoresons."

"Didn't see anyone else, apart from the five dead nomads scattered about your feet." They nodded as they looked around.

"Good work, sir!" one of the men said proudly. "Wish we'd been here in time to help you, or at least to see it."

"That's enough. Better gather their weapons and any food they have and get back to camp."

"What about the bodies?"

Lucius thought about the traveller and how they had treated him. "Leave them for the jackals and vultures. It's all they deserve."

"Yes, Tribune!" The two men began to search the corpses while Lucius climbed a high dune to scan the surroundings.

"He's gone…" he muttered.

"What's that sir?"

"Nothing…nothing." Lucius looked up at the full moon and found himself to be surprisingly calm, at ease in its silver light. He filled his lungs with a deep breath and realized, his hands were still.

VI

DECIMARE SABRATHAE

'Decimation in Sabratha'

Suspicions grew worse in Lucius' mind as more raiding parties somehow managed to penetrate deep within the province. Riders had been sent north to Leptis Magna with dispatches for the local governor informing him of the situation. The governor was outraged and humiliated and quickly sent word to the tribune that he should find out who was responsible and strike back. He would send four squadrons of troops to join the cohort and aid them in any way possible. 'The safety of Rome's grain and oil, Her dignity, are at stake!' he had written.

Lucius had been thrown headlong into a situation for which he had not been prepared and began to feel the pressure of his predicament acutely. After several meetings in the command tent, Lucius and his centurions decided upon a course of action. It was thought, by all of them, that the nomads were being let through by auxiliary troops at some of the frontier posts. That appeared to be the only logical explanation; the frontier forts were just too many, patrols too frequent to miss so many raids.

The action decided upon was a storming of the frontier forts directly to the south and west. No riders would be sent ahead to inform them of their arrival. The visits would be secret and instantaneous, only the commanding officers being privy to any plans. The auxiliaries, the cohort troops, none of them would know what was happening aside from the direction in which they were marching. Lucius was determined to bring the perpetrators to justice.

Many of the troops in the cohort were angry, frustrated; Lucius was forced to inflict disciplinary action on three especially mouthy individuals who had begun to spread their message of discontent. The flames of that fire did not spread too far into the ranks, especially when the men were told that the very security of the people of the empire was under threat if the insubordination was allowed to continue. The legionaries did not protest further to their tribune's actions; no doubt the sight of the three individuals' lashed backs also played a part in swaying opinion. The cavalry also followed suit, reluctantly. Within three days the four squadrons sent by the governor had arrived with orders to follow Lucius' every command.

In the regions south of Leptis Magna and Sabratha there were eight frontier forts suspected of being in a position to allow raiders through to the north. Beginning with the fort at Ghirza, the cohort moved quickly and relentlessly. Immediately, traces of treachery were discovered when an investigation of the Ghirza fort revealed a cache of gold coins in the troop quarters there. The troops there were taken into custody and replaced with some of the men sent by the governor until trusted substitutes arrived.

The next three forts yielded no evidence of treachery. A few more of the governor's troops were left behind at each fort for a short time. They would return to Leptis Magna a week later with their reports.

Wherever there were the slightest traces of acts against the empire, prisoners were taken and replaced. There was little or no resistance and the operation went relatively smoothly, that is, until the cohort arrived at the frontier fort of Tentheos, south-west of Sabratha. As the cohort came within reach of the fort, Lucius kept the cohort hidden from view behind the large rock formations that surrounded the sandy flatlands in which it was situated.

Two centuries waited in position to the south-west, two to the north and two centuries took up position to the south-east with Lucius and the cavalry.

Several horses could be seen outside the walls of the main gate. Lucius shielded his eyes from the dusty, wind-blown air to see what kind of harness the horses had. Pegasus shifted nervously beneath him. They had not expected to find cavalry at the fort.

"Well?" Argus asked impatiently, his men in ordered rows behind them. "Are they Roman or not?"

Lucius leaned forward, squinting. "They're not Roman. Nomad."

"Bastards!" Argus stepped forward for a better look, smacking his vinerod into the palm of his hand.

"Get back, Centurion!" Lucius tried not to yell. "I don't want them to see us until we're on the move. He looked over the faces behind him. "I want them alive. No killing. Antanelis, get your men ready. You too, Argus. On my signal." Lucius looked at Brutus and then at his cornicen standing on a rock behind him to make sure the man was ready to give the signal to attack; all centuries had to move in simultaneously. He tightened his grip on the reigns, unsheathed his spatha and raised it above his head.

He stayed his hand. A nomad and what looked to be the commander of the fort came out of the gate with several other men. *Now, Lucius! Now!* "Charge!" Lucius' sword swung downward and the cornicen gave the signal.

Lucius, the cavalry and all six centuries charged out into the open flats surrounding the fort. A cry of warning went up from one of the guards that sent the nomads coming out of the fort into a panic; they scattered quickly to their mounts and sped away in a cloud of dust. The auxiliaries manning the fort stood dumbfounded for a few brief moments of fear before retreating behind the walls. It was too late. They were surrounded. Lucius could see a ballista being readied on one of the ramparts and slowed to warn Argus and Antanelis.

"Ballista!" he yelled back. "What in Hades?"

Brutus and the rest of the cavalry continued their charge toward the fort, pounding full-speed into the gateway before it could be closed. *Damn the little bastard and his order!*

Inside, the fort commander stood with a few bedraggled men, their swords half-raised; they looked deathly afraid as the cavalry surrounded them, spears pointed directly at them.

"What the fuck are *you* doing here?" the garrison commander shouted as Brutus reigned in. The men on the ground lowered their swords.

Then it happened. Just as Lucius entered the gate, enraged that Brutus had broken formation, he heard Brutus give the command.

"Kill'em! Traitors!"

It was too late for Lucius to do anything or say anything above the yelling of the cavalry or the painful cries of the traitors as spears were plunged into their chests and bodies hacked to bloody pieces. It happened quickly and unexpectedly. Pegasus reared up and Lucius reigned in hard before the carnage. Time stood still for a moment.

"Stop it!" Lucius' words were too late. "I wanted those men alive, damn you!" He could feel his head pounding with rage. The cavalry stood all about, pieces of hacked limbs at their horses' hooves, like slavering hyenas above a fresh kill. He dismounted and walked over to the bodies. Not a single man left alive.

Lucius paced back and forth, his jaw tight with anger, as Brutus and the cavalry stood before him outside the fort walls. His centurions and the cohort troops stood behind him, watching. The situation was delicate. They still needed the cavalry to complete their patrol and yet there had to be an example. Then Lucius stopped in front of Brutus, staring into his dull, rebellious eyes. He wanted to cut off his smirking lips.

"Who in Hades gave you the order to execute them? Tell me!"

Brutus looked evenly at Lucius. He knew that this was not the time to speak out in anger or defiance for the tribune had every right to execute him. "I thought that we were to punish the traitors for their insolence." He held out his hands. "They were armed and ready to attack us. I gave the order to attack before they did."

"And now, thanks to your idiocy, they're all dead and we have no one to question! You would have been better off pursuing the nomads who ended up getting away. Now we're not any better off than before!" Lucius paced again. It took every ounce of will he had to calm himself. All eyes were on him. Alerio and Argus came over to his side. "I could execute all of you but, Gods help us, you're needed on this expedition. Therefore I'll be merciful for now and let the legate commander in Lambaesis do as he wishes with you when we get there." Brutus smiled triumphantly. Lucius tilted his head, mock amusement on his face. "You're not off easy Brutus. The punishment will be," he declared, "a hundred lashes each, latrine duty and denial of pay for the rest of the patrol!"

Lucius turned to walk away and Brutus spat. Argus, who was still standing nearby, unleashed his anger and landed a crushing blow with his vinerod across Brutus' spiteful face, knocking him to the ground before he knew what hit him. It felt good. The blood ran freely from the mouth of the unconscious man; his men did nothing, knew the consequences of retaliation. Argus stood above Brutus, stared the rest of them down as several of his own troops came to stand by his side.

At the gate with Alerio and Antanelis, Lucius looked back over his shoulder. "That must have hurt. Argus shows no restraint. He should've been a gladiator instead." He laughed, wondered if Argus had done it out of love for him or for the shear enjoyment of disciplining the Egyptian horseman. Nobody would ever get away with doing anything behind his back as long as Argus was around.

"You're late!" said a voice from the scattered boulders as the man approached from the north, the form of his dark cloak threading through the rocks and scrub. He breathed heavily, tired from the climb up the rocky hillside. The distant moon was shaded by clouds and a short way off, the flickering lights of Sabratha were visible along the sea's edge. The breeze was cool up there. Somewhere far below them a lamb bleated painfully, ripped at by a pack of dogs; an eerie chorus for the night.

"I had trouble getting out of the town, guards everywhere. Besides," he caught his breath, spat, "why should I come all the way out here to meet you? You're the one who needs my help." The newcomer sat down on a rock opposite the other. The man who had been waiting was a nomad, dressed all in black, armed from top to toe like a well-travelled mercenary. Out of concealment, only the worked silver of his buckles shone above the whites of his grinning teeth. His eyes were dark in the shadow cast by his linen head gear.

"Our plans were nearly ruined the other day when that patrol showed up. It'll take some time before anyone will deal with us at the frontier."

"Well you don't have to worry about anyone talking, it was taken care of and not without difficulty. You should thank me. This had better be worth it to us. We've helped you bastards for a long while now but things are getting too hot. This 'tribune', as he's called, has fucked us all good."

The nomad leaned forward, staring the seated man directly in the eyes. "You'll be rewarded if all goes well. Otherwise, you'll wake one morning with your throat gaping and your limbs cut to feed the jackals." The nomad put his hand to his ear and cocked his head, smiling, as the dogs below reached fever pitch. They were now into the herd. "Worry not. Besides, this is our last meeting before the attack on Lambaesis. You have the maps we have requested?"

The cloaked figure reached into the folds of his clothing, pulled out several rolled pieces of papyrus and handed them over to the nomad whose eyes widened. "You and your men will be rewarded a hundred fold if the information you have provided us with proves useful. In the lands to the south, you will live out your days as kings." He then tossed a heavy pouch of coins into the other's lap.

The cloaked figure jumped up and thrust a dagger against the nomad's neck. The nomad flinched only slightly. "I've risked too much for this and you'd better pay up, you piece of shit! Don't fuck with us! There's something else I want from you."

"If you remove that dagger from my throat I'll listen," he said angrily. "What do you want?"

"I want the young tribune kept alive so that I can dispose of him myself."

"Why do you not poison him now to make things easier for us? You were an assassin for the emperor they called Commodus, were you not?"

"Yes I was. Part of the Praetorian Guard until Severus disbanded it and replaced us with his own legions. After that I was banished from Rome to serve in the far east where I was put into the auxiliary units."

"Luckily for us." The nomad secured the maps in a satchel. "So, that is the reason why you are so eager to help us against the Romans. I still think it would be far easier if you were to poison this thorn in our side, this Roman *dragon*."

"Yes it would. But I want him to know it's me when I kill him. I want him to suffer and feel what real pain is. I want his blood to soak the desert and the memory of his screams to sing me to sleep every night."

"You are strange to me. But, our gods love variety. Just so long as you remember that your first task is to aid us. If these maps you have given me are correct, we will be able to approach without being noticed and take them by surprise. On the other hand, if the Legion is prepared for us, you will create confusion during the attack and turn on the Roman ranks. They won't suspect an attack from within their own forces. After

69

they are defeated, then will you be able to make this Tribune Metellus suffer for as long as you wish." The cloaked man pushed his hood back and smiled with evil joy at the thought of carrying out his bloody task. "If we capture him in battle, we will save him for you." He put up his hand. "*If* your information is correct."

"It's all correct. They won't know what hit them. As for the tribune, his days are numbered."

"Then, if all goes as it should, I will see you in a few months. Discuss the matter with your men so that they know exactly what to do when the time comes. There must be no mistakes. If there are, we will hunt you down to the last man." The nomad rose, nodded and then turned to disappear among the rocks and boulders.

The cloaked figure turned back to look toward the lights of Sabratha from where he had come. The town was still lively. As he made his way back down the rocky slope, clutching the pouch of coins, he was completely unaware of the man crouched down on the rocks high above the spot where they had finalized their plans.

The white-clad figure gazed down at the traitor with stern determination, watched him slink back to Sabratha like a thief in the night. He decided to follow.

Sabratha was another rich African city known for its production of oil and grain. It was also known as a city of monuments, adorned with various temples and baths, a magnificent theatre and a massive capitol. The city fell to Julius Caesar and grew over the years to become a prosperous centre of trade and provincial government.

The streets were not of the usual Roman plan, set out in a tidy grid pattern, but rather a confusing mix of criss-crossing streets that were problematic to anyone not familiar with its layout. However, not long ago the eastern part of the city was built up in a more ordered layout, the Phoenician pattern replaced with a true example of Roman ingenuity. In this newer sector were located the Temple of Hercules, the theatre, and a wondrous bath complex adorned with beautiful mosaics.

In the northeast sector, along the coast, was the beautiful sanctuary of Isis as well as more baths for the local citizens. All in all, this city in a far corner of the empire was a prime example of the Roman peace and prosperity that defined the civilized world.

That night, Sabratha was alive with activity. Rich citizens roamed the streets with their entourages mingling amongst each other, discussing various issues at many of the upscale taverns that dotted the main streets. There was also a special performance in the great theatre of classic Greek plays by Euripides that either dazzled, bored, or confused the audience. Patrons went to enjoy the performance, to be seen or to do business. There was always time to do business.

As the play let out and the viewers filed into the torch-lit streets, the taverns filled up and those merchants who had waited patiently for the end of the performance came alive, ready to sell their wares to any rich ladies who happened to pass within selling distance. Amid the raucous laughter and sparkling jewels dangled in front of rich customers, the white-robed figure picked his way through the crowd, never losing sight. Ghostlike, he followed like a shadow, never more than several paces away and yet completely unnoticed by anyone.

Once across the main street of the city, the dark figure suddenly turned down a street from which a great deal of laughter and noise emerged. This was the area most frequented by local and visiting soldiers. Here they could find many a tavern where they could drink and gamble amongst themselves, forget the harsh realities of war and spend their hard-earned denarii. They could also find the temporary companionship of a variety of women who lured them into several other edifices. All tastes were catered to and every soldier who went in with a heavy purse left with a smile, despite the relatively lighter weight of those purses. Being rubbed down with fragrant oils, massaged and pleasured by any woman, girl, eunuch or boy, was something for which most soldiers were willing to part with their money.

The pursued man slowed to a stop in front of the window of a particularly quiet tavern called "The Olive Branch", a rather unusual name for a tavern frequented by soldiers. This establishment was slightly cleaner than all of the others and had better food and wine. Here, officers gathered for a casual drink in their time off to talk, sit back with a cup of sweet nectar and forget being officers for a short time; this while their men caroused in some of the other establishments up the street.

The man pulled his hood closer over his head and face, peered inside the window, his eyes squinting to see something. His fists clenched momentarily and then he turned quickly to continue on his way. Keeping his eye on where he was headed, his pursuer stopped to have a look inside the window to see what it was that angered his quarry so. He rubbed some of the dirt from the window to get a better look and noticed that the tavern was not very busy at all.

Then, at the far left corner of the large room he noticed three men, two very large and the other of medium build. They were Roman officers. As they appeared to talk casually like friends something caught the man's eye. Beneath the red cloak of the central figure, only slightly covered and flickering lightly in the candlelight, was a large dragon with its wings spread. He realized he was going to lose the other and ran down the street to continue his pursuit.

After the incident at the fort of Tentheos, Lucius had led the cohort north to Sabratha for a three day rest and replenishment of supplies after their relentless sweep of the frontier. The men deserved the rest and a sampling of Sabratha's pleasures. Needless to say, most of them ended up in the neighbourhood surrounding the Olive Branch tavern in which Lucius, Argus and Alerio had sat for a few quiet drinks and several courses of good food.

They laughed and joked together in an attempt to forget the rigorous days that had passed. What was thought to be a long, boring march had turned out to be anything but boring. Now they relaxed and enjoyed a bit of idle conversation as friends are wont to do. The tavern keeper, a veteran by the name of Quintus Valerius, was a large, robust man. Occasionally he would sit down with the three friends and reminisce with them about his years in the service of the empire.

"See this?" Valerius put his leg up on the table's edge. "A German spear did that!" he said proudly, showing off a scar that carved its way up the inside of his leg from calf to inner thigh.

"Bloody hell Valerius!" Alerio cringed. The three lads recoiled in pain at the sight.

"Yup! Almost lost my balls on the edge of that one."

"Mars was watching over you that day, friend," Lucius said as the man lowered his leg.

"Nope. Not Mars."

"Who in Hades was it then Valerius?" Argus slugged his wine.

"I always thought it was that god with the great big prick, what's his name?"

"Faunus?" ventured Lucius, trying not to laugh.

"That's the one!" Valerius slammed his fist on the table. "Faunus! Bless his jingling balls." The three young men almost fell off their stools, spilling wine as they laughed. It had been a long time since they had done this together.

Funnily enough as it turned out, Valerius had served briefly with Lucius' father in the Legions, and so when he found out who Lucius was he promptly declared that the drinks and the meal were on the house. Lucius tried to decline the offer, felt uncomfortable with the reason for it, but the old veteran would not listen. Argus kicked Lucius under the table.

Apparently, in his retirement, Valerius had decided to settle down in Sabratha and open a tavern for officers and the high-ranking officials who frequented establishments in this sector of the city. He eventually married a freedwoman of Egyptian origin and had been happy ever since.

"I don't miss the crowded stink of Rome," he said. "Besides, I prefer the more gritty aspects of life on the desert frontier. Makes me feel like I'm still soldiering."

"Ha! So you left the thrill of battle and life in the army to run a tavern in this flea-infested province? Why in Hades did you do that?" Argus scoffed at Quintus Valerius who pulled his chair up next to Argus' and looked into the eyes of the young hot-blooded centurion.

"Because, my dear drunken centurion...when you've seen as much blood as I have, and looked death in the face too many times to remember, you'd willingly herd pigs rather than see another man hacked to bits by an enemy's sword or spear as their blood splashes across your face." Quintus Valerius felt pity and worry for the young soldiers and although he knew that they had been through more than most, there would most certainly be more to come.

The gathering grew suddenly sober. Argus, only slightly humbled, joined Lucius and Alerio in their quiet respect for a man of the world who had cheated death and chosen to live the life he believed in. "Enjoy the rest of your meal my young friends and stay as long as you wish. You're always welcome." Valerius rose from his stool and, patting Lucius fondly on the shoulder, turned to see to a couple of men who had just come in through the door and seated themselves at the other end of the room.

"Lucius," said Alerio. "When was the last time you heard from your father?" Lucius looked down into his cup of wine, swirled it about for a few moments.

"I haven't heard from him in, oh, I'd say a couple of years."

"Is it that long?" Argus asked.

"Yup. Quite some time. You know he was furious with me for leaving to join the army. He wanted me to become a politician to advance our family's position in the Senate. But it wasn't what I wanted to do. I wrote to him a couple of times since I left for training but each letter grew more and more bitter and frustrating. When I had proved to be so successful in the eastern campaigns I made sure he knew about it and told him he had been wrong about me from the beginning. That was the last letter between us. I suppose his pride kept him from writing back to me. My own pride prevented me from writing again too."

"Come'on Lucius! He treated you, and me, like shit. He's a bastard!"

Lucius shot Argus an angry look. "Watch it! He's still my father." Argus shook his head, frustrated, and poured more wine.

"Do you think you could mend the rift between you when you get back to Rome?"

"I hope so, Alerio. It's something I think about everyday." Lucius ignored Argus' rolling eyes.

The three sat in silence for several minutes, each of them no doubt remembering their families and loved ones wherever they might have been. Quiet and wine can have a strange effect on even the strongest warrior's mind.

The tavern door flew open suddenly and a cool breeze whipped through, extinguishing several candles. Quintus Valerius quickly set about closing the door and lighting the candles that had gone out. When he had finished, in the middle of the room stood a warrior clothed all in white, his face obscured by the hood that hung lightly over his head. At his side was a gold-hilted sword and a dagger.

Lucius and Alerio did not pay any notice to the stranger as they were too deep in their own thoughts. However, Argus turned to look at the man who stood facing them, discomfited by his presence. "Can I help you, stranger?" asked Quintus Valerius who stood, his thick, scarred arms crossed, suspicion in his eyes.

The stranger slid back his hood to reveal the strong dark features of his face. He had a dark beard and his piercing blue eyes were bright and full of life. "I seek the Tribune Lucius Metellus Anguis," the stranger stated calmly.

By this time Argus was making his way over to him, hand on the hilt of his gladius. "And what do you want with the Tribune, nomad?" Lucius and Alerio looked up. Argus had drunk too much, they all had.

"My message is for the Tribune alone, not you," he stated. Argus quickly drew his sword and rushed the white-clad apparition. In an instant, his sword was thrown to the side, stuck in the top of a wooden table, as the stranger flipped Argus over his head and back in one amazing, fluid motion so that he landed on his back on the table next to the two patrons at the other end of the room. The table shattered, Argus sprawling on the floorboards. Quintus Valerius drew a well-honed short sword from behind the counter, pointed it at the stranger.

"You shouldn't have done that stranger. These are friends of mine. Off with you or you'll leave in pieces."

"I mean no harm," he stressed. "I come with an important message for the Tribune Lu-"

"I'm Lucius Metellus Anguis!" Lucius stepped forward, his bright blade drawn and pointed at the stranger's throat. "An assault on my men is an assault on me," Lucius said angrily. Beyond the man he could see Argus shaking his head, trying to get to his feet.

"I was attacked first, Tribune, and merely defended myself." He stepped toward Lucius as Argus, Alerio, and Quintus Valerius surrounded him.

"What is it you want..." Lucius' sentence died out with a sudden realization. "I know you from somewhere..." The stranger smiled. He reached out and pointed to the dragon on Lucius' breastplate. "You?"

"Who is this Lucius?" Alerio asked. Argus' eyes narrowed as he made to grab the stranger again.

"Wait, Argus!" Lucius bellowed. "From the desert...that night..."

76

"Yes, Tribune." Everyone relaxed slightly, except Argus. "I am the one you saved in the desert that night."

Lucius was stunned. "But…but you disappeared?" The man smiled again.

"And yet, Tribune, I am here. For as you helped me once, I am here to help you."

"Lucius what's this nomad talking about?" Argus asked through clenched teeth. "Who sent you, pig?"

"I am not a nomad! I am no *man's* servant," the stranger stated.

"I saved him from some nomads who were torturing him in the desert weeks ago outside one of the oases one night." He looked to the man. "Your wounds seem to have healed rather quickly…you should've been dead."

"I heal quickly," he replied.

"It would seem so. Now stranger, tell me who you are."

"You may call me Ashur."

"And these are my centurions, Argus and Alerio, and this is our friend Quintus Valerius. I think you had better give us your message Ashur, before my friends here lose patience. Let's sit down." Oddly enough to Argus and Alerio, Lucius was calm and relaxed as he led the man to their table and although he seemed fine with this man they were going to keep their wits about them. They sobered up quickly. "Now tell me what this urgent message is, Ashur."

Ashur seated himself. He had a nobility and strength about him that the others had rarely seen in any man and although they were slightly awed by his noble demeanour they did not show it.

"I have come to warn you that you have traitors in your midst. They have been aiding the desert nomads and plan to kill you after a major assault on your legionary base at Lambaesis." The three men's eyes went wide at this news, though they were not sure whether to believe it. A nomad assault on Lambaesis? They would not dare! Lucius broke the hanging silence.

"And how do you know this, Ashur? Why should I believe you?"

"Because Tribune, since you have saved my life, I have vowed to the God that I would watch over you and save yours if I can."

"I have plenty of protection and can take care of myself."

"That's right, you nomad piece of camel shit! Let's take him out back Lucius, right now. Before he puts a knife in your back!"

"Argus, please!" Lucius slammed his fist on the table. "If there's a chance that Lambaesis is under threat, we must hear him out." He turned back to Ashur. "You still haven't answered my first question. How do you know of this plot?"

Ashur leaned forward, looked into Lucius' eyes. "I have been following a man for some weeks now who has been dealing with the nomads who have been attacking you. Tonight, I came upon this same man and a nomad leader while they met in the hills outside of the city. They did not know I was there. I heard of their plans and during their conversation your name was mentioned along with their plans to attack the Legion to the west. This man is among your ranks and has been giving the nomad army information on everything from troop movements and geography to strategy. He has even been telling them when and where to strike so that they could obtain Roman weapons and artillery. They spoke of plans to lead a surprise attack on the base at Lambaesis several months from now with the aid of some maps he gave them. He is to turn on you and your forces and when the battle is finished he has promised to kill you slowly and painfully. This man is very dangerous. I am here to ensure that he does not succeed and to forewarn you of this invasion in which many lives may be lost."

Everyone was quiet. The three soldiers looked at each other and knew the implications of what this man was saying, if he spoke the truth. "Who is this traitor? Could you identify him if you were to see him?" Alerio asked.

"I do not know him by name but if you will follow me I can lead you to him and his companions where they are discussing their plans."

"He's lying, Lucius!" yelled Argus. "You can't believe this man. Our troops are loyal!"

"I believe that for enough gold, many men would willingly sell their souls to the god of the underworld." Ashur looked to Argus. "Besides, it is not for you to decide but rather for your commander. Tribune? Time is short and if you wish to catch the traitor, I suggest we go now and that you bring some of your most trusted men." Ashur looked at Lucius almost pleadingly. Lucius stood, looking back at him and then to the others.

"All right. Show us Ashur. But! If you're lying, you'll regret it."

"I can't believe you're buying this Lucius!" interrupted Argus. "I'm leaving!"

"Centurion!" roared Lucius. "You'll do as I say! Now, you and Alerio go quickly and bring back Antanelis, Maren and their two centuries. Do it now and do it as quietly as you can. I'll wait here with Ashur and Quintus Valerius." Argus was red with anger and exploded out the tavern door without saying a word. "Alerio go with him and watch him."

"Lucius are you sure about this?" he asked. "Maybe I should stay with you. We don't even know this man."

"Don't worry, my friend I'll be fine. Now go and come back quickly."

"Don't fret centurion. I'll watch over him," said Quintus Valerius from across the room, still holding his short sword. Alerio looked at each of them, nodded and snapped a salute to Lucius before rushing out the door. Lucius looked at Ashur who nodded.

"You shall see the right of what I am saying Tribune."

Lucius placed his sword on the table. "We'll see."

79

It was not long before Alerio and Argus returned with Antanelis and Maren, the latter's men waiting in a nearby square. The four centurions were clearly concerned and came as quickly as they could to the tavern where Lucius awaited them. He and Ashur had sat in silence, regarding each other carefully, thoroughly.

As they made their way through the winding streets, Ashur told Lucius of the bag of gold that had been given to the traitor as a fee for his deed. Whoever it was, Lucius decided that they would need some kind of proof before accusing someone based solely on the word of a stranger who appeared out of the desert. Not even a Roman! They would wait and listen until they had heard or seen something to their satisfaction before arresting the perpetrators.

Ashur walked speedily until he came out of the city's eastern gate. On the plain outside the walls stood row upon row of the cohort's tents. Off to the side, in the direction Ashur now led them, were the stables and quarters set up for the auxiliaries. As they made their way over to the camp, Lucius motioned for Maren and Antanelis to hang back with their men until he signalled for them to move in. They were just too many to move into the camp undetected.

Lucius, Alerio and Argus now followed Ashur into the midst of the auxiliary tents. To their astonishment, there weren't any guards posted and the only activity seemed to be coming from the larger, central tent of the cavalry commander. Ashur halted a few paces from the tent's entrance which had been closed. The men looked to one another, each just coming to awareness of the situation and what was happening. Ashur motioned for them to listen carefully and pointed to a small, fresh slit in the leather tent that he had made earlier.

Lucius squinted as he peered through the small hole, searching the tent. It seemed as though the entire cavalry regiment were crammed in there, surrounding a central figure. *Brutus!* Lucius watched as the black-cloaked figure stood in front of the men, speaking in hushed tones. It was barely audible but Lucius managed to catch a few phrases.

"The nomads have promised…our help…giving maps…details…for the attack to come…at Lambaesis…" Lucius was livid and looked back at Argus and Alerio who were waiting to see for themselves. Alerio stepped forward now. Brutus talked on. "For myself…promise that…to kill Tribune Metellus…"

Alerio stepped back, shocked, and whispered in Lucius' ear what he had heard. Lucius turned and waved at Antanelis and Maren who were awaiting his signal. Slowly, quietly, they moved into position around the large tent. Gazing through the hole in the tent now, Argus glanced the final proof they needed and he nudged Lucius to look. He peered through once again to see Brutus holding the large pouch of gold coins, handing each man in the tent his share of blood-money. Lucius nodded to Ashur in thanks and then stepped back, drawing his sword.

"NOW!" On his command the legionaries drew their swords and rushed the tent. The men inside were totally taken by surprise. Some of them drew their own swords and rushed out to find themselves completely surrounded and outnumbered. Immediately they dropped their weapons in surrender. It happened quickly, efficiently. Lucius moved to the tent's main entrance, Ashur, Alerio, Argus, Antanelis and Maren just behind him. Everyone's eyes were on the traitor as he stepped out of the tent, the bag of gold still held in one hand, his sword in the other.

Brutus was speechless, gritting his teeth through his smug expression. He had gone too far and been too careless this time and he knew it. It enraged him that the one who should catch him this time was the man he hated most. "Well, Tribune? What's the problem? Sabrathan whores too dirty for your Roman sword?" Brutus moved toward Lucius who stood in front of a wall of flashing blades.

Lucius smiled, happy that he now had an excuse to deal with Brutus. "This time you've gone too far traitor. Drop your weapon." He did not. "Are you deaf as well as stupid? You have no rights now. Drop it." Brutus seemed to bare his teeth like a cornered animal, unwilling to give up. "Very well," stated Lucius flatly.

Brutus lunged, but in one smooth, deadly motion Lucius' gladius flew up from his side and knocked the sword from his hand. The traitor screamed and lunged again but the tribune's golden pommel landed square on his brow, knocking him backward into the tent wall so that he fell to the ground, dazed. At his feet the gold coins fell with a loud jingle, their luminous metal dusted over in black soil.

Lucius pointed to the traitor in disgust and motioned to two troopers standing nearby. "Pick up that filth and put him in chains!" He gazed around the tent at the cavalry troopers. They had paid dearly for their misplaced loyalty. "As for the rest of this scum, shackle them all to each other and to their dog of a leader. Guard them ruthlessly! If any of them tries to escape, moves or even breathes, RUN HIM THROUGH!"

Lucius turned toward the town with Argus, Alerio and the man named Ashur. Antanelis, Maren and their troops were left to see to the prisoners. Lucius walked speedily, forcing his way through the dwindling crowds in the streets. "Lucius, where are we going?" Alerio asked from behind.

"To the governor's house! We end this stupidity tomorrow!"

The forum in front of the Capitol of Sabratha, in the north west sector of the city, was usually a place where people gathered to discuss politics, buy and sell goods and meet with friends. However, that morning, the air was still and stale. Despite the throng of people that lined the pillared arcades beneath the massive temple, the only sound that could be heard was the slow, solemn and steady beating of a single war drum calling the Gods to bear witness.

Around the perimeter of the large courtyard stood the men of the cohort. In the centre of the forum, for all to see, stood the entire auxiliary cavalry, tired, dirty and full of fear. There, they awaited punishment for a crime worse than any other, treason against the people of Rome and an empire that was ruthless and unshakeable in the preservation of itself.

Among the accused stood Brutus, the once arrogant and proud Praetorian assassin, now a common criminal awaiting the military judgement of an army that had conquered the world. He stood among the others now, no different than them, not even a coin to put in his own mouth for his inevitable journey.

At the top of the Capitol stairs stood the Governor. He was a tall, dark man, his stature all the more impressive to the onlooking citizens because of his long white toga, lined with a broad purple stripe. He made his way slowly down the stairs, a grave look upon his face as he addressed the crowd.

"Citizens and people of Sabratha! Last night, the Gods favoured us in revealing an evil plot against our great empire." The crowd was silent. "Today, justice will be done. These men before you…" He pointed at the accused. "…are guilty of treason against the emperor, against this province and against you. They shall pay dearly for it." Cries of 'DEATH!' and 'JUSTICE!' went up among the crowd and the governor put up his hands in a plea for silence. "Luckily for us," he went on, "a cohort of Rome's finest soldiers, sent to us by your emperor and kinsman, has foiled this plot against our sacred Pax Romana. As these traitors are in the service of the army, it is for their commander at the time to pass judgement. I give to you the man who has saved you from treachery, Tribune Lucius Metellus Anguis!"

Lucius tried to hide the shock and fear he was feeling at that moment. *What? Me?* he thought. He could see the Governor avoiding his gaze. *This wasn't what we talked about. He's supposed to pass judgement! They're waiting, Lucius. Think!*

"Go on, Tribune," the governor whispered. "This mess is yours, not mine." He backed away smiling as Lucius stepped forward hesitantly, all eyes upon him.

Amid the scattered cheers of the crowd, Lucius turned to face the people and his men, look down on the accused. The life of each auxiliary cavalry trooper in that courtyard was in his hands. He stood tall and serious in full armour as his crimson cloak bristled in the dusty breeze. He pushed all his anxiety to the back of his mind.

He scanned the faces peering up at him and spoke. "The charges against these men are indeed grave and deserve serious punishment. They have treated with Rome's enemies, exchanged valuable information, supplied the enemy with weapons with which to threaten the security of our frontiers. For this they accepted gold and even the promise of killing fellow Romans. I say these treacherous acts are cowardly." Lucius stared icily at Brutus who met his gaze through beaten, swollen eyes.

"For all of this, a military punishment is called for." He paused, allowed the gravity of the situation to sink in. "Therefore, I, Tribune Lucius Metellus Anguis, of the Legions of our most glorious Emperor Septimius Severus, do accept the responsibility placed upon my shoulders. The punishment to be inflicted upon these men is that of Decimation."

The crowd gasped and many of the accused hung their heads in desperation at the utterance of the harshest military punishment that could be invoked by a commander. Without a word from Lucius, his troops set about lining up the accused the width of the forum. Then Alerio stepped forward, making his way down the lines of traitors, touching every tenth man with his vinerod. The crowd's attention made Lucius uncomfortable as he watched the selection of those who were to be executed. Then, to the disappointment of many, Alerio passed by Brutus who stood there, staring up at Lucius, a hateful grin on his face. However, Lucius tried not be moved in the least by this. He stared back coldly, further punishment coming to mind. He felt a strange power now. Brutus, felt fear.

The twelve men whose end was at hand were lined up before their fellow conspirators and made to kneel with their heads bowed. Behind each of them stood a stern legionary. The drum began to beat again, slowly ringing the death knell. Then, when the beating stopped, each legionary drew his gladius upward and all at once twelve blades were plunged downward into the necks of twelve traitors. All that could be heard was the sound of the blades withdrawing and the lifeless bodies falling limp to the dusty ground. Someone's baby wailed at the far end of the square.

After the soldiers returned to their positions, Lucius stepped forward again. "As for the rest of the traitors, you will not be so fortunate as to die like your companions. The punishment for those remaining is this; you will run out your days in the galleys as slaves. Never again will you see the light of day, nor set foot on land. Take them away!"

At that moment, the remaining traitors stared at the twelve dead men before them and wished that they could trade places. A life in the galleys was no life at all and most men didn't last more than a month. It was a life full of fear, pain and disease with harsh captains and even harsher slave drivers. Not even the sea air would cover the ever-present stench of puke, piss and shit. A sword in the back was a gift.

Lucius watched as the prisoners were rounded up and led away to the harbour. When they were out of the courtyard and the dead bodies were taken away, he turned to the governor.

"Satisfied, Governor?" He had to hold his temper and his tongue.

"Me, Tribune?" He held out his palms innocently. "I had nothing to do with this. The decision was yours, not mine."

"But you said that-"

"I said that justice would be done," he cut Lucius off, "and it has." He stepped back, nodded his head. "Sabratha thanks you for ridding us of this threat, Tribune Metellus. May the Gods go with you."

That was it. The Governor turned to leave, his secretaries in tow, Lucius left behind at the top of the marble steps. "Pompous bastard," he muttered. There was nothing more to say or do. Alerio waited for him at the far end of the square, waved for him to come. Reluctantly, Lucius made his way down to the harbour where his cohort was loading the prisoners onto the Imperial slave ships that were always awaiting new flesh for galleys.

Down on the docks, many of the former auxiliaries begged and pleaded like children not to be put on the ship but their cries went unheard. Some fought so violently they had to be beaten before they could be thrown into the hold. Lucius stood at the boarding plank with Argus, saw to it that all went as it should. It was not a duty that he relished, indeed the entire morning had left a bad taste in his mouth, but he knew it had to be done. They had questioned the prisoners all night and although they had not obtained any information about the enemy, they did know approximately when and where to expect the attack.

As the final few men were led onto the ship, Brutus, the last among them, stopped in front of him. He was not the man he had been but was not as broken as the rest. Only just managing to stand up, he stared coldly into Lucius' eyes. There in that moment, Lucius felt the anger and ultimate hatred that this man had for him.

"I'll kill you Metellus, one day!" Brutus mumbled through broken lips.

"I think not. You're dead already, traitor. Enjoy the underworld." Lucius could not help saying it. For the first time that morning, he felt a sense of accomplishment in carrying out his duty.

Brutus' eyes raged and he spat at Lucius' feet, screamed fury, unable to move his shackled hands. Argus grabbed him violently and pushed him onto the ship where he loosed several crushing blows to Brutus' ribs, the crack of bones clearly audible.

"Easy soldier!" yelled the captain of the vessel. "You beat him too much and he'll be useless!"

Argus ceased his onslaught, grabbed the broken man by his chains and dragged him across the deck to a square hole. "You smell that? Hmm? That's your home now, camel fucker!" He held Brutus' head by the hair. "I hear the rats down there will gnaw at your feet and hands while you sleep." All Brutus could do was moan. "Good luck in Hades!"

With those parting words, Argus pushed him down into the blackness of his new world. As he lay there at the bottom, half dead, Brutus caught his final glimpse of light as the heavy wooden portal fell with a crash. The bright, outside world he had once known, breathed, was no longer a reality for him.

VII

VIA PULVERULENTA AD OCCIDUM

'The Dusty Road West'

Sabratha had a profound effect on Lucius and it was with mixed feelings of relief, anger and dread that he left the city behind. *How could I have allowed the Governor to play me like that? Did I do the right thing? Will news of this go beyond Sabratha?* He pondered these questions and more as he rode at the head of the marching column.

The road would now hug the coastline for the next few days, run over sandy flatlands cooled by the sea's gentle breath. The men were in high spirits, happy to get on with things, but for all their jollity, Lucius was immovable in his stern silence.

He had not spoken of the incident since the last prisoner was pushed onto the galleys, had not sat quietly with any of his centurions, his friends, to get their thoughts on the matter. He remembered a story he had once heard about how some of the men in Aegyptus had returned from a patrol in the desert. They returned with the body of a massive lion, the biggest anyone had ever seen. When asked how they managed to trap such a fine specimen they recounted how they had not touched it, that the beast had trapped himself by somehow falling into a pool of quicksand. The men had heard the groans of despair across that sand and when they went to investigate they found the lion, exhausted from flailing around. 'He was helpless!' one of the men said. 'He stared at us, his face still, his eyes challenging us. We thought his skin might fetch a good price so we speared him where he was, threw a rope about his neck and pulled him out. Easiest kill ever!' *The bastard actually laughed.*

Lucius felt like that lion: strong but unable to move, helpless. He hoped no one would come along and spear him, drag his limp body out of the sand he had unwittingly fallen into. At the time, he thought he had done the right thing. *They were traitors!* he told himself.

He heard a rhythmic humming behind him, realized he had forgotten about him, the man named Ashur. He had been the only one with whom Lucius had felt able to speak the last few days, not Argus or Alerio, Antanelis or the others. Only Ashur carried with him an unexplainable sense of peace and ease of breath. It had been a last-minute decision to invite the fellow to ride with them for as long as he wished. The men had protested but Lucius remained firm. Ashur had warned them about the traitors, had helped them a great deal, the least they could do was allow him to ride with them for a spell.

"Your thoughts weigh heavily upon your shoulders, Tribune," Ashur said casually, trotting up alongside. "It is a beautiful day, no? Apollo's light shines brightly over the world." Lucius looked up at the sky but did not answer. "I see the dragon wishes to be quiet. Forgive me."

"Why did you decide to help us, Ashur?" Lucius asked. "Your people have no love of Rome."

"First of all, Tribune, I have no people." This was an odd thing to say but Lucius let it be. "Secondly, I helped you, as I have said, because you helped me that night in the desert."

"Quite. That night." Lucius remembered it well, had trouble forgetting it. "Do you think I did the right thing in Sabratha?" He did not know why he was asking Ashur this, he was not even Roman.

"It is not for me to judge, Tribune. You acted bravely."

"But foolishly. Out of anger."

"That is not for me to say." Ashur's voice was calm, almost soothing. "You are young but seem to have experienced a great deal of the world. The only ones fit to judge your actions are the Gods and yourself. None other."

"I hope the Gods are not offended."

"I have not seen any ill-omened birds fly across your path, you are not sick and you are still standing." He smiled. "I think the Gods are at ease with your actions."

"The Goddess Hera tormented Hercules for the whole of his life before he died," Lucius stated.

"Yes but, you are not Hercules, Tribune."

"No friend. I certainly am not." The thought frightened Lucius. His face grew dark. He was ashamed at all of his self-doubt. *By the Gods, I'm a Tribune, a Metellus!* he chided himself.

"Tell me about your name, Tribune," Ashur broke into Lucius' thoughts again, "about your family."

Lucius looked at him, his face quizzical. "Why?"

"No reason. Simply to know, to pass the time as we ride." Lucius saw no harm in talking. He had to do something, he realized, to stop himself from brooding. "Start with your name, Metellus. I believe that I have heard that nomen, as you Romans call it, spoken of a great deal in reference to Rome's past. Am I right?"

Lucius decided to entertain Ashur's question. He turned to look back and saw Alerio eyeing them. Lucius nodded to him and turned back to Ashur. "You're right. A long time ago, during the Republic, my ancestors were at the forefront of events." The names and honorific titles came rushing back to him as distant whispers…Dalmaticus, Macedonicus, Creticus and Numidicus. "They were warriors and generals, some politicians. Metelli have held the post of Pontifex Maximus as well as having been Dictator."

Ashur nodded as he remembered. "I have heard all of these names. You hail from a strong line. Was there not also a woman among them?"

Lucius had been waiting for that. Inevitably, people always thought of her first. "Yes," he replied. "Caecilia Metella, daughter of Dalmaticus. Her second husband was the dictator, Sulla." For Lucius, any connection to Sulla was not distant enough; the blood, the proscriptions, it had been well over two-hundred years since but not long enough to forget. His mind drifted again. He remembered what his old tutor had said about how important it was for him to remember all of his ancestors so that he might learn from their achievements and their mistakes alike. *The fault of many men,* Diodorus had said, *is that they either forget the past or long too greatly for it.*

"Tribune?" Lucius came out of his thoughts. Ashur watched him keenly. "And what of your cognomen? It is a strong and powerful name. Do you know of its significance?" Ashur indicated the dragon on Lucius' breastplate.

"Anguis is the ancient word for 'dragon'. It's the symbol of our branch of the family."

"It is also a symbol of power and wisdom," Ashur added.

Lucius looked at him. "Yes it is."

"Your family must be proud. Are there many people bearing the name of 'Anguis' in Rome?" Pegasus snorted and reared with impatience. Their pace had slowed and the troops behind were closer than before.

"No. I'm the only one. Hya!" Lucius dug his feet into his stallion's sides and the animal lunged forward into a sprint. Ashur watched him go, curious about the tribune's abruptness. Alerio walked ahead of the column to his side.

"What did you say to him?" he demanded.

"I merely asked about his family name."

"Don't. He's under enough pressure as it is, stranger." Alerio smacked his vinerod into the palm of his hand. "Why are you here anyway? You paid your debt to the Tribune when you informed us of the traitors. Isn't that enough?"

"Ah. I see. You are the dragon's loyal friend. Worry not. I will leave when He commands it." Ashur trotted forward on his mount before Alerio could say anything.

"Who? Lucius?" But the man had gone far ahead. "What the bloody hell is he talking about?" Alerio muttered. "Pick up the pace!" he yelled back at the column.

Half a mile along the sandy road, Ashur spotted Lucius gazing out to the distant sea from the top of a sand dune. He reigned in, did not want to disturb the young man further. "What is going through your mind, Tribune?"

Lucius stood on the sand next to Pegasus, stroking the animal's strong neck. He'd removed his helmet. "I wish you could advise me now, Diodorus," he said to the air as he recalled all of the lessons he had been given over the years. The greatest gift the old Greek had given him was a clearer understanding of life and the importance of being true to oneself and the Gods. *All heroes face tests, dilemmas along the way. They all fail at some point. What makes them heroes is how they overcome failure and turn it into a triumph.* The words echoed over the water like they were spoken yesterday. "I hope I haven't let you down."

Lucius's mind began to drift north across the sparkle of the sea, home to Rome. He could not think of that now. It was too far, in many ways. He took a deep breath and exhaled loudly. Pegasus' ear twitched and he nudged Lucius with his head.

"Time to go, boy." He hoisted himself up into the saddle. "It's a long way to Lambaesis." They turned to face west and spurred back to the road to join his troops with renewed determination. In a few days they would have to cross the burning salt flats and then make their way into the rocky mountains of Numidia, their new home.

VIII

IUGULA!

'Kill Him!'

The crowd roared and swelled, the sweaty populace on its feet, fists flailing above curses and oaths directed at either of the eques fighters charging around the arena. The two faceless combatants pleased the masses with a dazzling array of horsemanship, wielding their long hasta lances, each in an attempt to cut the other down off of his horse.

In a sudden and surprising move after dropping his hasta, the green rider leapt from the top of his black mount onto his red opponent. The fighters crashed to the ground with a hollow sounding thud. The crowd leapt to its feet once again with thunderous approval. It was a bold move. The two reeled on the sand-covered planks of the arena floor, a cloud of dust enveloped them in their grappling struggle to gain their feet and dropped weapons.

As the dust cleared and the sun's light filtered through, the two equites stood facing each other, their plumed, bronze helmets gleaming in the sun. From beneath their wide-brimmed visors and behind the honeycombed eye guards, the two seemed to anticipate the first move. The crowd sat silent for a brief moment, holding its breath just before the red eques slashed with his short sword at the other's face. The vociferous audience bellowed once again as the two engaged in a series of cut and thrust moves, parries and hits with sword, arm guard and shield.

The contest was evenly matched as the two men punished each other back and forth until at last the green eques stumbled backward over one of the stray lances that had been dropped earlier. The other moved in, kicked the sword from his hand. The crowd chanted, "Missum! Missum!" to let the brave fighter live. The red eques glanced up to the game's editor who looked rather pleased with himself as he nodded, giving his approval of the crowd's wishes. The bright blade was withdrawn from the fallen man's throat and he was helped up by his opponent. The men bowed to the editor and the crowd as cheers went up for the victor as he waved the prized palm branch above his head and stepped from the arena.

In anticipation of the next fight, spectators milled about the amphitheatre discussing the previous pairing. Music was provided by cornu, tuba, lituus, hydraulis organ and drum. Attendants removed any stray debris from the arena floor and bread was thrown to the audience by men dressed as satyrs and scantily-clad women dressed as amazons. Some spectators sat grumbling in their seats at the loss of money they had bet while others went to collect their winnings, to place bets on the next combat.

In one section of seating, beneath the sun awnings, sat a mass of crimson cloaks; a contingent of Roman troops on leave. Argus murmured to Maren beside him about the money he had lost. "Lose again Argus? Ha, ha!" Lucius came up from behind, slapped him playfully on the back.

"When did you get here?" Argus answered, nodding a greeting to Alerio who also sat down. "I thought you didn't want to see the fights today."

"Yes, yes, I know I said that but Alerio and I met the lanista who owns some of the gladiators. He said they're some of the best around and gave us a tip." Lucius shook a small purse of money to show his winnings. "He was right about the first tip anyway." Argus shook his head, his face reddening.

"We also saw the advertisements for the fight saying there would be sun awnings." Alerio glanced up at the fluttering white awnings above them. "This African heat just gets worse and worse."

"What have we missed so far? Maren, you've been here all day haven't you?"

"It's been an average day as far as games are concerned. First there were some animal hunts with some Numidian natives cutting down gazelles and ostriches. Then criminal executions; some were beheaded by a huge burly oaf and some were fed to lions. Well, actually the lions never really did anything. They were too damn tired and hot and half-dead. Mangy things; all they did was walk up to the criminals, sniff them, yawn and lay down to sleep. Even when they were prodded by the beast-master they still slept. So the lions were taken out of the arena and a couple of Nile alligators were let loose in the ring. They made short work of the criminals. Sucked the meat clean off their legs. After that there were some athletic contests, wrestling and pancration. Some comedic skits with dwarfs dressed as gods and then the gladiatorial fights began. This was the first one."

Lucius' smile left his face as he still pondered the alligator drama. "Sounds like we didn't miss much."

"Are you kidding me Lucius?" said Argus. "It was fantastic. I can't wait to see the next pairing. These provincial contests are great; no bloody referees to stop the fights."

"I'm going to put more money down on the next fight. Argus, I'll put some down for you. What's your preference?"

"Put a couple denarii on Caribdis for me." Argus leaned back in his seat to watch the sand. He loved the moments before a fight.

"All right, I'll be back soon." Lucius rose to leave, pushed his way through the returning crowd. Maren followed to place a last-minute bet.

As Alerio moved to sit down so did a dark, warlike man dressed all in white. His strange blue eyes greeted Argus.

"Alerio, what's *he* doing here?"

"We ran into Ashur this morning in the marketplace. He just kind of appeared out of nowhere."

"I'm sure." Argus' fists clenched around his knees.

"Greetings, Centurion Argus." Ashur bowed slightly, knew the greeting would not be returned. Argus grumbled something incoherent and took a bite of flat bread he had been saving. The music began to die down once more as Lucius and Maren came quickly to sit back down.

"Ashur. Have you ever been to the arena before?" Lucius asked.

"No Tribune. I must confess that this is my first time. It has never really interested me. I just don't understand the point of it all." Argus' angry breath could be heard in the background.

"Who did you put money on, Lucius? Caribdis?"

"Nope, on Neptune."

"Why am I surprised? You're pious even in your choice of gladiators." He cast a sly look at Lucius who pretended playfully to ignore him. Then the music reached fever pitch before dying away to allow the editor to speak. Lucius, Ashur and the troops quieted down to hear the introductions.

The editor licked the fish sauce from his fingers and strained to push himself up from his chair. He took his time, evidently enjoyed having the people's eyes on him. Despite the intense heat, he was lavishly dressed in layers of fine fabric. The light reflected off of his sweaty brow as well as the numerous gold rings and gems that bedecked his pudgy fingers. He raised his greasy hands for attention.

"Thysdrus!" he called out, his face red from the effort. "For our next fight we have brought in some of the best gladiators you will ever see. A duel!" He was suddenly very dramatic in his movement, his face extremely serious. There was a loud farting sound among the troops that reached his ears. He plodded on through echoes of stunted laughter, avoided looking at the sea of crimson. "From his underwater kingdom, the god Neptune will face off against the dreaded sea creature, Caribdis." His voice was hushed, as though it were a danger to speak the name loudly.

"Get on with it!" Argus shouted. There were more jeers from the troops. Lucius looked back at them but knew that it was harmless enough. The editor threw up his hands and plopped back down in his chair.

"Bloody soldiers," he grumbled to his aid. "Why cant they just shut up and watch the games? More food!" he barked, dabbing his brow.

In the middle of the arena floor, a scene of sorts had been set up with what looked like a semi-circle of rocks coming out of the sea. There was also a large wooden structure that resembled a dock built of wide planks resting on six upright posts. From one end of the arena, a massive cheer went up as a retiarius fighter stepped onto the sands and made his way onto the dock. As a net fighter, his only weapons were the trident, a weighted net and a small dagger. Apart from a blue loincloth he didn't wear much armour except for a manica and shoulder guard on his right arm. Cheers went up for the tall, dark, bearded god. He bowed graciously to the crowd, his muscles flexing.

Once the cheers for the god of the sea died away with the tide of excitement, a low chant rushed up from a group of supporters at the other end of the arena. At that moment all eyes turned to one of the trap doors in the floor which had opened in front of the rocks. From the depths of the sea emerged Caribdis. The secutor fighter moved slowly to stand on one of the large rocks and raised his massive arms into the air, waving them menacingly like a half-crazed beast.

He was faceless and terrible looking. Covering what must have been a terribly scarred face was the extra thick secutor's helmet, a roughly fashioned bronze with only two small, round holes for the eyes. The only ornament on the heavy helmet was what appeared to be a thick fin-like crest running from the brow to the back of the head lending its wearer some resemblance to a vile sea creature. In his left hand the secutor held a large scutum shield, on which were painted eight palm branches indicating his wins, and on his left leg a heavy bronze greave. The right arm was protected by a manica which led down to a hand holding an extremely sharp short sword.

Attendants fled the arena floor as the two foes stared each other down, Neptune's strong dark features determined and confident, the secutor deadly and ferocious, his massive bulk sweating in anticipation of the kill. Then the two leapt from atop their individual perches into the centre of the ring beneath a tidal wave of roars from the expectant crowd. Neptune moved lightening-like around the secutor swinging the massive net and thrusting with his deadly trident intermittently.

Caribdis, in a flurry of primal shrieks from himself and his supporters, tried to lure the sea god to within striking distance to plunge his deadly tooth deep into his flesh. Both god and beast struggled to stay ahead of the other and they manoeuvred in and out. By this time the retiarius was bleeding from a slash across his right arm. Caribdis had tasted blood and so had the crowd.

Lucius and the others watched as the sea god battled with all of his might against the creature. Then with a distracting thrust from his trident, Neptune's heavy net swung low and fast, entangling the unprotected leg of his opponent. In an instant several quick blows from the trident's point slashed across the secutor's heavily armoured face as he writhed, caught up in the net. Neptune quickly made his way around the back of his opponent, climbing up some of the rocks. To everyone's amazement, he leapt down from the highest point of the rocks to finish off his quarry.

Caribdis turned just as Neptune came crashing into him and in a spray of bright red blood the two collided with unspeakable force. The crowd leapt to its feet, waiting for the dust to clear and then, silence. Plunged deep and deadly into the secutor's small eyeholes was the retiarius' trident, two of the teeth forced through the small openings by the force of the onslaught. Beside the slain sea beast lay the once proud god, his convulsing body slowly coming to rest as the secutor's sword lay embedded through his now lifeless mass. They had been called up and had provided the entertainment at their own funerary rites. Both god and beast lay in the arena, joined in death.

The editor of the games motioned to the musicians to strike up a tune to break the silence. At the same time attendants entered the arena with two litters to bear the bodies of the fallen away to the bowels of the amphitheatre.

Lucius sat silent for a moment, shocked by the outcome of the fight and even slightly ashamed that he had placed money on it. Beside him Ashur looked sullen and severe.

"Well, I guess neither of us wins this one," said Argus. "Lucius, put my money down on the last combat, would you?"

"Not this time. I'm not betting anymore today. You take the money and do what you want with it." He tossed the pouch to Argus and watched as the arena floor was cleared.

"Suit yourself." Argus shrugged his heavy shoulders. "How about you, Maren?"

"I'm all out of money." Maren crossed his arms and leaned back. Just then Lucius turned to see Ashur had vanished.

"Alerio. Where's Ashur?"

"Not sure. He was here a second ago." Alerio looked about.

"Ach Lucius, who cares? I don't know why you trust him so much. He's bad news." Argus got up and went to place his bets.

"Alerio, I'm going to see if I can find him. I'll be back in time for the last fight."

"Good luck finding him in this crowd. Man's a bloody ghost."

Away from the crowd now, in the arched, peripheral corridors of the amphitheatre, Lucius stood gazing out into the sunlit afternoon. At that moment he wondered at the beauty of the structure he was in, arch upon arch filled with refined statuary and ornately carved columns supporting massive walls of perfectly cut stone. On all of this a heavenly light shining through every opening, casting an array of shadow and sun across the corridor floor and walls.

He felt the heat on his face, warming his skin and bringing it to life. Then he heard the roar of the crowd and the distant voice of the game's struggling editor introducing the next fight. Lucius found himself wondering how he could reconcile the beauty of life and even of the structure in which he found himself, with the terrible deaths he had just witnessed at the centre of it all on the arena sands. Was this life? In the arena had man simply decided to concentrate his attentions on one aspect of life for a short time, thereby making death more evident?

The tribune held out his hand to gaze at it, turned it slightly, noticed the thick muscles of his forearm stirring beneath his desert-darkened skin. He realized how far he had come, how much older he seemed. He had taken many men's lives and not only in battle as soldier, when a leader of men's duty was not only to himself but also to his fellows; in Alexandria he had taken men's lives in a fit of rage and passion. Was he any different than those who fought beneath the baying of the crowd in the arena?

Lucius looked out over the flat distance, pondering this not without some torment. His thoughts were muddled again. He hated that, especially since he had been taught to organize his thoughts and feelings in self-analysis.

He looked out over the town. The amphitheatre towered above the gathering of small villas and mud brick homes of Thysdrus. As far as the eye could see lay row upon row of olive groves, thousands of hectares. As his eye followed the length of the main road that came into town from the distance, Lucius spotted Ashur gazing up at him from the deserted streets below. His white robe fluttered gracefully in the wind like the sail of a Nile barge. Ashur looked up at Lucius with a degree of seriousness but behind the stern exterior was the friendly affection of a man taking his leave.

He bowed low to Lucius, not uttering a word. Lucius understood and raised his hand to bid farewell before Ashur disappeared as he had so many times since they had first met. The tribune stood there, lost in thought until he was brought to by the clanging of swords and the renewed roar of the crowd. The final combat had begun, the previous one all but forgotten.

Lucius decided not to go back into the theatre but rather to watch from one of the empty corridors that led to the arena floor.

He could see the two heavily armed gladiators moving about the sand in their dance of death. A murmillo and a thraex or Thracian fighter. Lucius watched as the two heavy-helmed gladiators pommeled each other relentlessly to the droning of drums and the cries of bloodthirsty spectators. Lucius wondered what drove these men and where they found their strength. Was it made easier by the fact that each was fighting a faceless foe? They dazzled the audience with an incredible array of slashes and parries, displaying their skills with incredible determination to win and live. Both were bleeding profusely, the murmillo from a cut to the right leg and the thraex from a gash across his muscular chest.

The sand went red about their shuffling feet, and in a barely perceptible instant, the murmillo's shield flew from his sweaty hand allowing the thraex to parry a desperate sword thrust and land a heavy kick to the vulnerable man's chest with the bronze greave covering his leg. The murmillo tumbled onto the ground, winded. He moved to get up but the thraex was upon him, knocked his sword from his bloodied hand. He made to get up yet again but the thraex smashed him in the centre of his face with the boss of his small shield, ripping his helmet from his head.

He groaned as he lay there on the clotted sand and raised his right hand in a sign for mercy and surrender. Lucius' heart began to pound, the blood flowing to his head and ears, as if he could feel the adrenaline from every person there present. Inwardly, he hoped to hear the word that would save his life, *missum, missum*, enough death for today. The thraex stood above the fallen murmillo, flipped him over onto his stomach and grabbed him by his bloody hair. He glanced up and around at the standing crowd. They cheered. Then, almost in total concert, they began to chant aloud, "Iugula! Iugula! Iugula!", Kill him! Kill him! Kill him!

The thraex looked to the editor who nodded gravely. The victor pulled the murmillo's head back to expose his neck and pulsing veins. Lucius could hear the shouts of his troops as the lethal blade was drawn slowly and cleanly across the fallen man's neck. His blood spilled out to soak the sand of the arena one last time before his head was released and he fell to the ground. The thraex made his way to the editor's platform to receive his prize, the palm branch for victory. Upon his head was also placed the valued corona, a laurel wreath for outstanding achievement; he had won ten consecutive fights and for the day he was the people's hero.

Dressed as the thraex, this man had appeared invincible and imposing, but with his head bared and his weapons shed, he was no longer a gladiator but a young man, no older than Lucius. The youthful innocence of his face and curly black hair betrayed the sight that all had just witnessed, adding to what Lucius thought to be the incredible juxtaposition of the Roman arena. Lucius turned to go out and wait for his men in the open air, away from the amphitheatre.

After Sabratha and the drama that had been played out before the Gods, which Lucius had decided to leave behind as done and not to be undone, the cohort had pressed on to Lambaesis to join up with the III Augustan Legion. From Sabratha, they marched directly westward along the coastline, passing through Tacape before turning into the desert once again, this time along the great salt plains. In that unforgiving environment where water was scarce and heat abundant, the crystalline glitter of surface-encrusted salt shone for countless miles with the intensity of Vulcan's forge. From the desert outpost of Nepeta they made their way into the province of Numidia.

For the men of the cohort, the Numidian desert was a rocky, lonely place. There was the fear of being set upon from all sides. This was the edge of the empire and not one of the men had been there previously. Fears however, subsided when the cohort encountered the legionary scouts from Lambaesis who had been expecting them. The base lay only one day's march to the north west between the mountains of the central Numidian plain.

Their welcome at the base was lukewarm, and although Lucius and his men were greeted with a degree of respect, due to what they had achieved and the news that they brought, they were also greeted with distant consternation and doubt. This was due in part to the youthfulness of Lucius and his centurions, but also to the age of the III Augustan troops. The III Augustan Legion was one of the oldest serving legions in the empire, formed by Caesar during the civil wars and later reconstituted by Emperor Augustus. It was old and proud and comprised mostly of battle-hardened veterans.

Upon arrival, Lucius and his men were promptly given a fortnight leave. They were told that this was a reward for the arduous journey they had just completed but Lucius and his centurions felt more as though it was a way of dismissing the *children*, to get them out of the way. Lucius wanted to voice his disapproval but Alerio advised him against it, said that the troops were in need of some leisure time after the long patrol and that they should ignore the disrespect. Time off would be good for morale. Lucius saw the truth of his centurion's words and three days after arriving in Lambaesis the men of the cohort set out for the games at Thysdrus.

The night before leaving camp, Lucius received an invitation from an old family friend who used to visit in Rome when Lucius was very young. The man's name was Marius Nelek and he was a veteran who had served in Germania with Lucius' father and become a very close friend of the elder Metellus. From Germania and Rome, Marius Nelek had been assigned to the III Augustan before retiring to nearby Thamugadi, a colonia near Lambaesis created by the Emperor Trajan for retired troops of the Numidian-based legion.

Marius Nelek had heard of the cohort's arrival in Lambaesis and of the commanding officer who led them. He

103

promptly sent a message to the young tribune inviting him to stop and visit him and his family as soon as he had time. Lucius remembered Marius' visits to their home in Rome when he was a child and how the old warrior used to dazzle him with battle stories, much to Quintus Metellus' dismay. As the road from Thysdrus to Lambaesis passed through Thamugadi, Lucius decided to take up the invitation on the way back from the games.

The games had been an escape and welcome rest for all of the troops in the cohort except Lucius, whose mind raced with all manner of thoughts. It was as though his soul was restless, not having rested once in the past months since Alexandria. It was not only the burden of command but something else, something elusive that nagged him in the depths of his being, something made worse since Thysdrus. His situation, the men's, was precarious at best.

Argus, Garai, Eligius and Maren, along with the men of their centuries had decided to stay on a bit longer in Thysdrus to see more spectacle, while Alerio and Antanelis with their men accompanied Lucius to Thamugadi. Some of the men also had relatives or family friends living there and wanted to visit, others simply wanted to see something new and enjoy the numerous bath houses of the colonia.

As Lucius rode, he thought of Parthia and Alexandria, the acts of bravery and heroism he had witnessed, the occasional savagery. He had been thrilled by his appointment to tribune and the patrol assignment. However, the patrol had only brought to the fore new confusion and strange events that he couldn't understand. His youthful enthusiasm had blinded him.

He remembered the deep desert...the sand, the heat, the blinding sun...but also the simple beauty and mystery by which it enchanted men at peace. Flashes of a dream leapt back to Lucius's mind as it raced. He saw the light of the full moon, a cool, silver orb hovering in the night sky as he came face to face with a god. *Apollo guide me*, he thought. Was it all real or just a dream? For Lucius, the veil between reality and the other realm had been thinned to the point where he was unsure where one ended and the other began.

And what of Ashur? Where did he disappear to and who was he? Since that fateful night in the desert, when their paths had crossed, he had come and gone like a spectre, a shade. In him Lucius sensed an ally, a friend, but he could not deem why. Why had this lone warrior decided to help him and why did Lucius feel that he could trust him so implicitly?

Breathing deeply of the warm afternoon air, Lucius tried to calm his mind and set all questions aside for the time being as he rode. The walls of Thamugadi soon came into view, in the middle of a vast, open plain surrounded by distant mountains. It lay amid groves of various fruit and olive trees and along the sides of the roads, outside each of the gates, were rows of gravestones and monuments dedicated to past troops of the III Augustan Legion and their families. After checking in at one of the gates, Lucius and his men were granted entry.

Thamugadi was a typical Roman colonia laid out in a perfect grid of intersecting streets surrounded by straight and high stone walls. Unlike most bases, the settlement had six gates instead of four, all manned. Locals came and went freely, to trade, visit friends and do other business with the retired legionaries there. The town was well equipped, housed a library, fourteen public baths and all manner of tradesman selling their wares and services. There were several inns as well, where Alerio and Antanelis saw to the billeting of those troops not visiting family or friends.

After making sure that Alerio and Antanelis had everything in hand and had obtained lodgings themselves, Lucius took his leave until the next morning. Then he saw that Pegasus was properly stabled for the night, gave the groom an extra denarius to take good care of him, and made his way up the street to find Marius Nelek. The main street was lined with shops and inns owned by the inhabitants who had obtained skills during their military service, carpenters, smiths, wrights and others. Marius, in his invitation, had asked Lucius to meet him at his shop, a forge where he made and sold weapons, and from there they would go together to his home.

Lucius walked slowly, searching both sides of the street for any sign of a forge. As he walked, many locals, both men and women, stopped to stare or nod greetings at the tall tribune. There was a respect for military men in Thamugadi that was rare in other coloniae. Lucius had made sure that he wore his full dress, perhaps, he thought, in a subconscious attempt to impress an old family friend. His crimson cloak stood out among the small crowds of people milling about him as he moved through the street. Then a loud, bellowing voice came from across the street.

"By Mars' hairy balls! It can't be? Is that…Lucius Metellus Anguis!" Lucius turned, surprised and somewhat embarrassed at all the eyes on him. From an open shop with smoke billowing out of a hole in the roof, came a dirty, burly man with a smile spanning his dark, weathered face. "It is! I recognize that cuirass anywhere." He walked over to Lucius and clasped his forearm tightly.

"It's good to see you, Marius Nelek." Lucius returned an uncomfortable smile; it had been years since he had seen Marius. "How long has it been? You're the same as I remember from my youth."

"I'm well, lad. The desert weather has pickled me like an Egyptian mummy. But you! Look at you!" Marius walked around Lucius, eyed him up and down. "You're your father's son, no doubt about that. But I must say that that armour looks a lot better on you. Ha, ha! It's been far too long, young Lucius, far too long. Last time I saw you in Rome you were as tall as my thigh and now, well…your father and mother must be very proud. Look at you! A Tribune! I heard about it when news of your patrol came. I drank a toast to you. There I go again, talk, talk, talk. Let's get out of the street. I'll go in the back of the shop and clean the soot from my face and hands and then we'll go to the house. Octavia will be thrilled to meet you. Wait here."

Lucius waited in the shop while Marius cleaned himself up. He breathed deeply, overwhelmed by such a public welcome. On the walls of the shop were many different swords, some finished others not, gladius, spatha and other types of African or eastern style weapons. The work was simple and strong. When Marius returned, he closed the shop and led Lucius down a small side street, turning corners a few times. He lived along the city's western wall and after walking and talking for several minutes they came to a clean and narrow street and an arched doorway flanked by a small torch. An inscribed clay tablet read "NELEK" in painted red letters.

The house was simple, just as the front entrance, but it was much larger than it appeared. Directly ahead of the front door was a small passage that led to an open, colonnaded peristyle with a small, beautifully crafted fountain in the centre. On the left were three rooms that comprised the baths, a study, and in the far left corner of the house the dining room. The entire back and right side of the house consisted of the cubicula, a bedroom for guests, two children's rooms and a main bedroom. To the immediate right of the front door was a large kitchen and storage area. The layout was simple and functional.

"Octavia! Kids! We have company!" Marius yelled. "We don't have any slaves in our home if you are wondering, Lucius. Damned nuisance they are, always nosing about when and where they shouldn't. I like to take care of things myself. I suppose it's all those years in the army, carrying everything and anything on my own back. Ah, here they come." Marius led Lucius into the garden of the peristyle to meet his family.

"Lucius Metellus, I would like you to meet my beautiful wife, Octavia..." Lucius bowed. "And these two little terrors are my children, Aeneas and Tulia. This is Tribune Lucius Metellus, Quintus' son that I told you about."

"Welcome to our home, Tribune." Octavia smiled and offered to take Lucius' cloak from him.

"Please," Lucius began, "call me Lucius. Marius knew me long before I was a tribune."

"All right then, Lucius." Octavia took his cloak and hung it up. Then the young boy, no more than twelve years of age stepped up, and saluted Lucius.

"Hail, Tribune Lucius!" He snapped his salute and stood at attention. Lucius snapped a salute back. Then he felt a tugging at his pteruges and looked down to see Tulia looking up at him. She was no more than six years old and beautiful like her mother with long dark hair, brown eyes and olive skin.

"Lucius?" she enquired. "Is that a bird on your shiny armour?"

"That's *Tribune Lucius* to you little ones," interrupted her father, half-joking. "And it's not a bird, it's a dragon."

"Forgive me father," Tulia replied, seeming to understand. She began again. "Tribune Lucius? Is that a dragon on your shiny armour?"

Lucius laughed. "Why yes, lady Tulia, it is."

"That's what I thought," she said. Her mother giggled at the puzzled look on Marius' face.

"Come my friend. We have much to talk about." Marius pat Lucius heartily on the back and led him to his study. "Octavia, can you bring some wine for the Tribune and myself?"

"Yes Marius. Come along Tulia, you can help me."

The study was a monument to service in the Legions. On the walls were hung various swords, spears and other weapons, pieces of armour, shields and both Roman and captured enemy standards. In the centre of the room was a desk with several open scrolls taken from a shelf on the back wall. On one corner of the desk were two silver armillae, decorations for bravery in battle. Marius pointed to a chair in which Lucius sat himself and then sat at his desk, busily rolling up the stray scrolls.

"So tell me Lucius, where have you been since you joined the army and how in Hades did you end up way out here?"

"Well," Lucius began, "after training was finished we set out directly with the emperor for Parthia-"

"Shit, thrown in at the deep end. Was that your first taste of battle?"

"Yes. And after having gone through that I have to say that no matter how prepared you think you are, you can't anticipate that first experience. I'm not sure I was totally prepared myself."

"Well, you're here and you're alive. That's enough, especially against Parthian cavalry. The first step is to survive the first battle and from there it all falls into place, Mars' grace."

"From there," Lucius continued, "we went on to Alexandria. We stayed there for two years."

"Great city, but a little too crowded for my taste. Were you appointed to centurion before becoming Tribune?" Lucius went on to tell Marius about how he came to be made tribune after centurion and of the patrol that the emperor had sent him on. Marius listened intently. While Lucius was speaking, Octavia came in quietly and laid down a tray of dried fruit and flat bread along with a pitcher of watered wine. Tulia followed close behind clutching two cups tightly, her tiny feet making carefully thought-out steps.

After Lucius had finished relating the story of the patrol, Marius took a sip of wine and was pensive for a moment. "Well, you're certainly on your way. Already rubbing shoulders with the emperor? Phew! What does your father say about all that?"

"Hmm," Lucius stared at the geometrical mosaic on the floor. "To be honest, he and I aren't exactly on speaking terms."

"Why? What happened? Wait, let me guess. He didn't want you to join the army. Is that it?" He leaned forward on his desk, hands clasped.

"That's it exactly," Lucius sighed. "I haven't spoken to him for a long time. In fact I haven't spoken to him or any other members of my family for quite a while." He regretted that, knew that he should at least have continued to write to his mother and sister. "I'm afraid I can't give you any recent news."

"No matter. I'm sure good old Quintus is the same as ever, which is why I'm not exactly surprised at his reaction to your choices. He sits in the Senate now, reading and making laws along with all those over-fed, fat asses. That's all he ever wanted to do though. I think he's better than that." Marius leaned back, sipped more wine and ripped a piece of flat bread from the tray. "Did you know that I served as contuburnium in his century?" Lucius shook his head. Although he knew Marius had served with his father he had not known that he was in charge of eight men within the century himself. "Yup! Those were the days. Your father could have been one of the best centurions around. Instead, he did his minimum of five years and then went straight into politics." Marius looked into his cup, swirled the wine about slowly. Lucius noticed a sad, thoughtful look on his face.

"I'm afraid Marius, that my father is even more against the army than before, or at least my serving in it. I could never have a decent conversation with him about it. Sometimes I wonder whether something happened to him while he was serving, something that turned him."

"Not that I know of. Ach, who can say Lucius? War does strange things to a man." Marius went over to the wall and took down an old, battered gladius, the sheath worn through and blood-stained. He drew out the blade. It still looked sharp and deadly. "You see this? My first gladius. This blade has been everywhere with me, from the beginning." He swung it around, remembering the weight of it. "The day I took another man's life with it was a day I shall never forget. Some men can accept the act of taking a life, reconcile it as something that had to be done. 'It's them or me' you say to yourself. Other men however, are tormented by every life they take. For them, it's personal, and it either drives them mad or hardens them to the point of losing all emotional ties to the world; if you don't you can't go on living for all the guilt and fear that plague you. Other men are just cowards who piss themselves the moment they face down an enemy." He hung the sword back on the wall.

"I was able to deal with it, your father too I suppose. Perhaps after a while it got to him. I don't know. He was at odds with the other officers a lot of the time. He laughed a lot less. I remember the day he met Antonia, your mother. He seemed transformed for a time but hated having to go back to war. He resented it. I can understand of course. Your mother was one of the most beautiful women in Rome, still is I'm sure." He smiled. "By Mithras, it would be good to see them again some day. How's your sister, Alene right? She must be a grown woman by now, and married?"

Lucius was warmed by thoughts of Alene. He wondered how she was, what she had been doing all these years. "Oh Alene is great, we're very close. That's right you never met the other two!"

Marius' eyes went wide. "The other two? You mean there are two more Metelli in the nest! That is good news. What are their names?"

"Quintus Caecilius and Clarinda."

"Ah, I see. Another boy and girl. Wonderful! I see that your father gave your younger brother the ancestral name. He must have big plans for him."

"Especially since his eldest son has proved such a disappointment to him." At that moment Tulia came quietly into the room to inform her father and *Tribune Lucius* that dinner was ready and that they should move to the triclinium for the meal.

"Thank you Tulia," Marius said as he got up from his chair. "We'll be along in a minute." Tulia went skipping into the kitchen to tell her mother. "Wouldn't worry about it Lucius.

Your father, much as I love the old goat, is stubborn and even if he is proud of you, he won't say it. All parents want to live through their children, especially their first-born sons. He just needs time to get used to the idea that you're a man and will go your own way." Lucius got up.

"I hope you're right, Marius."

"Ah, for now let's put these heavy matters aside. I'll show you to your room so you can remove your armour and get into more comfortable clothes. After that, you can tell me about *your* battle stories over dinner. We can compare scars." He led Lucius out of the study, the two of them laughing.

Dinner was, much to Lucius' delight, the most scrumptious meal to grace his stomach in a long time. Spiced lamb and suckling pig were accompanied by a variety of fresh and dried fruits, warm bread, goat's cheese and honey cakes. There was also plenty of watered wine which was surprisingly good, especially in such a distant corner of the empire. "It was made by one of the retired legionaries in town," Marius said. "Man can't piss straight but makes excellent wine. Go figure." The boy Aeneas chuckled while his mother and sister buried their faces in their hands, embarrassed.

Lucius enjoyed the warm, welcoming environment provided by an old acquaintance and his family. He felt safe, at ease. The triclinium was medium sized with couches on three of the four walls and a large table in the middle on which all of the food had been laid ahead of time. Lucius sat on the right couch by himself while Aeneas and Tulia shared one and their parents the central. They ate, drank and laughed. It was nice, Lucius thought, to talk of nothing. Eventually night came and Marius lit a small brazier in the corner of the room to beat away the evening chill that had slunk into the room from the courtyard.

Octavia began to clear the dirty plates before putting the children to bed. Their small heads had begun to bob up and down in their struggle to remain awake to hear more battle stories. Orpheus eventually took hold and they both collapsed in a sleeping heap on their couch. Octavia bid good night to Lucius and Marius as she knew the two of them had much more to talk about. Lucius thanked her wholeheartedly for her hospitality.

"Well now, Lucius. How much time did you spend in Lambaesis before going up to Thysdrus? Did you get to know anyone there yet?"

"Not much time at all, only three days before leaving. Or should I say, before being dismissed." Lucius told him that he felt that they were not taken at all seriously by the men of the veteran legion. Marius laughed.

"Ha, ha. I wouldn't worry about it too much, Lucius. They're an old, proud bunch, but tough as Hades. To them, you and your men are grandchildren. Once you prove yourselves in a battle, they'll warm to you. Just give them a bit of time. Besides, without the information you've brought about this nomad army and the attack, their old, wrinkly butts would be in big trouble. When's the force expected, do they know anything?"

"Within the month, although if word has gotten out that we discovered the traitors and the plot, the nomads may change their plans. The legate at the base has patrols out all the time."

"Flavius Marcellus is Legate Commander now, right?" Marius' eyebrow arched questioningly.

"Yup, that's him. Didn't seem to like me much."

"He doesn't like anyone. He's a ruthless son of a bitch but a brilliant tactician. He's far more suited to command than that shit-for-brains Anicius Faustus who was there before. Just stay on Marcellus' good side, if that's at all possible. The III Augustan is a strong legion and with Marcellus commanding they would be better used on the Rhine frontier or in the East. But, if there's going to be an attack out here, the III Augustan will tear those sons of whores to bits." Lucius laughed as he noticed Marius had returned to his soldier's role as soon as his wife and kids had left the room. The two men reclined on their couches, quiet for a few minutes, sipping their wine in comfortable silence, each lost in his own thoughts.

The night had grown still and that mysterious feeling Lucius had felt so many times before in that land began to cover the world. Beyond Thamugadi's walls he could discern the faint echo of chanting by some of the local tribesman where their fires dotted the darkness of the surrounding valley floor. Then Marius' voice cut into Lucius' drifting mind.

"Lucius, about your father…if he's changed it's because he's been dealt some heavy blows by the Gods in exchange for all his blessings. In Germania…in Germania after returning to the front from Rome and your mother, he felt abandoned. On a patrol he was leading through the forest at night…" Lucius listened intently, struggling to hear Marius' suddenly faint voice. "Our century was set upon by a large force of tribesman. It was dark, we were confused and your father struggled to keep things together. We were on the edge of a ravine, Quintus slipped and fell back from a heavy hitting sword thrust. Who hit him I don't know, must have been an enemy sword out of the dark. He yelled and before I could reach him to catch his arm, I was knocked unconscious by some bastard's war hammer. I found out later that Quintus had dragged me to safety beneath a fallen tree where he waited till the enemy was gone before carrying me back to camp on his back. Turns out most of our century was slaughtered. Only about twenty of us made it."

"I never knew about this." Lucius was incredulous. He had a hard time believing that his father was able to carry Marius on his back through the German forest while being hunted down. "It just doesn't sound like my father."

"Well it was. The only reason I'm alive is because of what he did for me. Stuck his neck out he did and I won't soon forget it." Marius poured them more wine. "He was different after that. Don't know why…six months later he pulled out and went back to Rome. Five years was up." Marius was moving slowly, dazedly, as if remembering and regretting.

Lucius, on the other had, was stunned and if his mind drifted before, it now spun out of control.

"He never told me any of this."

"That's Quintus for ya! Always keeping things to himself."

"Why are you telling me this now, Marius?"

"Because you're his son but also because you are a man and a soldier. You deserve to know why your father is the way he is. Honour him, Lucius. For all his stubbornness and harsh words, he's still your father." Lucius watched Marius rise uneasily from his couch. "Think about what I've said," he slurred, pausing for a moment. "Think we should turn in. Are your quarters suitable?"

"They're perfect, my friend. Thank you." Lucius gave Marius his arm as he climbed over the couch. "I'll have to leave early in the morning to gather the men and get back to base. I'll try not to disturb you."

"We'll be up with you. There's no way you'll leave without saying goodbye. We'll all be up to see you off. I'm going to bed now, before I fall down. Goodnight." Lucius bid him good night as well and Marius stumbled down through the peristyle to his bed and his wife. Lucius took one more sip of his wine, blew out the lamps and made his way to his room. A brazier had been lit to provide heat and as he lay in bed, gazing at the red and white painted walls, his eyes closed to thoughts of his father and the tale his host had just related. He thought he had known him, that he had been right to shun him the past years. *Was I wrong about him?* Part of him hoped that were true.

Lucius rose before the cock crew, a habit of being in the army. His hosts were already astir, ready to see him off, no doubt Marius still rose early too. After putting on all of his armour and gear, Lucius stepped into the open courtyard at the centre of the house. In the sky above, the stars still twinkled brightly, day was still two hours away. He inhaled the smell of jasmine from the garden and walked to the entrance where Marius and his family awaited him. The children struggled to stand as they were still half asleep, leaning up against their mother.

"Well Lucius, it was good to see you again after so long." Marius was wide awake.

"Yes Lucius, thank you for coming to our home, you are always welcome here." Octavia's soft features looked on him as if looking at her own son. "Take this." She held out a small bundle of food. "You will need your strength for the march." Lucius accepted the bundle gratefully.

"Thank you, lady, for this and for welcoming me into your home. And thank you, master Aeneas and mistress Tulia." He looked down at the two nodding heads, their eyes barely open. Faint smiles spanned their little faces as they managed a weak sounding "you're welcome". Lucius secured his cloak over his shoulders, put on his helmet and turned toward the door where Marius waited to show him out.

Marius leaned forward to whisper to him. "Remember what I told you about the Legion. Stay strong and show them what men of young blood can do. Also, if you should happen to write to or even see your father anytime soon, please give him and your mother my love and tell them I miss them."

"I will indeed. Thank you for everything." Lucius stepped through the door's arch into the darkness and quiet of the street.

"And remember what I told you of your father! You must understand and try to forgive him."

"I will, my friend." Lucius began to walk slowly away but Marius was not finished.

"Remember, out here nothing is as it seems. Watch your back and look out for yourself. Danger lurks in the shadows of peace." He waved to Lucius, who was already several paces away.

"I'll remember. Farewell." Lucius responded faintly from down the street as Marius closed the door.

Lucius struggled at first to find his way back to the main street. There was a deathly stillness in the chill air of the morning, the only sound being the hollow clanging of his hob-nail boots on the flagstones.

He felt suddenly cold, despite the thickness of his cloak, and his breath could be seen as its warmth penetrated the cold. He slowed, suddenly aware of something, someone…a noise from around the corner, up ahead. The noise stopped as he drew closer and stopped to listen. A cold breeze flooded into the alleyway, heightening his senses and causing the hairs on the back of his neck to prickle. Then, in a flash of glinting steel Lucius found himself on the ground, being kicked.

He didn't know what was happening but several voices, foreign voices, were discernible in the background as he struggled to get to his feet, avoiding the shining blade that jumped in and out of his field of vision, hitting him several times in the breastplate. He managed to gain his footing, his eyes jumping left and right, the faint images of six black figures, blades drawn in the cold light of the moon.

Lucius backed away slightly, they had the advantage, who were they? Under his breath "Apollo guide and protect me." Then a loud battle cry from behind him as another attacker grasped his arms tightly, holding him for the others. The reflexes sharp, Lucius' great crested helmet hit backward to stun his rearward attacker with a blow to the face. Before the man knew it he had been spun around just as one of his fellows came charging in and impaled him on his sword. Lucius let the wounded man go quickly to deal with the others.

His heart pounded, the sound of blood deafening to him with every movement to save himself from death's grasp. He could see his end hovering near him, reaching out. Lucius managed to shed his hindering cloak and draw his short sword but not before being knocked to his knees again. He grasped frantically where a dagger had been thrown and embedded itself in his thigh. The burning pain was excruciating as he tore it out. "Kill him now!" one of the dark attackers yelled as three more moved in to finish him off.

For a brief, fleeting moment, Lucius' strength waned, almost giving way. Hope reared its head in that second, with the speed of a god's ethereal force, a flash of white out of the sky. A dagger in one attacker, then another. The two corpses stumbled over Lucius who fell sideways to avoid another attacker. His sword came to life and swung up and down to take his life.

Across from him, only several feet away, a white-robed phantom battled furiously with the remaining three. Blood stained the ground and shrieks of pain polluted the morning air as the figure seemed to fly and leap about the three evil shades punishing them furiously with deep cuts and broken bones. Before Lucius could reach the scene, it was over. He held his sword up, pointed at the robed man, beast, god...what was it?

Amid the tangle of death at its feet stood the white being, a deep, rhythmic breathing emanating from its now still form.

"Who in Hades are you?" Lucius demanded, limping his way over, sword still drawn.

The figure turned slowly and beneath the white hood of the robe revealed himself.

"Ashur!" The amazement and shock of the situation registered on Lucius' cut and bleeding face. Ashur closed his eyes, trying to bring a sense of calm down on himself. He was weakened from the fight and bled from a deep slash across his cheek. "By Apollo my friend! Where did you...I mean how did...thank the Gods you came when you did." Ashur's eyes opened slowly, happy as he realized he had not been too late and that Lucius was safe. "Who were those...men?"

"Nomads, friend. They followed you from Thysdrus, and I them. Are you badly injured?"

"I've been better, a dagger to my leg muscle. I didn't see them...I...I couldn't..."

"Calm my friend." Ashur's voice was strong and reassuring. "You were not supposed to see them. They were assassins. They are gone now. Come, we must go. I'll help you." Lucius agreed and accepted Ashur's shoulder for support as they made their way through the misty, early morning streets.

IX

LEGIO III AUGUSTA

'The III Augustan Legion'

The wound burned and itched without end, unbearably so. Lucius sat in his quarters eating, had been unable to sleep. He was ready for the day's exercises on the training ground, hoped that doing something would keep his mind from the annoyance in his thigh. Luckily, the care he had received in the past few days was good, due to the Legion's head physician, a Greek named Loxias.

He had cleansed the wound thoroughly with a mixture of rosemary and other healing herbs, cauterized it and sealed it with four staples. "A serious wound can fester," he had said, "if it's stitched with gut. Then I'd have to cut your whole damn leg off." It was said with a smile, nevertheless, Lucius was perfectly happy with the staples.

He wanted to scratch, rip the stiff staples out himself, but he refrained. Walking was much easier now, as was riding. In fact he had been amazed at the speed with which his wound had healed. A little exercise on the training ground with the troops would do him some good and hopefully distract him. It had been several days since the incident in Thamugadi. He had tried to hide his limp but it was impossible. Upon arrival, he happened to meet the legate along the Via Praetoria. When Flavius Marcellus saw he was wounded, he didn't ask how but grunted and said "Get yourself to the infirmary, Metellus." That was it. Lucius was relieved.

The fort was immense, about thirty hectares, so it had not been a problem for the camp prefect, Lartius Claudius, to find quarters for the extra cohort that Lucius had brought in. Amid the grid of streets leading away from the central Principia, the headquarters building, a couple of empty barrack blocks were given over to Lucius' men while a pleasingly comfortable dwelling had been provided for the young tribune in the officers' quarters along the Via Principalis.

Lucius didn't know how long their stay in Lambaesis would last, he was happy to have comfortable quarters in the meantime. The tribune's house comprised several rooms around a rectangular courtyard. The largest rooms were a bedroom and a meeting room with a large table. There was a triclinium with couches, a kitchen and a storeroom where one of the Legion's slaves could prepare food at Lucius' request. Most impressive to Lucius was the fact that he had his own private baths and latrine. He could now avoid crowded baths with the rest of the men and even empty his bowels without being cheek to cheek with them too.

He did not socialize a great deal with the other, older tribunes. Like most, they seemed unconvinced that he deserved his rank. Occasionally, when he bumped into one of them in the street, he would engage in a short conversation. They seemed to be probing him for signs of military knowledge; his once great family name made expectations that much higher, and life much tougher. Apart from brief periods of interaction on duty, the older officers had no time for a young tribune. Many of them had their families with them in their own quarters. It was no longer thought that wives and children were a distraction for the officers; many of the women and children who did not live within the base lived outside the walls or in Thamugadi. There was immense gratitude that Emperor Severus had lifted the ban on wives.

Lucius sat at the large table in the centre of his meeting room, suddenly lonely. Scattered on the tabletop were several open scrolls he had been reading the previous night: Thucydides, Caesar and Arrian. These had been gifts to him from his tutor. Lucius smiled, thinking of his old, white-bearded mentor, now long gone. Diodorus was, he thought, one of the only people, other than his sister Alene, who seemed to believe in who he was and what he was capable of.

That gentle Greek saw something in Lucius that few, if any, ever did. *If you have faith in yourself and the Gods Lucius, anything in this world will be possible.*

The words echoed in Lucius' mind, a distant voice, a whisper, calling to him, reminding him. Was Diodorus actually there, on the other side of the River? Lucius preferred to think that such a kind soul lived not in the shadows but in some ethereal paradise, admiring the world he loved so much from above, in the Gods' company.

The cock crew and the cornu sounded. The pre-dawn call to drills. Harsh voices of centurions rang through the camp, shattering the still morning air. He rose to put on his armour and cloak, took a last bite of dried fruit from a nearby plate and made his way out into the cool morning air.

"Good morning Xeno," he greeted the kitchen slave who had just come out of the storage room.

"Good morning, Tribune. Did you sleep well this night?" The old man was hunched over slightly, twisting his neck to look up at Lucius.

"No, Xeno, another sleepless night I'm afraid. I'm going to Loxias this morning to get these damned staples removed. Hopefully that'll help."

"I hope so, Tribune." He stood there holding a bucket of water, the weight of which pulled the man closer to the ground. "Shall I clean your quarters today, Tribune?"

"No, no Xeno. That won't be necessary. Just leave the day's bread ration on the table in the kitchen and then you can go." Lucius had felt awkward lately about having a man three times his elder cleaning for him. But, it was the man's only job and so Lucius accepted his service, as long as Xeno took some money from him occasionally; it was their secret. "I'm sure you have better things to do than wait on me. Spend the time with your family instead."

"You are very kind, Tribune. May Jupiter and Juno bless you."

"You as well, Xeno. You as well."

122

The Via Principalis was already bustling with troops making their way to the training ground. Lucius crossed the street and made his way to the Principia to check in with the commanding tribune, Cornelius Ciceron. Just off the inner courtyard were located the offices of the six tribunes, the camp prefect and the legate commander of the III Augustan.

Around the edges of the courtyard, scattered groups of soldiers stood conferring or waiting to see their officers. In the centre stood a large bronze tripod, smoke wafting to the rooftops of the Principia, the strong smell of eastern incense permeating the morning air.

As he passed through, Lucius received two or three reluctant salutes to a superior officer from the lower-ranking troops. The older veterans ignored him. Any desultory remarks didn't even warrant reprimand. His situation among the legionaries was tenuous enough. Lucius simply stood tall, shoulders back, and marched into the senior tribune's office. The room was dimly lit, empty. Two small braziers sputtered in the far corners, either side of the entrance to a back room.

"Tribune?" Lucius called out.

"Who's that?" A bored voice from the far room.

"Lucius Metellus, sir."

"What in the name of Jupiter do you want, Metellus?" Impatience and frustration crept in upon Lucius. He fought them down.

"Yesterday, Tribune, you said I should report to you first thing this morning. Something about training?"

"Ah yes. You're early!" A tall skinny man of about thirty-eight appeared in the doorway at the back of the room. Beneath a perfectly shorn head of blond hair the man's beak-like nose and beady eyes glared at Lucius with disdain. He moved across the room to his table, very careful of the folds of his clothing, the broad stripe of the senatorial aristocracy was a deep, dark purple around the edges of his tunic. He was not a soldier. He was an aspiring politician serving his minimum length of service as a tribune to gain respect.

Lucius had not talked much with him, but he didn't need to to know that Cornelius Ciceron had never been in battle. He would be back in Rome, in the Forum, as quickly as he could.

"So, Metellus. Is that leg of yours working again?

"It's fine now, sir. I'm going to Loxias this morning to get the staples removed." Cornelius Ciceron sniffed loudly.

"Well, after you're done playing around with that old Greek you can tell your men that their training time has been increased. They're not good enough." Lucius could feel, and enjoy, having this man's throat in his hand.

"But Tribune, my men have been training harder than most!"

"Not hard enough, Metellus."

"They're good troops."

"I don't think so. You'll work them all day today and all day tomorrow. Standard drills."

"Yes, sir." Lucius snapped, fists clenched behind his back.

"Oh, one more thing, Metellus. This so-called nomadic army. There's no sign of them yet. They've scattered to the winds in my opinion."

"Thank you, sir," Lucius blurted sarcastically.

"For what?"

"Your opinion, sir."

Cornelius Ciceron was taken aback. "Yes well, I just hope you didn't decimate a whole cavalry squadron for nothing. Dismissed." Lucius didn't reply. Simply saluted sharply and turned to go out. The anger at the man's pomposity was too much. "Look out for assassins Metellus!" Ciceron chuckled as Lucius went out the door, knocking over one of the younger troops who bounced off of his bulk like a sack of grain. He was happy to be out in the street again, and tried to calm himself. Suddenly the deep desert seemed like a better place.

Loxias, the chief medical officer of the Legion, shuffled across the room, dragging his enfeebled leg behind him. From out of a wooden box on a nearby table he pulled a pair of bronze tweezers and some clamps.

"Don't worry, Tribune, this won't take long at all. I know you have drills out on the parade ground." He fumbled about for some herbs and oils, throwing them into a large mortar and pestle to grind them together.

"This mixture will help ease the itch around the wound after I remove the staples."

"Thank you and Asclepius for that, Loxias." Lucius was relieved to hear it and the Greek gave a slight nod of respect at the mention of the god of healing. As Lucius looked about the room, waiting, patient, he noticed other implements hanging on the walls or sitting on shelves among jars and pots of herbs. Most disturbing among them were the large knives used for amputating mangled or gangrenous limbs. He suddenly became grateful of his small, insignificant wound that itched. At least he still had his leg.

That thought hit him as he looked at Loxias limping about. "I was born like this, Tribune. In case you were wondering." Loxias took Lucius completely by surprise. He felt badly, being caught staring. "Don't worry. I'm used to people staring at my leg and the way I walk."

"Forgive me, Loxias."

"No need, Tribune."

"So why did you decide to become a physician?" Lucius was curious but also wanted to change the subject.

"Well, it wasn't so that I could heal myself. I knew my leg wouldn't get better early on. I enjoy science; in Greece it's an important part of study."

"Were you educated in Athens?"

"No. At the sanctuary of Asclepius, on the island of Kos. One of the teachers there specialized in war wounds. I found that I had an aptitude for it and here I am. Don't know what I would have done if I weren't a physician. I love it too much.

Besides, I believe my leg helps to remind my patients how fortunate they are most of the time. They leave with a greater appreciation of their physical selves I think. What would you say?"

Lucius looked down at Loxias' crooked leg and then at his itchy wound. He would heal soon, Loxias would not. "Definitely," he answered.

On the way, he had seen Alerio who had come looking for him. He wanted to know what the plans were. Lucius recounted his meeting with Cornelius Ciceron and the orders for extra drills.

"That arrogant, Patrician bastard," he muttered through clenched teeth as he thought about Ciceron. Lucius told Alerio he would meet them on the field after the infirmary. He had also asked Alerio if he had seen or heard from Ashur. He hadn't.

"OUCH!" Loxias pulled the edge of the last staple from Lucius' skin, leaving a small hole.

"It's always the big ones who make the most noise," the hunched over Greek murmured, smiling to himself. Lucius cringed, trying to hide the pained expression on his face.

As soon as Loxias covered it in the ointment he had prepared however, the pain and itching stopped almost immediately.

"I'll sleep well tonight," Lucius sighed with relief.

"Yes Tribune, I suspect you will. Just watch yourself on the training ground. A direct blow to the wound will reopen it. Here." He handed Lucius a small pot with some of the mixture. "Keep clean bandages on it and put more of this on every morning for the next couple days." Lucius rose, feeling better on his leg.

"Thank you, Loxias, really, thank you." The old man nodded and led Lucius to the door where he called in the next patient.

Lucius rode out of the fort in the direction of the training ground walls. Dust from the drilling troops within clouded the sky above. When he had first arrived in Lambaesis, Lucius had been amazed that such a complex should be located there, on the empire's edge. Its thin stone walls formed a large square, two hundred meters on each side with fourteen round, evenly-spaced towers used by sentries and by officers so that they might observe their troops more critically from a higher vantage point. There were only two gates, flanking the eastern and western sides.

The training ground served the Legion well; parades, manoeuvres and all manner of military tactics for both infantry and cavalry were practised. It had been dedicated over seventy years before by Emperor Hadrian when he made his rounds of the empire. It was because of this imperial visit that the most striking feature of the training ground was erected; a large podium in the centre of the mud floor, supporting an imposing equestrian monument of Hadrian himself. Because of this *presence*, the troops seemed to work harder, as though Hadrian's shade blanketed the grounds with a spectral eye.

Once inside, Lucius searched for his cohort in the dust-choked air. Then, a loud voice rang out.

"Move! Move! Together! That's it! Testudinem facite!" The sound of interlocking shields penetrated the air as a tortoise shell formation was put into action. "In numerum ite!" The sound of Argus' vinerod smacking the shields could be heard clearly as he ordered the stragglers to stay in step.

"Ha, ha!" Lucius smiled and rode in the direction of Argus' exacting voice. He reigned in hard next to Alerio who watched intently as three testudo formations marched past in perfect concert.

"Attention!" The troops stopped immediately and saluted their tribune sharply as he rode up.

These are good men, Lucius thought. "Centurion!" he called to Argus. "Carry on!" The men returned to their drills.

All day Lucius watched, observed and corrected movements wherever he saw fit, ever mindful of the need for unison, discipline and accuracy. Each centurion had to lead his century into battle with trust and absolute certainty of their skills. Lucius looked on with pride as his men moved flawlessly. *All this skill*, he thought, *despite their youth*. The men too were proud when their tribune got down from his horse and joined them. He felt his leg growing stronger with each step, enjoyed sweating it out on the dusty field. He remembered how he felt when he first held a short sword, the weight, the beauty, the perfect balance and simplicity. He still enjoyed sword practice, especially with Argus.

The second day of intense training was nearing its end, the sun grew red in the distance. As Argus and the others formed up the men to march back to the fort and hit the baths, there was a raucous laughter from a group of veterans several feet away.

"Metellus? What a name!" yelled out one grunt. "Your family's nothing now! Give it up and go back to your cushy house in Rome." The man's friends chuckled.

That was it. Since arriving, Lucius had bore the brunt of a lot of bad jokes and insults. But this was his family they were talking about now, his warlike ancestors who had built this empire; they were listening, and speaking to him in faint, ghostly echoes. Before Alerio could stop him, Lucius had already reached the loud mouth, Argus right behind him. The man was not small. He was an older, muscular man with an ugly scar rippling across the left side of his neck.

Lucius stood directly in front of him, eye to eye. The man's rank breath polluted the air between them. The other centurions caught up.

"What's your name trooper?" Lucius mustered the most commanding voice he could.

"Gordianus Porcinus," the man grunted, flexing his thick forearms.

"Ah well, that explains it!" Lucius grinned with disgust.

"Yeah? What's that?"

Lucius stared into the man's bloodshot gaze. "The only way your mother could have begot you *Porcinus*, was to have fucked her peasant father's pigs in the haystacks where you were undoubtedly born." Lucius knew the words were a mistake, that they undermined his rank, as soon as he had uttered them. But it was too late.

The anger rose so furiously in the man that he resembled a rabid dog, foaming at the mouth. His eyes twitched in shocked fury at the response from such a young puppy. Lucius waited for the lunge and the instant it came he sidestepped and brought his clenched fist down on his assailant's head. He fell in the dust, scrambling to his feet. Argus shook his head at the man's companions. It would be stupid for them to intervene.

The two men circled each other. Lucius could feel his heart pounding so hard he thought it would break his ribs. A handful of sand blinded Lucius and then, pain. A pain that tore through him like firestorm. He clutched at his thigh where a hobnailed boot had kicked him. *Calm Lucius, calm*, an inner voice spoke to him. He tried to ignore the pain. He had to. Then he stood up and let the man come at him again. *Don't draw your blade!* the voice yelled. He was tempted. As the man rushed, out came Lucius' powerful leg, the heal of his boot striking the man's knee. He stumbled forward uncontrollably, Lucius catching him by the throat.

Porcinus gasped for air as Lucius crushed his windpipe between thumb and forefingers.

"Tribune!" Alerio yelled out. "He's not worth it!"

Argus' head turned to Alerio and back to Lucius. "Squeeze the life out of that son of a bitch Lucius!"

Lucius looked down at the fading life he held between his fingers, his arm clenched in rage. "I won't soil my family's name with a pig's blood. Talk to me again though and I'll sacrifice you to the memory of my ancestors."

Drop him, advised the voice. Porcinus fell with a thud on the ground, his shocked companions trying to revive the unconscious man. *Yet another enemy.* The distant voice faded away in the numbness of Lucius' mind.

He turned and made his way back to his men where they still stood in perfect formation. Although they had not moved, he knew that everyone of them would have been at his side in an instant had his life been in danger. Their strength and discipline were a tribute to him, their loyalty a sign of their affection.

As they exited the training ground gates, ten riders sped by in a cloud of dust, sweaty and exhausted, toward the fort's gate. They had come from the south, out of the desert.

"It's begun," Lucius muttered to himself.

The trooper who had called on Lucius in his quarters looked hurried and concerned. "Tribune! The Legate commands all officers and senior centurions to the Principia in an hour's time." That was all he said but the urgency with which he spoke confirmed Lucius' suspicions. The nomad army had been spotted.

An hour later, Lucius and Alerio approached the torchlit entrance of the Legate Commander's offices. From within, they heard raised voices, arguing and excited. Lucius nodded to the two guards at the door and they entered. The room was full, forcing them to find a space along the wall to the left of the entrance. For several minutes they stood there listening to the remarks of incredulous officers that the nomads had actually managed to muster themselves for an attack.

At the front of the room behind a large table, stood the Legate, Gaius Flavius Marcellus. He had replaced the former Legate, Quintus Anicius Faustus, just over a year before; the latter was an African commander who had built several new forts in southern Numidia and Tripolitania. He was now in Rome. Gaius Flavius Marcellus on the other hand, was not concerned with pushing the frontiers. Rather, his concern was with maintaining the integrity of the existing frontiers as well as maintaining the discipline in his ranks. He was a tall and imposing man, despite his greying appearance, and his voice managed to cut through all others. When Flavius Marcellus spoke, men listened. Beneath a white cloak with a thick purple stripe he wore a black, Greek cuirass with a large gold eagle on the chest that seemed to glow in the lamplight. Behind him, standing prominently was the III Augustan's Aquila standard, the sacred golden eagle that was their symbol. It had been in many battles and had always come home.

About the room, Lucius spotted all of the other tribunes of the Legion, Miles Octavius and Idaeus Ignatius, two of the older officers. Balbas Ascanius too, who was said to have killed one of his own centurions for insubordinate remarks. There were also the two younger tribunes Tertius Sabinus and Aufidus Brenca who were the only officers who actually acknowledged Lucius' rank. On the right side of the legate's table stood Cornelius Ciceron, arms crossed as he gazed about the room. Lucius sighed as Ciceron spotted him and grinned.

"Well, Metellus!" All heads in the room turned to Lucius and Alerio. "Good of you to join us." Flavius Marcellus stopped talking, suddenly very impatient. Ciceron went on. "We hear that you and your men were involved in some trouble on the training ground today. Care to explain?"

Flavius Marcellus raised a hand to silence the impudent senior tribune beside him. "Tribune Metellus. Come to the front of the room so you can hear what's going on." Lucius stepped forward and saluted the legate respectfully. He ignored Ciceron, heeding the legate's commanding presence, and remembering what Marius Nelek had told him about the severity of the man before him.

"Legate. My men were not involved in any trouble today." He glanced sidelong at Ciceron.

"I know, I know, Metellus. I've received a full report. That troublemaker Porcinus is the one who attacked you. You defended yourself. That's fine. It might have been different if you'd killed him."

"But Commander!" Ciceron butt in. Flavius Marcellus silenced him with a raised hand.

"When Porcinus wakes up, I'll have him flogged for good measure. I don't care how old he is. Your men behaved admirably Metellus. Word is that they didn't even move."

"I must protest, Comma-"

"Ciceron if you interrupt me one more time I'll have *you* flogged! Is that understood?" Flavius Marcellus' voice rang through the Principia.

"Yes, Legate Commander," Ciceron replied obediently. The other tribunes smiled slightly. They all knew Ciceron's kind.

"Now back to the task at hand." The legate cleared his throat. "As you all know by now, our scouts reported having sighted the nomad army about fifty miles to the south of here. Their numbers are much greater than we had thought and it appears that they've acquired some of our artillery. Metellus." Lucius stepped up. "According to the reports from your patrol, the nomads had been supplied with siege engines."

"Yes, Commander."

"What about weapons and armour? Did you get anything out of the auxiliaries who dealt with the nomads?"

"We questioned several auxiliaries, Commander, and it appears that the nomads had bought both weapons and armour as well as siege equipment. As to numbers, I don't know, but it must be a lot. There were several frontier forts supplying the enemy for some time it seems."

"Fine." Flavius Marcellus breathed deeply, pensively. "We have to assume then that they have more rather than less. From what the scouts have reported, the nomad army numbers around nine to ten thousand troops, mostly cavalry." The officers in the room began to grumble either in agreement or surprise. "We have close to nine thousand men plus artillery. In the past, the desert armies were ill-disciplined, easily routed. Now, however, they've learned from us over the years and many of them have served in the auxiliary forces." There was more talk among the officers. "I think, gentlemen, we should discuss our strategy."

Flavius Marcellus unrolled a large map of the plain south of the fort and proceeded to draw out their position and the enemy's approach. "They will be here in a day and a half. That gives us tomorrow to get together and mobilize. I want to be here before they arrive." He pointed to a position on a slight rise on the north end of the Numidian plain. "Scipio's tactics won't work here. There will be too many of them. So, standard arrowhead formation, auxiliaries first, to cut into their centre and disperse them. Cavalry on the wings to keep them from wrapping around us." The tribunes nodded their agreement, Lucius included. He could tell that Flavius Marcellus had been through countless engagements and had learned from each one. He had everything well thought out. "Cohorts, of course in the centre. Our backbone. Ascanius, take the two cohorts at the front centre. Octavius, our front right and wing, Ignatius, left front and wing. Brenca and Sabinus the four cohorts at the rear." Lucius wondered what he was doing there, what his cohort's role would be. He dared not say anything. Then the commander looked up. "Ah yes, Metellus. Your cohort will be split in two to support the wings. Your senior centurion," Alerio stepped forward to show he was listening and nodded in understanding, "will command three centuries behind the Gaulish cavalry on our right flank while you will take the other three centuries in position behind the Numidian cavalry on the left. You'll stay there, reserve. You probably won't have to fight but I want the backup. All agreed?" All the officers nodded their approval.

What a waste! Lucius thought to himself. *The best men left out of the fight.* He couldn't understand why their resources, their skill, were being wasted. The cavalry would hold the wings without a problem. He knew however that his position was such that he could not say a word and so, kept it to himself.

"What about myself, Commander?" Ciceron broke his silence for the first time since being threatened with flogging.

"Hmm. Ciceron." The commander rubbed his chin. "I need you on the field." Suddenly Ciceron regretted having spoken up. "You're a good rider. You'll head the Numidian cavalry on the left flank." The senior tribune felt faint but tried to fight it back, visibly shaken for a moment. He had hoped to be at the top of the hill with the commander, observing the battle from a distance.

Some of the officers had lingered in the legate's offices to discuss further plans. Others had gone to brief the rest of their men and get some sleep, Lucius among them. Somewhat angry at the position his men had been given he wanted to confer with his centurions, his friends, and asked Alerio to get them and come to his quarters after they informed their centuries of the preparations to be made for the campaign.

Lucius paced the room. The fresh bandages he had wrapped around his wound were bloody again and he made to change them before the men arrived.

"Still not healed, Tribune?" A familiar voice from the doorway leading to the courtyard.

"Ashur? Where in Hades have you been?" Ashur entered the room, hung his thick white cloak on a peg on the wall.

"Not in Hades, my friend. The desert."

"Yeah, well I guess you know that the nomad army is coming. We fight the day after tomorrow." Lucius was feeling differently toward Ashur, angry, and he didn't know why exactly.

"My friend, I have to tell you something. You must be careful in the battle because-"

"No! Don't say anything. All you do is talk in riddles. You show up mysteriously and then disappear without a trace for days, weeks at a time. Now you show up with some excuse and another ghost story just before I go into battle. Forget it! I don't want to hear it!" Lucius took a gulp of wine from a jug on the table. Ashur stood there, arms crossed, impassive. He had come to warn Lucius of something important, vital. He had been turned away.

"As you do not want me here I will go, Lucius Metellus. But hear this for your own sake. I have been told that there are forces working against you in this battle. It is a neutral foe, who feels nothing for you, not love, not hate. His power is endless and he waits for you while others support you, from a distance." Lucius was not listening. He was too angry, his judgement clouded by the officers' meeting.

"You see! More riddles. I've had enough. Just go. I have business with my centurions." Ashur bowed his head out of respect for Lucius' wishes.

"Very well. I pray...that we shall meet again. Take care...mighty dragon." Gravely, Ashur donned his cloak and disappeared into the darkness of night. Lucius, sat in his chair, hunched over, head in his hands. Suddenly realizing what he had done, said, to the man who had helped them uncover the auxiliaries' treachery, he ran into the courtyard.

"Ashur?" There was no answer. Only a howling wind.

"What in Hades is wrong with these fucking people?" Argus slammed a fist down on the wooden table. "Do they think we're women?"

"Easy, Argus. There's nothing we can do about it."

"No, Alerio! I won't take it easy. You and Lucius should have said something in there."

"Lucius did what he could. Right, Lucius?"

"Oh come on, Antanelis." Garai rubbed his temples, trying to soothe a headache.

"I think you men are forgetting what the tribune has done for us." Eligius walked around the room. He's gotten us out of a lot of bad situations and stood up for us countless times." The men nodded in agreement, except Argus. Maren chewed on a piece of salted meat, silent as usual.

Lucius stood up, looking at them all. "If I could have done more I would have. The fact is that Flavius Marcellus' strategy is impeccable. We just happen to be the newest and youngest in this legion and so we get put in reserve."

"We're also the best," Maren finally added.

"I won't disagree with that, Maren. Who knows what will happen in battle. It'll probably be over in a matter of minutes. We just have to do as we're commanded. I don't want my troops getting a flogging for insubordination." Lucius walked around the table. "What's the attitude among the men?"

"They grumbled a bit, Tribune, but you know they would follow you anywhere." Lucius patted Antanelis on the shoulder.

"I know. We'll just have to wait out the battle in the back." Lucius looked for Argus' reaction. Argus slumped back onto his stool, arms crossed, thoroughly fed up with the entire situation. "It's out of my hands, Argus. I have my superiors too."

"Yeah. Don't we all." He rose to leave. "I'm going now. I need some sleep." Lucius went to see him to the door but Argus simply headed straight out. "I'll see you all tomorrow."

"Don't worry about Argus, Lucius. He always comes around." Eligius was trying to smooth things over.

"If you ask me, Argus has a real problem with authority. Especially lately," Alerio remarked. Maren frowned. Lucius shook his head.

"We're all upset at the situation. Here we are, on the edge of the empire. We have no real objective except to sit and wait. I can see where Argus is coming from." After so long, Lucius still wouldn't hear anything bad said of his adopted brother.

Maren, Garai and Eligius then rose to leave. "We'll have everything ready tomorrow, Lucius, don't worry about a thing. You take care of your officer's duties." Eligius slapped him playfully on the back as the three of them went out.

Alerio, Antanelis and Lucius were left sipping their wine. He thought of telling them about Ashur's visit and what he had said but decided against it. Even though the two of them were the most accepting of Ashur, they still had their misgivings. He kept it to himself.

Shortly after, Alerio and Antanelis departed, leaving Lucius to his thoughts, to sleep. Usually he prayed, dutifully, happily, but lately his mind had wandered and he had forgotten. It was not like him. His thoughts raced once again, an inner fear manifested. He needed strength but he did not find it. He had become withdrawn somehow, had neglected his family, his friends. Even, it seemed, his gods. He regretted this most of all. That night, he placed the two feathers that were dear to him beneath his pillow. In that hazy state between awake and deep sleep, he dreamed of a day many years before, when two eagles soaring in the sky above came down to earth and blessed him, his strength, his innocence. They were still there, had not left his side.

X

FACIES MARTIS

'The Face of Mars'

The men of the III Augustan stood on the rock and sand of the Numidian plain. The sun had not yet risen to greet them in the small hours of the morning, leaving each soldier cold and alone beneath the distant moon. The Roman force numbered close to eight and a half thousand men, all tense, all waiting for the enemy to announce itself.

The auxiliary forces stood at the front of the ranks; nine hundred African spearmen and six hundred German infantrymen. On the left flank were one thousand light Numidian cavalry led by Cornelius Ciceron and on the far right, one thousand heavy cavalry from Gaul.

In the centre were laid out the ten cohorts in checkerboard formation. They were the strength, the heart of the Legion. Divided up on either side of these cohorts were Lucius' men. *Have I led them across all of North Africa to act as bystanders during the fighting?* he asked himself. On the right flank were Alerio, Argus and Maren with their centuries while on the opposite side Lucius headed Antanelis, Garai, and Eligius' forces. In all likelihood, they would not fight. With such a large force of auxiliaries, it would be over before the legionaries drew steel.

At the rear were rows of Roman artillery, scorpions, onagers, and ballistas, their heavy bolts and boulders in ordered piles beside. Behind these, on a rise, their banners fluttering peacefully, stood the legate and the prefect along with their staff and personal guard. At their centre of this oasis of command stood the aquilifer, holding the sacred eagle. It shone even in the darkness, a beacon for the thousands of men laid out before it.

Among these thousands, Lucius felt truly alone and for the first time in years, he felt fear; not the fear of battle itself but of something more elusive, more powerful. It was as though a shadow that had been closing in on him for years had finally caught up. All his childhood nightmares had come to the fore. He felt cold.

In the midst of this foreboding feeling, he looked up to the still-glistening stars of the dawn sky. Inwardly and with great respect, he prayed to Apollo and hoped he would be heard. The first time such fear is felt, it is a time of reckoning. Thus far the Gods had been gracious and forgiving, but had they been too lenient, too dispassionate? Perhaps this was the time? Lucius had lived and fought honestly. But, was it enough to warrant the good graces of Apollo and satisfy the scrutiny of the other Gods of the Pantheon?

If my blood is to be shed, let it be for the good of my family and ancestors, my men and for Rome; an inner thought, a declaration to the heavens that he would not go easily. Lucius breathed, attempted to fight the tightness in his chest, the dark thoughts of shadowy death. *I am not afraid*, he told himself, gripping the reigns tightly. Pegasus shifted uneasily, as if trying to bring Lucius out of the darkness. He looked at the sky; the sun seemed unwilling to begin a new day. He sensed a burning and felt for it dazedly at his thigh, something warm and wet. His wound had ripped open again and started to bleed. He cut a strip of fabric from his saddle coverings with his dagger and tied it about the wound to stop the bleeding.

Suddenly thoughts of eagles soared through the haze that had clouded his mind and he felt the two feathers beneath his cuirass, held to his breast. He smiled, remembering. His gods would not desert him now, he had to believe that, having come so far. Lucius no longer felt alone. He managed to find that peaceful state where soldiers run to for sanctuary, a place to fight from, in which one's sanity remains intact. He felt for his spatha and drew it out, sharp and bright, gripped it, felt its weight. Some of his men behind him glanced at each other, puzzled. He knew they were thinking that he was exaggerating, that they were not even going to fight. He did not care. He felt the image of the dragon on his cuirass, felt the strength of generations.

At that moment, as if in reply to his defiance, the morning sun peaked over the distant mountains, red and gold flowing slowly across the dunes and the plain. The day was to begin at last. In that early morning light, as the sun climbed, the enemy was revealed. Almost magically, like a shimmering oasis they appeared in their thousands, silent and deadly. They had been there all along.

As the sun's light covered the opposing armies, an ominous chanting went up from the still, nomadic ranks, prayers to dark desert gods. From the Roman side, cornuii and drums sounded the solemn death knell, calling on the God of War to preside. In the midst of these opposing prayers and chants, out walked a centurion of the first cohort, followed by two troopers leading a nomadic prisoner. The centurion, now in front of the entire army, drew his dagger and pointed to the opposition. Then, slowly, coldly, he turned to the prisoner who had been made to kneel, and slit his throat for all to see. The body fell with a thud on the sand. A silence fell over the nomadic ranks momentarily, before cries for vengeance and destruction replaced prayers.

The nomad force was huge. Nearly ten thousand. It was made up of several of the desert tribes, mostly Berbers and Garamantians but also Phasanians, Libyans and other minor tribes. Of these, the Berbers were especially superstitious. Flavius Marcellus knew this; the symbolic sacrifice to the Roman God of War of one of their own on the battlefield would either enrage them or strike fear into their hearts. They were also supposed to have little stamina in battle but with numbers such as theirs, reinforcements would be readily available.

In their centre were one thousand horse and eight hundred camels; their large round leather shields and broad-bladed javelins bristled like a forest of young palms. Behind these were two thousand bowmen in front of another sixteen hundred reserve troops. Their strength however, was on their wings; two thousand light cavalry on either side, some armed with bows and swords, others with long spears. As Flavius Marcellus observed the ground from his position, he spotted the stolen Roman artillery behind the reserve troops, on a slight rise below the chieftains' position: two scorpions and one onager. The legate's face was silent, determined. If he had his doubts, they did not show. A lifetime of fighting had shown him that anything could happen and that most things did.

"Hmm. Camels." The legate looked annoyed. "Lartius," he addressed the prefect. "Make sure the German infantry take out the camels quickly. I don't want the smelly beasts being used as a barrier to frighten our horses and break the charge."

"Yes, Legate Commander." The camp prefect sent word. Then to another aid, the legate nodded the go ahead for artillery fire to commence.

"Ballistarii!" the artillery commander yelled out. "Iacite!" The sound of missiles threading their way through the air above the Roman lines cracked the air so loudly it caused some men to duck. The deadly bolts and boulders struck like comets out of the heavens among the enemy ranks, the earth shaking on impact. The voices of centurions in the front ranks steadying their men could be heard faintly beneath the artillery fire.

In his first battle as an innocent youth, Lucius had experienced death and battle with a sort of numbness. Time then had no real direction, no sense of itself. It had been too overwhelming. He had been a singular leaf on the rushing wind of war. This time, it was different. He wasn't numb, senseless, but wholly awake, aware of every sound, command, every one of his actions and those of his men. This consciousness was either a comfort to men or a source of deep fear and anxiety. Despite the dark feeling within, he decided to light his senses, to allow the flame that burns in all men to spread throughout his being, guide him, strengthen him.

The moment the Roman artillery began to shower bolt and boulder upon the enemy, darting overhead like a flock of migrating birds, the sounds of war rang clearly and sharply in Lucius' ears. The steps of warriors on the crusty ground, drums and horns, the neighing of horses, the screams of men. The drama played itself out before him as his cohort watched, waited.

The nomads had been prepared for the flight of artillery, hiding behind shields and toughened hide panels to cheat Rome's deadly prelude. Then, down the centre, the first attack came from a direct assault by the nomad horse and camel squadrons. They were met by the Roman auxiliary infantry, Africans and Germans. In the middle of the plain, dust clouded the air, hiding the violent clashes between man and beast. Cries rang out amid the clanging of sword and spear. The African spearhead faltered slightly but the German vanguard held them there for the time being. Lucius strained to see what he could clearly hear.

As the forces collided in the middle, the nomadic cavalry charged out on the wings, beneath a hail of their archers' covering fire. The stolen scorpions and onagers did little damage to the Roman forces, their range miscalculated; the Romans had to strike before the nomads readjusted. To meet the right and left assaults, Flavius Marcellus signalled for the cavalry charge by the Gaulish and Numidian troops on the wings. The Legion looked on as Cornelius Ciceron led the thousand Numidian horsemen into the fray, riding hard at their head, his spear balanced in wait for its release.

The battle raged on all fronts, neither side breaking. The command was given for the first lines of the cohorts to enter into battle with the far right and left cohorts moving in to support the cavalry. As the sun gained its height, Lucius and his men could see more of what was happening. It seemed like a mass of confusion and disorder, but it wasn't. Every movement, subtle or not, was calculated. Each side countered the other's movements, unrelenting in the slaughter.

At the moment the rear cohorts were given the order to march into the middle to support the slightly faltering centre, the unthinkable happened. Lucius watched in horror as the Numidian cavalry suddenly turned to ride back along the left. Amid the wheeling horses, Cornelius Ciceron's arms went up, his sword falling from his hand as several Numidians thrust their spears into his body from all sides. As the foremost cohorts were occupied keeping the nomad cavalry at bay, the Numidian traitors rode hard around the far left in an attempt to hit the Roman rear. Ciceron's body lay lifeless and trampled in the dirt.

Lucius watched as several horsemen broke through the other cohort's defence, cutting many of them down. On the far right, the heavy Gaulish cavalry held and dispersed the nomad horsemen before cutting inward and across to the centre. Both horse and rider went down around the field and the few remaining nomad bowmen loosed their straight shafts. Lucius looked to the legate but he was busy with the right, sending Alerio's reserve centuries into the centre to bolster the force.

"Tribune!" Eligius yelled. "On the left! Cavalry!"

"I know!" Lucius wheeled Pegasus to follow the movement of the oncoming enemy. They were partly hidden by a cloud of dust, unnoticed by military command. "Damn!" Frustrated, Lucius decided to take a chance, not wait for orders as he was supposed to. The legate did not see what was happening. "Pila tollite!" he ordered the men to ready their spears. "Pila iacite!" A few stray horsemen were taken out as some released their pila but the rest were moving too quickly.

"Tribune! They're turning in now!" Garai strained to see above his men's heads.

"Move in! We'll head them off!" Lucius commanded. "All three centuries together side by side. Prepare to repel cavalry! Break their line of attack! Advance!"

143

The fighting was fierce on both sides, death and dismemberment inherent over the gory plain. Lucius spun, leading his men quickly, desperate to head off the flanking Numidians.

By this time, several of the legate's men had noticed the enemy manoeuvre and formed a small wall of locked shields. They were however, too few. The Numidians would ride them down easily, slaughter them. The small group of Romans ran holding a tight formation as best they could. Lucius charged on ahead of his men, his eye on the Numidians.

Men who have fought, and lived, have learned that the unexpected can occur at any time. One must be ready, aware. Despite Lucius' consciousness of the battle raging all about, the rush of his men to meet the Numidians, he was not prepared for the shining broad-bladed spear that came from his right and, narrowly missing his leg, imbedded itself in Pegasus' side.

The stallion reared up uncontrollably, racked with pain, heaving a gorgon's cry. Eight of Lucius' troops noticed their fallen leader trapped beneath his dying horse. The younger men broke off from their century flank and rushed fearlessly to their tribune's side. Two helped to dislodge him while the other six shielded them.

"Garai, Eligius, Antanelis! Keep moving!" Lucius commanded as he was helped from the ground. A rush of blood suddenly wet his face and, for a fearful moment, the world turned to crimson darkness. Lucius rubbed his sticky, stinging face, clearing the hot blood away from his red-shaded eyes. He looked up to see the source of the spear, this new attack.

Four nomad horsemen stabbed and slashed at his defenders, their essence showering bloodily over him as they fought to their deaths. The riders were not Numidians. The six young Romans took out two riders before they died themselves.

Lucius and the two who had helped him rushed in. His companions were killed and he picked up one of their scuta to repel the enemy blows. The sound was like a summer hailstorm, forceful and unexpected. These riders were apart from all others on the field. They were not after the legate, they wanted Lucius. The fury of battle welled up inside him, the fallen youths bloody at his feet. He wrenched a spear from one of his men's limp bodies and hurled the weighty shaft, Achilles-like, so that it impaled one rider through the neck. The remaining one leapt from his horse onto Lucius, knocking the wind out of him.

The deft wraith was strong, he pushed Lucius to his limit. The Roman cut, thrust, jumped and lunged, attacking and avoiding the thrashing spear that sought his death like a serpent's fang. In a fleeting moment, a chance. Locked together, arms clasped, Lucius found his assailant's throat and crushed it. There was no time to think, to feel for his fallen men, for Pegasus. He picked up the shield and rushed to meet the others who had at that moment clashed hard with the Numidians.

Bravely, brutally, the three centuries blocked the Numidians' way. Their shield wall swayed back and forth but remained solid, impenetrable. Lucius moved to where the wall seemed to weaken, encouraging his men. Twice the Numidians moved to attack, twice they were held by the red-shielded legionaries. The third time, a few broke through and rode hard to the legate's position, the golden eagle gleaming above him. Sword drawn, Flavius Marcellus ordered his guard around the Aquila; to lose the sacred eagle in battle was an utter disgrace, a sacrilege. He had signalled for the Gaulish cavalry to cut back to his position.

Roman and Numidian war cries rang deafeningly in the desert air. Lucius spotted the movement and detached half his men to follow the Numidians who were locked between them and the arriving Gauls. The slaughter was quick, fierce, bloody. The traitors were cut to pieces on the offal-strewn sand.

Marcellus sat tall upon his white charger, expertly hiding the pang of fear and extreme shock he had felt at almost being cut down by his own auxiliaries, men bought by the enemy. In all his years of command, never had he come this close to losing his standard, his life. He scanned the plain, ordered the cornuii to ring out. The remaining nomads, including their proud chieftains, fled into the desert from whence they came, disappeared as they had come, as ghosts. The battle was over.

The bloody day gave way to orange evening and starlit night. Detachments of men had been organized to help the wounded from the field while others gathered the bodies of Roman dead to be buried or burned outside the Lambaesian walls.

Quietly, secretly given over to sadness, Lucius walked across the plain to the site of his fallen men, his own heroes. The taste of their blood still lingered in his mouth, bitter and warm. He felt ill as he came to the spot where their eight bodies lay, lifeless, their souls now lingering shades before journeying to the underworld. And Pegasus, friend and companion. Warlike and gentle, the noble stallion lay on the sand, in a pool of his own blood.

Lucius wept, remembering that first day he saw him in Alexandria. It seemed so long ago. He ran his hand over the bulky muscles of Pegasus' shoulder one last time, a final farewell. He wiped the blood from his hands on his torn cloak. There were cuts on both his arms and his thigh hurt intensely but he ignored the pain, concentrating instead on the brave men, boys, who had saved him. He went over to each one, closing eyes where he could, placing severed limbs with respect, next to their own bodies. He felt like fainting. The world spun momentarily.

Across the littered sand, on the other side of the plain, came an eerie wailing. Lucius forced himself to listen. It wasn't easy. The shrill keening of the nomadic women over the thousands of bodies of their dead men shattered the post-battle silence. Whatever world these people's shades retired to, Lucius thought, their mournful songs would be heard there.

He stood up, made an attempt at a show of composure and signalled Alerio to bring the men and a wagon they had obtained to carry away the bodies of their Roman brothers. Then another song reached his ears, not mournful, not victorious, a prayer of thanks. An ancient language Lucius had no knowledge of. He searched the line of peaks of the surrounding mountains and spotted it. A single, luminous fire, among the crags and rocky outcrops.

The distant voice rose and fell melodically, humbly, beneath the starry sky, the moon in the infancy of its nightly brilliance. Lucius knew that voice, looked to the limitless expanse above as he was comforted by white-robed Ashur's prayers to Apollo. He was grateful then, to his brave men, to swift-footed Pegasus, to Far-Shooting Apollo.

Deep within however, he knew he owed thanks to another. He was also grateful to the harsh God of War, despite all the loss upon that field. The choking within had subsided. Mars had reared his warlike face and Lucius Metellus Anguis had won his favour. His life was permitted to go on...for now.

Three days later, the entire Legion was gathered on the field outside the fort to bid farewell to the shades of the departed warriors. Several had been interred, ornate gravestones of cavalrymen, infantrymen and seventeen centurions standing tall to mark where they lay. Others were burned, in the old Roman practice. The numerous biers lit up the night as the flames cracked and wept fiery tears for the brave.

Among these, the body of Cornelius Ciceron crumbled to ash. Although not well liked among the troops, he was given respect in honour of his station, his ancestors. Around another bier stood the men of Lucius' cohort, honouring those with whom they had eaten, slept, fought and lived through the desert to that place. At the front stood Lucius, the warmth of the flames sweeping all around him as some of the men sang verses from a song they had sung on the march across Africa.

Lucius raised his hands to the fire and spoke, "Remember them, their bravery, what they did for you and for me. Let their memory inspire us always." He then poured libations over the red and blue flames, offerings to them, to the Gods. When the flames died away the following morning their ashes were buried beneath a grave stone in their honour. On it were carved their names, beneath sand dunes and a palm tree. The final inscription read: *In Defence of the Empire the Romans here interred Willingly, Dutifully, Fulfilled their Vows.*

"Tribune?" Lucius had been standing there a lot over several days. He felt it was his duty to his men, a way of giving thanks. "Tribune. Are you well?" Alerio waited patiently.

"What?…ah…yes. Sorry, Alerio. I was lost in thought."

"I know. Me too. Quite a bit lately."

"Is everything all right, Alerio?"

"I'm not sure. Lartius Claudius came to see me with a message. You're to report to the Principia in an hour. Garai, Eligius, Antanelis, Argus, Maren and myself are to accompany you."

"Did he say why?"

"Nope. Said it was very important though and that we should be in formal military dress."

"I swear if we get one more reprimand from any one of these fucking veterans I'll go mad. I won't have them dishonour *them*." He pointed to the gravestone. Lucius shook in anger at the thought but Alerio calmed him, a friendly hand placed gently on his shoulder.

"It'll be fine, my friend. Come. Let's go."

An hour later Lucius and his six centurions made their way along the Via Principalis to the headquarters building. They were resplendent, their armour polished, their newly-issued crimson cloaks clean and brilliant. Lucius wore his flowing white cloak with the thin purple stripe around the edge, a symbol of his equestrian rank. He had wanted to wear crimson like his men but Alerio had advised him against it, just this once. Lucius' demeanour was grim. He was prepared to argue, even with the legate, on his men's behalf.

They were the last to arrive at the Principia and as they entered they were met with stern-faced, silent disapproval. Around the edges of the courtyard and beneath the peristyle stood all the Legion's centurions and tribunes. Lucius stood in front looking from face to face. He wouldn't be pushed around, not this time.

A moment later, the officers surrounding the courtyard snapped to attention, Lucius and the others too, as the legate commander and the camp prefect came out of the main offices, into the open, sunlit courtyard.

Gaius Flavius Marcellus approached the group of young officers, brow furrowed, lips pursed. Lucius looked into his piercing eyes, his heart beginning to pound. And then...a smile. A broad, happy, warm smile cracked the legate's warring face.

"Ave Lucius Metellus Anguis!" he shouted unexpectedly, deep and resonating.

"Ave Lucius Metellus Anguis!" The cheer was taken up by all officers there. Three times they cheered, smiled, praised. Marcellus raised his hand for silence.

"Metellus. You and your centurions have proved yourselves in battle in your service to the empire and to the III Augustan Legion." More cheers from the men as Lucius' centurions looked from one to the other, confused. Only Alerio, smiling to himself, had known of this. "Step forward Lucius Metellus and bare your head." Lucius removed his crested helmet, tucked it under his left arm and stepped forward. The legate continued, "For decisive action in battle and extreme bravery, I present you with this corona, a symbol of your deeds."

Lucius leaned forward as the corona aurea, a crown of golden leaves, was placed upon his head. It felt heavy he thought, but it also felt wonderful. A chill went through his body as the men roared their praise in his honour. He stood tall and proud. The legate raised his hand again as the prefect handed him something else.

"In addition to this corona, the men of the legion present you with this hasta, a symbol of your warlike skill." The cheer went up as the spear was handed to Lucius. Its wooden shaft was smoothly polished, its bronze head sharp and brilliant. Lucius saluted the legate sharply as Flavius Marcellus now eyed the centurions before him.

"Would centurions Garai, Eligius and Antanelis step forward." The three men moved up, saluted, stood at attention. "For your courage and for saving the life of a citizen, we present you with these coronae." Lartius Claudius stepped forward to place the oak leaf crowns on each of their heads. Lucius looked on proudly as well deserved cheers went up once again. The legate went on, "To centurions Alerio, Argus and Maren for their part in the battle we present you with these silver torques." The prefect presented them to each man, they saluted in return. The legate and prefect stepped back and saluted all seven men, the other officers there following suit.

"In an hour," Flavius Marcellus began, " we shall all dine and drink together in the Praetorium in honour of our victory." With that he turned and went out. The courtyard then filled, the officers offering more personal congratulations to Lucius and his men.

"A measly silver trinket! That's it?"

"What did you expect Argus? They did save the legate's life. Besides, we were engaged in fighting elsewhere." Maren tried in vain to calm Argus as they stood together in a small corner of the legate's home, sipping wine.

Argus looked up from his cup and stared across the room. "Look at him. Surrounded. Now that he's decorated, those who hated him before are now his friends." Lucius stood in the centre of the room, chatting with some of the other tribunes.

"Where did you learn to throw a spear like that?" from one. "I knew your father you know, a great man." From another.

Argus rolled his eyes in disgust. The compliments were cursory. "They probably don't even know our father." Maren went back to his drink.

"If it had been me on the other side of the field, I at least wouldn't have fallen off my horse." Maren's turn to roll his eyes as Argus marched over to a table set with food. The smell of honey and spices lingered in the air with that of roast pig and other meats. As Argus hoisted food onto a plate, he scanned the room for the others.

Antanelis was caught in heated conversation with four other centurions. He was far younger than any of them, but also far bigger, muscular. He seemed to nod in agreement as someone spoke, said something, then a loud burst of laughter. He was enjoying himself.

So too were Eligius and Garai who were engaged in broad-smiling conversation with a few of the tribunes' wives and that of the legate. She was a proper Roman woman, tactful and graceful. It seemed she would have been more at home in Rome, attending state functions and banquets, but as it happened she stood strongly by her husband. Aelia Sophonisma had an imposing but beautiful presence, despite her age. She had a refinement seen mostly in the aristocrats of Rome; her bearing was perfect in every way, her manners flawless. Her personality demanded an immediate respect that was rewarded with genuine kindness of heart; Lucius, Garai, Eligius and Antanelis had each felt it as she moved to thank them individually, discreetly, for saving her husband's life and congratulate them on their honours.

A few times other centurions had approached Argus to congratulate him. He was unmoved, unimpressed by their sudden wish to be friendly. For so long they had been given a cold shoulder...but now, after a freak occurrence in the confusion of battle the other officers were their best friends. To boot, Lucius had received high honours where Argus had not. It was unjust. He clenched his clay cup, threatening to crush it.

"Argus? What's going on? Aren't you enjoying the banquet?" Alerio came up beside him. He knew what was on his mind. Knew him too well.

"Why are you so cheerful? Don't tell me you're happy about that *thing* around your neck." He flicked at Alerio's torque.

"Actually, Argus, I am. You should be too after so long."

"Humph!" he grunted.

"Besides, you should be proud of Lucius. He's fought hard and finally has the recognition he deserves."

"Lucius is no better than any of us, Alerio, you know that. He got his recognition when the emperor made him a tribune."

"He's got far more responsibilities than we do. I don't think you or I could do as good a job." Alerio was suddenly very serious.

"That's horse shit, Alerio." His voice was low, aggressive. "If any one of us had been in the right place at the right time like Lucius, any one of us would be tribune. We'd do better probably." Alerio moved in close, chest to chest with Argus, eye to eye.

"Lucius is a good tribune and a better soldier, warrior or commander than either of us is capable of being. Maybe if you hadn't raped your way through the streets of Ctesiphon you might be a little better off!" Alerio's patience had grown unusually thin now. "Besides, you have to be of equestrian rank to be a tribune."

"Go fuck yourself, Alerio." Argus bumped hard into his shoulder to pass him and left the room. Lucius had seen this from where he stood and cast a questioning glance at Alerio who simply waved it off as if everything was fine. He wanted Lucius to enjoy the evening.

Once most of the other officers had finished speaking with Lucius, Flavius Marcellus came over to him, laid an almost fatherly hand on his shoulder.

"Well, Metellus, are you enjoying yourself?"

"Yes, Legate, very much. Thank you for your hospitality."

Flavius Marcellus laughed. "Be at ease Metellus, I'm not the emperor. No need to be so formal all the time." He sipped wine from a silver cup and called for a slave to bring another for Lucius. "To your ancestors, Metellus." They both drank. Lucius enjoyed the legate's personal store of wine. "Ahh. Fine Gaulish wine. You see, even out here on the frontier, on the edge of Hades, there are still some luxuries to be had." He cleared his throat loudly and those standing near to them moved away, allowing for them to speak more privately.

"I know it's been difficult here for you and your men. A tough bunch here in this legion. But, as you can see, they have their moments. A strong heart. A close-knit unit. If I can manage it, I would like for you and your cohort to join the III Augustan permanently. What would you say to that?"

Lucius was filled with shock, surprise, honour and a bit of dread all at once. "Well, Legate, I hadn't really thought about it. Since Alexandria I was under the impression that the emperor intended to keep us moving around."

"You have to settle somewhere you know. What better place than with one of the best and oldest legions? Think about it. We could use some fresh, strong blood in the ranks. You've got a lot of potential, Metellus. What is it?" Lartius Claudius came walking up. In his hand was a document, the Imperial seal on it.

Lucius watched as the legate read it, his intense eyes moving steadily over the words. When finished he rolled it up and was quiet for a moment before looking back at Lucius, an eyebrow raised.

"That settles it then." He looked like he was biting back something, frustration, annoyance?

"Settles what, Legate Commander?"

"It appears you won't be staying here after all."

"No?" Lucius was worried now. First an Imperial dispatch, now this.

"No. You're going back to Rome."

The words seemed to linger in an unending echo through the caverns of Lucius' mind. *Rome. You're going back to Rome...Home.*

The legate waited patiently, allowing it to sink in. In all his years of experience he had come to learn and expect that it was always a shock to a soldier who has spent a long time on the front, to go back to Rome.

"Metellus, are you well?" he placed a hand on his shoulder. His grip was firm.

"Yes...yes, Legate. I...I'm just in a bit of shock. It's been so long since..."

"I know. We've all had that shock at one time or another." He unrolled the scroll again. "It says here that the emperor has had word of your deeds here...By Mars word travels fast! It also says that your presence is requested at the unveiling ceremony for his victory arch in the Forum. You may bring one centurion and leave the rest of your cohort with me until you return. Your ship leaves in a week from Carthage, bound for Ostia." He rolled the document up once again, handed it to Lucius to read.

"Well, I won't say I'm happy about this. I'd rather have you here, especially with Ciceron gone. But, it's out of my hands." Lucius finished reading.

"I'm not sure I want to go, leave my men. Legate?"

"Ha ha! By Jupiter you're an honest soldier." He took a deep mouthful of wine. Lucius did the same, he needed it. "A piece of advice, Metellus, before you go into the lions' den. Keep your nose out of politics. In Rome, honest men have a habit of dying, especially honest soldiers. Play the stupid grunt and you'll live longer." He leaned closer to Lucius, so that none at all could hear. "Tribune. Emperors are dangerous

154

enough as enemies, but even more dangerous as friends. That goes for anyone close to the emperor too; they're all waiting like dogs for scraps from the Imperial table and will rip your throat out to get it. Remember what I've said." Flavius Marcellus stepped back, and laughed out loud, the severity of the moment utterly shattered. Lucius looked at him, incredulous at his sudden outburst but he quickly saw his reason and laughed along with him. Flavius Marcellus was protecting himself and Lucius by disguising their conversation to seem like relaxed banter. The emperor had eyes and ears everywhere, even on the very edge of the empire, in that fort, in that very room.

"I wonder what this is all about? Rome? Jupiter and Juno, I wish I was going with you!" Alerio paced the stone floor of Lucius' quarters. The others had not yet arrived.

"I had thought to bring you, Alerio. You're my first centurion after all."

"And Argus is practically your brother. I really think you should take him, Lucius. He seems a bit...withdrawn, lately." Lucius shrugged. He could see the truth in what his friend said. "Besides, I can keep an eye on things while you're away."

"All right. I'll take Argus. Maybe it'll be good for him to see the family."

"How long do you think you'll be away?"

"Haven't got a clue. A month? A year? Don't know. I'll send dispatches to keep you and the men informed. I really don't know what to expect."

"Well, my friend, whatever it is, between you and me, I think you should listen to what Flavius Marcellus said." Alerio sat across the table from him. "He's been around, knows how things work." He whispered now. "Emperor Severus is good but he is an emperor and has uses for everybody he surrounds himself with. Just be careful."

Lucius smiled. "You're talking like I'm going to join the Imperial court. All I'll end up doing there is standing with all the other grunts for hours during the Triumph and then sent back here. I doubt if they'll let me stay for any amount of time. Don't worry so much."

"Whatever you say. The sooner you come back the better. We're just getting a foothold here. It's not right that the men should lose their commander so soon."

"I know." Lucius thought about it for a moment. Alerio was right. They had just gained acceptance within the Legion but would it last? He hoped so. He had not been apart from his men for so long. "Just one thing, Alerio."

"Sure, what's that?"

Lucius rose from the table, quiet. He looked at the spear he had received where it hung on the wall, the corona on the table.

"If...if you see Ashur at all...tell him I'm sorry. Tell him where I've gone and that I'll not forget him. That I'll see him again." Alerio thought of asking why. Why was Lucius so upset, guilty? But he decided to accede to his wishes. He did not understand his attachment to Ashur but knew there was more to it, something only Lucius could understand.

"Don't worry. I'll tell him if I see him." There was a noise from the courtyard. In walked the others, laughing. Only Argus was quiet, sullen. He had missed the rest of the banquet, had left after his conversation with Alerio.

"You wanted to see us Tribune?" Antanelis was still wearing his corona. Eligius and Garai carried theirs and placed them on the table as they all gathered around. Argus leaned against the wall, just inside the doorway. Lucius spoke.

"I have some news. I'm not sure you'll like it."

"Well? What is it?" Eligius was curious.

"Are we finally getting out of this shit hole?" Maren blurted out.

"No." The intense smell of wine filled the room. They had all drunk a lot.

"Don't tell me," Argus said. "You got another kiss ass promotion?" Lucius ignored that one, without thought.

156

"At the banquet earlier, the legate received an Imperial dispatch."

"What did it say?" Garai's head picked up.

"I'm going to Rome." He let that sink in. "Argus is to come with me." The others were in shock, even Argus' face softened.

"Rome? Why?"

"I don't know, Antanelis. The emperor has asked for my presence at the unveiling of his victory arch. Other than that, I'm in the dark. We leave tomorrow."

The buzz of conversation grew loud in the room then. Questions of "why now?" and "for what reason?"

"The rest of you are to remain in Lambaesis, under Alerio's immediate command until Argus and I get back." Maren rolled his eyes. Lucius always favoured Alerio. There was an air of jealously in the room, they all would have liked time in Rome. Antanelis on the other hand, looked sullen; he had not been separated from Lucius since Parthia. Despite his own personal strength, the young man saw Lucius, who had saved his life, as a sort of beacon on which he could set his gaze in a cloudy world. He knew that Lucius did not have a choice, decided then that things would be even better when Lucius returned.

"We won't let you down, Lucius," Antanelis said as he stared across the table to his tribune, ignoring the others' banter. "The men will be in even better shape by the time you get back."

Lucius looked at his youngest centurion and smiled knowingly. Antanelis meant what he said, always did. "Thank you my friend." Lucius inclined his head. The scar across Antanelis' forehead seemed to redden then, as though he held something back. Lucius felt badly for him, knew that he would feel alone. In some ways, Antanelis was older and wiser than any of them. At times, he was Lucius' only true friend. He looked at the others. "I do have one piece of good news!" They quieted down. "The cohort has been granted permission to escort Argus and I to Carthage for a day or two of leisure time before we sail for Ostia."

Eligius and Garai smiled, looked at each other. "Hear that brother!" Eligius burst out. "I can see them now. Carthaginian dancing girls shaking their bits for us all night long!" Garai then proceeded to jump about in a mock dance that only the brothers' uncouth minds could conceive of. The men laughed at this and joked about what else they might do in the city when they arrived; it was a small consolation for being left out there in the desert, while Lucius and Argus lived well in Rome.

The journey to Carthage had taken only a few days. The roads Rome had built made travelling easier, swifter.

Mixed together, as olive oil and water, emotions of sadness and uncertainty mingled with the excitement of Carthage. Every member of the cohort felt this. What would happen to them? The question pestered every man. Lucius felt more uncertainty than any other. What sort of welcome awaited him in Rome? How long would he be gone? He even wondered whether he would see his men again. So long, so much time. He missed his family, no question. But, had they changed? Surely, all people do. He had.

Carthage was to many the second city of the empire. It swelled, bustled with people from all over the world. From rich Romans to the lowliest eastern harlot. Thousands and thousands of merchants. They were all there, conjoined in a massed confusion of sound, smell, light and colour.

In that place, the glories of the Barcas, Hamilcar and Hannibal, were overshadowed. Distant memories, swallowed by the sands of time. Forgotten on the desolate plain that Rome had burned and salted hundreds of years before, when Punic honour was blown to the winds.

For the two days they were there, Lucius and his men enjoyed life among friends. They were as young men; not a care in the world, at least outwardly. They feasted and drank, competed on the palaestra, gambled and brawled in the taverns and brothels. It was as though each one of them was a green recruit, tasting the pleasures of the world for the very first time. The laughter never ceased, as is usual when all worldly realities are forgotten for a time. Even Lucius, the burdens of command set aside, could not remember ever having a better time than during those precious few days.

When the day came for Lucius and Argus to depart, there were fond farewells. Lucius had made sure to say his goodbyes to each and every man of the cohort, encouraging them, assuring them that he would be back very soon. He wasn't sure about that, but they were and it was good for morale. The thought of it kept them together, kept them strong, and to Lucius that was what was important.

From the Antonine Baths, the force of men escorted their tribune through the streets, past the forum and on into the crowded agora. Lucius had no words left, he had spent them all. Before leaving his troops, he turned and saluted them and they, respectfully, lovingly, returned the gesture.

Alerio, Antanelis, Eligius, Garai and Maren followed Lucius and Argus to the great, circular military harbour of Carthage where the massive trireme awaited its military and political passengers. Many of them were also heading to Rome for the ceremony.

The group bid the two travellers well. Wishes of fortune and guidance to Rome, and for their return. They parted as friends, as a close knit group who had been to Hades and back, together.

As five of them stood on the dock of the harbour, the other two ascended the gang plank. A horn blew, row upon row of oars splashed downward into the water and the ship lurched forward, angling its way out of the harbour. The centurions turned to go back to the cohort, except Antanelis who stood still, watching Lucius wave to him, to his scarred face.

"Gods, protect you on your journey," the young man whispered as he waved back, watched the ship disappear among the masts of a hundred more.

Lucius and Argus made their way to the prow as they passed through the rectangular merchants' harbour, crowded and noisy. Each was silent with his own private thoughts as the great bulk of the trireme passed out of the last set of docks and the sea opened up. Gulls hovered high above the sails and spray wet Lucius and Argus' faces as they pushed out.

Lucius looked back briefly, the walls of Carthage, the province of Africa growing smaller and smaller. He turned his gaze to the sea now, thought of his family, his friend next to him, his father. He looked ahead to Ostia, to Rome.

Part II

VENUS AND ROME

A.D. 203

XI

ADOLESCERE CUM AQUILIS

'Growing up with Eagles'

The Gods have a wondrous view.

From Their realm beyond the strain of human vision, They sit atop whispering cliffs. Stretched into the infinite expanses of the world, laid like a sheet of silk beneath Their naked feet, is the vibrant sea of life. A glimmering pool larger than the imagination can conceive, and yet, to be read in its entirety in the dewy gloss of a single flower petal. Within the sea, the lives of mortals take shape, those of the past, the present and those yet to be born. Each life can be viewed individually or as part of the whole.

Each life has a song and these songs can move the Gods in Their far-removed peaks. The Gods laugh and dance, They sing. They also weep and tremble with fury, depending on the song of the life They are hearing. Some families' songs are ever pleasing to immortal ears, others never so. Those songs with heavenly potential draw the Gods into them, beg Their aid with the beginnings of a hopeful melody, one that if nurtured and blessed, will please Them for all eternity.

It was a day like any other, and yet, not. In a room in Rome, to the descendants of a family whose fire and song had faded away for an age, a son was born. The Gods turned Their heads to listen when that melody began, the people in the room smiled and uttered blessings to Them.

"You have a son, Lady," said the midwife as she wrapped the child in warm linen and handed him to his father.

"A son!" Joy crossed the man's face. He dabbed the sweat from his brow with the sleeve of his immaculate toga. He had been nervous for his wife.

"Mother," spoke a little girl, "does this mean I have a brother now?"

"Yes, Alene, dear. It does." The mother accepted the child in her arms and though exhausted, she held him close and kissed his forehead.

"What will we name him, father?" asked the girl, her face red with excitement as she caressed the baby's hand.

The Roman crossed his arms and looked at his wife, displeasure entering the song. The Gods listened. He had promised. "He will be named at the lustratio."

"Is it the one I heard you and mother say before, father?" The girl and her mother looked at him expectantly.

"Yes. I suppose it will."

"Lucius Metellus An-gu-is," the child struggled with the strange name.

"Alene! I told you, not until the lustratio."

"But we have to call him something until then, don't we?"

"Yes, Alene," the mother soothed. "But we must also abide by the traditions. Call him 'Brother' for now."

"Yes, mother."

It was on a cool autumn morning when the young boy had risen from his bed, dressed and been drawn out of doors. He had had another dream and could not sleep. He always had dreams. In them he heard soft voices and beautiful music. He did not want to wake from dreams such as these but he always did. That morning, the music he had heard continued once his eyes were open. He rubbed them, stuck his fingers in his ears, but the music was still there.

He peered out of his window on the upper floor of their home and spotted the Palatine Hill. He liked that hill, had been told that their ancestors used to live up there, above the city, like gods. But that was long ago. Restless and unable to sleep longer, he dressed himself, laced his boots and put on his thick cloak.

The air outside smelled sweetly, like honey. He took the path he knew best, the quickest path to the steep staircase that mounted the hill to the square in front of the temple. The music seemed louder as he entered the gleaming courtyard in front of the temple. It was the place where he felt safest. He looked up at the pediment, the image of the God Apollo, their family's patron. The music stopped almost completely, only the resonance of a single string lingered.

He hummed, tried to emulate the music but it was too difficult. He was happy though, the restlessness having quit his body as he looked toward the Tiber, the Circus. He nodded off, restful against one of the massive columns at the top of the temple's stairs. An hour later, the sun higher now on the horizon, he felt a breeze on his face, soft like the kisses his mother used to wake him. *Rise*, a voice said. But nobody was there.

Startled, he moved to the centre of the courtyard and looked up at the morning sky. Something whirled and swooped, sang. It flew directly towards him but he did not feel fear, it was beautiful. He recognized it as something from his dreams. An eagle.

It came to land in front of the temple, a few feet away.

"Good morning," the boy said. The great bird turned its head sideways, his golden eyes observing him. They were almost the same size. "Don't fly away my friend. I won't hurt you." The boy began to move closer and the bird, rather than flying away, began to amble slowly toward his outstretched hand. The eyes were hypnotic, familiar. They contained an accumulated wisdom of ages. "You seem very smart to me," the boy smiled at the sense of joy he felt within. "I sure wish you could talk."

He wanted the moment to last forever. It was like one of his dreams, the good ones he had all the time. But this was real. He couldn't wait to tell Diodorus.

"LUCIUS!" The harsh sound broke into the peace like a rock shattering brilliant blue glass. It was his father. The bird

164

began to squawk angrily at the intruder, causing Quintus Metellus to stop in his tracks. "Get away from that thing, Lucius! How dare you leave without permission."

"It's fine father, look, he's my friend." He stood next to the bird proudly.

"It's not *fine*. Leave that animal be, you don't know what you're doing!"

"I have to go now," he whispered to the eagle. "Please come and see me again." Lucius began to walk to his father but stopped. "Go ahead. Fly!" The bird flapped its massive wings, ruffling the boy's hair, and climbed into the sky in the direction of the rising sun.

"Come, now!" He felt his father's cold hand grab his neck and squeeze hard as he dragged him home. "Nine year old boys don't walk around the city by themselves. Your mother has been worried sick," his father muttered.

That evening, lying in bed, the boy smiled as he remembered the beautiful eagle. He would never feel the same after that, would never forget that perfect morning before his father had come. Nor would he forget the ruthless beating he had received when they got home; some things were meant to be remembered, others forgotten.

"Your father had always been kind and gentle, Lucius, that is, before his five years in the army. He has always felt at home in the Senate, hopes for the same thing for you some day." Lucius' mother tried in vain to smooth her son's impatience with his father. He would not have it.

"Mother, he just doesn't understand. I don't want to go into politics. I want to join the Legions. He can't stop me." The young man held out his arms as his sister adjusted the folds of his first toga.

"Have it your way, Lucius," his mother conceded. "But, you will have to tell him yourself. You're a man now and you have to act like it. I'm not going to tell him for you."

"I will, mother."

"Just remember that your father has worked very hard to bring this family some measure of prominence again, to make a good life for us. He does not want anything to ruin it."

The young man could not say anything more, did not want to hurt his mother's feelings. Of course he too wanted the best for their family. Without question! It was just that he wanted to do things his own way, the way he dreamed, not his father's way. They never saw eye to eye.

"There!" Alene stepped back. "You're ready, Lucius."

The thick folds of cloth were heavy, pulled down on his shoulders.

"How do I look?" he asked.

"Like a Roman." His mother beamed with pride. "Sixteen years," she mused. "I can't believe it's been that long. Let's go and see your father."

The three of them went down the staircase to the courtyard where Quintus Metellus was seated in the garden going over some scrolls.

"Look, father," Lucius said as he came to the edge of the garden.

Quintus looked up from his work, eyed his son and got up. "Looks good for now. Let's see if you can keep the folds as you walk through the Forum. The real thing is much different from that bed sheet you practice with." He looked past his son to his wife and daughter and the slave who was holding their youngest two. "Are we ready to go?"

"Yes, husband."

"Good. Let's get this done before it's too hot." He pushed past all of them and made directly for the atrium and the front door. Everyone followed.

The folds of the toga did not slip once as the small procession made its way through the streets to the Forum Romanum. Citizens greeted Lucius as he walked in front. He was met with nods of approval. Lucius looked back at Argus who walked with the rest of the family. Quintus had thought to have the other boy stay at home but Lucius had asked that he be allowed to join them. Actually, Lucius thought, his father had given in rather easily to that request.

They all turned onto the large ramp that led up to the Palatine Hill and into the various palace complexes. Many families made the walk to the Capitol and the Temple of Jupiter but their family had always made offerings on such days at the Temple of Apollo. The augur would be waiting for them now, to read the omens for Lucius' future as a man. He walked on, feeling nervous, hot beneath his unfamiliar garment. His eyes glanced skyward, they always did, especially in that place. It had been years since he had dreamed of eagles. Lucius prayed the omens would be good for him.

Upon reaching the temple, everyone remained outside while Lucius mounted the steps and was led inside by the head priest. It was pungent and smoky inside, dark. The priest stopped and indicated the great altar beneath Apollo and his muses. The god stared down at him expectantly while the beautiful nine seemed to smile at him, as if sharing some mysterious secret. He even blushed.

The sacrifice arrived, a small goat. It was hoisted carefully onto the altar and Lucius was handed the ceremonial dagger. This was his first sacrifice, he was nervous. He knew that the life of the small creature was in his hands and he felt his heart begin to pound in unison with the goat's as he stroked its soft head to soothe it, as he thanked it for its life. Lucius looked up at Apollo, offered his prayer and drew the blade quickly across the neck in one fluid motion. The blood spurted out quickly at first, then slowly, until the animal went on to eternal sleep, its blood running over the white marble surface of the altar. Lucius bowed to the god and backed away, trying to hide his shaking hands.

Outside in the square, everyone was waiting at the bottom of the steps. The augur, who was dressed in long white robes, met Lucius half way up the steps and turned to look at the sky. The air was still, no one spoke and all Lucius could hear was the augur's breathing. Lucius looked about, his bloody hands ceased their trembling. A wind picked up and the augur raised his arms skyward, casting oak and bay leaves into the air. They waited.

Then, high above, a shrill song echoed among the scattered clouds. "There!" the augur shouted, pointing in that direction. A moment later, two eagles dove out from their white, lumbering shelter in the direction of the temple. Everyone gasped as they circled before landing on the temple's pediment. "By Jupiter and Apollo!" the augur whispered, humbled by the holy birds' intense gaze. Lucius fought back the tears of joy that trembled behind his eyes. For years he had hoped, wished that the bird would come back to him and now there were two on the day he became a man. The birds flapped their wings and two feathers glided down onto the steps above him.

He moved carefully to pick them up, bowed to them when he had. "Thank you," he said below his breath, his heart heaving joyfully. The eagles then swooped down over the square and were gone again.

Nobody had words for a few moments. Lucius could see the tears in his sister's eyes, the pride on his mother's face, the fear in his father. The augur managed to compose himself, walked up the steps to Lucius and turned to face the others. "The omens, Lucius Metellus Anguis," he declared, "are good." That was all he said. That was all anyone said.

As the family made its way back home for the celebratory feast, Lucius dropped back to where his father was walking in the rear, lost in his thoughts. Quintus had not said anything to his son as they left the temple. It hurt Lucius to think that he did not want to be near him then, on that day of days.

"Father, I have to talk to you about my plans." Quintus' face lit up for a moment. Plans indeed. He had great plans for his son.

168

"Quite right, son," he began without allowing Lucius a moment more to speak. "Now that you are a man, Lucius, you will be able to go to the Senate with me and listen to the sessions. If you are to be involved in Roman politics you must become acquainted with the protocols involved, see how things work."

Lucius knew he had to tell him now, not a year or two hence, now. He stopped walking and held his father's arm to stop. "Father. I do not intend to enter into politics as you have." Quintus looked genuinely surprised. "I want to...I'm going to join the army. If Septimius Severus wins out over his enemies and defeats Albinus then-"

"Are you mad?" his father cut in, teeth clenched. "There might be a civil war! It's suicide to even choose a side or speak about it. And in the streets of Rome of all places!"

Lucius pushed on with his speech. "I'm not going to join right away. I'll wait two years to join. In the meantime, I'll train and continue my studies. I enjoy them."

"It's time to begin doing something with your life Lucius, not waste your time and my money for two years on books, races and baths while you dream of a fantasy career in the Legions. Besides, you wouldn't last a month!"

"Yes I would, father. I will. I'll make myself in the army, like our ancestor who carried the dragon with him at Zama."

"You'd do better to follow in the footsteps of those of our ancestors who weren't mad and prone to Punic superstitions."

"You won't change my mind," Lucius knew he was sounding like a petulant child now. But how else could he say what he wanted to say to convince the man before him? "I'm going into the army, father, not the Senate. You don't have to agree with me. I'm telling you that's the way it is."

His father seemed to deflate on the spot, as though the pride and hope of years of planning had suddenly sputtered out of him. Then, his anger rose. "Very well then. When you *truly* become a man, you will see how stupid you are being. Go

ahead and disgrace yourself! That's fine. But if you disgrace
this family, you'll be no son of mine. Understood?"

The two of them stared at each other, their words spent.
Finally, Quintus turned and went after the rest of the family.
They would have been home by then. Lucius followed an hour
later.

*All that time, all those angry words, wasted. For what? To go
back to it all?* Lucius stood alone on the deck of the trireme as
it cut through a choppy sea in the direction of Ostia. Most of
the passengers were below deck. He needed to be alone,
needed a view of the sky and the scent of fresh air in his lungs.

As the spray hit his face he remembered the last time he
had seen his family, the day he and Argus had left for Parthia.
His mother had thrown a great feast for them, a feast fit for
returning heroes not departing youths. Alene and his mother
had been sad to see him go but as ever, had put on their bravest
faces when the time came.

After having said goodbye to little Quintus and Clarinda,
Lucius moved to Alene. He remembered her face like it was
yesterday, the sea droplets that hit his face on the deck of the
ship reminded him of the tears that ran down his sister's
cheeks when he had hugged her. She had wrapped his eagle
feathers in a swathe of white silk and tucked them into the
pouch at his side. "Apollo bring you home safely, Lucius," she
had said. They were still comforting each other when the door
to his father's office had opened and he stepped out, silent and
severe. He held a large, plain-looking bundle.

"This was your grandfather's a long time ago. It's useless
to me. You can have it." Lucius had accepted the gift. He
remembered his father looking more tired and angry than ever.
He had wanted to make peace with him then and there but his
father spoke. "Try not to get yourself killed." After that, he
turned and went back into his office, to his scrolls of accounts
and Senate business.

170

"It is your father's way of dealing with things my son," his mother said as she walked with him to the front door. She pointed to the bundle he had been given. "I convinced him to give you that. For once, he agreed."

"What is it?"

"Your grandfather's armour and sword. It is very special." Lucius looked at the unassuming bundle. "You can wear it when you make tribunus." Her confidence surprised him.

He felt a weight upon his shoulders. "I won't disgrace the family, mother. I promise," he said, his lip quivering slightly as he realized that it might be the last time he saw her. She shook her head, stared him in the eye.

"My son. Never did I think for an instant that you would. Simply by being, you rain glory upon this house. I will miss you. But we will see each other again, I am certain." She then wrapped a new cloak around his shoulders, a black one, the one he wore as he thought of this on the deck of the ship.

"Goodbyes are always difficult," he said to himself.

"What's that?" Argus said as he came up on deck. "Are you talking to yourself again, Lucius?" He smacked him on the back.

"Just thinking of the last time we were home, that's all."

"Seems like ages doesn't it?" Argus was actually giddy.

"What are you so happy about then? Did you get close to that Mauritanian girl below deck?"

"Ha! Not quite. Her husband keeps getting in the way," he joked. "I'm excited to be back in Rome! Aren't you?" He put up a hand. "No, wait. You're stuck in that shit hole you always fall into when you think about the family."

"I'm happy to see them."

"All of them?" Argus shook his head. "You're so full of shit sometimes, Lucius. I don't know why you worry so much. We won't even be there very long, so you might as well enjoy yourself before we have to go back to camels and ass-nippers." Lucius remained silent. "Personally," Argus went on, "I'm happy to see good old Quintus again."

"Bugger off, Argus."

"Ha, ha. I knew that would get you. Ach!" A gush of sea spray soaked his face. "I can't stay out here any longer. I'm going back down." Before descending the steep steps, Argus watched Lucius where he stood, huddled in his cloak as he leaned against the mast, silent. "Miserable bastard," he muttered as he went down.

XII

OSTIA: PORTUS ROMAE

'Ostia: The Port of Rome'

The sky above shone gold in the waning hours of the afternoon sun as the trireme, its sail now hoisted, entered the preliminary harbour. The entrance, precarious enough with all the water-bound traffic, was marked by a tall lighthouse, its beacon ready to guide all manner of people into the port of Rome.

"Strike oars! Slower!" the voice of the captain commanded the rowers, the steady, slowing beat of a drum determining the concerted, rhythmic movement of the oars as the galley came into the huge hexagonal port of Trajan.

The harbour was manic. People from all over the empire and beyond milled about, loading and unloading massive trade ships. At one side of the docks, several detachments of troops oversaw the unloading of a precious cargo from Aegyptus: corn. Six enormous Alexandrian shipping vessels were tied up, bobbing lethargically in the murky water as the holds were emptied. Their cargoes were taken under guard to the various horrea, granaries located throughout the town, until shipment to Rome herself.

Ostia was a small version of its Imperial mother, a teasing taste for the senses prior to the great feast that was Rome. With over fifty-thousand inhabitants, what had originally been a military camp near the mouth of the Tiber, was now a rich city where anything could be bought, any service had.

The extremely rich and Imperial patrons of the city had crowned it with numerous temples, baths and theatres; the temples of Hercules and of Rome and Augustus stood out to inspire, awe those from the outside world who had come to trade goods from their own, comparatively poor nations. Nightly, the people of Ostia were witness to acts of tragedy, love and comedy as they sat transfixed in the seats of the theatre erected by Pompey the Great and Marcellus; it was now under full renovation by order of Emperor Severus. Building and renovation churned up the dust of almost every street.

Any traveller who came to Ostia was struck by the richness of the homes. In Rome, homes were tucked away on the hills or lost in the maze of streets and squares. The inhabitants of Ostia flaunted their wealth. Family homes lined the main streets displaying colourfully painted walls, columned balconies and marble facades of every colour. Alongside the homes of senators and rich merchants were the tenement insulae, four and five story blocks of brick and mortar which, despite the occasional fire, provided reliable housing for the majority of Ostians. On the ground floors of these insulae were the tabernae, over eight hundred in total, where merchants and traders had their shops and workshops. Anything from pastries and pottery to weapons and clothing could be obtained by anyone with enough of a jingle in their purse. The clinging of sestertii and denarii were tangible in Ostia, as normal and frequent a sound as sailors' whistles to passing ladies, the laughter of children, the moaning of slaves.

The sea voyage had passed quickly for Lucius, more so than he would have liked; he was not yet prepared for his return home and the accompanying feelings. Neptune's deep, which had always been a great mystery to him in the past, now floated by unnoticed in foam-crested waves. The god's presence was there to be felt but the Roman's mind was adrift off a more distant shore. Even the darting of dolphins as they danced in the trireme's wake could not pull Lucius from his pooling thoughts; Neptune's messengers, carriers of souls to the underworld, soared and squealed and splashed and all the while he thought of home.

Throughout the entire voyage, as Lucius leaned against the swaying mast, Argus puked; he cursed and spat, his stomach churning, spinning, a sickening whirlpool from within. When he had finished, he would return below deck until he became sick again. Some people were not made for the sea, even the toughest of soldiers. Argus was one of these and as soon as the ship docked in Ostia, he headed up the street to the baths to clean himself up.

Lucius walked on alone for a while, having arranged to meet Argus at the inn where they would spend the night before departing for Rome the following morning. It was in a quieter part of town, away from the harbour and the dockside brothels; a soft breast and a warm thigh always awaited the weary seamen who came to port. Argus would visit that particular stretch of Ostia later on. He had asked Lucius to come with him, "You could use a good rub-along," he said. But he was to be disappointed. Lucius was too pre-occupied for women, usually was since he became a tribune.

Ostia was a shock to the senses after the remoteness of the desert towns. People paid no attention to a young tribune passing through the crowded streets. He walked slowly, took in the intricate mosaic signs that advertised the tabernae dotting the thoroughfare.

The sweet, warm smell of fresh honeyed pastries finally drew Lucius into one shop where he was welcomed enthusiastically by an elderly woman who promptly shoved a piece of something delectable into his salivating mouth. He came out with several things wrapped carefully in large palm leaves.

That evening, after having visited the baths himself, Lucius ate a simple meal with Argus.

"You're not talking much. What the hell's wrong with you? The trip over was more exciting than this."

Lucius realized that it was the first time the two of them had been alone in a long while, that Argus was trying to talk with him. "I'm sorry, Argus. I'm just a little nervous about tomorrow. I haven't written since Alexandria, not once."

"So what? Do you really think that your mother and Alene are going to care? They used to dote over you for shitting. You're overreacting, as usual."

Lucius shook his head. *Why is it he never understands?* he thought. "I suppose I'm more nervous about meeting with father."

Argus leaned forward. "Who gives a shit about him? If he can't see what great things we've done while away that's his fucking problem. *Make* him see. That's how you have to deal with him."

"Since when are you an expert in oratory?" Lucius' tone was slightly bitter, biting.

"Who said I was? I've just thought about it from time to time. Doesn't mean I can't enjoy myself. Besides, with all your moping, how can I not think about it?"

Lucius did not answer, the conversation was not helping. They were busied with all of the racing thoughts that accompanied their return to Rome, their reunion with a family they had not seen in years. It was evident that each dealt with those feelings in a different way.

Lucius also realized that he and Argus had grown distant, with jealousies and misunderstandings between them, resentments and frustrations. It hurt, could be felt in every word. Together, they had left Rome as the best of friends, as brothers. Now however, the divide seemed great as too many thoughts went unsaid, too many feelings unheard. He wanted to avoid arguing with Argus. What was the point?

They were no longer equals. This saddened the one, angered the other. One was a tribune who had gained respect and honour in the field, the love of his men, the attention of the emperor. The other was a centurion, one embittered by the thought of being passed over, denied what he deserved. The same training had been completed, the same battles fought, and yet he had to follow the orders of his one-time equal. His men did not love him, they feared him and although they followed his commands, he wondered, would they die for him?

For Lucius, men had gone to Hades. Argus knew they wouldn't do as much for him. Anger built upon jealousy within his confused heart and unfounded fears of a dagger from behind were with him now, always. In his time off duty he took out his frustrations, his resentments, in the whorehouses of whatever town they were in, the seedy gambling establishments frequented by the lowest ranking grunts. Ostia had plenty to chose from.

"I'm leaving now!" Argus blurted out suddenly as he rose from the small table, popping a final piece of squid into his mouth.

Lucius, startled, looked up. "Where are you going now?"

"Where do you think? Down to the docks. I need a little female companionship and some sour wine." He gathered up his money bag and cloak.

"Remember Argus, we leave early in the morning. Since you don't want to sail up river it'll take longer and-"

"Yeah, yeah. I know. You've reminded me three times. I won't be late."

Lucius quieted. "I'll have the horses ready. Don't worry."

"Why should I worry, Lucius, you always have everything under control," he said sarcastically. For a brief moment however, Argus' face, his features, softened and Lucius wanted to smile, having caught a glimpse of the boy he had grown up with. He wanted to rise, to embrace him and tell him he loved him… but, the moment passed, as such moments tend to. "Maybe," he began hesitantly, "we can go to the Colosseum together, before we go back to Africa? What do you think?" He was like an excited child.

"I don't know, Argus. We'll see how much time we have when we're there." Lucius pushed around some of the remaining food in his plate.

"Fine. See ya in the morning." Argus' face hardened once again and he went out into the street. He ran as fast as he

177

could, as though he were trying to outrun the feelings of sadness in his soul, the tears that formed in his eyes.

That night, Lucius lay in his bed on the third floor of the inn. From the distant harbour came the faint sounds and screams of night revellers, penetrating the quiet of the neighbourhood.

He stared out the window, the moon bright, the sea calm and reflective, its otherworldly aura beautiful. Lucius thought of his men, of Ashur. Were they watching that same moon? Did they also have trouble sleeping? He hoped they did not resent his leaving, prayed that they would not forget him while he was away.

In his half-sleep, he wondered, curious to know: Did the Gods sleep? Or was their gaze constantly fixed upon the lives of men? The coming days would be trying, would hold much that was not known. Anything could happen. In his uncertainty, Lucius hoped that the Gods did not sleep, but would watch over him, guide him day and night as he tread the shiny streets of Rome, as he slept beneath the roof of his father with whom he had not spoken in years.

XIII

CAPUT MUNDI

'Capital of the World'

Morning sun shines golden, heralding the birth of a new day and seven hills rise up from awakening streets. Brilliant temples to gods, goddesses, monuments to men, homes of people of little consequence, the mob, and palaces of the mighty – a world of contrasts that only hints at the power, wealth and dangerous beauty that would always be, Rome.

The Tiber flows on, winding its way through the city of Caesars, smoothly, like a singular silver thread uniting the heart of an empire. Daily, the people of Romulus go about their business, their lives. Daily, people from around the world pass through one of Rome's many gates, having travelled various roads to this spot, all with their dreams of fortune, their hopes and their regrets intermingled in a satchel that each carries the length of their long journey.

The two young soldiers had entered the city at mid-morning and crossed the Tiber over the Pons Sublicius, the oldest bridge in Rome. The first thing to awaken a sense of familiarity as they made their way through the busy Forum Boarium was the smell. The old neighbourhood filled their nostrils, then their ears. The cattle market and the Circus Maximus a short distance away made for an interesting mixture. For those unused to the scene it could be quite overwhelming. For others, it was the smell of spring, tinged with the sounds of life reverberating all around. It felt strange to be home.

A shaking hand reached for the large, bronze griffin knocker that hung menacingly on the crimson doors. In the background, as if the hand were being encouraged, came the roars of the crowd within the Circus. The emperor's celebrations had already begun.

"Well? Go on, Lucius. Knock! What in Mars' name is wrong with you?" Argus reached for the knocker himself, impatient, but Lucius stayed his hand.

"I should've let them know we were coming, Argus. Why didn't I?" Lucius fidgeted with the pommel of his sword.

"I don't know but you better knock soon. I'm getting hungry and we look like a couple of idiots standing in front of the door like this." He looked across the street and up to see an old woman staring at them. She was a permanent fixture of the neighbourhood, the source of much gossip. "Look, see? There's that old crone up there. Still!" he yelled at her. "Maybe we should *call the urban guards on her*!" The old woman promptly busied herself with something and closed her shutters.

Lucius knocked twice. The solid sound of the bronze seemed to echo in his head as the blood pumped in his reddening ears. They both stood up straight as the doors creaked and an unfamiliar slave girl opened.

"Erm. Hello." Lucius stepped forward slightly but was unwilling to push his way inside. "I don't believe we've met. I'm Lucius Metellus and this is Argus. Could you tell the Lady Antonia, my mother, that we are here?"

The girl looked momentarily unimpressed until her large green eyes opened wide in shocked recognition of the names she had just heard. The mistress often spoke these names when conversing with her eldest daughter. "Oh yes...yes...ww, welcome home, masters." She averted her gaze and backed up to allow them to enter, bowing as she went. "I am new here. My name is Ambrosia. I will go inform my mistress, your mother. Please come, come. It is quite beautiful in the garden at the moment."

"Thank you, Ambrosia. We'll wait here." Lucius smiled as she turned to go. Argus continued to stare at her, watched the curves of her body beneath her plain stola until she disappeared around a corner.

"Hmm. Things have changed here, and for the better."

"I guess so. I don't know. It doesn't feel like home."

"Well what did you expect? We've been gone for a few years."

The house was quiet, as though it had been deserted for some time. Perhaps everyone was out? In a way Lucius had hoped no one would be there, time for him to get accustomed to the surroundings again. He looked to the atrium where the afternoon sun was angling its way in, illuminating the marble floor, smooth and glasslike.

Then, as out of a dream, a happy, rejuvenating wish fulfilled, Lucius heard quick footsteps and then saw the people he had missed most. Alene came running from the lighted corridor, tears of joy glistening on her cheeks.

"Lucius! You've come home!" Lucius ran to her and she threw her arms about him tightly, lovingly, as she laughed. He spun her around in a frenzy of youthful happiness and buried his face in her comforting hair.

"I've missed you," He tried to keep his voice from shaking as he stepped back to look at her. "You're more beautiful than ever, sister." The sight of her was warming, as it always had been. He felt at home.

"Hm. Hm." A voice cleared behind Alene as Antonia Metella, shocked and overjoyed, called Lucius' attention to her.

"Mother!" He stepped towards her and, quite unexpectedly, smiling like a happy child, picked her up as if she were a feather. She laughed and laughed.

"Oh Lucius, stop! Put me down. I'm too old for this!"

"Nonsense, mother! You look perfect!" He put her down and she looked upon him proudly.

"My son, a tribune! You have grown into a formidable man." She looked to where Argus was standing, quiet, trying to smile. "And Argus, you too have grown strong and imposing. Welcome home." Antonia embraced him. "I wish you would have informed us of your visit. The house is not prepared for you."

"Don't worry, mother, everything looks great." Lucius looked down the corridor. "Is…father here?"

"No, Lucius, he's at the Senate house today. He took your brother with him. They'll be back this evening. But Cla-"

"Lucius! You're home!" Clarinda came running up to them. "You too, Argus?" Lucius knelt down on one knee to look his younger sister over. She had grown and had adopted many of their mother's mannerisms, proper and graceful. "Are you staying this time Lucius?"

"Not for long, Clarinda." He stood up again. "The emperor has summoned me, us, to come to the unveiling of his victory arch and-"

"The emperor?" Alene blurted out excitedly.

"Yes." Lucius nodded.

"Well, it seems we have much to talk about. Let's go into the garden. No, wait! You must be exhausted from the journey. Do you want to sleep first?"

"No, no, mother. We've slept enough. I want as much time with you as possible."

"Wonderful." Antonia Metella clapped her hands. "Ambrosia! Bring food and wine."

"Yes, my lady." The girl left quickly for the kitchen but not before flashing a slight smile at Argus. It did not go unnoticed.

Alene took her brother's arm and they followed their mother to the garden where couches basked in the sunshine.

For hours, the four of them sat together on sunlit couches, talking, the gentle splashing of a fountain echoing in the background. Clarinda lay up in her room to sleep in preparation for a late night of feasting.

It had been a long time since Lucius had felt so relaxed, at ease. He enjoyed the simple things that came with a return home; his favourite bread and olives, fresh fruits, the soothing voices of his mother and Alene and the simple joy that could only be had with family. Mother and sister asked all about their experiences over the past years, campaigns, exotic places like Alexandria, friends they had made, and lost. Despite their decision not to overwhelm the two young men with questions, they could not stop themselves. Simply too much time had passed, without a word or letter.

"What was Alexandria like, Lucius?" Alene's eyes sparkled as she spoke. "Was it beautiful? Oh, it must have been."

"Is that where you were promoted, Lucius?" his mother asked.

Lucius made himself comfortable. "It's quite a story," he began. Argus poured himself a full cup of wine; he knew it would not be short. "Aegyptus is a very ancient land that mesmerized me from the beginning. Even before we set foot in the province, my imagination had run wild with images of all the things Diodorus used to tell me: giant temples to strange half-animal gods, the pyramids, the people even. It was all true."

"All of it?" Alene asked. She remembered asking Diodorus a question or two in passing when he was around for Lucius' lessons.

"All of it. Even the Pharos; it pierces the sky like a titanic candle. Its light is reflected out into the world by immense bronze mirrors at the top where the beacon fire blazes night and day. I was centurion then." Lucius decided to spare them the details of battle, opting to relate the more pleasant things he had seen. We had marched through Syria and on to Caesarea where we stayed for a month or so. From there we marched through Palaestina until we entered Aegyptus."

"Tell us about Alexandria."

"I'm coming to that, Alene." Lucius slowed down intentionally, took on the air of an orator. He wanted to laugh at seeing his sister ready to explode with curiosity. "Alexandria is beautiful and busy, full of colour. The Canopic way, the city's main street, is very wide and flanked by splendid monuments, temples and marble and limestone villas. Along the street are numerous pools of fresh water that are constantly fed by underground canals running from neighbouring lakes."

"Sounds interesting," Antonia said. Argus yawned.

"Come now, Lucius!" Alene chided. "I don't want to hear about villas and canals. We have those in Rome. Tell us about the Alexandrians themselves. Is it true that they are as ill-bread as people say, that they have no morals?" Alene looked like the thought tickled her.

"Even more so." Lucius remembered the outrageous parties that used to be given. "It's a playground for the rich and pleasure-seeking people of the empire. Sumptuous. Alexandrian women are very tall and go about in golden litters carried by sleek-looking Nubians, faces permanently painted and their breasts bare to the sun for all to see."

"Good Gods, Lucius!"

"Ha. I'm only teasing mother. They are more lax than we Romans but they are also very proper, especially when it comes to their religion." An image of Brutus flashed in his mind and he shook it off. "Um, where was I?"

"You were talking about religion," his mother reminded him.

"Ah, yes. The Egyptians worship our gods but they also maintain their old religion. In fact many Romans living there have adopted everything from Egyptian dress to Egyptian worship of the more obscure gods other than Isis." He looked at Alene, who had seemingly given up. He'd missed the brotherly teasing he used to inflict on her. "The place to experience Alexandria is not in the temples or lavishly debauched parties," Alene's ears pricked up, "but rather in the streets. People from countries you have never heard tell of are there, bodies glistening with sweat. The light is tinted with the colours of their exotic clothes and the reflection of jewelled arms. Rubies, emeralds and other precious gems bedeck every woman of quality. The richest of men can be seen dealing with the meanest of merchants for everything from grain and ivory to poison and papyrus. The air is sense-tickling and smells permanently of incense and exotic spice."

"Ohh…" Alene reclined again, looked up as she tried to imagine such a world so far away. "I wish I could have seen it with you, Lucius."

"You would have loved it."

"Now, Lucius," his mother finally spoke. "Tell us about your promotion. Your last letter informed us you were a tribune but how did that come to pass? And so quickly too!" She beamed with pride.

"Well, we were two years in Alexandria. Patrols, training exercises and helping with public building projects. The slaves there are useless for building roads and aqueducts. At any rate, one day our cohort was out on patrol when we engaged a large remnant of the Parthian forces we had defeated before. We repelled them, but our tribune, Livius, was killed. Stuck through with two spears at once. Most of our centurions were killed too."

"How horrible!" Antonia gasped.

"It was. I managed to regroup our men and retrieve the tribune's body. Then, we formed up and broke the Parthians' second offensive. On our return, the full II Traiana was dispatched to pursue the rest of the enemy into the desert. Apparently, news of what we did reached the emperor's ears because a Praetorian messenger arrived at my tent with orders to present myself to the emperor at the palace near the harbour."

"The emperor called for you personally?"

"He did mother," Lucius said proudly. "I wore grandfather's armour for the occasion. I was presented to the emperor; he was dressed in flowing purple robes trimmed with gold. He spoke to me by name and asked me to approach."

"You were face to face with him?" Alene asked.

"Yes. I could see the curled hairs of his dark beard. Severus is an imposing man, friendly to soldiers though. But I was still uncomfortable. Apparently he was good friends with the tribune, Livius, who had told him good things about me." Lucius' thoughts were interrupted by the sound of heavy breathing. Argus had fallen asleep on the couch across from him. Antonia waved it off and asked her son to continue. "He told me that he had chosen Livius to undertake a crucial patrol across the African provinces to the west to investigate the rumours of plots against the empire. The emperor has many spies, I suppose. Anyhow, Livius had mentioned promoting me to the emperor and after what had happened the day Livius was killed, the emperor said that..." Lucius paused.

"What did he say, Lucius?" mother and sister asked.

"It was hot. I was sweating and nervous. The emperor rose from his golden chair and said, 'Lucius Metellus, you are now Tribune Lucius Metellus Anguis of the Imperial Legions. Do you accept this office?' I said yes of course but tried my best not to faint. He gave me my orders for the patrol and told me that I could assign my own centurions. Argus was one of them." He looked over to where Argus' head twitched at the mention of his name. "Welcome back." Lucius shook his head and rolled his eyes.

"Did you leave Alexandria right after that?"

"We set out a week later. The next day I bought myself a horse in the markets." Lucius imagined Pegasus then, how he had first seen him. "My cohort was joined by a force of auxiliary cavalry..." He remembered them too.

"We took care of them though, didn't we Lucius?" added Argus.

"Yes well, we can talk more of your exploits later," Antonia interjected. She had, of course, heard about what had happened in Sabratha. Everyone had. But, in her mind, it was too beautiful a time to mar it with what had been such a touchy topic in their household. "What do you think of what we have done with the garden Lucius? Beautiful, is it not?"

"Yes, mother." He nodded and smiled at Alene.

They talked further of more trivial things then, in comfortable, familiar surroundings. Lucius watched his older sister speak and move, remembered her sadness when he had left. Thoughts of her love had kept him strong and guided him through darkness as much as the moon or any god. She shone in the sunlight, her blond hair cascading to her shoulders in golden waves that framed her soft, comforting face.

"Well," Alene said at one point, noticing Argus nod off again. "It seems as though the celebrations over the next few days are going to be something to look forward to. There are so many people for you to meet." Lucius smiled at her. Socializing in particular circles now would be very different from before, considering how far he had come. Argus finally spoke.

"It feels strange to be here, in Rome. Has much changed?" he asked Antonia.

"Not really, Argus. The city is as beautiful as ever and there are plans for the building of another massive bath complex; the emperor's son has been placed in charge of overseeing that."

"Caracalla?" Lucius was surprised; he had not heard news of him for some time.

"Oh yes, he has many duties. He was given the title of 'Augustus' the year after you left. So young too, only about eighteen years old now. Quite strong willed by what they say."

"Times are changing quickly," Argus noted. "I feel old already."

"Please dear boy, you haven't even a grey hair on your head, despite all the awful things you've seen."

"What other changes, mother?" Antonia sat more upright and put her plate on the small table to free her hands; it had always been easier for her to speak with her hands free.

"The emperor's new palace on the Palatine Hill is nearing completion. He began it, oh, about two years ago. They have actually built it *out* from the hill, extending it to the Circus. Supposedly quite elaborate, but not too ostentatious, tasteful,

Roman. Nothing like the golden monstrosity they say Nero built years ago."

"By Apollo, that sounds like a massive project! There won't be any room left on the Palatine." Buildings went up faster and faster. "Who'd have thought there was any room left to build in Rome?"

"It was a huge undertaking," replied his mother. "But that's not all. The empress has provided funds, at the same time the palace was begun, for a new Temple of Vesta in the Forum. It is quite beautiful and has classic designs." Antonia quieted for a moment, thinking. "Despite all these physical changes to the capital itself, what has changed most in Rome is her politics."

"Fortunately, soldiers aren't concerned much with politics," Argus scoffed slightly. Lucius eyed him, annoyed at his disrespect. Antonia continued.

"Don't be so sure, Argus. The emperor has made the army a massive political weapon and not in years has an emperor held sway so strongly over the Senate."

"Mother? Since when are you interested in politics?"

"Why, Lucius, I'm a senator's wife. It is my duty to know what is going on. Do you think I sit around embroidering all day and gossiping with the other ladies about who is sleeping with whom?"

"Mother! My ears," Lucius mocked her playfully.

"Oh come now. We Roman ladies gossip about more than affairs. We also gossip about politics. It just so happens that most of the time the two are interconnected." They all laughed. "Have you met the emperor's wife, Julia Domna?"

"No. Not yet. Don't know if I will."

"I wouldn't be surprised if you did. She's very involved. If you do meet her, look out for her accent. Apparently she speaks Latin very peculiarly."

"Oh really, mother! You're terrible. What a way for a virtuous Roman woman to speak." Alene teased, well-knowing that she was the one who had told her mother that juicy morsel.

"What did I say?" Antonia mocked disbelief, dismissing her daughter with a playful wave of her hand.

As they sat and talked some more, Lucius' thoughts inevitably returned over and over again to the moment when he and his father would meet.

"Mother?"

"Yes, my son." She knew immediately from the tone of his voice.

"What should I expect from father? How will he react to seeing me?" Antonia placed her cup on the table and sat up again on her couch. A serious topic had been breached.

"He has refused to speak of you since your last letter. He is bitter, Lucius. He is upset at losing you, as he sees it, and feels betrayed in a way."

"How so? What have I done?"

"To start with you entered the army, which for some reason he never wanted you to do. To make matters worse, in his eyes, you have had much success and have been favoured by the emperor. You have done this on your own, without his help or blessing. It is difficult to explain and even more so to understand." Argus was listening suddenly. "You serve an emperor, might I add, whom your father does not support. Your father has strong republican views, always had. He longs for the days of old, or at least the days of Marcus Aurelius who also had republican leanings. Every time word of your deeds would come to Rome, especially...the incident in Sabratha...his mood would sour to such an extent that he would stay in his study for hours on end." Antonia looked at the ground, the colourful mosaics at their feet; a scene depicting Jason's return home with the Golden Fleece to confront his uncle. "You two have much to talk about. I cannot interfere."

"I know," he said thoughtfully. They all sat in silence for a while, the same thought on each of their minds: How would

Quintus Metellus react to his son's return? It was something they had to face although they dreaded the encounter.

"By Jupiter! How many sestertii must be spent on these ridiculous celebrations! The streets are full of riotous drunkards." The evening calm was broken as Quintus Caecilius Metellus and his younger son came through the doors at the front of the house. His angry voice bellowed from the atrium. Lucius sat up quickly, tried to compose himself, Alene next to him to soothe his nerves.

"Ah." Argus slapped his knees as if in anticipation. "And here he is."

"Where in Hades is everyone?" The voice stopped short and as Lucius stood up his eyes met the stern, shocked gaze of his father, all too familiar, harder than ever.

"Hail, father." Lucius stood tall, could not smile or say much else.

"Father," Alene began. "Lucius and Argus have come home."

"So I see." His brow was tightly creased, his jaw rigid. Quintus Metellus, wrapped in his thick toga, looked at Argus. "Welcome home Argus. Are you well?" Argus glanced at Lucius before answering.

"I am well, sir, thank you. It's good to be home." He was showing more decorum than usual.

"Hmm…is it?" Metellus pater's nostrils flared slightly as he eyed Alene holding Lucius' arm. Finally, Antonia spoke, breaking the tensity of the moment.

"Don't the two of them look magnificent, Quintus? They've grown and have much to tell. I've asked the servants to go to the marketplace and buy food and wine for a special meal tonight to celebrate."

"Not much need for further, unnecessary celebrations in here. There's enough of that in the streets. Still, do as you wish."

Lucius stepped forward not wanting to stand mute, ridiculous. "Father, Argus and I were asked to come to Rome by the emperor for his celebrations." This was the wrong thing to say.

"Hmph! You mean the emperor's secretary invited you along with hundreds of other loyal servants. Well, I can't say I'm surprised. How good of you to grace us with a visit." He turned brusquely to his wife. "Antonia I'll be in my study working. Have one of the slaves call me when food is ready." He turned and walked away without another word or look.

"It will take time Lucius. He'll come around." Antonia tried to comfort her son but she knew it was no use. Quintus had actually been better than she had supposed he would.

"I'm not so sure mother." Lucius left the courtyard to go to his rooms but not before meeting his younger brother who had remained silent behind their father. "Hello, Quintus. You've grown. Almost a man." He stood before Lucius, much shorter, dressed in a very proper rust-coloured tunic and a thick brown cloak with gold borders, pinned with a small enamelled brooch.

"Hello, brother," was all he said before turning with disdain and going away.

Lucius walked off to his rooms. "Lucius, wait!" Alene ran after him.

"Well my dear, Argus," Antonia began as she rose to leave, "it looks as though the wars have followed you home. I shall see you this evening."

"Yes, lady." Antonia left him alone in the middle of the courtyard, the sun disappearing behind the peak of the terra cotta roof tiles. Argus laughed to himself. He found that he enjoyed not being berated for once. He chuckled at seeing the *tribune* chided by another man like a runny-nosed trainee. He tossed another olive high in the air as he reclined and caught it between his teeth so that he took on a mischievous grin. From behind one of the columns of the peristyle he noticed a pair of eyes and two glossy lips.

Ambrosia giggled as she stared at him and went away to her slave quarters. Argus smiled, his grey eyes following her. "Being back here's going to be better than ever, in many ways," he said to himself.

The evening meal wasn't a celebration for the family, but an uncomfortable gathering in which every word was well thought out, measured. Antonia had done her best to arrange a pleasing meal. Everyone lounged on the couches in the triclinium, the main dining room of the household, enjoying a luscious variety of sweet meats, fresh bread, fish, snails, sea oysters, fruits and wine from the family estate.

The large square room had six couches arranged in a horseshoe shape, the food laid out on a table in their midst. Three and four-spouted lamps burned here and there and two flickering braziers, one on each side, lit up the painted walls; behind silent diners, creatures and heroes of ancient realms and worlds danced and frolicked amid idyllic gardens. Lucius gazed at the image of a small dragon on the wall across from him. In the dancing light, its wings seemed to flap rhythmically.

Young Quintus and Clarinda sat on the couch opposite, Antonia to his right and his father, quiet and sullen, to the far left. Argus was sprawled out on the couch between Lucius and Metellus pater with whom he spoke brokenly on topics of little import. Lucius paid no attention to them, enjoying instead answering his mother's questions and talking with Alene who reclined at his side.

"When you were in battle, Lucius," Clarinda spoke up, "did you kill many men?" The question was unexpected, a child's musing. Everyone turned to look at him, even Quintus.

Lucius finished chewing a piece of meat. "Yes, Clarinda, but only when I had to."

"Were they all bad?" she persisted.

"Yes. They tried to kill me and other Roman soldiers, and so I had to kill them first. That is war."

"Hmm..." She wasn't finished. "...but didn't you kill Roman soldiers too?"

"Of course he didn't!" Alene entered the conversation but Clarinda was curious and not to be deterred.

"But father said that you executed-"

"Clarinda!" Antonia snapped, casting an icy look at her youngest. "That's enough. You shouldn't speak of things you know nothing about."

Lucius then realized that his young sister was referring to Sabratha. Decimation was not a punishment to be undertaken lightly; it wasn't always a popular decision either. Clarinda couldn't possibly understand. She must have overheard her father talking about the incident.

"It's all right, mother," Lucius said calmly. He would address his father through his sister's question. "You see Clarinda, those men were traitors and received the punishment they deserved." She listened intently while their father chewed loudly. "They had been helping Rome's enemies and if they had not been stopped, many good Romans would have lost their lives." He looked to his father. "Those men were traitors to the empire and they got what they deserved." Lucius remembered not really believing that himself after the fact, but he had made his mind up since then. He had done the right thing. Quintus eyed his son coldly in that moment and the room turned icy.

"Pardon the interruption, master," Ambrosia poked her head through the door and addressed Quintus as she stared at the floor.

"What is it?" replied Antonia, heading off a heated response from her husband.

"There is a Praetorian messenger in the atrium with a message for master Lucius."

"Thank you, Ambrosia. Tell him I'm coming." Lucius rose swiftly, straightened his thick tunic and went out to meet the messenger.

"Look at him!" Quintus scoffed. "He runs like a faithful dog when the emperor whistles."

"Father," Alene objected. "Lucius has his duty to consider."

"The boy sickens me." He got up and left the room. Antonia remained silent, sipping her wine while the two children elbowed each other. Argus continued to gorge himself on milk-fattened snails; his mouth glistened as he slurped them down.

"You certainly have not lost your appetite, Argus," Antonia observed, appalled by his manners.

"I'm always hungry, lady," he answered cheekily.

"I can see that."

The messenger waited patiently in the atrium. He wore a long, white knee-length tunic with thin purple borders beneath a cuirass of bronze scale armour, brown leggings, closed hobnail boots and a yellow-brown cloak. Lucius saluted him and the man saluted in return.

"Hail, Tribune Metellus. I have an Imperial dispatch for you." The stocky soldier handed a small scroll to Lucius.

"My thanks." Lucius opened it, read slowly, then turned back to the messenger. "Tell the emperor I am at his service and will be in attendance at the specified hour." The messenger saluted and turned to go out. Another slave locked the door behind him.

The civility and respect he had received from the Praetorian messenger had surprised Lucius at first; most of the time the Praetorians saw themselves as superior to legionary officers. Emperor Severus had replaced the old Praetorians with soldiers from among the Legions on the Danube when he came to power and had made his closest friend and kinsman sole Praetorian prefect. The days of a strictly Italian Guard were a thing of the past. Lucius breathed deeply of the cool evening air, rolled up the message and returned to the triclinium.

"What is it, Lucius?" Alene looked concerned, although for no reason. She was still upset at her father.

"The emperor wants to see me in the morning at the palace. It doesn't say what about." He sat back down on the couch.

"I'm sure he only wishes to congratulate you on your mission in Africa." Antonia was calm, even proud. "How exciting."

"Where's father?" He suspected already that his father had stormed out of the room the first chance he had.

"He wasn't feeling well. He's probably asleep already. Some days the Senate can be a trying place for him." Their mother was always trying to keep the peace in the family.

An unusual quiet fell on Rome that night. Where the day had been eventful, loud with the sound of the Circus crowds, the night was calm, its silence unspoilt. The crisp winter evenings were beginning to melt away, slightly warmer nights in their stead, hints of spring's renewal on the air. In this lull between the cold months and the blazing heat of summer when men's blood boiled and violence was always on the doorstep ready to erupt, Rome was quiet, calm.

It was however, still cool enough for the sky to be crystal-like, clear, illuminated by the myriad stars that graced the heavens. The moon was small, but its crescent ever so bright. From his room on the upper floor, Lucius watched the flickering stars, the Gods' celestial lamps. Up and to the right rose the Palatine hill with its complex of palaces. Home to the emperors of Rome, he would go there tomorrow.

He felt uncomfortably young at that moment, naïve. Man was perpetually harried by a state of unknowing. Why? Was there such a world, a time, when one could know all and be comforted, at peace just for being? When he was young, he remembered, he had posed that question, or something similar, to Diodorus. The old man had looked him straight in the eye, put his hands on Lucius' shoulders and said "Lucius, the day we know all there is to know in this universe is the day we die. Learning, the search for knowledge and truth, never stops. It is

195

a driving force behind human existence. We are not gods...we are men. The world is beautiful. Enjoy discovering her."

The world was beautiful, Lucius knew it, but it was also terrible, brutal and unpredictable. To remain strong and compassionate, to have faith in oneself and in the Gods was man's salvation through life. Lucius sighed, looked over to where the effigy of his beloved Apollo stood proudly on a side table, two small lamps burning on either side. Before the god were laid the golden corona and the eagle feathers.

"Are you nervous about tomorrow?" Lucius, surprised, turned from the window, Alene stood in the doorway, her silhouette tall and slender. He had not wanted to sleep yet, nor did she. They hadn't had time to talk alone.

"A little, I suppose. I don't know why." He looked up at the sliver of moon again. "Sit with me a while?"

"Of course." Her face lit up.

He smiled as she came in and sat in a chair to his right, next to the window, a warm brazier sputtered in the nearby corner. She wore the same gown as earlier. Her green eyes looked very happy, observing.

They sat in silence for a time, gazing out at the sky, pleased to be alone again, to enjoy each other's company. Alene had known since the time Lucius had arrived that he had much to tell her, and she him. He had to lighten his heart of things that could not be said to his friends, to their parents. She put her soft hand on his stubbly cheek. It was warm.

"Tell me everything, Lucius. I want to know about what's happened to you, what you've been through. I love you, I want to help if I can." She could always tell when his heart was heavy with some thought or other. Her compassionate smile could always draw it out of him.

"I've missed our talks." He breathed deeply, exhaled as if letting out pain-wracked memories, closed his eyes and remembered. "Well..." he began.

Thoughts and emotions poured from Lucius' mind, his heart, as cool water from an overflowing spring. He spoke, Alene listened silently. He told her of his rise through the ranks, his experiences in leading men, meeting the emperor, the Parthian wars, Ctesiphon. She listened to Lucius as he recounted the horrors of war, the aftermath of victory, the sacking of a city. Alene could hardly believe the things her brother had been through. Life in Rome seemed so sheltered in comparison. Lucius also spoke of Argus, the growing rift between them since Parthia. She had suspected as much since they arrived, but not to such an extent. The truth was that ever since Argus had come to live with them all those years ago, she had not liked him much. He made her uncomfortable, tried to manipulate Lucius, take him away. She continued to listen.

Her brother spoke of the beauty and mystery of the desert in detail, captivated her mind; the fine sand, a long march, the nightly moon above the oases of the powdered dunes. The fear rose in her breast as she learned of the attempts of assassins on his life, of treachery in dark corners, of the one called Brutus, of decimation. She had thought that hearing about Sabratha from his own lips would ease her heart. It did. But, to think that her own brother had been faced with such a decision; the thought was sad and unnerving. The desert however, was something that intrigued her and she wanted to hear more.

The desert had given many gifts to Lucius: the presence and grace of Apollo, who seemed to protect and guide Lucius, answered Alene's own frequent, humble prayers. There was the man named Ashur, no matter how strange or inexplicable; he had saved her dear brother and she thanked the Gods.

"I don't know if I'll ever see Ashur again..." a great sadness intruded upon Lucius' thoughts, his voice as he spoke. "He arrives in darkness and leaves on the wind. I have my suspicions of...his purpose...but I dare not say." Alene looked to the effigy of Apollo on the table.

"Just accept the gift of friendship that the Gods have given you, Lucius. It isn't up to us to choose the vehicle of their

197

graces. You must see this! Thank mighty Apollo for this man, whoever he is. Go to the temple tomorrow and make offerings. If by some amazing twist of fortune, he *is* the god's messenger…" she paused. Alene was not usually this outspoken but she wished to help. "…you must do justice to the gift, to Apollo."

"I only pray that I haven't driven Ashur off for good."

He described the battle in Numidia and how Ashur had tried to warn him, how he treated him in return. He was ashamed. Alene listened fearfully to how the four riders appeared in the battle, set on killing Lucius.

When he had finished explaining such events, those that had shaped him in the last few years, Alene, traces of tears on her cheeks, wrapped her arms around him tightly. He was safe now, but only for the moment. Fears within her went unvoiced, she did not wish to tempt the fates.

Calmer now, she sat back again and dried her eyes, looked at him, her expression tender.

"And what of…love, Lucius?"

"What? What do you mean, Alene?"

"Everything you've just told me is either terrifying, inspiring or mysterious. You've told me about your battles, traitors, Ashur, and Argus. There must be more. Please, Lucius. Talk to me. What about love?" He could not understand why she was so concerned about it.

"Are you sure you haven't been reading Catullus or Ovid again?"

"Don't joke, Lucius. I'm serious. Does your soul not long for something more?"

"I'm sorry." He could see how concerned she was. "I haven't much to say about that, Alene. I never had the time really, to get to know anyone." His thoughts drifted back to Alexandria. In his mind he saw Medea, sad, alone. "There was this one woman but…I was sent on the patrol and… Oh, it doesn't matter really." He didn't want that memory of blood on the mosaic and marble floor. "She was someone I just spent some time with, someone to talk to, someone kind."

"What happened?"

He told her. His heart pounded and his fists clenched as he spoke. He had been a part of that horror, saved her life.

"Did you love her?" Alene held his hand as he stared into nothingness.

"She brought me much joy and happiness, caring, at a time when I needed it. We gave to each other. I don't think I loved her. How do you know? Diodorus spoke of love but how do you recognize it? I would say no, I didn't love Medea, but I did care for her. It saddens me to think of it, of her. I fled, afraid and angered by what had happened to her."

"But you saved her, Lucius! Because of you she went on living. You may not have truly loved her but you sacrificed yourself for her. You showed your caring for her and I'm sure she will remember you for it."

Alene remembered how Lucius used to pelt her prospective suitors with pebbles to save her. He hadn't changed too much. He was, she thought, stronger now, braver, a true hero, grown into a man of honour and virtue. Not many could see it in him, certainly not their father. But she could.

"And you?" he asked. "How many hundreds of suitors have lined up at our door to ask for Alene Metella's hand while I've been away?"

"Quite a few I suppose. Most of them only want the family connection to our name." She looked sad.

"Anyone worthy?" He felt like that protective little brother again. "Was there anyone that you actually liked, or were they all morons that father brought home?"

"Mostly greedy imbeciles." She looked down at the floor. "There was one man, Gallus; he was from Massilia. We saw quite a bit of each other for a time, mother liked him too. He was the fifth son of a merchant." Alene stood up and went to the other side of the room. It was obvious to Lucius that she had liked this Gallus very much. "We talked briefly about

199

getting married. He was the only man who ever showed interest in me and not my name. Anyway, one night he came over for dinner so that he could speak with father about the marriage. I was excited but quite nervous. Father hadn't been too pleased when mother had discussed the prospect with him beforehand."

"What happened?"

"We sat down to eat. The meal was quiet. After the last course father and Gallus went into the study to speak and-" her voice broke and she turned away from Lucius. "I heard the front doors slam. Father came back in, without Gallus. I asked where he'd gone and father said he had left and wasn't coming back. I asked why. Father said that he had told Gallus that he could not afford to give me a dowry. He said that he'd told Gallus he had to give him something to marry me." Lucius could hear her sobbing now, the hurt in her voice. She turned now to face him, her cheeks soaked. "Who does that? Who refuses to give their daughter a dowry?"

Lucius moved to put his arm around her. "I'm sorry I wasn't here."

"I was wrong about Gallus, Lucius. He wasn't any different from all the others. He played me for a fool. The whole time he was telling me how much he loved me and wanted to be with me always. He only wanted to make a fortune. He didn't even say goodbye." She sunk in her brother's arms. Lucius searched for words of comfort, like those she always managed to find for him. Alene had really cared for the man. "Father should've given you a proper dowry. He's a greedy bastard."

"Shh! He'll hear you. Besides, if he had given me a dowry then I might never have known that Gallus only cared for my money and my name, not me." Alene dried her eyes and went back to the window. "After Gallus left, I gave up on all the others. It's the same everywhere. Everyone wants to marry for profit and prestige, nothing more. If I don't marry someone who truly loves me, I won't get married at all. I know that sounds romantic but, I just couldn't live with myself, Lucius. Am I wrong to think that way?"

"No. I'd hate to see you live the rest of your life with some whoreson who locks you up at home while he's at the brothels. I'd kill him."

Alene put her hands on his shoulders. "I know you would." She laughed. "You'd throw pebbles at him like you used to." Lucius smiled. He could imagine doing much worse but let the thought lie. He sat down.

"Lucius," she knelt before him, held his hands and kissed them. "A life without love is not complete. I believe that!"

"Alene, you're an idealist at heart."

"Absolutely! So are you!" She seemed to have found a new strength within all of a sudden. It always amazed him how she could do that.

"I know. Perhaps that's why father shuns me, us."

"That's beside the point. Lucius, the Gods work in unclear ways. Venus is mysterious, Eros fickle. But at times they show us the way."

"Alene, what are you talking about?" She was like an excited child at his feet.

"Months ago, when the moon was full, bright over the city, I had a dream. I saw you alone in the desert, sad. I cried for you. But then I was in a land to the east; it looked like Italy but it wasn't. The sun was bright and the water clear and blue. On a cliff was an ancient temple. I looked down to a pebble beach and there I spotted the most beautiful woman ever. I didn't see her face, for she was gazing out to sea, looking for something. Suddenly a light flashed in the sky and something splashed into the water in front of her, something alive. It appeared to be drowning. She waded out, picked it up fearlessly and held it to her breast lovingly. I saw that it was a young dragon, gold and red."

"What did the dragon do?"

"It lived! It seemed revived, happy, and flew up in the air above her as if to thank her. Then, as if by magic, the dragon turned into a brilliant golden-hilted sword and plunged down into the ground at the girl's feet. She picked it up carefully, wrapped it in her silk stola and turned to come up the path. Just as I was about to see her face something tapped me on the shoulder from behind." Alene breathed excitedly as she described all of this. "It was the Goddess of Love. I've never seen or imagined such beauty. Her smile and her eyes were bright and brilliant, and she nodded as if to say 'yes' before pointing to the girl as she came up the path toward me. Instantly I saw you on a ship, crossing the sea."

"What? What about the girl?" Lucius thought there had to be more.

"Before I saw you I caught a glimpse of the girl's face, her smile, her dark rich hair wet from the sea. She smiled at me, as if in recognition. That's all I remember. After seeing you on the ship I woke up."

"What do you think it means? Who was she?" Lucius was entranced and excited at once.

"The strange thing is that I woke up not sad or lonely but full of joy. I hadn't been that happy since before you left."

"You knew. You could see that I was coming home, Alene!" He hugged her.

"Perhaps, but there's more."

"What else could there be?"

"Alene smiled. "Hmm. I can't say now." Lucius hunched back exasperated. She put her hands on his cheeks and kissed his forehead. "Oh how I've missed you for so long. And now you're back."

Alene stood again and went to the window, silver moonlight falling onto her features. She turned to him. If she could not have love in her lifetime, she prayed more than anything that her brother would.

"Lucius, there's someone I want you to meet."

XIV

PATER ET FILIUS

'Father and Son'

Storms gather and dissipate in the stillness of night, in the busy minds of men. Jupiter, father of all, Optimus Maximus, raises the deserving and condemns the worthless, and every man wonders which one he will be. The Capitol glistens white over Rome, and from within the sacred space the spirits of Jupiter, Juno and Minerva hold sway over the populace. This godly triad and their peers keep the heart of the empire in check; for men are men and gods...are gods.

Morpheus had not cast his spell on Lucius until the smallest hours of morning. He and Alene had spoken for a long while. However, when sleep did come, it was a short but calming journey. Lucius woke early, fresh and rejuvenated despite an inkling of worry at the back of his mind about his imperial audience.

After a quick meal of bread, goat's cheese and fruit, Lucius washed and shaved and polished his armour which he then put on over a clean tunic. The last time he had seen the emperor was in Alexandria when he had been given his promotion and new orders. Now they were in Rome and he was to meet the emperor in the palace. He was a tribune and needed to look it; he carefully arranged his crimson cloak over his shoulders, fastened it with a blue and red enamelled brooch and stopped at the main doorway of the atrium where his mother and Alene were waiting for him.

"Don't be nervous son, all will be well. Be proud of yourself, and what you've accomplished."

"I know, mother." Lucius smiled and hugged her. He then turned to Alene "I'll see you later?"

"Of course you will. Good luck." She kissed his cheek.

The city was awake with citizens going about their daily business. Farmers who had come in the early hours of the morning had already set up stalls to sell their goods; they had to arrive early as carts were forbidden in the streets during the day to avoid congestion. The only carts permitted were those carrying building materials for public works. Lucius noticed many of these headed toward the Forum and the Palatine hill.

The Vigiles, city police, were already busy checking for merchants' carts in the streets; just one cart blocking the way could lead to frustration and violence in the ensuing congestion. Butchers, knife makers, cloth merchants, potters, all were open for business on the sunny morning of what promised to be a pleasingly warm day, the first of the year. There was still time before his appointment and so Lucius decided to go through the Forum on his way. It had been a long time since he had passed through the heart of Rome, seen politicians and priests and the massed mob milling about the paving slabs. As Lucius passed through the narrow street between the Temple of Saturn and the Basilica Julia, he was greeted by the familiar play of sunlight and shadow cast by the towering white columns that reached to the sky, ornate pediments and godly statues.

He stepped onto the Via Sacra, a gust of cool morning air rippling his cloak and the horsehair crest of his helmet. The crowd on the street parted for a procession of priests and augurs who were making their way to the Capitol for their daily sacrifices and readings of the omens. A beautiful lady accompanied them, obviously wealthy, not necessarily Roman, because of her dark complexion. She was veiled by a rich, yellow, hooded cloak over a white and purple stola. She held her head high as she walked alongside the priests and another gust of wind came rolling up the street behind them, like a divine breath urging them toward the temples.

Once they had passed, everyone went back about their business and the street filled up again. Lucius however, kept watching, curious. As he peered over the tops of the crowd's heads, he spotted the Senate house, and the Curia, where senators' litters were parked. Their slaves waiting patiently - Nubians, Gauls and Germans - as their masters conversed on the steps before going inside to discuss the business of the empire. One of the senators pointed at something large directly in front of the Senate, his hands waving madly in a fit of angry gestures. "It's an outrage! Completely inappropriate!" he bawled. The structure was covered with scaffolding and leather sheets to restrict the public's view. Only the sound of chiselling could be heard above the old man's ranting just several paces from the numerous artisans' carts at the base of the structure.

The street grew more crowded and where before people avoided bumping into an armed tribune, they now pushed Lucius from every side in their efforts to get by. His reverie broken, he pressed on to his right where he spotted the new Temple of Vesta next to the house of the Vestal Virgins. The round temple was beautifully ornamented with pure white columns supporting elaborate friezes around the top. He remembered his mother mentioning that the emperor's wife, Julia Domna, had paid for its construction. She had spared no expense and it showed. What sort of woman was she?

Farther down the street, Lucius came to the large paved ramp that led up onto the Palatine and the imperial complexes. As a child, he used to marvel at the thought of the hill, the place where Rome was born, a small village. From huts hundreds of years ago, to this: ornate gardens, fountains, exotic orchards, baths and stadiums surrounding the most ornate, luxuriously marbled palaces. *And to think, the Metelli used to live up here.* The thought still took his breath away. It was quiet on the hill. All that could be heard was the splashing coming from tucked-away fountains and the song of birds singing in the approach of spring. Lucius enjoyed this as he walked, breathed it all in but he felt his nerves begin to take hold on him and his heart begin to pound as he came under the watchful eyes of the Praetorian guards lining the hedgerows above the street.

"Ah yes, Tribune Metellus. There's your name, almost at the top of the list." The centurion on duty rolled up his papyrus scroll listing the various visitors who were to be admitted to the palace that day. "You're right on time. Not like the politicians and merchants who come here; always early, hoping to cut in the waiting line, or always late. 'Takes a soldier to be on time', that's what I say. At any rate, the emperor is in the new palace now so you'll have to pass through the old gardens first. One of my men will show you the way." The centurion raised his vinerod and the trooper behind and to his right snapped to attention.

"My thanks, Centurion." The man saluted Lucius casually and the trooper walked on, motioning for Lucius to follow.

As they made their winding way through various groomed gardens and colonnaded walkways lined with statuary, Lucius was struck by the remarkable condition of the old palace built by Augustus so long ago. The Romans who must have tread those pathways, smelled the citrus-tinged air, heard the wailing of the peacocks roaming the grounds. This had been home to the greatest and most infamous of Romans, and Lucius passed this way now, to meet with the current emperor, a man who had come to power not through inheritance, but civil war. He had fought for the imperial seat and had crushed his enemies, Pescennius Niger and Clodius Albinus, in the process. It was said that Severus had seen his victory in the stars, that he knew he was destined to be emperor. Truth was, there were all manner of rumours about the emperor and the rest of his family and Lucius had heard many of them. Among the troops however, Severus was loved; he gave them victories to be proud of and payment aplenty. In the end, that was all that was needed. Stars or no stars, Lucius thought, this was a man who was firmly planted in the imperial seat. His legions made sure of it.

The soldier leading Lucius looked back sternly, making sure he was still following. Finally, as they came out of a vine-covered walkway into the sunlight, the new palace came into view. It was not yet complete and workmen scurried about to the sounds of chisels, hoists and grunts. And yet, it still loomed large above the gardens.

Lucius was led up a short flight of steps to an enormous atrium lined with massive Corinthian columns. Their footsteps echoed on the marble floors as they turned left down a corridor, right up another. Eventually the trooper stopped, pointed to a large waiting room that was already half full of people seeking an audience with the emperor.

"Wait here, Tribune. The Praetorian prefect will be along shortly to take you to the emperor." The man saluted, turned and made his way back to his post. His footsteps could be heard for a few moments before disappearing into the maze-like structure of the palace.

The Praetorian prefect! Lucius thought, discomfited by this turn of events. He was not prepared to meet the one who was thought by many to be the second most powerful man in the empire. If memory served him correctly, the prefect was Gaius Fulvius Plautianus. He didn't know much about Plautianus except that he used to command in the Vigiles and was a kinsman of the emperor from Leptis Magna. He was recently made a senator and there was talk of him running for the consulship. Lucius had never met or seen the man and so could only guess at what he was like. Having been away from Rome for so long he didn't have the advantage of rumour and so had to decide for himself. *Odd,* he thought, *that there are so many rumours about the imperial family and almost none about the Praetorian prefect.* He gazed about the room at what were mostly hot, tired old politicians who didn't give him a second glance, or young, favour-seeking nobles who looked at a young tribune with disdain, jealousy. He was comforted by the fact that he had been summoned and was not seeking an audience like most of the men in the room.

"Tribune Lucius Metellus Anguis!" He stood up, slightly startled by the loud, harsh voice. "The emperor will see you now." Across the room, from a high, open doorway, a tall, imposing man in full Praetorian regalia eyed Lucius suspiciously. He was dark-skinned with piercing black eyes and closely cropped black hair. He turned and Lucius quickly followed Gaius Fulvius Plautianus down another corridor.

The Praetorian prefect didn't look back once as he led Lucius to the emperor's rooms. When they reached a tall doorway flanked by two guards, Plautianus turned and led Lucius between the green marble columns. The troopers saluted as they passed.

Once inside, stillness and quiet could be felt immediately, the sort of feelings one has upon entering a sanctuary. It was not necessarily a religious air, but rather one of respect in the presence of the father of the empire. Lucius waited for the prefect to say something but he did not. He stared straight ahead in silence, his gaze floating across the enormous mosaic of golden laurels in the middle of the floor to an open balcony where rich, saffron-coloured silks hung, blowing in the gentle breeze. As the soft fabric floated on the warm air like feathers on Zephyrus' breath, Lucius glimpsed a figure standing off to the left of the balcony. It was the emperor standing there, draped in a brilliant white robe with purple borders and intricate gold brocade in the shape of laurel leaves. He seemed to be in a contemplative, almost meditative state. Plautianus waited.

Lucius felt the presence of two others behind him on either side of the door, tall and powerful. He wanted to turn but decided it would not be wise, in case the emperor entered and he was looking elsewhere. What surprised him was that the room before him was not so much the rich, ornate chamber of an emperor but rather the study of an intelligent man, a warrior.

To the left and right, nearest to him, Lucius noticed enormous olive-wood cabinets, the pigeon holes filled to capacity with hundreds, even thousands, of scrolls. The only other place he had seen as many was in the Palatine library where Diodorus used to take him. Further up the left wall were old legionary standards and pieces of exotic and ancient armour collected over the years. Next to these, displayed on a wooden stand, brilliant in the angling light, was the emperor's own armour, silver and black, a golden horsehair crest on his helm, magnificent. A memory flickered in Lucius' mind when he saw that armour, of the battle in Parthia, Severus urging the troops on from his white steed, a light in the dust-choked air. His memory was jogged even further by the displays on another wall of Parthian weapons, armour and standards. What an irony that they should now hang in the imperial palace, trophies to be admired, no longer feared.

Plautianus suddenly snapped to attention and as Lucius peered over the large table that stood before the opening of the balcony, the silhouette of the emperor came into view. He walked over to them, a slight limp in his step, Lucius bowed deeply, his crested helmet held firmly beneath his left arm.

"Tribune Metellus." Plautianus' bland introduction was routine, unimportant. But the deep, almost friendly voice of Septimius Severus broke the silence.

"Welcome, Tribune. Welcome to Our new palace." He moved around the table to the centre of the room, Plautianus stepping aside so that Lucius was now face to face with the emperor.

"I thank you for your invitation, Sire. The palace is truly remarkable."

"There is still much to be done but it should be finished soon enough. Come, sit. Gaius, tell the servants to bring some wine for the tribune and myself." Plautianus nodded slowly and went to do as he had been told. The emperor moved back to the other side of the table and took his seat in a solid wood-framed chair covered in black hide; it was the sort of chair he would have had on campaign, perhaps it was the same he did use. Lucius in turn sat at a backless folding chair. Just then Plautianus returned and stood off to a corner of the room.

"Don't mind Plautianus here, what I know, he knows." The prefect looked at Lucius with his dark, shaded eyes. The emperor rubbed his thickly bearded chin. "Well, Metellus, you must be wondering why I summoned you here this morning, to Rome for that matter?"

"Yes, Sire." Lucius began to measure his words carefully. "Although, it is my duty not to question. When my Imperator calls, I come. It is good to be back home after so long."

"I'm sure." Just then a richly dressed slave entered with a jug of wine and two red cups decorated with gladiatorial scenes. The emperor paused for a moment, coughing badly, as the wine was poured. The slave handed Lucius his cup. *That's a bad cough,* Lucius thought. Indeed, he had noticed that the emperor had aged much since Alexandria; pock marks dotted his face with scars, he was limping and leaning on things to hold himself up. This deterioration was due, it was said, to his having contracted smallpox while in Egypt. His mind however, was as sharp as ever.

"To Mars and Jupiter." The emperor raised his cup to Lucius but seemed to gaze past him, probably watching the slave leave the room.

"To Mars and Jupiter," Lucius reiterated and drank. The wine was sweet, refreshing for his parched, nervous mouth.

"Now, one of the reasons I wanted to see you this morning is to congratulate you on your patrol in Africa. It was a good thing you did, to root out those traitors. Excellent work."

"Thank you, Sire. Although, many have disapproved of the punishment I deemed necessary."

"To Hades with them! They got what they deserved." He leaned back in his chair. "Congratulations also on your victory in Numidia. Your corona was well deserved, and the reports from Gaius Flavius Marcellus have been exceedingly good."

"Again, thank you."

"Don't thank me, Metellus, thank Marcellus. That old goat never gave praise lightly." They drank again. Lucius could feel Plautianus' gaze on him. He sat up straight, tried to ignore his sudden discomfort. "Well, Tribune," the emperor began again, "what did you think of Africa Proconsularis?"

"When I wasn't fighting, I found it to be the most beautiful place on Earth. The desert is very...mysterious."

"Indeed!" he smiled. "There's something about it. I must confess that I miss my homeland often." Another coughing fit consumed Severus' attention. "Gaius too. But Rome beckons as always. However, I may go back to Leptis Magna in the new year. My astrologer says it is a good time to go and my Greek doctors say the climate would be good for me. But enough of that."

He rose from his seat and, with his wine, moved toward the light of the balcony. Lucius was on his feet and looked to Plautianus who stood motionless, arms crossed. Lucius followed the emperor through the wavering saffron silks into the sunlight. Once his eyes adjusted to the light, he noticed a brilliantly detailed mosaic beneath his feet depicting a victorious chariot team. As he came to the columned railing at the emperor's side, he was amazed at the beauty of the view.

"A wondrous view, Sire."

"Yes it is."

Below the balcony, Lucius could see just how high they really were; the palace was indeed built straight out from the Palatine Hill and in full view was the Circus Maximus; one could see the sands being groomed for the afternoon's races. In the distant haze of the late morning sun, the walls of Rome seemed to shimmer above the rooftops, and beyond that, the rolling green countryside, with its long roads and aqueducts, seemed endless. Lucius, taken with the sight before him, suddenly realized the emperor was looking at him.

"I knew I picked the right man for that patrol, Metellus. You proved yourself as a warrior, a leader, and as a Roman. That's why I wanted you to come to Rome. My Triumph and

211

the unveiling of the arch in the Forum are in three days and I want all my good commanders to be here for it. I want to show not only the people of Rome but also the Senate that Rome's military might is greater than ever, that her emperor has chosen from among the best to keep the empire in check, protect her within and without."

"I am honoured that I was counted among such a group, Sire."

"Think nothing of it. You earned it like the others. You have a bright future, Metellus, no doubt. I need men like you. Strong, loyal. I'm not sure where you'll end up with your men yet but there's time enough for that. For now, enjoy being in Rome again. There are plenty of celebrations until the unveiling in the Forum."

"I'm looking forward to it, Sire. By the way, where is your arch to be?"

The emperor smiled. "At the end of the Via Sacra, right in front of the Senate steps." Lucius couldn't hide the surprise on his face. "Don't look so shocked, Metellus. It's the perfect place. A central spot in full view of all the politicians. It will remind them who is master of Rome, who saved her from her enemies."

"That it will Sire. Did the Senate oppose the location?"

"Of course they did but in the end they yielded. Some of those old men really put up a fight." He paused for a moment. "Actually, your father was one of them." He gazed at Lucius as if wanting to confirm something.

"Oh, Sire, my father is old and has old ideas, he's harmless enough and-"

"Don't worry, Tribune, I don't hold any grudges against him. It's good to have a little opposition from time to time, especially from the old families. It reminds me of how far Rome has come."

"My father and I rarely see eye to eye, Sire. He wanted me to be a senator but I wanted to be in the Legions."

"And rightly so! I'm glad you won that argument with the old Senator." The emperor walked back into the room where Plautianus waited. "Well, Metellus, it's been good talking with you but I had better see some of the tired old men in the waiting room now or I'll never hear the end of it. I shall see you in three days."

"I look forward to it, Sire."

"Oh, and you will of course attend the banquet here in the palace the night of the Triumph. Everyone on the Palatine is coming as well as your fellow officers." Lucius stood again in the middle of the room with the emperor standing behind his table. "And bring your entire family."

"Thank you, Sire. Until then." Lucius bowed, backed up several paces, saluted. "Hail Caesar!" As he made for the doorway he stumbled slightly at the two figures who met his gaze. What he had taken to be two enormous guards watching him the whole time, silent, still, were actually two statues. Jupiter on the right, Mars on the left. The gods had stood there the whole time watching Lucius in the presence of the emperor. Their robes seemed to flutter slightly, their hair shine, their weapons glisten. Indeed Lucius had never, ever seen such lifelike features in a statue. He averted his eyes from theirs as he exited the room, for they seemed to stare deep within him. He came to, humbled not only by his audience with the emperor but also with the sentry gods who had watched him. Another soldier outside the door led him out of the palace into the gardens.

"Are you sure it is wise to speak so openly with a lesser Equestrian tribune, Septimius?" Plautianus asked when they were alone again.

"Don't be ridiculous, Gaius."

"I just think that you should not show so much dislike for the Senate in front of people, especially the son of a senator with republican views."

"My friend, you are just being paranoid, as usual. That boy's a soldier, loyal to me. I don't feel I have anything to worry about with men like him in the ranks. Just like I don't worry with you watching over my back here." Severus sipped some wine. "Really, Gaius, you need to know when there are people you *can* trust."

"I still think it unwise to speak so openly. I don't trust this one." The prefect looked to the door through which Lucius had passed.

"Bring in the next person now, Gaius," the emperor commanded, not wishing to carry on their conversation.

As Lucius walked across the Palatine, among the various homes and other parts of the palace, he remembered what Alene had said the night before about giving his thanks to Apollo. His meeting with the emperor had gone well and thanks were in order. He decided to make his way to the Temple of Apollo to spend some time in silent meditation and make his offerings. Years had passed since he had been there and he felt drawn to it, just as one is drawn to people and places of the past that have given the greatest joy, the warmest of memories. That place had become a part of him, an important link to his past, to what he viewed as part of his destiny.

"Read them again, you imbecile!" The augur stumbled slightly as he was pushed by the angry man whose son trembled beneath the folds of his new toga. A group of black ravens fighting over a dead rat could not have been an inspiring sight to anyone there, frightening almost. "Check the signs again! I tell you I saw an eagle high above!"

The father pushed at the augur once again, his family trying to restrain him. The small crowd swayed to and fro, shattering the sacred silence of the square in front of the temple. Lucius' hobnails clicked on the paving slabs. The crowd quieted slightly, embarrassed. He looked over, curious more than anything but thought he would leave them to it. Bad omens and sacrilege; best to stay away.

"Never mind them, Tribune," a voice called from the far left of the temple stairs. "They've been arguing like game cocks for a long time. Most entertaining."

"Bad omens?" Lucius ventured.

"Of course. What else?" Lucius walked over to where the man had a large table set up, several cages of chickens, and a small goat. The vendor wore a simple brown, knee-length tunic belted at the waist and a cloak of the same colour. A man of about thirty-five or so, he seemed to enjoy watching life go by day after day, selling his offerings, inconspicuously chuckling to himself at the absurdities that inevitably unfolded before him.

"Would you care for something to offer to Apollo today, Tribune?" He pointed to various items and vials on the table. "I have bundles of sacred herbs, oils...or if you prefer, a chicken?"

"No thank you, no chickens today. But I'll take some of that Greek oil and a large bunch of the rosemary." Lucius reached for his purse.

"Ah, an excellent choice, Tribune. The God will be pleased and his muses will sing your praise." The man paused for a moment, peering at his client. "Say, aren't you the young man who was here several years ago for his readings when two eagles came down out of the sky?"

Lucius was surprised by this sudden recognition by a total stranger. "I, I suppose I was. Why?"

"I was here with my father, working that day. He said you were truly blessed by the Gods, protected, a rare and inspired omen. Where have you been all these years?'

"Parthia and Africa." Lucius put out his hand with the money.

"No, no, Tribune. I would like to give the offerings to you. No charge." Lucius however, wanted to give him something. The man needed to make a living.

"I thank you..."

215

"Numonius. My name is Numonius." He smiled a big white smile.

"Thank you, Numonius. But I insist on making a contribution to your family." Lucius placed the money in his hand and Numonius took it gratefully.

"May the Gods bless you and guide you, Tribune."

"You as well."

The smell of frankincense and pine permeated the air of the temple, the lingering smoke fluting its way in and out of the rows of columns on either side, adding to the mystery of Apollo's sanctum. Shape and form were only slightly discernible, as in a murky swamp after nightfall or a misty field before daybreak. Several torches and braziers glowed in sleepy hues of orange and pomegranate.

On the far left, between two columns, Lucius laid the offering in the concavity of the altar, kneeling.

"Thank you, golden Apollo, for your help, your guidance. Make me strong and wise. Keep me from the shadows with your light. I offer this sacred herb and oil to you and my ancestors who also benefited from your grace. My life is yours." Lucius poured the oil from the small blue glass vessel over the sweet smelling sprigs and placed his hands on either side of the altar, head bent in heartfelt humility. He rose, strengthened by his prayers; he always felt his words reached Apollo's ears more clearly in that particular place, a resounding note for the God of Music. He turned to look upon the likeness at the far end of the temple, above the main altar. Amid the wafts of smoke and muted firelight, the figures of Apollo and his muses seemed to float. At their feet, in obedient supplication a dim figure was bowed.

"You there!" Out of the shadows a priest appeared to address the shrouded suppliant. "It is not proper that you prostrate yourself before the main altar. Citizens only are permitted and even they use the lesser altars. There are plenty of other temples in the city for you. Do you hear me?"

The figure made no reply, did not move. For some unknown reason, Lucius made his way through the haze to address the priest.

"I have seen many a person before this altar before and not all of them necessarily Roman. He harms no one." The priest looked at him indignantly at first but once his eyes adjusted and the tribune came into view, he curbed his annoyance.

"But, Tribune, that fellow has been there for several hours, since the first hour of the day in fact."

"Has he disturbed the peace of this place?"

"No, Tribune."

"Has he shown disrespect?"

"No," he whispered.

"Then I see no reason why his devotion should not be respected." The priest conceded with a slight nod. "If anything, you should see to that bunch outside the temple. Their disrespect is unforgivable."

"I shall see to it, Tribune." Lucius nodded and turned to look at the praying figure several feet away. As he approached, not willing to disturb him, the figure's head turned forward. Had he been listening? No doubt, for even whispers were carried on the smoky air amid the temple walls.

"I knew you would come," the man said softly, rising to his feet, his shrouded head gazing up to Apollo.

"Excuse me?" Lucius approached a little more.

"The dragon may leave his friends to fly on his own...but his friends will never leave him." He turned and slid back his hood.

"Ashur?" The soft-spoken name rang through the temple and the two men gripped forearms in affectionate reunion.

"By the Gods! What are you doing here?"

"As I said, Tribune, the dragon's friends will not leave his side."

The day wore on with a renewed sense of comfort for Lucius as he and Ashur wandered the thronging, sun-drenched streets of Rome. Even in the empire's capital, where people of all races and countries gathered, Ashur proved an interesting sight for the populace in his white desert garb. Lucius noticed at one point that people moved out of the way, the crowd parting slightly, like the forest air giving way to the sure-footed leopard. Ashur claimed that the city had changed a great deal since he was last there. Surprised that Ashur had been to Rome before, Lucius didn't dare ask when, for an incredible suspicion at the back of his whirling mind restrained him in anticipation of an unbelievable response.

Earlier he had been contemplating his meeting with the emperor, Plautianus breathing down his neck like a curious dog. Now, he had all but forgotten it. Instead, his mind was back on his friend, the desert, and the men who awaited his return. At times, Ashur grew silent, sullen. He claimed that despite the great beauty of the place, the pulsing of life within it, there was a looming darkness hanging over Rome.

"But how did you know where to find me?" Lucius finally asked.

Ashur smiled. "Let us sit away from the crowds for a few moments. There is much less freedom of movement here than in the desert." The two of them moved across the street to a bench beneath an olive tree. It was pleasant. Lucius always liked to watch the people from just such a spot when he was younger.

"All right," he said to Ashur. "Tell me."

"Our last parting saddened me," Ashur began. "I am not usually disposed to this emotion." He closed his eyes momentarily. "I watched the battle from the top of the surrounding cliffs. I watched you and your men fight, I saw you fall."

Why is he talking about all this? Lucius wondered. He was not too happy to relive all those memories again, so soon.

"I watched as Mars brought you to trial and prayed for your victory. I sang."

"I heard you," Lucius said. The song among the rocks was clear in his mind. "But, why didn't you come to see me after the battle?"

"The time after blood is a lonely, personal time. I did not wish to intrude. Not much later, I dreamed of Carthage and of you and knew that you must have gone there. So, I went. I must have just missed you and Argus, for I met your eagles in the city and spoke with Alerio who told me where you had gone. I followed."

"But why, Ashur?"

Ashur looked at him as though the answer were as obvious to him as sunlight. "Because you are my friend, that is why. Because Apollo, for whatever reason, has crossed our paths." Lucius still looked confused. "I watched your ship set out to sea and trailing it, among the white gulls, was a black crow. The crow is Apollo's messenger, his watcher. Once they were purest white, that is until one day when the crow brought Apollo terrible tidings concerning the lady Coronis. In his anger, the god struck the bird black and now all crows suffer the same fate."

"But what does that story have to do with anything?"

Ashur looked up at the sun through the leaves of the tree, his eyes drinking in the light. "For reasons known only to Him, Apollo has shown me that I must protect you. I must not fail in this. I must not bring him terrible news of you...my...friend." What appeared to be fear crossed Ashur's face then, something Lucius had never thought to see. Ashur looked at the ground, the dirt between the paving slabs at their feet. "I would not suffer the crow's fate and be struck into darkness. That is why I am here."

Lucius stared at the man next to him for several moments, not quite sure what to make of his strange words. They were haunting. Then he realized how happy he was to have him there and smiled. "I've missed your riddles." He stood up. "I don't see a shadow over the city of Rome, my friend, but it certainly is a better place with you here now. Come, let's walk some more. I'm hungry."

The two men walked for a while longer among the market stalls and shops, taking in the city. Before they knew it, the light of day had begun to dwindle and redden in the sky, casting the temples and buildings in pink. Despite Ashur's protestations, Lucius insisted that he be his guest in the Metellus household. He conceded, reluctantly.

The cool stillness of the atrium, its small mosaic pool mirroring the sky above, was a different world after the sweaty streets. Ambrosia, having opened the door to Lucius and his new guest, had slunk back against the wall, wary of the exotic foreigner.

"Where is everyone, Ambrosia?"

"Your mother and sisters are up the street at the Lady Claudia's house. Your father and brother have just returned from the Senate. They're in the master's rooms now with Argus." Lucius noticed her familiar use of the name.

"Very well. Ashur?" Lucius turned to his calm companion. "Ambrosia will show you to the garden. I'll take off my armour and join you." Ashur nodded. "Ambrosia, bring food and wine to our guest and prepare his room in the guest wing."

"Yes master. This way please." The girl flitted across the marble floors almost as though she were running away from Ashur.

Lucius made his way down the hall to his rooms and stopped briefly in front of the row of imagines, the busts of his Metellus ancestors. They peered at him, called to him from their individual niches. The stern eyes of Dalmaticus, Macedonicus and the others, ages of ancestors, beheld Lucius and whispered to him on hushed winds. They were expectant, severe, heroic. Men of war and of thought. Lucius remembered how Diodorus had told him to never pass by his ancestors without stopping to acknowledge them. So many times had they been Rome's hammer against her enemies and although many believed the Metelli's flame to have died out long ago with the last embers of the Republic, Lucius felt, could not help but feel, that his family was still great, deserving of respect, that he too was...destined for some purpose. With ancestors such as those before him, watching him, expectations of the young tribune were high, but not so high as those he had of himself. He looked at all of them but noticed that one was missing, not where it used to be. He moved down the row until he reached a corner in the wall and there he found it, tucked away, hidden from sight.

The bust of Quintus Caecilius Metellus, who fought for Rome at Zama, had been left unclean, dusty. Lucius turned the head so that its pooling eyes and thoughtful brow faced him. When he had ever thought of his ancestors, the man before him was the one he always measured himself against. He had been a friend of Scipio, a warrior and philosopher. Diodorus had also told Lucius, in confidence, that this particular Caecilius Metellus had been the first of their family to carry the dragon into battle, that he had been the one to pass on the power of that image to a favourite, more distant cousin rather than those of his immediate line. Lucius' father had called that man 'insane', had instructed Diodorus never to reveal that information to his son. But, Diodorus had known Lucius' grandfather and, before dying, the old man had instructed the Greek to one day tell the grandson he would never see about who he really was. Lucius picked up the cloth that the slaves used to dust the busts and wiped the dust from his ancestor's face. His father might try to hide it out of embarrassment, but not Lucius.

Hushed voices suddenly reached his ear and he started back, moving from one gleaming bust to the other but he soon realised they weren't the ghostly voices of the past but the harsh voices of the present. He moved further down the hall until he came to his father's door.

"He's as inept as a woman. Causes me no end of embarrassment and disappointment." Lucius couldn't help but listen. "You must have noticed this yourself?"

"Of course I have. Even his men see this."

What? Lucius' mind spun. *Argus? His voice and my father's!*

"Argus tell me. I'm curious. Who was this ex-Praetorian traitor in Africa?"

"Oh some dark-skinned grunt. Alexandrian or something. Headed up the cavalry squadron."

"Yes I've heard that but what was his name?"

"Ah,...Brutus. Yes Brutus, that's it. Why?"

"No reason. Just a common grunt's name. Did you know it means 'stupid'? Hmm, decimation...maybe I should have called my idiot son the same. Even executing a common grunt can be bad for one's image."

I can't take this. There's the door. Kick it in. Now! "That's enough!" The door to the room suddenly burst open and broke the arm off a marble statue of Jupiter that stood behind it. Lucius' large frame, heaving with rage, filled the doorway. A voice inside, called out to him; *composure, calm, no anger.* Argus looked surprised, Quintus junior cowered in a corner like a rat and Quintus senior remained at his desk, arms crossed, disgusted and defiant. His look dared his son to speak.

"Well, well. The emperor's faithful hound returns. You certainly didn't learn any manners over the past few years."

"I learned more on campaign, *father,*" he spat the word, "than I ever did from you."

"I certainly hope so, young puppy, because I couldn't have cared less." The words were meant to cut deep, sting. Lucius couldn't allow that.

"Argus, Quintus. Get the hell out of here!"

"You might as well leave boys, it seems my son finally has the courage to speak to me. Or is it to apologize?" He glanced at Lucius who restrained himself from pummelling Argus as he went into the hall. His words had hurt even more than his father's.

"An apology is the one thing you will never get from me. Your son I may be, unfortunate yes, but I'm also a tribune in the Legions, chosen by the emperor himself. When you speak ill of me, you speak ill of him. Call me traitor? I think, dear father, that you are more deserving of the title. You're jealous of my success under an emperor who has saved this empire, brought it out of civil war, consolidated power for the Senate and people of Rome. It's your own failure as a soldier that's driven you to petty jealousy and resentment of your own son."

A vein in Quintus Metellus' left temple pulsed momentarily as he looked up at Lucius in that damned armour, looking down on him, arms crossed. Lucius felt confident, powerful, unwavering.

"An emperor who has 'saved' the empire? By the Gods you're an ignorant boy!" Quintus barked. Then, as if addressing the Senate he rose from his chair, holding the folds of his toga, and began to pace slowly. "Let me tell you about your beloved Emperor Septimius Severus…He is a man. That is all. And like most men he is susceptible to greed, jealousy, malice and brutality. Do you know how he became a consul thirteen years ago? I'll tell you. He bought his way into it. Commodus' scheming chief of security, Cleander, was selling posts for personal profit and Severus took advantage of this." Quintus stopped pacing to check Lucius' expression. Nothing. He paced on.

"You say that he saved the empire from civil war? It was he who plunged it into war. The Senate, after his legions in Upper Pannonia had declared him emperor, labelled him a public enemy. Like a cornered animal he struck out, sending assassins to kill Niger in the East, who was supported by many in the Senate."

Lucius butt in. "You forget father that Niger and Consul Julianus sent assassins to kill him. He struck back in defence."

"If that's what you call civil war, defence?" Lucius let him ramble on. "So nervous was he, so afraid, that he sent his lap dog Plautianus, brutal and blood-loving, to seize Niger's family. With Albinus in Britain and Niger in the East, he entered Rome under arms, with his troops, breaking the age-old law that no commander may do so. His entry into the city aroused hatred and terror, his men stealing and threatening to sack the city. He revenged himself on many who had opposed him, inflicting penalties on cities that had sided with Niger, even going so far as to put to death those senators who had served in Niger's army as generals or tribunes. He took Roman justice upon himself, as have other power-hungry men." The implication that Lucius had decimated men for power was not missed, just ignored. "Once Niger was defeated, Albinus finally saw reason and rebelled against this tyrant in Gaul. His sons were put to death and he was declared a public enemy. It was at this time that Severus attempted to tie himself to the house of the noble Marcus Aurelius by naming his son Caracalla, Aurelius Antoninus, Caesar. Severus had even gone so far as to name himself the 'son of the deified Marcus.' What arrogance!"

Lucius wondered where all this was leading. His father paced, head up, a gesture here, a facial expression there. Had he practised this speech? Was he addressing Lucius, the Senate, or the shades of their ancestors out in the hall? It seemed he had forgotten Lucius was there. It occurred to him that his father was a ranting has-been.

"Eventually, out of fear, many of Albinus' friends defected to Severus' camp and so he lost at Lugdunum in Gaul, his head sent on to Rome for display." Quintus paused for effect before continuing. "Severus enjoyed likening himself to a great man such as Marcus Aurelius. Why not? He was loved by all, but Severus' true self came through in the other men in whose paths he followed proudly. After Lugdunum he held proscriptions! He even praised the severity of the dictator Sulla. Of all things! A telling choice but that was not all. In a further attempt to legitimise his associations with the Antonine dynasty he announced the deification of Commodus to the Senate. Commodus! His savagery destroyed the world his father Marcus had created. A god? He claimed Commodus to have been unpopular only with the depraved. No one opposed for it was suspected that Severus was in a rage. Those senators who had opposed him were in fact killed, without trial. Claudius Rufus, the Pescenni, the Cerelli, Antonius Balbus and more that were of consular and praetorian rank. He even cast Narcissus, the man who had strangled Commodus, to the lions.

"In Africa, among the savages, Severus is a god! In Rome, he is a man whose dependence on the army for his position is both blatant and pre-meditated, violent, selfish and barbaric. He holds Rome prisoner beneath his boot with the largest Praetorian force ever of thirty thousand men and his II Parthica Legion not far off in Alba. And you think *me* a traitor for being a Republican at heart, for wanting a return to the days when the Metelli fought for the Roman people, for the Republic so that men could live freely? I tell you this, *young tribune*, this emperor's actions have set the empire in a downward spiral that will bring Rome crashing to her knees." He looked at Lucius squarely for the first time since he had begun his diatribe, moved to his chair and sat down. It was evident that he was pleased with himself, that he believed his son speechless, dumbfounded.

Normally, Lucius was not one for words, for arguments expressed clearly, concisely. For the last few years, a sword had been his argument. Not now. He knew that only words would do. His hand rested naturally on the pommel of his gladius. Consciously, he removed his hand and clasped both behind his back so as not to fidget. He paced once or twice, a few feet, then stopped. His father was almost smirking.

"A fantastic speech, father. A pity it was in the safety of your rooms rather than on the Senate floor." The smirk quickly died away from Quintus' face as his son proceeded to speak, never taking his eyes away. "Much of what you have told me is true, I admit, but a lot of it is also based solely on malicious gossip, rumour and hearsay. As for myself, I decide on what I see and experience. Today I've met with the emperor; he has never been anything but gracious and forthright toward me. He has made me a tribune, yes, in his service. But more than that, a tribune in the service of Rome, of the empire. Just as a legion needs a commander, so does an empire. Not a group of men arguing matters in the Senate but a strong leader, at the front, on the field. I was there in Parthia. I witnessed Severus achieve what so many commanders had not: the defeat of the Parthian Empire. Marcus Licinius Crassus and Mark Antony had failed where Severus succeeded. And why? Because his men love him and follow him." Quintus looked disgusted.

"Yes, one reason he is emperor is because his troops are loyal to him, back him up. He isn't the first Roman to see the importance of the army, certainly not the last. Julius Caesar is a prime example. If anything Emperor Severus has saved the empire as Caesar did, with his legions, through civil war. Once opponents were eliminated as needed, he could begin to clean up the mess left by Commodus and the Praetorians. As for the deification of Commodus, it is not for me to say or judge. As for Severus' praise of the dictator Sulla, I would bear in mind, father, that the Metelli served Sulla, our ancestor Caecilia Metella was married to him! Whether right or wrong is not for us to decide. The Gods will do that. My duty is to Them, my ancestors and family, and my Imperator. In three days I will stand by him in the Forum for his Triumph. It is my duty, my honour to do so and I will, proudly. The shades of those great Romans outside your door will be there, in silent watch, as a Metellus once more is honoured next to his commander along the Via Sacra. I would that my own father were there to share in this."

Lucius surprised himself, shocked by the words that had just left his mouth. His father looked old, tired, beaten. Lucius had decided to reach out, extend to him an olive branch of peace. Then, a mistake. He pitied the proud Roman before him.

"Father, I know that you hated being in the army, that that's why you didn't want me to join. But, hear me when I say that I love it and I excel at being a soldier-"

Quintus Metellus jumped to his feet, his face suddenly red with rage, his anger swelling. "What in Hades do you know? You're nothing but an ignorant, self-indulged swine hiding behind your emperor. The best place to serve your family is in the Senate, not the Legions. I will not be there to watch you in three days, for I have no son apart from Quintus. How dare you storm in here, dribbling virtue like a salivating cur! You know nothing of the world, of men, of character. You disgrace our family name and make our ancestors cringe from beyond. I suppose you would like to be called 'Africanus' for decimating Romans across the sea." Lucius stepped to the edge of the desk, his strong fists resting on the table.

"I'm a Metellus *Anguis*, father! And I know who I am and that our ancestors are proud. Can you say the same of yourself?" Lucius did not give his father a chance to retort. "The world changes and so men must change with it. You can't long for the days of a time that won't come again. Our ancestors lived in their time with honour and I live now, with honour. Unlike you I don't live in jealousy and bitterness of the past and present."

"Get out of my sight!" Quintus' fist slammed down on the table, scattering several scrolls. "By the Gods if ever you speak thus to me again I'll box your ears so hard you'll wish that-"

"Wish what, father? That I were dead? I'm not the little boy you used to beat around when I wouldn't do your bidding. You can't hurt me."

"You're a swine, an insult to the family and-"

Lucius cut him off again. "Farewell, father. Thank you for the pleasant conversation." Lucius turned his back and made his way out of the room, leaving Quintus alone to stew in his rage. Outside in the hallway, it seemed to Lucius the busts of the Metelli were silent, pensive, as if deliberating. He bowed to them and went to his rooms. Would he stay longer? He wasn't sure.

An hour later Lucius entered the garden. How could he have forgotten Ashur? On a couch between the lemon tree and jasmine bush, Ashur sat sipping wine. Across from him, on the facing couch, sat Antonia and Alene.

Lucius stood behind a column and watched for a moment. The three of them smiled and laughed, even Ashur. *From one extreme to the other,* he thought. An hour ago he had been locked in a battle of words with his father, defending who he was in a dark, dour room. Now he came into what seemed a sort of paradise, a place of happiness and laughter with people who loved him. Such a contrast under the same roof. He was now steeped in a sense of calm and peace as he moved from behind the column into the enclosed part of the garden.

"Ah, Lucius! There you are. You should have told us you were bringing a guest home." Antonia rose, embraced her son. He felt her grip him tightly. There was worry in it. She must have heard. "Had you forgotten about Ashur? We came home to find him sitting here all by himself."

Lucius turned to Ashur. "Forgive me, my friend. There were matters that needed to be tended to immediately." Ashur nodded gravely.

"No apologies needed."

"What happened, Lucius?" Alene came over to him.

"I'll tell you later. For now let's sit some more. Have you become acquainted already?"

"Well," began Antonia, "Ashur has been telling us of his travels in Africa and how you both met." Lucius registered surprise.

"Oh… really?"

"And," she continued, "I must say I'm grateful that you did meet. Imagine coming to each other's rescue at different times. It seems fated. Of course Alene told me that." Alene smiled demurely at Lucius. "Ashur speaks only of you, never of himself. Like yourself. At any rate, Ashur, I am grateful for your presence and aid of my son. You are welcome in this house."

"Thank you, Lady Metella. I am honoured." Lucius smiled at his friend's gracious treatment of his mother. Antonia rose.

"Now if you will excuse me I must see your father about a few things." Lucius dropped his head slightly. "Until later." She made her way out of the garden.

"So, Lucius, how was your meeting with the emperor?" Alene was very curious. She really couldn't wait to hear what happened, what was said. And so he told her and Ashur as they sipped wine and listened.

XV

ARGUS

The Colosseum had been packed to capacity, the crowds spilling out after the day's events like grains of wheat from a hemp sack. The corridors of the amphitheatre resounded with the people's pleasure at the skill and unusual viciousness that had been displayed on the sand. Some sang the praises of their favourite athletes while others lamented the loss of funds bet on the losers, the dead.

Argus had been very excited about being back in the stands of the Colosseum and even more excited about his winnings. He counted several coins in his hand and dropped them into his leather pouch, grinning like a child who has just escaped with a stolen pastry from the marketplace. The few coins he had taken from Lucius' coffer for the occasion would not be missed.

"Looks like you did all right there, Argus!"

"Yeah. Seems the Gods have forgotten about me today. My luck's changed. What about you Didius?" He looked at the Praetorian's meagre handful. "Not so good, hmm."

"Not today. Come. The least you can do is buy me a drink with your winnings. I know a great place!" The man named Didius turned to his comrades. "We're going for a drink. I'll see you back at the mess." They waved him off and went on their way.

Argus had met Didius in the stands during the fights. He and his fellow Praetorians were off duty for the day and had been given permission to attend the games that were part of the emperor's celebrations. When Argus had sat down, the two had got to talking. Argus did not mind that Didius had insisted on talking with him the whole time. He had been a bit angry at having to attend the games by himself. It was always more fun when one had someone with whom to harangue the gladiators.

As they walked along, Didius decided to make conversation. "So, which was your favourite fight of the afternoon?"

"The third combat. The one with that murmillo, what was his name?"

"Atlantis."

"That's it. His cut and thrust moves were inspiring and best of all he didn't kill quickly. He drew it out, nice and long and painful. Even above the voices of all those sweaty asses you could still hear the poor bastard's screams."

"You can say that again! A broken arm, then a leg!"

"When Atlantis slit open his opponent's groin and the guy's balls fell out onto the sand I thought I would die laughing, watching him grope around the sand, crying like an exposed baby."

Didius regarded Argus strangely, a little apprehensively. He needed to find out more about him. "Finally, someone who likes the games a little more bloody than usual. I'm glad I ran into you. Look, there's the tavern I was talking about. Let's sit outside. We can watch the whores walk by on their way to the public latrine over there." Didius pointed to a small tavern with several benches outside and a rickety sign that said 'Bacchus' Balls' hanging above the small door.

"Is the wine any good here?" Argus looked sceptical. "Looks like a shit hole."

"It is. But the wine's good and the view even better. Hi girls!" he called over to two prostitutes coming out of the latrine, their legs glistening after washing.

"Piss off!" one of them yelled back.

"That's Mina," Didius said. "She's fantastic." Argus couldn't help but laugh. The man was a riot, no inhibitions it seemed. Didius wore the off duty colours of a Praetorian, a brown tunic and yellow cloak. Argus was surprised to see that Didius and his friends seemed to do as they pleased, address whom they wished. They seemed far less restricted, people got

231

out of their way. "So, Argus. Where was it you said you were stationed?"

"In Numidia with the III Augustan."

"And you're a centurion."

"Yes. What's it to ya?" Argus did not like all the questions.

"Nothing, nothing. Just curious why a huge son of a bitch like yourself, who obviously knows a thing or two about the world, is stuck in the middle of nowhere with a bunch of old geezers."

"Not sure of that myself," Argus said, happy to have an ear to speak to. "It's boring as Hades down there."

"What are you doing here then?"

"My bro-," he caught himself, "my friend's a tribune and was told to attend the celebrations here in Rome. I was allowed to come too."

"Ha," Didius laughed coldly. "Allowed to come to Rome but not allowed to be in the Triumph with the rest of them."

"Yeah, well I didn't know it was only going to be for any damned primus pilus or higher to attend."

"Would you rather have stayed in Numidia?"

"Not a chance! I'll take Rome any day."

Just then one of the tavern servers arrived with a tray of food, two cups and a beaker of wine. "Bout fucking time!" Didius scowled at the server.

"Your pardon sir, your pardon, your pardon," the server repeated fearfully.

Didius and Argus set to drinking. "So, who's this tribune friend of yours?"

"Lucius Metellus. I grew up with him."

"Lucius Metellus! The one who decimated that lot down in Sabratha?"

"Don't tell me you've heard of him?" Argus hated the thought that even this fellow, a Praetorian, had heard about Lucius.

232

"Damn right I've heard about him. Everybody was talking about the hornet's nest he stirred up down there. So you were with him?"

"Yes." Argus drank some more. "Actually, I was the one who helped nail the fucking traitors. Lucius wouldn't have done it without me."

"I'm not surprised," Didius sympathized. "It's always the higher rankers who get the credit."

"No kidding."

"So you said you grew up in the Senator's house?"

"Yup."

"What was that like?"

"Fine, I guess. Better now actually. They've got this new slave girl since I've been away. I've got her dying for it all the time now. Whenever the Metelli are out for the day I just take Ambrosia into my room to screw."

"Sounds good. What's she like? Sweet, I bet."

"Oh yeah. She's clean, smells good and isn't bad to look at. A lot better than the flea infested women down in Africa or Numidia. And she's free."

"Now, you're talking Argus. A free fuck always feels better, that's what I think anyway." The two men laughed, the sound carrying across the square. They whistled at another of the girls running to the latrine. She was so distracted that she slipped at the entrance and cursed in some foreign language. They laughed even harder at her. "So Argus," Didius began after catching his breath. "Since the Metelli are your foster parents that must mean that you get some sort of inheritance from them, no?"

"Foster parents? Oh, right. Umm, nope. All I have is my soldier's pay to live on."

"That's practically nothing!" Didius looked outraged. "You should get something!"

"I don't get anything."

"You know Argus, a Praetorian gets more than three times what army regulars get, seventeen-hundred denarii, and that's if you're a standard guard."

"And you stay in Rome?"

"Yup. Well, we're in Rome most of the time but we do have to go wherever the emperor or prefect are. But yeah, most of the time, we live it up in Rome."

"Unbelievable." Argus poured more wine, downed it and shook his head.

Didius leaned back against the wall, rubbing his chin. "You know, the prefect is always looking for exceptional men for the Guard. I could put a word in for you. You'd make a lot more money."

"I've got plans for getting my hands on money." Argus looked as though he were far away for a moment, outside the conversation. Then he turned to Didius. "Actually, I wouldn't mind getting the fuck out of Numidia. Would you put a word in for me with the prefect?"

Didius smiled broadly. "Absolutely, my friend. You're perfect material for the Praetorians! Just get a recommendation or a probatus from the Senator and it'll better your chances. Could you do that?"

"That won't be a problem." Argus was confident of that.

He thought about it as he said it. Staying in Rome, more money, doing whatever he wanted: it all sounded perfect and would provide him with many opportunities to advance himself. Besides, he was tired of Lucius, already tired of being in that house with all of them bitching at each other, especially Lucius and his father. It was funny for a while when he had heard them the day before but that got tiring very quickly. He was sick of getting the cold shoulder from all of them. *Bunch of snobs!* he thought. Even Alene, who at least used to feign courtesy toward him, now ignored him outright. There was Ambrosia to consider but Argus knew that he could always count on her to let him in whenever the urge took him and whenever the Metelli were out.

234

"Do it, Didius!" Argus blurted out. "Talk to whoever you have to, but get me a chance at the Guard. I'll make it worth your while."

"Don't worry about it. That's what friends are for." Their eyes strayed across the way to where some of the girls hung out of the upper windows of the brothel, waving at them.

Argus finished the last of his wine. "Well, the least I can do is treat you to a little fun over there." He pointed to the hooting women.

"I certainly won't say no to that!" The two men rose from their benches, strode across the square to the brothel and disappeared into the building's steamy innards.

XVI

ALENE

It had been a bad night. Restful sleep had not graced Alene's mind and body as she tossed and turned in her cubicula, in her bed. Occasionally, she had nightmares but this one seemed too real, like a cryptic message. The odd thing was that the darkness was intermingled with moments of inspiration and joy. But it was the sense of dread and despair that she remembered when she had awoken, her shift soaked with sweat, her ears ringing with the sound of yelling, her face wet with tears. It was about Lucius and a dark cloud that seemed to be rolling in from the hills to overwhelm him but for a light that surrounded him. She did not want to speak to him about it for fear that some dark god might be listening.

Instead, Alene decided to go immediately to the Temple of Vesta to make an offering. It comforted her to be there. She put on a long, wine-dark tunic and matching mantle, the edge of which she put over her head to hide her hair and face. She came down the stairs to the first floor of the domus to find that no one was around. Lucius and Ashur were likely out already but where were her mother and father, the children? She stopped at the bottom of the stairs and listened. Nothing. Earlier, she thought she had heard angry voices coming from the atrium. It had sounded like her mother and father were arguing again. This time however, it seemed very bad. Their voices got higher and higher. Alene suspected it might have been a part of her whirling dream, about Lucius. It did not matter. She could not remember now and the house was quiet. She walked passed her father's study door.

"Ambrosia?" she called into the kitchens.

There was no reply for several moments but then came hurried footsteps down the corridor from beyond the garden.

"Coming, mistress!" the slave called. She arrived panting, her hair dishevelled and her tunic a bit ragged-looking.

"Are you busy?" Alene asked.

"N...no, mistress." She brushed back her hair and tied it with a plain ribbon.

"Good. I'd like you to accompany me to the Forum. I need to go to the Temple of Vesta and then we need to buy a couple of things in the market. Get your things."

"Yes, mistress." The girl hurried off and came back a couple minutes later. She was rosy-cheeked and smiling. Alene frowned at her and the girl bowed her head. She had been acting very strangely the past days.

"Let's go."

She walked ahead of the slave, slowly, lost in thought. She tried to push back thoughts of that terrible dream. *Perhaps it was because I heard Lucius and father arguing so violently?* she wondered. *Let it be, Alene.* She had missed her brother for so long, years, had been sad beyond knowing when he had left for war. Her mother had told her that the women of Rome had always dealt with loneliness and hardship, the absence of husbands, sons and of brothers. It had always been so when the men of Rome went far away to defend her borders. The only difference was that now, those borders were infinitely farther away than before. Her mother was right, of course.

She came around the bottom of the Capitoline and into the Forum. There were people everywhere, most pointing to the draped edifice in front of the Curia. Alene hoped that she would not meet any of her former suitors and picked up her pace slightly as the round tholos of the temple came into view. A voice called to her as she was just about to walk up the short flight of steps.

"Alene Metella!" the voice was rude, always had been. It approached her. She stopped and turned.

"What do you want, Raxus?" she said coldly. "I'm busy."

"Just a friendly greeting is all, Metella." He always said her name with such smugness in his voice, resentment. She tried not to look at him. He disgusted her with his shorn, bulbous head, the stink of garlic that emanated from him and the gaudy rings that he had on every finger. She had been grateful to her father for not forcing her to marry this one. "No need to be so snooty with me, Metella."

"Oh no?" She beckoned Ambrosia to stand behind her, away from Raxus' eyes. "You never have anything pleasant to say so don't bother."

He grinned nastily. "I've just been talking with some of the other young citizens of Rome."

"Really? And what have you and your lackeys been talking about? How you can weasel your way into the Senate?"

"No. Actually we were talking about your brother." Alene's face coloured red and Raxus smiled; he'd hit the mark. "I've heard that he's back in Rome for the Triumph."

"Yes he is." She tried to control her anger. She hated it when people spoke about Lucius behind his back. "What of it?"

"Oh, nothing. We were just thinking that it must be difficult for him to come back, what with that embarrassing incident in Sabratha." He shook his head, eyes closed. "Quite difficult, I should think."

"Only to jealous gossip-mongers like yourself, Raxus." Alene held her head up. "You really are pathetic." Behind her, Ambrosia gasped at her aggressive tone.

"Such anger doesn't become you, Metella. Still, I'm sure that you are happy to have your brother home. Perhaps he can...comfort...you."

Alene wanted to slap him hard across the face. She hated that malicious rumour and did her utmost to remain still, visibly unmoved. She stared coolly at him. "You're even more degenerate and disgusting than I'd thought. Why don't you run along and play with the other ill-bred children of the city?" By the look on his face she could see that that remark did it;

Raxus was one of these 'new men', another merchant's son, who was obsessed with their lack of noble lineage and tried to make up for it by marrying into an old family.

"No wonder you can't find yourself a husband," he answered through puffed-out lips before turning back to his friends. They all watched her as she turned up the stairs and went into the temple.

"Wait there, Ambrosia," Alene muttered, pointing to a small bench near the door as she went across the temple floor to the other side.

"Yes, mistress." Ambrosia sat down, laid her basket on the floor and leaned against the wall. She was happy to be near the door, the smell of the incense was very strong.

Alene moved to an altar and placed a small bunch of flowers she had been carrying on it. Her hands were shaking terribly and her voice trembled accidentally as she said her prayers.

"Alene?" came a soft voice from behind her. Alene did not hear or notice until she felt the priestess' gentle hand on her shoulder. "Alene, are you unwell? What has happened?" It was Vergina, a young Vestal about the same age as Alene. She was dressed all in white, her pale hands were healing as they touched Alene's wet cheek and pat her shaking shoulders. "Tell me," she urged.

Alene got to her feet and stopped her tears. Her eyes were red from crying. "Vergina. I've just seen Raxus outside in the square." Vergina nodded. She knew about Raxus, about his kind. "Such hateful words, such jealousy. I can't stand it when people speak badly about my family."

The priestess' tranquil features held so much compassion for someone who would likely never have personal knowledge of such matters. She always knew what to say to Alene. "Such people are ignorant of their shortcomings. Do not let them fill your heart with anger, Alene. You are above such baseness."

"Am I? I'm not so sure." Alene looked confused.

"I know you are. You doubt it but I see how good you are. The goddess Vesta holds you dear. The sanctity of this place is only enhanced by the presence of mortals such as yourself. Let your mind and heart be at peace."

Alene looked down at the floor. "Perhaps I should have been a Vestal Virgin," she wondered.

Vergina smiled. "You were not meant to. If so, then you would be wearing these robes instead of me. Be happy with the life the Goddess has given you."

"Oh, I am, I am," she stressed. "Actually, I've been very happy these past days because my brother Lucius has come home. That's the reason I was upset; they were talking about him outside."

"They have small minds with nothing else to do. It is no matter." Vergina smiled. "But how is your brother? Is he well?"

"Yes, he is." Alene was already feeling better. "But last night I had a terrible nightmare about him." She related the dream she had had to the priestess. "I don't understand why I should think such things because he seems so well and has been telling me about the wonderful places he's seen over the years. I was ever so worried when he was away so it does me good to see him home in person, safe."

"I'm sure. Do not worry about such dreams Alene. Oftentimes they come when we are happiest. Perhaps it is the Gods' way of making us appreciate the blessings we enjoy by day." Vergina looked at the flowers on the altar and turned slowly when a group of women came into the temple. "I must go now." She placed her hands on Alene's head. "The Goddess blesses you and thanks you for your offering. I will pray for your family."

"Thank you, Vergina." Alene turned, feeling much better, and went out of the temple, motioning to Ambrosia to follow as she passed through the doors.

Alene was happy to see that Raxus and his cronies were gone when she came outside. The day seemed much more beautiful after her visit to the goddess, the sun was out and the birds singing from the temple rooftops. *Vergina is right*, Alene thought as she walked, *perhaps my dream was to remind me of the blessing that Lucius is to me.* She slid the mantle back from her head. *I'll protect him and help him.* The thought gave her a sense of purpose. He needed her, just as she needed him. She began to hum.

"Come, Ambrosia. Let's go to Trajan's market. I told my friends that we'd shop together. We should just make it on time."

"Yes, mistress."

"By Apollo, it's a beautiful day!"

XVII

CIRCUS MAXIMUS

'The Great Circus'

With the approach of each new season, every memorable event, there is a build-up, an anticipation of something big, the promise of something better. Just as before a great storm there is a cool breeze and then a rushing wind. On the wind there is a murmur, the sound of a god awakening from a dream. You can smell something in the air, danger, excitement, uncertainty. A restlessness overtakes man and beast with the clamorous stirrings of the Gods until finally the skies open up, the rain upon the earth, furious lashings and bolts of colour in rhythmic pounding.

If a furious winter storm over Rome brought flooded streets, panic and flurries of otherworldly predictions and ill-omens, the days leading up to the triumph of Septimius Severus brought an increasing sense of anticipation, of tangible elation that was thick in the air of every home, street and public place. It was the month of Martius and the celebrations coincided with the twenty-four day Festival of Mars. Rome had not seen such a wonderful and varied display for years. With each day that approached the triumph, the games were indeed bigger and better. It was assured that even the planets and constellations of the heavens were positioned so as to guarantee success. For an emperor who viewed life through the stars, this was paramount. The day before the main event was to be the culmination before the climax. The city smelled sweet, pulsed with life and a sort of social intoxication. In the fora, sweet breads, cakes and even coins were handed out to all free citizens as speeches were made to thronging crowds.

Morning had dawned bright and clear. Alene was not up yet when Lucius made his way to the peristyle garden with a plate of honeyed figs and oats, some cheese and a cup of milk. He enjoyed the peaceful hours of morning, the time when the world slumbers and all is still. It was a soldier's time, he felt, quiet, the darkness of night and memory left behind. Ashur, he knew, was already gone, as he said he would be for the first half of the day. No doubt he was at the temple again, drawn to it as ever, like a bee toward a sweet, fresh flower. Lucius had decided, after Ashur's arrival in Rome, not to question him about his mysterious ways or cryptic words. He did not want to judge or make presumptions, only accept the warmth and honest, strong friendship that he had been offered.

Lucius reclined on his couch, eating and enjoying the chance to be alone for a moment in the contemplative stillness of the garden. He had no idea whether his mother was up as yet; he had heard movement in the house and voices in the atrium even before the sun had risen but he was not sure what it was about. Perhaps Antonia was out or still asleep?

As morning moved on, the sounds of Rome's streets finally penetrated the house, the air was tinged with jollity. It was to be a grand day. Lucius remembered the emperor's talk of festivities and decided to go out and enjoy himself, be a Roman among Romans. First a trip to the baths and from there to whichever spectacles attracted him. He put on a cloak over his soft tunic and breeches and laced up his black Athenian sandals; like a playful dolphin to the waves the young tribune plunged excitedly into the sea of people.

A couple of hours later, exhausted by physical exertion at the gymnasium, having lifted weights, stretched his limbs and wrestled with some of the athletes, Lucius enjoyed the soothing waters of the Baths of Titus where he spoke casually with several citizens. While conversing with one fellow who was being massaged on the table next to his, Lucius learned of a special unveiling along the Via Appia, just next to the new palace.

"You really should go!" the man said. "Apparently Rome has never seen anything like it." He started to sit up, fully enthused, but the giant of a masseuse pushed him back down kneading his shoulders deeply. "Hey! Not so hard!" he whined. "Anyway after this I'm going to pick up my wife and kids to go see it."

"Sounds interesting," Lucius said, grunting slightly as his thigh wound was massaged, his leg pulled; the winter had been rather painful on it. "I'll definitely head there myself." The other man rose to leave, a little shaky on his legs.

"Well, maybe I'll see you there. Good day, citizen."

"Good day to you." Lucius closed his eyes, utterly relaxed. Shortly after, two women being massaged on nearby tables glanced over at him as his muscled body was oiled and rubbed.

"Oh, Celara! Look at that one," one of the women said a bit too loudly.

"Hmm," the other replied as she turned to lean on her elbow for a better view. "He looks like he could go all night."

Lucius shifted uncomfortably, his eyes closed. He knew they were looking at him, could feel their eyes all over him. His masseuse even giggled a little. Normally the attention would not have bothered him but he was unprepared for this. He was curious though and opened his eyes to see the women. They smiled and nodded.

"Hello, ladies," he greeted them.

"Hello to you, soldier," answered the one sitting up now, her breasts bare for him to see. She was older, not unattractive. She shamelessly played with one of her oily nipples. "Do you have plans for the day?" Lucius had heard about this sort of thing. Married women, bored of their husbands, flirting with younger men in the baths. He felt his loins stir a little.

"Maybe he didn't hear you?" her friend said.

"Strong and silent. What do you say to joining us for the day soldier?"

Lucius looked at the pair of them and smiled. "Thank you, ladies," he said graciously, "but I have plans. Maybe some other time." He thought it would not hurt to flirt back a little.

"Maybe," she said as she lay on her back. "Pity though." The woman stretched her naked body and her friend giggled. Their masseuse returned and quickly covered her again with the towel she had so easily shed for Lucius. "How terribly boring," she complained to her friend. When she looked back, Lucius was gone.

"Perhaps the next one will be more amenable," her friend soothed as they continued with their massages.

Anyone trying to get into Rome along the Via Appia that day would have found passage next to impossible. It seemed to Lucius that half the city had turned out to see the midday unveiling of this curious wall-like structure that provided a façade for the southern end of the new palace overlooking Italy's most famous road.

A contingent of the urban cohorts was on hand creating an arching barrier in front of the silk-covered structure. Citizens, pressed up against the guards' shields, waited expectantly, cheering and laughing. Several sailors from the navy then came out from behind the structure and picked up ropes that were attached to the massive silks. Horns suddenly rang out loud and clear and with quick precision the sailors pulled simultaneously on the ropes bringing the great silk sheets down to the base of the monument. Lucius stood at the centre of the crowd. At first there was an awed silence but when water began to dance and play and flit to and fro from arch to arch, the crowd erupted in a mass of cheering.

Lucius, indeed everyone there, had never seen anything like it. It was a lofty decorative façade that took the form of an elaborate columnar screen not unlike stage buildings in theatres. Only this was magnificently unimaginable. The entire display consisted of three massive storeys with three recesses flanked by two shallow rectangular wings. It was like a colossal nymphaeum intended to impress a sense of unearthly power upon travellers coming along the road, from Africa, the emperor's homeland.

The crowd gazed admiringly at the rich colours of the columns, all of African marble. Within the recesses were representations of the seven planetary divinities, orbited by streams of water and which in turn seemed to hover around the central figure at the top of the monument: a statue of Septimius Severus as the Sun-god, the light of the empire, the universe. Everyone whispered of his superstitious beliefs in exotic Eastern gods, his dependence on astrology and now it was displayed for all to see.

As Lucius looked up smiling, admiring the beauty of the thing before him, cool drops of fresh water sprinkled his face and those of the other bystanders. The horns blasted again, a fanfare, and behind the crowd on a high balcony across the street, the emperor, his wife and their two sons Caracalla and Geta appeared. All heads spun wildly and cheers went up again. They were barely discernible in all the confusion but their presence and the feel of the crowd was unmistakable. The people lauded the beauty of the Septizodium.

From there the crowd began to disperse and flow back toward the Forum. Lucius followed and decided to treat himself to some sweet breads and grilled meat on skewers. Several of the conversations going on around him were of other events that day, mainly shows in the theatres, gladiatorial combats and of course chariot races. The latter were the most widely spoken of and many were saying the emperor had brought back some of the greatest charioteers in recent years. It promised to be a most memorable and invigorating occasion, one not to be missed. It didn't take much deliberation before Lucius decided. He would definitely be there but first he would go to get Ashur from the temple so that he might show him the splendour and pageantry of Rome's greatest spectator sport.

The sound of excited voices was deafening. The smelly mix of sweat, perfumes, cooked meats and a tinge of horse manure was something that could only be experienced in the great Circus.

"Right this way masters, just along this row." The slave led Lucius and Ashur down the narrow passage, through the press of spectators to some seats about ten rows up in the middle of the Circus, facing the central spina. "Here we are," the young man said happily, relieved to have made the circuit without stumbling. "The prefect has set aside hundreds of seats for all military personnel in Rome and their guests. The view will be fantastic."

"It definitely looks that way," Lucius replied as he scanned the seats around them, nodding politely in the direction of several faces he thought he recognized.

"Enjoy the races." The slave then went off in another direction, back to his posting to seat other citizens.

"Well Ashur? What do you think?"

"My friend, I think that sometimes Romans have far too much time on their hands." Lucius saddened a bit but then a rare smile cracked Ashur's normally serious face and he picked up on his companion's dry humour. "I am capable of making a joke, Lucius. Actually I'm looking forward to this a great deal. It has been many years since I have been to a chariot race."

"You've been before?" Lucius thought he was treating his friend to something new. "Where? Not here! Don't tell me you've been in the Circus Maximus before!"

"No, do not worry. Elsewhere…ah, in Caesarea, long ago."

"Ah." Lucius was relieved. "Well then, let me tell you about the games in Rome." Ashur smiled as he sat back in his seat to listen to Lucius explaining like an enthusiastic child. "Chariot racing is the oldest game in Rome and was first held by Romulus in honour of the God Consus, equated with Neptune, and in honour of horses."

"Indeed," Ashur added. "The most noble of beasts."

"Quite. Now there are four factions in Rome: the Veneti, Blues, the Prasini, Greens, the Russati, Reds, and the Albati, Whites. The Blues and Reds are allied as are the Greens and Whites. I've always preferred the Blues myself. Each faction can enter up to three teams of aurigae, charioteers, and the prizes can be from fifteen thousand to sixty thousand sestertii."

"That much?" Even Ashur found it difficult to hide his incredulity.

"Of course. The aurigae become some of the most popular people in Rome, even around the empire. Much of the time particular horses become so well loved by the people that they are even given victory palms, oats in golden containers and luxurious retirement to countryside estates. The standard, most used chariot is the quadriga, a Greek four-horse chariot. You see the large central structure there in the middle?"

"Yes. The one with the giant obelisk and other buildings."

"That's the spina. The teams must complete seven laps around that which are counted down on those suspended objects in the form of dolphins at either end. The obelisk was brought from Aegyptus to commemorate Rome's conquests there; it's from the reign of the Pharaoh Ramesses II."

"It's magnificent." Ashur gazed at the monument while Lucius continued.

"I used to come here all the time when I was young." Ashur turned to him again. "Some of the most memorable times of my youth were spent in these seats, cheering until I lost my voice. Sometimes I miss those days…few worries or responsibilities, just enjoying the games with my father and Argus… How times change. The Gods sometimes play with me I think." He hung his head.

Ashur laid his hand on Lucius' shoulder. "Times do indeed change. It is the way of things. You're a good man, Lucius Metellus. The Gods reward men such as you so long as you remain true. If you do this, the change in your life will be for the better and your heart and your soul will fill up once more."

"I hope so. Thank you." Lucius felt better. The groomed earth and sand of the Circus seemed to sparkle in the afternoon sun and in that moment the sights, smells and sounds that surrounded him all melded into one, inexorable feeling of youthful comfort to ease his mind. In a way, that's what the games were all about. In a world where men and women were burdened with worrying, fear, violence and even simple distrust, there was a place where they could go to forget their troubles for a short time and be entertained alongside each other and their emperor.

The horns began to blare loudly from every corner of the hippodrome and the acrobatic riders who had been entertaining the crowd sped from the sands. On the Palatine side of the Circus Maximus, Septimius Severus appeared with the rest of the Imperial family, shining and resplendent, to the adoration of the people. With youthful exuberance, two hundred and fifty thousand Romans leapt to their feet, chants of "Caesar! Caesar! Caesar!" rising up to the sky in honour of the games' host. Ashur felt the hairs on the back of his neck tingle and a shiver run down his spine as he found himself on his feet as well, next to Lucius, peering over and between heads at the scene before him. At that moment he understood, he thought, something of what it was to be Roman, something of his friend.

My Gods, he thought.

As the emperor, clad in purple and gold, took his seat in the imperial box, more music rang out, flutes, drums, tambourines, water organs, horns and other instruments in a great fanfare. The swinging starting gates, the ostia, flew open and out came the twelve aurigae and their teams to parade their colours, their horses and themselves. Each faction had three teams, all well known from around the empire.

The teams rounded the track slowly, the Blues and Reds, the Greens and Whites. The chariots themselves were small and compact like war chariots, fast. The stallions were all perfectly groomed, their bridles and tack decorated in the team colours with ornaments and charms to their protective gods.

But it was the aurigae themselves who received the most adulation from the people who waved silky banners so that the stands were awash with colour. Over top of brilliant tunics, the drivers wore polished leather armour to protect their torsos, heads and arms. The cheers were deafening and while Lucius struggled to see if he recognized any of them, he heard various names yelled out by adoring fans.

For the Blues came "Diomedes! Poseidon! Charon!", for the Reds "Cupido! Atlas! Tigranis!" Loud cheers came from the Green supporters in honour of "Victor! Ariadne! Maximus!" and their compatriots, the Whites, "Flaminio! Britannicus! Porcius!"

The revered came from all over the empire; Africa, Palestine, Greece, Gaul, Iberia, Britannia and of course Italy. Each one had at one time or another held aloft the victor's palm, felt the roar of thousands fill his veins. Bets had been placed for hours before but due to the uncertainty of the outcome, for they were all heroes, it was difficult to know who would win and who would lose. It was whispered that the emperor would give the victor a record hundred-thousand sestertii.

"There! Ashur look!" Lucius pointed. "See there, the main rider for the Blues. I knew it, that's him!"

"Who?" Ashur was puzzled.

"That's Charon. He was always my favourite. I tell you, I've seen him drive to victory more than once."

"He is a formidable man. Interesting name too."

"Yes well, let's hope that today he speeds along the sands and not the Styx. I believe he'll win."

"It won't be easy, my dear Lucius. True his horses are magnificent but look at the other teams, all equally imposing with beautiful stallions, spirited."

"Care to wager?" Lucius ribbed Ashur playfully.

"Tribune I would not think of betting on games. How could you think such a thing. I don't wish to take your money. Besides, I told myself I wouldn't enjoy this Roman spectacle; I've already lost *that* bet. I'm enjoying myself already!"

"Fine then, have it your way." Lucius lowered his voice. "Let's sit. Here come the priests."

Ashur gazed curiously onto the sands. The chariot teams had completed their lap and were now taking their positions in the starting gates. At each side and end of the Circus white-robed priests came out to perform the preliminary sacrifices. The entire crowd fell to respectful silence as a lamb, a goat, a chicken and a bull were offered up to the Gods Jupiter, Neptune, Juno and Mars. Libations were poured onto the bloodied sand and the priests spoke several cryptic words before departing, the carcasses carried off by lesser of their order.

The people began to murmur, then chant and then, when the emperor stepped forward again with his sons, they roared. Ashur was somewhat amazed that when the emperor raised one hand the crowd quieted immediately. Then with the other hand he held aloft a pure white cloth and dropped it. Like a soft feather it glided gently downward, all eyes on it.

It fell to earth and simultaneously the ostia flew open. The Circus Maximus erupted in an explosion equalled only by Vesuvius. The twelve teams charged out toward one side of the spina, all competing for the first few positions. Horses' hooves pounded the earth, their manes like wings as the aurigae drove them on in various tongues.

Immediately, there was an accident as Porcius of the Whites and Diomedes of the Blues collided, their wheels locked. Diomedes' wheel came off and Porcius' chariot flipped, bringing his team down. The crowd loved it and cheered for more.

The whole world seemed to shake with all the excitement, as if the Gods themselves were cheering on man and horse. Victor and Maximus kept the Greens in front blocking in turn

Cupido and Charon who each lay attack upon attack, harrying them for first. In the rear, Tigranis and Atlas had Ariadne between them. Several punches were thrown back and forth and Ariadne fought hard to hold his charging team steady. The two remaining Whites saw their chance and Flaminio and Britannicus moved along the outside into place ahead of the duelling trio. They cut back in tightly at the same time, and in the squeeze, Atlas' sleek wheels rolled up onto the edge of the spina, flipping his chariot and himself. Ariadne, whose chariot began to wobble and bounce uncontrollably, saw the danger as Tigranis moved in for the crush, and jumped from his quadriga onto one of his horses an instant before his chariot broke loose and toppled.

The crowd cried out jubilantly at this acrobatic and daring feat. He was out of the race, but what an exit! The fourth out of seven dolphins was flipped over, the race sped on. The horses' lungs heaved and their coats glistened with sweat as their bloodied riders whipped and yelled. Cupido had succeeded in breaking through, ahead of Victor and Maximus. His white Iberians, like the wind, were hard to catch.

Lucius watched as Charon held back in fourth behind the two Greens and ahead of the two Whites. His team-mate Poseidon held to the outside, equal with him and blocking Tigranis who was trying to move up. The sixth lap came and the tide of the Circus began to change. Poseidon moved up to squeeze the Greens, Victor and Maximus, so tightly that their wheels began to rub the spina. Charon watched, waited and when Victor reigned in to avoid smashing into the spina, he shot to the outside and sped up to the front past Poseidon who was now pressing Maximus against the spina. Charon's black chargers moved like winged stallions to catch the leader Cupido.

"What beautiful magnificence," Ashur admired, his face and Lucius' alight.

"Go! Go!" Lucius yelled and yelled on his feet.

The other riders abandoned their own battles and struggled to reach the front and hopefully third place. To every Roman there that final lap seemed to pass both with the speed of a bolt of lightning and with the slowness of a lumbering cloud. Their heroes fought admirably, fiercely. Cupido and Charon rounded the final corner, perfectly equal, their wheels on fire across the sky. Two battling gods.

It was said that Cupido had tired his horses too soon, for in that final stretch in which Victory came down to crown a champion, his team faltered, almost tumbling, allowing Charon, the "ferryman" as he was called, and the Blues to drive to victory with Britannicus in second from the outside and an exhausted Cupido in third thanks to the hard-fought endurance of his ivory team.

All two hundred and fifty thousand spectators cheered on the brave aurigae and their noble horses, voicing their praise and muttering for their lost sestertii. The three winners pulled up in front of the imperial box where they entered a doorway and appeared above, before the emperor and his sons. Few could hear what was said but the actions spoke much. Caracalla and Geta each placed laurel crowns on the heads of Britannicus and Cupido and the cheers went up.

When the emperor stepped forward he placed a crown of golden laurels on Charon's sweaty brow and in that addictive moment, to which all charioteers strive, the champion was handed the palm branch for victory. Thunder spread through the stands to cover the whole of Rome with cheers in honour of the day's god.

The three aurigae saluted the emperor once more and made their way back to their teams to be congratulated by their fellows and factions. The horses were watered and Charon's team was awarded well deserved oats, fed to them in golden containers upon which their names had been hastily etched. Charon took it upon himself to feed each of them as the people continued to cheer, sing and praise.

It took some time for the thousands of spectators to begin filing out of the Circus. No one wanted to leave the scene of such a spectacle. Eventually, Ashur and Lucius made their slow way out through the gates into the streets.

"Well, Ashur? What did you think? Quite an experience isn't it?"

"Lucius, it was unlike anything I've seen before. I feel that the Gods are most pleased."

"The Gods? What about you?"

"Me?... When can we go again?"

XVIII

TRIUMPHUS ET CONVIVIUM

'Triumph and Banquet'

"Antonia, I've made up my mind. I cannot abide him any longer. I'm leaving."

"But, Quintus, tomorrow of all days, he will stand as a tribune in the ceremonies."

"Especially then. He's dishonoured me for the last time and I'll not have him do it in public. Our family name can't take this humiliation-"

"We have no family if you leave, if you break your bonds as father."

"Enough!" Quintus shuddered and rubbed his temples. His outburst did not phase Antonia, she simply stared at him. She wasn't sure if she wanted to cry for her husband and youngest son who were leaving, for Lucius, her family or for herself. Self-pity was not an honourable indulgence for a Roman matron.

"When will you return?"

"Send word when he has left Rome. Then will I come."

"You will take care of young Quintus, won't you?"

"Of course I will. He is all that I have left in this world."

"All? But what about-"

"He doesn't exist, not now. Antonia I must go before the streets become too busy, young Quintus is waiting." Husband and wife stared at each other momentarily, painfully. Quintus shook his head, went to go out, paused just inside the doorway, then left his house.

"But what about me?" she finished. As the slave closed the door behind Quintus Metellus the atrium rang with the sound of emptiness. Outside, the wagon carrying father and son rolled uneasily down the street and around the corner. "Leave me," she said to the slave. "I wish to be alone."

The following day, Antonia was reclined on a couch in the peristyle covered by a thick blanket, gazing silently out at the garden, the blue morning sky above. She heard some hesitant footsteps and then the sound of a packed satchel being laid on the ground.

"Come here, Argus." He stepped out from behind a column, fully dressed, his armour packed up. "Are you leaving so soon?"

"Yes, lady Metella. I, uh, I'm to report to the Praetorian camp this morning. Is Metellus pater here at all? I need..."

"No. He is not here, Argus. He has gone with our younger son to our estate in Etruria for a while."

"Oh? Did he, by any chance leave something for-"

"Do not worry, he didn't forget your letter. Here." She held out a scroll with Quintus' seal on it. Her words were short, cutting. "He left this for you. Of course, he had already spoken to the right people for you. That's why you leave earlier than expected."

"Thank you, lady."

"Do not thank me. May the Gods guide you on your way and Fortune love you."

Argus was confused by this treatment from a lady who had always been kind and gracious to him, the only real mother he had ever known. He had wanted to leave that household for a while, to be off on his own, away from Lucius and the rest of the Metelli. But now, as he stood on the threshold of making that break, as he stared at Antonia Metella sitting there hard and saddened, he was afraid.

He forced his legs to back up, his arms to pick up his belongings, his shivering neck to bow his spinning head one more time to the lady of the house. Argus turned then and, Quintus' letter in hand, he moved forward slowly, and then quickly through the house to the atrium where he pushed the door slave aside to let himself out.

"Argus?" Ambrosia appeared in a small doorway. "Are you leaving?" He turned to look at her, his free hand clenched, his eyes cold as winter ice. He spat at her feet before slamming the door and running up the street.

To the eye, morning dawned over Rome as it had on any other day, the sun's orb peaked the distant hills, creeping slowly along the land, down the streets, into the windows of citizens and slaves, the rich and the poor. The gift of morning light was free to everybody and the crisp cool air of the early hours hung silently over the city.

Through the peaks of the temples, to the palaces and gardens of the Palatine, to the arched openings of the Colosseum, the sound of birdsong from fleet-winged flocks heralded the new day as they passed above the still-quiet world. Asleep in their beds or on mattresses laid out on floors the people of Rome would awake. With the first flickerings of eyelids they would believe it was the start of yet another ordinary day. A beam of sunlight might warm their faces, a lover's sleepy groan awake their ears. Shifting in their beds, rubbing their eyes, they would realise that it was not an ordinary day.

The movement of slaves would become more hurried, the voices of masters more demanding. It was the day of the triumph and there was much to be done. It was a day to be out, a day to be seen. There were places to go, duties to perform. In the Forum, officials and organizers were already milling about, sacrifices were made and the omens read. Slaves sat lazily in folding chairs, sent early in the morning to reserve spots for their masters for the day's celebrations.

In the Praetorian camp, the emperor's guard prepared for inspection, received orders. Every invited soldier from prefect to common grunt, young muscled man to scarred veteran, each polished his armour, sword and helmet. To stand next to the emperor, in his honour on the day of his triumph was to stand next to the sun.

Before anything else, after awakening to the sound of larks in the garden, Lucius Metellus rose from his bed, crossed the room to the small altar and poured a libation to Apollo, praying that the day would be a good one. In the warm morning light coming through his window, he gathered all his armour and polished it lovingly until he could see his reflection, until the image of the dragon on the cuirass and cheek pieces came alive. Yesterday he had felt like an excited child going to the games with his friend. Today he was a tribune once more and would march through Rome and down the Via Sacra with his comrades, into the Forum, to salute the emperor.

He sighed, breathed deeply three times. Having strapped on his breastplate, hung his sword at his side, and fastened his crimson cloak at the shoulders, he gazed into a bronze mirror to see if all was well. How much older he looked, not weathered, just burdened. He didn't feel older, but he was. He hadn't noticed until then. Had the Gods chosen that moment, that day in particular to allow him to see? Was he on the verge of something? As he moved closer to the mirror, gazed fixedly at the dilating pupils set in brown eyes, he realized that all he could do was go out and see what the day had in store.

"Mother are you sure you're all right? You look very pale. I'll have some camomile flowers and hot water brought for you. It will calm you." Alene sat on the edge of the couch fussing over Antonia.

"You'll do no such thing, Alene. Please. I'm quite well thank you."

"Oh mother come now! Something's wrong. Why did I find you out here by yourself, shivering under a blanket? What's happened?"

"What's going on?" Lucius stepped around the corner.

"Lucius, something's wrong with mother. I found her out here alone and-"

"Will you two stop it!" Antonia smacked her hand against the edge of the couch. "I am not a child!" Lucius placed his helmet on the floor and knelt beside her, reached for her hand.

"Please mother, tell us what's going on." Antonia closed her eyes and sighed.

"Your father has left." It took Lucius and Alene a moment to register the news.

"Where did he go?" he asked.

"He took your brother with him and left for Etruria."

"But why mother? Why would he do such a thing?"

"Because Alene, he said...he said that as long as Lucius was here he would not be. He won't return until Lucius leaves Rome."

Lucius' heart sank then, not because his father had shunned him, that was expected after the other day. He was sad because of the effect it was having, would have, on his mother.

"I'm sorry, mother." He bowed his head. "I should never have returned." Antonia lifted her son's chin.

"Don't say such things my son. Since your return, this home has known a happiness, as I have, that has not been felt in a long time. The Gods have brought you back to us for a short time at least, and for that I am grateful. Times are changing and I must deal with change in my own way, as you must. As for your father and I, who knows what the fates have planned? Today is your day!" Antonia, suddenly full of life, threw off her blanket and jumped up from her couch. "Today my son, like so many of your ancestors, you will stand in the Forum, in front of all Rome and *I* shall be there to see it!" She clapped her hands loudly and the slave girl came running. "Ambrosia, come! I must dress now. Bring my finest stola!" With that, Antonia Metella went to her rooms to prepare, leaving Lucius and Alene dumbfounded.

259

Midday arrived and a hum of anticipation rang through the streets. Thousands and thousands of citizens and their families stood, sat or perched precariously on the edges of buildings in wait for the procession. Rome was a busy hive that day, the buzzing throng awaiting their leader. The sun was warm and the sky deep blue above.

Near the Septizodium, where the Via Appia enters Rome, the procession stood in wait for the order to move. All were a bit confused and uncertain except for the soldiers who stood in orderly rows, some chatting with their fellows, others silent, eager to get it over with. They would be some of the last to go, prefects and their staff, standard bearers, tribunes, centurions and other troops. Each group had been given their orders and signals. Firstly, the crowds lining the streets would be dazzled with dancers, acrobats and other displays.

In the midst of glinting armour and crested helms, Lucius stood patiently. He didn't know any of the men around him, mostly older men. Some exchanged pleasantries with him before continuing conversations with their friends. The fact that he was there seemed to earn him a measure of respect; no more the young boy to be taunted by veterans.

He gripped the handle of his sword and suddenly found himself wondering about his men back in Numidia, especially Alerio and Antanelis, Garai, Eligius and Maren. Without any of them he knew he wouldn't be where he was at that moment. He honoured them, and as if by winged messenger he sent gracious thoughts to them. There was a sudden drumming and then an explosion of music that brought him and everyone else onto their toes to peer over and between each other's heads. The procession was setting off.

"Listen, mother! It's starting." From where they sat in the sections reserved for senators' wives and military families, Alene and Antonia Metella, two shining Roman women, looked down the Via Sacra for any sign of movement. "I wonder when Lucius will come in."

"Alene, I don't think that will be for some time. I've heard that there's going to be much ceremony and display. We're going to be here for a while."

"Not to worry mother. The day is warm and the sun shining brightly." Although, she would not say as much to her mother, Alene was feeling extremely light-hearted since hearing that her father was gone. Had Antonia stayed at home to skulk she would not have felt like that but, as she was out with her, her feelings felt warranted.

"Hmm. Quite a beautiful day for this. Well, let's sit and enjoy the show." The crowd gazed on in delight as dancers and acrobats from various lands, mostly of Africa and the East, bounded and glided before them, scattering flowers and showering all with newly minted coins to commemorate the event.

Then came troops of Numidian horsemen, the hooves of their stallions clicking on the paving slabs as their twisted locks bounced up and down. The senators were seated on the steps of the Curia; many watched excitedly, laughing, talking. A few sulked silently. Above all of them loomed the triumphal arch, now draped in long-flowing silks of purple and gold. It stood where, it was said, Severus had a dream that Pertinax fell from his horse which he then mounted himself.

After over an hour, the troops began to make their slow rhythmic way through the streets. Lucius' legs woke up, the blood flowing after standing for so long. They had not yet seen the emperor or his sons. The moment they came onto the Via Sacra at the end of the Forum, the music changed distinctly from something playful and jumpy to the solid sounds of cornu and drum. The scene sent shivers up Lucius' spine and he stood as tall as he could, shoulders wide, his chest out. He thought he'd never seen the Forum so full.

Antonia and Alene finally spotted him. They were proud, and for the first time that day, their mother smiled and came to life. The troops lined up on the edges of the Sacred Way, a wall of honour for their commander. The music slowed and then exploded as two four-horse chariots came around the corner in front of the Colosseum. Caracalla and Geta drove on their purple and black quadrigae, one with black stallions, the other with white. They each saluted the crowd to either side and were greeted with adoring shouts of "Hail Caesars!" or "Long live Caracalla and Geta!" Many were surprised to see the two young men playing such a prominent role in their father's triumph but then, they were the nominated heirs.

Lucius stood at attention, watched. Then an odd feeling crept upon him and his eye was drawn to the middle of the crowd across from him. He became unaware of the proceedings, his mind uncontrollably bent in that one direction. The sun came down hot and bright and intense, the air smelled of sweet perfume though he did not know why. A pair of eyes flashed momentarily among the throng, but were lost in the mix. He looked back at the procession.

The two chariots pulled up to the base of the shrouded structure, near a dais where several dignitaries and other persons of great import sat, including the empress dressed in robes of Tyrian purple and gold. The young Caesars dismounted, saluted the senators and went to stand near their mother to look down the avenue for their father. On the tops of the buildings, men and women with floral crowns appeared with large baskets. Horns blared out and a golden chariot drawn by eight silver-coated stallions, their manes shimmering, came into view. Lucius and the rest of the troops saluted, following Caracalla and Geta's lead. The entire Forum was on its feet, drenched in showers of scented flowers from the hands of those on the rooftops.

Everyone looked for the emperor, many further back pushed their way forward to see more clearly. The chariot was larger than usual and in the back of it, in a golden chair on a raised block, sat Septimius Severus all in the purest white robes with brilliant golden laurels of victory encircling his head like a sun.

Lucius realized that he was sitting because of his ailing health which wasn't a secret any longer. Yet, the people roared and were blinded by his image, a sun before their eyes. Once the emperor came even with the Temple of Antoninus and Faustina, the Praetorians pulled sharply on the silks covering the arch, revealing its ornate beauty. Caracalla, Geta and all the troops hailed their Imperator.

"Hail Caesar! Severus Imperator!" Instantly everyone present took up the salutation, raising it to the heavens so that the Gods themselves took notice. Behind the emperor's chariot came wagonloads of spoils, gold, arms and armour, and slaves from Parthia; trophies to be gawked at.

The sheer size and uniqueness of the arch struck all. It was seventy-five feet high, eighty-two feet wide and all of highly polished Pentelic marble. It was not composed of the usual single opening but rather three monumental gateways, crowned by statues of the emperor and his sons in a six-horse chariot flanked by other equestrian statues. On the faces of the arch were representations of military victories over the Parthians and their allies, dramatic moments frozen in time, intended to be remembered. Artistically, the style was a new perspective reflecting a new age.

The inscription on the front of the monument read: "Erected by the Senate and People of Rome in Recognition of the Restoration of Rome and the Extension of the empire."

After several sacrifices to the Gods and even more speeches, the crowd began to disperse slowly. Some went home, others lingered and admired the monument and more went to the various baths around the city. Lucius was one of the latter. Standing for so long he had grown sweaty and tired, and if he was going to attend the palace banquet, he needed to revive and refresh himself.

Alene enticed their mother to go to the baths with her as well, hoping it would help her relax; they would meet with Lucius back at the house later in the day.

Before leaving the Forum, Lucius searched one more time for any sign of the eyes that had caught his, but it was in vain.

After they had all visited the baths, been oiled and rubbed and scented, Lucius, Alene and Antonia met at home. Ashur too had appeared as usual after spending most of the day at the Temple of Apollo, chatting, he said, with the priest there.

After endless debate on the matter, Alene had not succeeded in convincing her mother to come with them to the Imperial banquet. The triumph was one thing, but she said she had no intention of standing about all evening as people gorged and gossiped, especially after what had happened at home; Quintus was gone and she wanted to be alone for a while.

"Please go, both of you! I'll be fine. Besides, if I need help with anything Ashur will be here."

Ashur nodded and smiled. "Of course, dear lady."

"You're sure?" Lucius was a bit sceptical at first.

"Of course I am, Lucius. Now go. You of all people should be there tonight. The emperor has his eye on you and it wouldn't do to shun his invitation. You too, Alene."

"All right, mother. But, should you need us send one of the slaves to call for us."

"Don't be ridiculous! Go and enjoy yourselves. Please." They knew that their mother was not to be swayed and ceased their attempts to persuade her. So, Lucius, in his finest toga, and Alene in a radiant yellow stola with her best jewels and finest scent, made their way to the Palatine Hill for the Imperial banquet.

Evening had already fallen, the stars gleamed brightly as they walked along the torch-lit paths of the gardens to the palace. Many other guests were also making their way to the banquet; some husbands chided their wives for having taken so long to prepare, others arrived fashionably late. Alene walked proudly with her brother, arm through his. She couldn't remember the last time they had been out together, her happy eyes matched the stars above.

"Are you nervous?" she asked, nudging him playfully.

"A little. I don't know why though. I suppose it's been a long time since I went to such a formal gathering. Are you nervous?"

"No, not at all."

"Just like you, Alene. Sometimes I think you thrive on these occasions, enjoy watching me squirm and sweat."

"Don't be silly. But this is an important night. I mean, everybody who is anybody will be there, politicians, philosophers, generals, poets etceteras, etceteras...and then there's the Imperial family."

"Now I'm nervous. I'm already sweating under my toga."

"It'll be fine, not to worry. This is going to be a wonderful night."

"Sometimes, Alene, I think you know things that I don't."

"Of course I do. I'm a woman. What would you do without me?

Lucius laughed.

"By Bacchus, look at this place!" Lucius was not prepared for the sight before him, let alone the size of the room. It was like a basilica, teaming with hundreds of Romans. At the entrance, a Praetorian asked for their names and announced them, though few would have heard above the din.

"Tribune Lucius Metellus Anguis and Lady Alene Metella." Just then Alene seemed to acquire a sophisticated air, she held her head higher, a slight, amused smile on her face as she nodded to acquaintances here and there. She had shed her youthfulness and sisterly laughter like a true performer. After all, banquets such as these were indeed sharp social performances.

Lucius on the other hand was already dizzy with the sounds and smells and when Alene left quickly to meet some friends, he felt even more lost. Confusion in battle was one thing, confusion at a party with strangers was quite another. So he did the only thing any soldier would: he went straight for the food.

He was sweating more now. When finally he reached the centre of the room, a small opening in the crowd allowed him to look around and find his bearings. It was almost difficult to believe they were indoors. In the centre of this grandiose banquet hall there was a large garden rounded by a peristyle. He moved closer to this, thankful for the breeze, however slight. Within the garden was a fountain with several olive trees, delicate and small. Above the fountain loomed a large African date palm, its branches groaning with fruit for guests to pick at. Within the hall, at the edge of the peristyle, were two fountains, one of Bacchus, the other of Venus. What was different about these was not the sculpture but rather the fact that they were spouting wine and not water. Slaves moved back and forth filling silver cups and ewers with fine Falernian wine.

To the western edge of the room was a large balcony overlooking the Circus Maximus. To the east were four large anterooms filled with dining couches for the more prestigious guests. Briefly Lucius wondered where in all the confusion was the emperor but then he spotted a long line of people leading to a large group of couches at the southern end of the hall. People were lining up to pay their respects and congratulations to their emperor on the day. Lucius knew he should do so but he wasn't ready yet. He decided to walk around the room and avoid standing in one spot. As he made his way between the groupings of couches and bodies, he found himself admiring several larger than life sculptures prominently displayed.

The sculptures were of various scenes of mythology and history and in each there was an essence of life he had not seen before. One in particular grabbed his attention; a scene from the Iliad in which the goddess Aphrodite is carrying her son, the Trojan hero Aeneas, wounded from the battlefield. The artist who had created the sculpture had captured the goddess in a moment of pain and anguish that made her almost human as she risked herself for her son. Aeneas' pained expression revealed his human side but the straining of his muscles and the perfectness of his form hinted at his half-mortality.

"I believe this is my favourite. Do you like it?" A calm voice came over Lucius' shoulder. Behind him stood a middle-aged, bearded man with strong hands and a slight twinkle in his eye. Lucius turned back to look at the sculpture.

"Well, um, I think...I've never seen anything like it."

The man nodded. "But what do you *feel* when you watch them?"

"Oh it's silly." Lucius felt embarrassed. Who was this fellow?

"No feeling is silly. Tell me," he said expectantly.

"Well, I think I can hear them; the goddess speaking softly to her son, his groans of pain as the battle rages all around them. It is a peace within the storm."

"Hmm." The man rubbed his chin thoughtfully. "You know, you're the only one to have felt that. Wonderful! The only other person to understand is my apprentice, Carissa."

"You mean you did this?"

"Yes, I did."

"And all the others around the room?"

"Yes. But this is my favourite." Lucius was shocked that someone so unassuming had created such beauty.

"They're magnificent!"

"Thank you." The sculptor took a sip of wine from his cup and stepped forward to brush away some flower petals that were sprinkled about the base of the statue. "My name is Emrys. I'm from Britannia. And you?"

"Oh, ah, Lucius Metellus."

"So Lucius Metellus, are you a politician, a soldier, what?"

"I'm a tribune in the army but as yet not attached to any particular legion. For the moment my cohort is stationed in Numidia. I'm here for the triumph."

"I see." He turned toward a young woman who approached them. "Ah, there you are, Carissa! Come, I want you to meet someone." A young woman with short hair, delicate hands and intense grey eyes came up. She was dressed in a simple white tunic, knotted at the shoulders. "This is Tribune Metellus. He's managed to appreciate our work as no one else has."

"Lady Carissa." Lucius nodded politely and smiled.

"It is not our work, Tribune, it is my master's. I am but an apprentice…and pleased to meet you." They were so alike Emrys and Carissa, that they could have been father and daughter.

"Well, Carissa, with a teacher like Emrys your creations will be just as stunning I'm sure." He turned to Emrys. "Where did you learn to do this? I haven't heard of any sculpture coming out of Britannia. I'm not an expert but…"

"You're quite right, Tribune. I'm from Britannia, Dumnonia to be precise, but for the last twenty years I've travelled the world, every part of the empire, studying the artistic styles and techniques of various lands; Greece, Aegyptus, Africa and parts of Asia. Of course I learned the most in Greece, but each culture has something to offer." Lucius listened, very interested and relaxed now, as Emrys spoke about techniques, images and feelings, not the usual artistic temperaments. Emrys appeared to be something of an enigma.

Their conversation was eventually interrupted by a loud fanfare as the first course of the evening was brought out by an army of slaves who offered platters to those standing or reclining on couches.

"Before you go," Lucius said quickly, on impulse. "Would you both honour my family's home by joining us for dinner a week from now? If you are still in Rome that is." Lucius found he was interested by the sculptor and his apprentice and had a feeling that his mother and Alene would enjoy the artistic company for a change. He had a good feeling about them.

Emrys looked at his apprentice. She did not seem very keen on the idea, they did not go to other people's homes often. The sculptor looked at Lucius a moment. "We'd be honoured to join you at your home, Tribune."

"Great." Lucius shook his hand. "I'll see you then." Emrys thanked him and moved to take his place for the beginning of the feast, disappearing into the mingling, munching crowd. Lucius gazed for another moment at the sculpture and was not surprised when he recognized the lifelike quality of the statues of Mars and Jupiter in the emperor's study in the one before him. *What talent!* he thought.

The first course of the evening was a feast in itself with more than enough for the entire assembly. There were several varieties of olives from all over the empire, especially from Africa, Syrian sausages flavoured with plum and pomegranate, small garden birds in delicate pastry, and spiced chick peas with mussels. These were but a few that Lucius tasted. It was going to be a long evening.

After a while, Lucius decided that he could not relax and enjoy himself until he and Alene had presented themselves before the Imperial family, their hosts. He searched the crowd for his sister and caught sight of her golden head in the midst of a gathering of togas. *What's going on there?* He began to edge his way through the crowd to where they were.

"So, Metella, your tongue is not as sharp inside as it was outside. What's the matter, you too good to speak with us?" Alene looked around vainly for a friendly face, tried to ignore Raxus and his followers as they crowded around her. She felt faint, like crying. But she would not give them the satisfaction. "Tut, tut. All alone are we? Where's your precious brother?"

"Right here!" Lucius' voice cut through the gathered men as he pushed two of them aside to reach his sister. "What's going on here?" Lucius stood close to Alene, stared Raxus in

269

the eyes. They were all shorter than him, skinnier beneath the thickness of their togas.

Raxus looked unperturbed, his thin nose in the air. "Little Lucius Metellus, or should I say, Tribune," he mocked. "To what do we owe the honour, *hero* of Sabratha?"

"Come Lucius," Alene whispered, fearing a scene. "Let's go. He's not worth it." She knew that look in her brother's eyes.

"Wait, sister. Why don't you introduce me to this little clique of peacocks?"

Raxus' friends began to mutter at the insult but none save their spokesman spoke up. "My name's Raxus. Your sister here decided some time ago that I was not good enough for her to marry. She's insulted me and my family."

Lucius rubbed his chin and spoke lowly. "Raxus...Raxus...oh yes! I've heard your family's name." The peacock puffed up proudly, as best as his scrawny body could. "Family of merchants, am I right?"

"You are."

"Very, very wealthy?"

"Indeed. Quite."

Lucius nodded. "No decent breeding. Descendants of country bumpkins and former slaves, is that not also true?"

"How dare you!" Raxus' bony arm creaked out like a whipping branch to slap Lucius in the face but before he knew what had happened his wrist was caught in the tribune's iron grip, his cracking arm bent painfully behind his back. He heard Lucius' voice hot in his ear.

"Listen here, you arrogant bastard. I've faced down Parthian cavalry while on foot. Do you think you and your little bedfellows frighten me in the least?" Raxus shook his head and tried to cover his pain and fear with a smile beneath his sweating head. His friends backed away. Lucius squeezed his wrist harder, almost to breaking. "If you ever," he said slowly, "approach or speak to my sister again, I will personally dismantle your bony corpse piece by pitiful piece. Do you understand?" Raxus nodded. People around them were starting to stare. "Good. Now get away from her." Lucius pushed the squirming Raxus into the crowd and turned to Alene. "Are you all right?" He held her hand.

"I'm fine. He's been doing that for months now."

"I doubt if he'll do it again."

Alene looked up at him, holding back her emotions. "I'm glad you're here."

"Me too." Lucius looked at the line of people waiting to see the emperor and his entourage. "Are you able to go through with this right now?"

"Are you kidding?" Her smile returned. "After that, this is going to be fun. Let's join the line before the main courses are brought out. They both moved forward to wait nervously for their turn to approach the imperial gathering.

Spread out on six couches, eating and drinking casually, were the emperor and his wife, their sons, the empress' kinswomen Julia Maesa and Julia Mamaea, Prefect Plautianus and his daughter, Plautilla, Caracalla's wife. Also present, in heated discussion with the empress, were several other men of repute: the lawyers Aemilius Papinianus, Julius Paulus and Domitius Ulpianus, the rhetoricians Philostratus and Philiscus and two well-known historians, Senator Cassius Dio and a Syrian by the name of Herodian. Also there, seemingly content to watch the magnanimity around him, was an author by the name of Longus.

To Lucius and his social-minded sister, approaching this gathering was a test of both nerves and etiquette. Did they interrupt? Did they wait to be announced? Finally, just as they were starting to feel very ill-at-ease, the emperor's aid approached.

"Caesar, the Tribune Metellus and Lady Metella." Lucius wondered how these people managed to know who was who. He and Alene bowed deeply and slowly, feeling many pairs of eyes on them. Lucius spoke first.

"Hail Caesar, Parthicus Maximus." Caracalla and Geta sniggered slightly. Little did Lucius know the emperor had decided not to use the title outside of the ceremonies; he tried to stay composed. "Many congratulations on your Triumph and a magnificent day, Sire. Our humble thanks for your hospitality."

"We are indeed honoured to be here, Sire," Alene put in. The emperor rose to sit up.

"Most kind, Tribune. You and your sister are welcome." His smile faded to a slight, momentary frown. "But where is the rest of your family?"

Lucius began to sweat again and felt his ears burning. Finally words came. "Sire, my father has taken ill and my mother has remained at home to care for him and our younger brother and sister. They send me in their stead to offer you their warm thanks and congratulations." Plautianus and the emperor exchanged brief looks while the empress spoke on with the academics, although with tilted head, she listened to every word. Lucius hoped his excuse would suffice. The emperor spoke again.

"Quite a shame. At least you and your charming sister were able to come."

"Charming indeed," Caracalla muttered as he stared intensely at Alene, making her shudder. Plautilla jabbed him with her elbow but he dismissed her with a sharp scowl. The emperor turned to his wife.

"My dear? This is the young tribune I told you about, the one who routed out the traitors in Sabratha."

Julia Domna was a woman who held herself extremely well, confident, with a dark beauty about her. She and her sisters were distinctly eastern with dark skin and hair that was short but elaborately styled. She looked at the two suppliants and Lucius realized then that she was the one he had seen in the Forum that morning in the procession going to the Capitoline. A powerful, intelligent woman who made a point of knowing everyone and everything.

"Your deeds in Africa and Numidia have been widely spoken of, Tribune." Not knowing how to respond, Lucius simply bowed. The empress' kinswomen didn't pay him much attention but some of the learned group with the empress were fixed on him more out of curiosity, finally able to put a face to the name. "You are of course acquainted with our distinguished group here?" She gestured to the men on her right.

"Only by their work and reputations my Lady." This was a bit of a lie but Lucius saw no harm in some idle flattery. "Gentlemen, it is indeed an honour." Longus, Dio and Philostratus nodded politely, the others looked unamused. Then the emperor spoke again wishing to move on to the next people in line.

"Well Tribune, you must listen to Longus here recite from his latest work later. Enjoy yourselves. Tribune, Lady Metella…"

"Sire," they said in unison, bowing once again and backing away.

"Lucius, you're getting better at this. Actually, I'm glad you were with me, that way you had to do all the talking. The emperor's son though, made me very uncomfortable."

"I noticed." Lucius' jaw grew taught. "We'll talk about it later. Just keep clear of him if you can."

"Don't worry. There are so many people here, it shouldn't be a problem." They each accepted a cup of wine from a passing slave dressed as a nymph. "So, who have you talked to or met? Anyone interesting?"

"I talked to a few of the troops briefly, no one important. Um, I did however meet the artist who did all the magnificent sculptures around the room."

"Oh wonderful! You've met Emrys. Isn't he an amazing man?"

"Yes, quite. I also met his apprentice, Carissa."

"Yes, yes, she and I have spoken several times."

273

"Alene is there anyone in Rome you don't know?"

"When I meet them I'll let you know."

"You're hilarious. At any rate, I've invited Emrys and Carissa to our home next week for a meal."

"What a good idea! I'll arrange it all, not to worry. Did you tell them when and where we live?"

"Oh, ah, well I forgot that."

"Oh Lucius, I think you're the funny one. No matter, I'll find Carissa and tell her. There she is over there. Mingle. I'll see you later." Alene dashed off, elegantly so, to speak with the young artisan, leaving Lucius on his own once again.

Lucius went back to the centre of the garden to pick more dates from the tree and fill his cup at the fountain of wine. To his amazement there were still people arriving, thus restricting the floor space more and more. He had forgotten how useless he was at mingling with strangers; he felt particularly ridiculous after meeting with the emperor's entourage and thought it was obvious he was in over his head.

"Tribune Metellus." A man came up from his right.

"Oh, Senator Dio, forgive me. I'm afraid with all this noise I can't hear much." What was he doing away from his couch?

"Not to worry. May I speak with you for a moment?" Lucius looked surprised, checked in the direction of the emperor. "They know where I am; making my way around the room, speaking with many of the soldiers here about their experiences. I'm writing a history of the reign of Severus."

"Of course, Senator. Although I'm not sure I'm the best man to talk to." Cassius Dio was one of the most learned historians of the time, having written a history of Rome and a history of the civil wars which he presented to the emperor himself only recently; he admired Severus although his dislike of Caracalla was no secret. He had also written a biography of Arrian as well as a book about the dreams of Septimius Severus. Dio was a man much respected by Rome.

"The main course is being served. Come, let's sit at these couches and we can talk and eat." The smell of food filled the air as they made their way to a group of couches. Lucius' stomach began to growl. Too much wine, not enough food.

Dio was about thirty-nine years of age, of medium height and a little large around the waist. Not fat but not fit like a soldier. A Bythinian Greek, he was the son of Caius Apronianus, a Roman senator and governor of Dalmatia and Cilicia under Aurelius. Dio himself was a young senator under Commodus; the turbulence of the time no doubt added to his strong interests in historical and political developments. Ever the historian, he was very thorough with his questions, jotting notes on a wax tablet with a stylus. And so, over several main courses consisting of ostrich brains, shellfish, boiled chicken with olives, bull's testicles and goat's meat with African grains, Dio plied Lucius with questions about his experiences in Parthia, Africa and Numidia.

"You see, Tribune, you are from one of the oldest families in Rome, and your actions, experiences and views help provide a different perspective on the development of Rome."

"I'm not so sure, Senator. I mean, I've had an average upbringing, as much as any other man in the Equestrian class."

"Yes, but how many families still hold strong Republican views?"

"I believe my father is the only one who holds such views. I do not, I assure you."

"Would it surprise you if I said I know this? That it is a point of contention between the two of you?"

"Of course it would!" *How in Hades does he know all this?* The realization that a man he had never met knew so much about him struck him like a slap across the face.

"Well, do not be. Your father's views have always been well known in the Senate. He is not the only one." Dio sipped more wine and put a piece of roasted peacock in his mouth. "You may not know this but your experiences in Sabratha were widely spoken of in Rome."

"Really?" He was finding that out more and more.

"Oh yes. And since your actions in Numidia, many eyes have been on you. The fact that you're a Metellus in favour of empire, rather than republic, has drawn the critics' attention away from your father."

"Why though? I don't understand. How did all this get out? I don't remember speaking about politics with anyone, I'm a soldier."

"You are a young tribune of an old family, who has shown much potential. People are interested. One piece of advice though: be careful what you tell to whom. Nothing new, but every once in a while I find I have to remind myself of that. For instance, everyone knows of this person staying in your household right now and that he helped you in routing out the traitors in Africa."

"Ashur? But how did-"

"Ah, remember, Rome is a small world inhabited by wolves and cackling hens. Everyone knows everything as I'm sure you are beginning to see by the look on your face."

Lucius realised his mouth and eyes were wide open in shock and promptly took a large gulp of wine to wet his dry throat. He was worried.

"Senator, with all due respect, may I ask that you not mention anything personal or any names I have mentioned."

"Of course, Tribune. I'm a historian not a gossip monger." Dio rose from the couch. "I must speak with some more people but I am grateful for the campaign details you gave me. Very interesting." He turned to leave but returned a moment later. "Before I forget, please give my regards to your father." He raised a dark eyebrow. "That is, when he returns from Etruria."

Lucius' heart sank and he felt ill. How did Dio know his father was in Etruria? If he knew, then others must. A nervous sweat began to trickle down his back as it dawned on him that he and Alene had outright lied to the emperor about the absence of his parents. His appetite gone, he rose to get some more wine.

The evening seemed to lumber and drag slowly, Lucius' mind reeling from what Cassius Dio had told him. Life was indeed simpler for a soldier and so he made it a point to mingle only with soldiers. There was a group of them seated around couches in a corner of the hall.

Most of them were drunk and traded slurred battle stories. There was interest in Lucius' experiences but for the most part each man talked about himself. The soldiers were clearly uncomfortable on such a social occasion and seemed to find a degree of comfort amongst their own kind. Dessert was brought out, paraded around the hall by slaves while lively music was played on flutes and tambourines and scantily clad dancers moved gracefully among the guests, spreading flowers at their feet and feeding them sweets. The air was strongly perfumed.

His appetite back, Lucius left the gruntish gathering to get some food. There were cheese-stuffed figs, honey cakes, pastries and dates filled with nuts and pepper. Slaves also moved around the room carrying fruit-laden orange and pomegranate branches from which guests helped themselves.

There are times in life, unexpected occasions, when one is drawn to a place but is fully unaware of the reasons why. Could it be luck...fate...or some god's pleasure? Despite questions in the mind, protestations, the heart insists otherwise and what might have seemed pointless turns out to be quite the opposite. For Lucius, the evening took such a turn.

He had been leaning against a column of the central peristyle, debating whether he should leave when it happened. From the garden behind him, a cool breeze blew softly, rustling the branches of the huge date palm. The hairs on the back of Lucius' neck stood up, stunning him to awareness. His heart pounded and he felt as though someone was behind him...but he dared not turn to look.

Gentle whispers reached his ear. Not in words but in feelings. All around him the once loud and numbing room went quiet and a feeling of utter serenity came over his entire being as the mass of bodies before him seemed to part like blades of grass in the wind.

The young woman moved smoothly, gracefully among the guests, her long stola gently brushing the multi-coloured mosaics beneath her. She was accompanied by several others as they approached the Imperial hosts. Entranced, not knowing why or what he was feeling, Lucius moved forward so as not to lose sight of her.

"By the Gods..." he said to himself, his heart pounding in his breast like Vulcan's hammer upon the anvil. Never in his life or mind or imagination had he seen so beautiful and perfect a being. Momentarily he thought her a goddess, come down to earth to mingle among mortals. But, something inside told him it was not so. He moved around the room, as she and her companions stood before the emperor, hoping to get a glimpse of her face. Suddenly she turned and Lucius' eyes were met with a blinding beauty.

She appeared to be about one or two years younger than he, tall and lithe with pale olive skin brought out by a stola, blue as the sea, that clung to her body. As she moved, long, shiny deep black curls swung elegantly around her head. Her face shone with an otherworldly light, eyes like green emeralds sparkling and bright. Beneath those eyes, in the midst of her perfectly proportioned features was a smile full of joy that lit Lucius' heart and made him smile in thanks to the Gods above for even this one, fleeting glance.

But sometimes it is within the Gods' capacity to be generous and caring, benevolent to the deserving. As she passed only ten feet in front of him, time slowed to a standstill. He wanted to speak, to reach out, but he could not. Within, his heart cried out. She slowed to a stop, alone now, and turned hesitantly as if something had attracted her attention. Their eyes met and they held each other's gaze tightly. They felt they

278

were dreaming, strayed from reality, but they were not, they had not.

The palms of the date tree rustled once more and all was still. Their mouths were open slightly, each wanting to say something but words did not come, not easily. Lucius breathed deeply, moved closer, his heart still pounding. *Speak Lucius! Speak!*

"I...I'm Lucius. Lucius Metellus." His eyes widened in relief.

"I am Adara Antonina."

They stood there in a state of pleasurable hypnosis, smiling, trying to make sense of the situation, the raging feelings within when...

"Adara! There you are! I've been looking for you all night." Alene came from behind Lucius, not noticing it was him from the back, and ran to embrace the young woman. The room grew loud again in Lucius' ears. The girl smiled warmly, joyful to see Alene, but still looked to Lucius. Alene turned to her confused brother.

"Lucius? What are you – oh. By Venus! You've met?" Alene put her hand over her heart, her eyes flashing excitedly. "Lucius, this is Adara, the one I wanted you to meet!" He blinked, looked at the two women standing next to each other. "Adara, this is Lucius, my brother."

The rest of the evening passed in a swift instant for both Lucius and Adara as they talked and became acquainted. Neither had expected such a connection to ever grace their lives, but it had and now, inwardly, they thanked the Gods for it. As the entire banquet slowed to a halt and listened to the poet Longus' recitations, Lucius and Adara stood outside together, alone on the long balcony facing the Circus, beneath the stars and the moon. Both had experienced a sort of silent recognition, highlighted by the fact that though they had not met before, they were completely at ease and happy in each other's company.

279

She wanted to know all about Lucius, his life, family, beliefs, everything. In turn, he asked her all that came to his mind. She came from Greece, the eldest daughter of a Roman father and a Greek mother. Adara's father, Publius Leander Antoninus, was a Roman magistrate in Athens, formerly a soldier. Her mother was Delphina Antonina. She grew up near the sanctuary of Apollo at Delphi and had become one of the foremost artistic painters in Athens where she later moved. Adara spoke of them with both love and appreciation. She also spoke of her two younger sisters, Hadrea and Lavena. They had all come to Rome for the Triumph.

Lucius found great happiness merely in watching and listening to Adara speak; captivated by the movement of her soft mouth and held by her bright, sympathetic eyes. It was the same for her as he spoke. However, as most things do, the evening came to an end and the guests began to leave, full and content and drunk.

"I have to go now," Adara said reluctantly. "I see my father, mother and sisters looking for me. Lucius looked into the hall from the darkened balcony to see the people she had come in with.

"When will I see you again?" he asked eagerly. She smiled warmly, indecorously held his hand.

"Alene will make sure we meet again. I think she's been planning this ever since we became friends." Adara's laugh was like soft music.

"Well, I'm glad she did."

"Me too." They looked longingly into each other's eyes before she spoke again. "I really must go now. Goodnight, Lucius."

"Goodnight." He watched her join the rest of her family who were speaking with Alene inside. Lucius stared as Adara walked away, turning her head several times to see him once more before she rounded a corner.

Alene walked over to him. "So?" She stared expectantly at her brother. "Was I right?"

"Inspired, Alene. Inspired. I don't know if I can wait to see her again."

"Don't worry. I've already invited all of them to come to the house for the dinner party you've begun planning this evening."

"They're going to come?"

"Yes. All of them. Are you happy?"

"Very!" He hugged her tightly, took her by the hand and led her out into the cool night air to make their way home.

That night Lucius found very little, if any sleep. His mind and heart were racing. He knew that it must be the same for Adara and could feel her calling out to him as she too lay sleepless.

On the way back home, Alene had decided to remind Lucius of her dream in which the woman had saved the dragon. She was certain that the goddess Venus had shown her Adara, that she was meant to introduce them; the fact that they had found each other without her only served to reinforce this. Lucius thought again of the cool breeze and the rustling palm at the banquet. He felt certain the evening, their meeting, was fated, that it was a gift.

As he sat back in bed remembering all this, staring at the lamplight, visions of Adara filled his mind. She had more than just a perfect, natural beauty; every aspect of her, the person she was, had grown to be, her shining spirit, caring nature, strong sense of self, and a keen intellect all made her unlike anyone he had ever met. Each different quality was a coloured tessera in a mosaic, brilliant and perfect. But like a caringly crafted mosaic, when the tesserae are combined, they provide the world with an otherworldly, stunning work of art that lifts the soul and celebrates life. Lucius was filled with a deep admiration and a love that felt true, strong.

He believed, and was grateful that, in Adara, the Gods had truly outdone themselves.

XIX

VENUS ET ROMA

'Venus and Rome'

Like so many things in this world, Love is a mystery only to be guessed at, felt. She is varied and strikes in different ways, at different times; the effects upon the mind, heart or soul cannot be explained or escaped. Like a naked mortal or a lone, shuddering ship swept away in a heaving sea, it is useless to fight the torrent, fruitless. Better still to let oneself be carried on the rushing tide with the possibility of discovering a distant, soft shore on which Love might beach us. That, or to drown in the fighting of it, pale beneath the sparkling foam.

Love takes many guises; from childlike infatuation and admiration to a passionate longing that sets all of one's being on fire so that separation is unimaginable. Time spent with the object of one's affection passes with the speed of a ray of light, time apart flows ever so slowly, an interminable loneliness until an awaited reunion. It may be that Love, the world's mistress, rarely looks upon a mortal but when she does, the warmth of her gaze and the coolness of her breath is worth lifetimes of waiting.

It was with great impatience that Lucius waited the entire day after the banquet before he couldn't bear it any longer. He had to see Adara, hear her, bathe in her presence. Neither food nor wine passed his lips. He wanted water, cool and clear after a trek across the fiery desert. To him, seeing Adara again was like a single, life-giving sip of pure water.

For Adara, her heart had not stopped its continuous fast-paced beating since the night when they met. Such feelings were infinitely new to her, but unmistakable. She tried reading and singing, but to no avail, her concentration wracked by an incessant chorus of longing deep within. Finally she grabbed a piece of parchment and a stylus from her table to jot down a hurried message:

Alene Metella from Adara Antonina,

My dear friend,
It was wonderful to see you again last night, brief though it was. I must speak with you as soon as possible. It cannot wait. I am too excited. Please come to our house and I will explain.

Sincerely, Adara.

She rolled the message up carefully, sealed it and, slightly breathless, she handed it to a slave to run over to the Metellus household.

A knock on the door turned Lucius from where he was staring out of the window in his cubicula. "Come in!" His voice was a thoughtful sigh.

Alene poked her smiling face through the door, then entered. "Lucius? Are you well? You've been locked in here all day."

"Well? Well! Of course not... I mean... of course I am. Oh! I don't know Alene. I'm going mad. I can't eat, I can't sleep, I get dressed to go out, then I get undressed. Ahh! What's going on? I'm so restless!" Alene chuckled, her cheeks rosy with mirth. "What's so funny?" Flustered, Lucius had to sit down. Alene sat next to him on the edge of the bed.

"You're what's funny!" she laughed again.

"Me? Alene stop laughing and tell me!"

"Oh, Lucius. Don't you see?"

"Well, I don't eat or sleep; why should I be able to see as well?"

Alene turned toward him, put her hand on his burning cheek.

"Lucius, you're in love."

"Is that what you call this, this madness?" He rubbed his face manically.

"Of course, what else?" She pulled a small parchment from a fold in her stola "Well, I just might have a cure for you."

"What? Can you speed up time, make Adara appear out of thin air?"

"After a fashion. Here, read this." Lucius took the message and read it. When he had finished, he jumped up and he started pacing about the room.

"Oh, Alene, I knew it! She feels the same!"

"Of course she does, silly."

"You have to arrange for us to meet! Yes, that's it. You... you have to-"

"I've already thought of it Lucius. Listen, I'm going over to her house. I'll suggest we go for a walk in the Forum, to look at silks. You'll be there waiting."

"Perfect. Yes! But you should stay with us, you know, for appearance's sake."

"Yes, yes, don't worry. I know how things work."

"Alene, what do I wear?"

"Oh, Lucius, for Venus' sake! A warrior tribune reduced to an indecisive love-struck boy. I never thought I'd see the day!" She ran excitedly over to a large chest on the floor and pulled out some off-white, knee-length trousers with a thin purple stripe, a matching tunic and threw them on the bed. "Here, wear these with your clean crimson cloak and your nice boots. Simple but refined, no armour."

Lucius nodded his head vigorously. "Good! Good. Now where do I meet you?"

"Umm, on the steps of the Temple of Venus and Rome, so you'll see us coming toward the Forum."

"Perfect." Lucius beamed with happiness. "Well, what are you waiting for? Go! Go!"

Alene remembered herself. "I'm going! I'm going!"

Once she had left the room, Lucius busied himself with getting ready, fumbling about for his clothes, awkwardly lacing his boots and trying to fasten his cloak with a brooch. Once ready, he dashed eagerly out the door for the Forum.

The square in front of the Colosseum was busy as usual with vendors and performers scattered in small pockets. The amphitheatre loomed overhead, its many niches lit by flickering torches. Across the square, next to the entrance of the Via Sacra into the white marble of the Forum Romanum, the Temple of Venus and Rome reflected the waning sun in tones of pink and amber.

On the wide stair leading to the temple doors, Lucius had picked a row without loiterers on which he paced the full width over and over. Now and then, a lone pigeon would wander over, join the nervous tribune for a few paces, tire and fly off to find a vendor who might toss it a few stray crumbs. He knew he had arrived far too early, probably even before Alene had a chance to reach Adara's house. Now, he had to wait and sweat and pace. The temple was bigger than he remembered. Not having been there for some years, he looked up and admired it, the way the light played upon it; very fitting he thought, for the temple of the Goddess of Love. Quite a contrast also, with the roars of fans baying for blood in the Colosseum as the afternoon's gladiatorial combats reached their climax.

Lucius' heart didn't care for that and the harsh screams pushed him farther up the stairs to the goddess' sanctuary. It seemed right that he should be standing there, in wait for the one who had him so hopelessly enrapt. No small thanks, he believed, to Venus herself. Had the Goddess come to involve herself directly in his life? Had she really revealed all to Alene in her dream? He was happy to be caught up in this particular mystery.

"No, no sir. Trust me now. Chickens are not suitable sacrifices for the Goddess of Love. Nor piglets! What you want are some flowers, perfume, oil, or even a small ruby. Yes, that would definitely help in securing the young lady's affections."

That voice. Lucius recognised it from once before. But where? Who?

"Ah! The ruby!" The voice came from the top of the steps. "An excellent choice! The Goddess will be most pleased by your offering."

"Ha!" Lucius remembered. "Numonius! That's who it is!" he pushed his way to the top of the steps and found the vendor as he had at the Temple of Apollo, his tables set up, selling offerings to love-sick pilgrims.

"Hail, Numonius!" Lucius came up to him, happy to see a friendly face.

"Tribune!" He came around the table this time to greet Lucius, leaving several customers waiting. Lucius extended his hand in greeting. "Good evening to you. The Gods bless you now and always."

"Oh they do Numonius, they do. But what are you doing here? I thought you were usually up on the Palatine."

"Well, Tribune, it seems that lately citizens' embassies to Apollo are few and far between. You and your family friend, Ashur, are his most loyal suppliants these days." Lucius was surprised to hear that Ashur had mingled with the locals but said nothing. Numonius went on. "It seems that every citizen in Rome wishes to make offerings to the Goddess of Love. Always the same this time of year. With the approach of Spring, love seems to permeate the very air we breathe. Every young hopeful wants help ensnaring the heart they desire most." Numonius paused and smiled. "Actually, Tribune, by the red glow on your cheeks and the beading sweat on your forehead I would say you too have been touched by the mysterious mistress."

Lucius laughed. "And you'd be absolutely correct! Although I'm here to offer my thanks to Lady Venus, not ask for her help. She has already helped me without my asking." Numonius' eyes widened.

"Well, that is special. I have just the thing here. My wife made it yesterday evening." Numonius scanned the tables and picked up a delicate wreath of daisies and bluebells woven together with golden thread.

"I'll take it!" Without hesitation Lucius reached for his purse, gave Numonius more than the wreath was worth and took the delicate circlet with both hands.

"May the Goddess continue to bless you, Tribune!" Numonius yelled as Lucius made his way into the temple, through the great bronze door.

Once inside, Lucius moved quietly beneath the lofty, timber roof of the temple, not wanting the sound of his footsteps to disturb the serenity of the goddess' domain. Small fires burned on either side of the main isle before small images of Venus and sweet incense smouldered like beacon fires in bright, bronze tripods on either side of the central altar. The gentle sighs of love-struck pilgrims resonated in a beautifully painful chorus; men and women prayed nervously in private corners, some on their knees, others standing with their arms spread wide to expose the heart that had been struck through. Lucius approached the cella to place his offering on the altar, adding it to the myriad other flowers whose dazzling colours radiated upward to the goddess where she stood. He looked up to take in her beauty and was forced to his knees like so many others, another petal at her feet.

Love watched him from her marble likeness, her gown clinging, drenched with the sea from which she had been born. Her left breast was revealed and she held out her right hand, the delicate fingers reaching to touch the crowns of her admirers. Above her right shoulder, Cupido fluttered, poised with his bow. Lucius could almost see his arrows being loosed on the unsuspecting pilgrims gathered in the temple's haze.

Lucius wondered what to say, but when he looked up from his knees to speak, words came not easily. There was only the beating of his heart, the overflowing well within, the cover of which had swung open. *Lady Venus,* he prayed. *I do not know what to say except, thank you. Thank you for this gift. I offer you my feelings and my hopes. I never want it to end. Let her be mine if she wishes it.* He bowed his head for several moments, then felt it, that cool breeze from the night before, a loving caress that sent shivers through his body. He stood up again to leave. "Thank you," he whispered.

By the time he exited the temple, Numonius had packed up for the day and the people that had been milling on the steps had cleared. He wondered briefly whether he had missed Alene and Adara but quickly dismissed the thought. He felt otherwise and so, waited.

They appeared up the road soon after and he felt a rush of excitement heat his face. He started to run but stopped, not wanting to appear childlike. He turned to walk away, pretend not to notice, but didn't want to appear rude. Before Lucius could decide how to present himself, his sister and Adara had already reached the bottom of the steps. He smiled and she smiled back. Little did he know, Adara was just as happy and nervous.

Lucius made his way down the steps, trying not to trip, as his eyes took in her beauty. She wore a simple long white stola bordered with blue and gold waves. A long blue silk cloak draped from her shoulders and her smooth black locks were tied up loosely with a blue and gold thread.

Alene spoke first as they approached. "Have you been waiting long?"

Lucius spoke, still holding Adara's gaze. "Oh, about an hour or so." He took Adara's hand, held it gently. His touch made her heart race as she ventured to speak.

"I'm sorry you had to wait so long...Lucius..." She found she liked saying his name. "My mother was talking as usual. She likes Alene very much".

"It wasn't long to wait. Not at all. Actually, I would wait forever."

Alene cocked her head slightly, surprised by her, supposedly shy, brother's boldness. "Well," she said. "Let's walk. I want to look at some shops in the Forum before they pack up for the day." She walked on, leaving the two to follow her at their own pace.

I can't believe this is happening, Lucius thought.

The Via Sacra, the Forum, rarely appeared so perfect, bathed as it was in the angling rays of the evening sun. The columns of the buildings cast long shadows and sleepy birds cooed and sang softly from the trees in the gardens atop the Palatine. The air seemed scented, sweet. It was as a dream for both Lucius and Adara, a familiar and comforting dream. For some time they walked in silence, words unable to justify their feelings. There was an odd relief to the anguish each had had, merely by being in the other's presence. They were oblivious to all others around them, passing entities, blurry apparitions.

As they passed the arch of Titus, Lucius' right hand ventured out from beneath his cloak, his fingers stretching desperately for a single touch of her own hand which hung gracefully at the end of her smooth slender arm.

To Hades with convention! thought Adara. Slowly, she too reached out and clasped Lucius' hand tightly, her eyes closing momentarily with the joy it caused within her. She felt like crying, she was so happy, so inexplicably, uncontrollably swept away. She hoped that he would give voice to her thoughts, the happy, shocking hope that had come upon her the night before as she lay in bed. *I've never felt so strongly about anything or anyone before*, she told herself. *It just feels right.* She tilted her head to look sidelong at the man next to her.

289

He's so beautiful and kind. Just then, Lucius smiled and turned his head to look at her.

"Adara," he began, voice a soft whisper. He was neither ashamed, nor cautious or hesitant. His voice was gentle.

"Yes, Lucius." She felt his hand hold hers tightly, full of caring.

"I know that we've only just met and that..." He stopped walking and turned to face her. They were alone. "...I know that things work differently than this but something inside me tells me that, well, there's no sense in waiting when things just feel so...right." He paused, felt his words were jumbled and that perhaps he was being silly. Then he looked into her eyes, that far away place beyond the lids where only a certain person was allowed to see. She looked back, not an inkling of doubt or disappointment. He continued, had to. "I'm a soldier and I know that makes things uncertain but...I guess what I'm trying to say is that...I don't want to be away from you."

He's going to say it, Adara thought excitedly. *Please say it.* She felt her eyes close and open again, slowly. Time seemed to slow itself.

"I don't want tomorrow to come, or the day after that, or any other day when the time to say 'Goodbye' arrives. I never want to say such a word to you. I never want to let go, Adara." Lucius turned to look down at their clasped hands, half covered by their mingling cloaks. "Ever since the first moment I saw you, found out who you are as we talked, I haven't been able to stop thinking about you."

"Nor I, Lucius," she said, gazing into his dark eyes.

From a silk stall just up the road, Alene, pretending to browse, watched them from the corner of her eye and thought she had never seen her brother standing so tall, strong and proud, unencumbered by the duties of his rank, his class or his name.

"Will you have me, Adara? Will you stay with me, go through this life with me?" In that moment before she answered, Lucius had expected to feel anxious, afraid she would decline but, her eyes, the way they spoke for her, the tilt of her head, it all said otherwise and he was calm.

"I…" she began, unsure of how to express her thoughts and feelings. "Life, would be incomplete if I were not yours and you mine." She knew that sounded strange, knew that he understood. "I want to spend every waking moment of this life with you, Lucius," she leaned closer to him, looked up, "if you will have me. Never any goodbyes." He brought her hand to his lips. They both felt something inexplicable in that moment, as though the Gods had opened the Elysian doors for them alone, a place for them to wander as they pleased, free of cares or worries, an untouched garden.

They did not say anything else as they turned to walk again toward Alene where she had been watching. "Hmm," Alene sighed.

"Have you made a decision? I'm about to close up for the day," the vendor said as he was folding up a beautiful length of red silk.

"Oh, sorry." Alene hesitated. "Nothing today." She had not really been looking. "Will you be here again tomorrow?" she asked out of politeness.

"Of course, lady. I'm here most days."

"Fine then. I'll come back another time." The merchant finished packing up his stall and Alene turned to see several groups of citizens watching Lucius and Adara walk toward her. She recognized a few faces, all gossips. There would be talk of this in Rome, slanders on the lips of many a nosy matron, but what of it! Lucius Metellus was in love with Adara Antonina. Alene also realized as she watched them walking together, that in the short year she had known Adara, she had never seen her so happy, glowing, possessing a strength of which even she was envious.

The Gods were rejoicing in their work.

XX

VERTICORDIA

'The Changer of Hearts'

At first, Antonia was taken aback when Alene informed her of the small banquet she had planned for the evening. Her daughter had decided not to tell her until the day so as not to cause undue worrying, or give her a chance to decide against it.

After a short burst of ranting, and an hour of feeling too lonely for her husband, Antonia decided it might indeed be a good idea after she heard who was coming. Alene decided to secure her still unsure mother's mind by telling her, secretly, that the young lady Antonina and Lucius had fallen in love and that she wouldn't be surprised if Lucius were to ask for her hand.

"He's that taken with her?" Antonia had asked her daughter.

"Yes. I think he is. I know he is." Alene seemed quite certain.

"And so quickly?"

"What does it matter, mother? If they are both utterly sure of their feelings time itself is irrelevant."

Antonia went and sat down in the garden to look up at the sky, feel the sun on her face. "Thank you, Apollo," was all she said. Her own marriage had been decided and she had been fortunate enough to be happy most of the time. She thought to herself that if her husband was not going to be there to support his son, then she would definitely make sure that her son did not need for anything. Of course she had met Adara before when Alene had brought her home but things were different now, new eyes were required to imagine her married to her eldest son. If the young woman was worthy, she would give her blessing.

She went immediately to the sitting room to compose a letter to Quintus, informing him of the small banquet and of the wonderful news concerning Lucius. Quintus would not be able to complain that he was not informed beforehand, even though it was extremely short notice. *What does it matter? He doesn't care anyway,* she told herself.

She put the letter into the hands of the house steward to give to a mounted courier for delivery and busied herself with organizing the household for the evening. Sure, Alene said she would take care of everything, but she was the mistress of the house and as such she would see that their important guests were well received.

If there had ever been a day of utter chaos in the Metellus household, this was it! Antonia had the slaves running to and from the Forum collecting whatever foodstuffs or other goods she could think of. The problem was that she never thought of everything at once; a little bread here, some dates there, a spice, some fish, the list went on. Alene was pulling her hair out, all her previous plans totally forgotten, since her mother decided she wanted to "help". However, summoning all the patience she could, Alene told herself it was better that her mother be busy with some chore (or fifty) rather than sulking in some room by herself.

In the triclinium, Lucius and one of the slaves were trying to decide how to arrange the couches for twelve people. It was not an extremely large room so they had to be economical with the space while still allowing the guests to be comfortable while they ate.

"It's going to be tight, Master. I'm not sure everyone will fit." The slave rubbed his chin in worry as he gazed about the room, trying to figure out how they would be able to fit twelve people, two per couch, while still allowing himself and the other slaves enough room to serve without disruption.

Lucius scratched his head. "It has to work, Cato. Tonight must be perfect!" He looked around the room, Cato watching. "When you were out in the Forum earlier, Cato, how was the weather?"

Slightly confused, the servant answered. "Well, uh, actually quite fair for this time of year, Master. No breeze and not a dark cloud in the sky."

"Do you think it will remain that way?"

"Most definitely Master. At least for a couple more days."

Lucius clapped his hands. "Very well! We'll remove the two braziers and put them outside the door. That will allow the two extra couches. Will you have enough room to move in and out easily?"

Cato looked around, frowning in thought. "Yes, should do, Master. We could even leave one brazier inside the room until the guests arrive, to keep it warm."

"Good idea!"

"Thank you, Master. Don't worry, I'll see that everything goes without a flaw."

The rest of the slaves hurried about the house dusting the busts of ancestors and the statues of gods, polishing the marble floors and tidying the garden of dead leaves and foliage after the winter.

In the kitchen, Antonia and Alene were busy with the two cooks, Apulius and Pollux, arranging the menu for the evening. "Right, now. I want a constant supply of stuffed dates, spiced olives, grapes and breads on the central table. Keep them replenished at all times. Also, bring out the wine from the estate. Last year's batch, that was a good one." Antonia paced around looking at all the ingredients. It had been some time since she had entertained; never such important guests either. Future family? The thought gave her joy but also worried her in a way. What were they like? What will they think of Quintus' absence? She pressed on with her plans. "Apulius, Pollux, the usual order of courses: salads, seafoods and small fowl first, then the boiled and roasted meats and finally the cheeses, sweetmeats, cakes and fruit. Do you think you can handle this?"

"Yes, Mistress." they said in unison, trying not to look annoyed at the fact that she was panicked and stating the obvious.

When Antonia and Alene left the room, Pollux turned to Apulius. "Does she think we've never done this before? As if we're amateur cooks!"

"Shh! Keep your voice down, Pollux. Since the master's been away, mistress Metella hasn't been herself. To be honest, I prefer it now that he's gone." He waived a leek in Pollux's face. "At any rate this is an important evening! Ambrosia told me that Master Lucius' possible future wife is coming with her family."

"Really? Well then, we had better prove our worth and give them a feast to remember."

"Absolutely! The young master deserves the best and we'll make sure he gets it." Apulius slammed the leek down onto a cutting block. "Now let's get to work. Go into the store room and get the chickens so you can start on the livers."

Antonia appeared at the door of the triclinium, eyeing the activity within. "How is everything in here? Lucius? Will the couches fit?"

"Yes, mother. They should be fine. Cato and I have worked it out."

"Good, good." She looked her son up and down, her brow creased ever so slightly. "Hmm. Lucius, Cato can handle the rest, why don't you go to the baths and tidy yourself up? You look a bit, well, rough."

"You look nervous too," Alene added, a slight giggle breaking loose. "I wonder why?"

"I suppose I should. I want to be perfect for her... I mean for tonight!"

"Oh, Lucius, Alene told me all about it. We'll make sure all goes well, trust me." Antonia took her son's hand. "Now go and leave everything to us."

Lucius felt much better after his visit to the baths for a little exercise, a good cleansing, massage and shave. He realized that he had grown a bit loose of late, his muscles lax. After all, in Numidia or on campaign he and the cohort were always engaged in their manoeuvres and exercises on the parade ground, honing their skills for the possibility of battle. In Rome, people tended to sit around a lot and eat and talk about the cushy lives they lived. A young tribune needed to maintain a level of fitness second to none; Lucius wanted to be perfect for the woman he had fallen in love with, a woman who was coming to dinner that night.

Suddenly reflective on his walk home, he thought back on the last few months, amazed and overwhelmed by the changes in his life, the contrasting worlds and experiences he had visited. A part of him missed the desert, its beauty and magic; and yet he had found both beauty and magic right there in Rome. *I must be dreaming all of this?* he thought. But he wasn't, it was all real and that night he would likely make one of the most important decisions of his life.

He knew how marriages worked, how they were supposed to. *What is her family like? Should I ask her father about a dowry? What if I displease them?* Lucius wasn't rich. Despite being of an old, distinguished family, even a more distant branch of the tree, he was not moneyed like a "New Man" or an African merchant. Lucius Metellus Anguis was a soldier. *Hopefully,* he thought, *that will be enough.* All he knew was that he wanted nothing more than to marry Adara, dowry or no dowry; it did not matter and he knew she must feel the same, that she must be as sure as he.

In the house of Publius Leander Antoninus, husband and wife chuckled lightly to themselves at the sight of their usually quietly-controlled daughter as she ran about the house, changing outfits five times, blush-faced all the while.

In the garden, Publius gently caressed his wife's artistic hand, both of them aware of the immense importance of the night. In a way, they held the happiness of their eldest in the palms of their hands, fragile and hopeful like a single blossom of jasmine that is ready to bloom and grow on its own.

Adara had told them everything, her hopes and feelings concerning this young tribune. They were very unusual as far as Roman families were concerned. Some said it was due to the lax and overly-passionate Greek influence of Delphina. Others believed that the heat in that country drove even the most respectable citizens to embarrassing extremes. Publius Leander Antoninus knew it was neither. He knew that it was due to the respect each family member had for the other, the pride he had in his three intelligent daughters, in his wife who had shown him how to feel and love and honour. Life was a waste if all good qualities were swept aside in favour of conformity and conservatism. They didn't always see eye to eye but he wouldn't have it any other way.

Delphina leaned against her husband, resting her head in the crook of his neck as he put his arm about her. "Maybe I should see if Adara needs my help?"

"She's fine, dear. Lavena and Hadrea are helping her. A little sisterly fun might ease everybody's nerves." Delphina breathed the evening air, exhaling loudly.

"Publius, do you think it will go well tonight? Look at her, she's so excited, permanently breathless. It means so much to her but…"

"But things have moved so quickly?"

"You always could read my thoughts."

"Only yours, my dear. I'm not fully in the dark. I spotted the young man she was speaking to at the banquet and he behaved very well. From what people have been saying he's a great asset to Rome, has proven himself. I know that these are merely whispers and gossip but our daughter sees something wonderful in him and so…"

"And so my husband, we must trust to her judgement and see for ourselves this evening."

"Now who's reading my thoughts?" He laughed. "I know we can't ignore the details of marriage, dowry, income, so on and so forth. Yes, we come from an ancient family but we are of distant relation, sharing the name, not the funds. We need to bear in mind that we have three daughters who will get married, who will require some kind of dowry. If Quintus Metellus wishes to speak of these matters I'm prepared. They're an even older family and no doubt wealthy. He would expect a large dowry." Delphina was suddenly worried.

"What are you saying Publius?"

"I'm saying, my love, that this is Rome, not Athens, and that I'll do all I can to ensure our daughter is happy and well taken care of. Come now, let's get ready."

With a still-lingering shade of pink and orange far to the west, darkness came over Rome, the stars and moon ever increasing in brightness. The city was alive, for Romans loved to shed the toils of work, their daylight images, and head out into the night to visit friends, feast and carouse in one form or another. Now that Spring had arrived, this nightly ritual became possible once more.

This night was made even more special for it was the first day of Aprilis, and the beginning of the festival of Veneralia. This festival was a favourite among Romans because it was held in honour of the Goddess, Venus Verticordia, 'The Changer of Hearts'.

On this special evening, the house of the Metelli was bedecked in a beauty so simple it seemed a world of its own. Outside the front door, two torches were lit and a slave dressed and groomed in a white tunic, a crown of flowers on his head, stood calmly at attention, ready to receive the guests. Inside the atrium, two more slaves waited silently in a corner to accept the cloaks. In the small mosaic pool in the floor, tiny oil lamps in the shape of lotus flowers floated sleepily. Along the corridors of the peristyle hung more oil lamps every few feet, offering a warm glow that was reflected on the marble floors. The faces of the Metellus ancestors were serene, at peace. In the garden, light wisps of smoke from sweet incense fluttered about to the gentle trickling of the fountain. The flowerbeds and foliage had been raked, pruned and refreshed with new blossoms. Just off the garden, the triclinium was lit by more lamps and heated to comfortable perfection by the brazier in the doorway.

As he strolled the edges of the peristyle, Ashur hummed a gentle, solemn tune from some distant land; he had adopted this quiet, reflective habit of late. It helped him to think.

"From the East you come, my healing sun, Phoenix and Griffin and Dragon become..." he sang.

"That's beautiful, Ashur. Lucius never told me you sang." Alene came out of her room into the corridor.

"I don't believe he's heard me sing that tune before," Ashur answered.

"Is it from your native land?"

"No, no...I suppose I just picked it up somewhere along the road over the years. It is soothing, no?"

"Yes, very." Alene breathed deeply of the air.

"Is our tribune about ready? He was quite nervous earlier."

"I think he's fine now. I just finished helping him with the folds of his toga."

"Ah yes, the Roman man's best attire. He will look magnificent for his bride-to-be."

"So Lucius has told you about Adara?" Alene had not seen much of Ashur in the past few days and so was unsure of what he knew.

"No," he smiled, also a new habit he had adopted since being among them. "Something inside tells me it is going to be a momentous evening."

"Let's hope so! How do I look?" Lucius surprised them both as he came into the garden where they had sat themselves. The folds of his narrow-stripped toga hung perfectly, held up with his left hand, his dark hair had been trimmed and his face was smooth, highlighting his strong jaw.

"Perfect, Lucius! Absolutely wonderful." Lucius noticed Alene as well in her green silk stola with gold highlights that matched her smooth hair.

"You're a vision, sister." He turned to Ashur. "And you my friend, are the image of an Egyptian Pharaoh. I don't believe I've ever seen you so resplendent." The lone warrior bowed graciously.

"For your special night, Lucius Anguis." Ashur had shed his usual desert garb for a long tunic in blue and silver, belted at the waist and complemented by a Greek-style cloak fastened at the shoulders with silver brooches of desert design. He had also trimmed his usually long beard to a shorter style, the sharp lines revealing his ageless skin.

"Well, everyone? What are we standing around for? Did you not hear the door?" Antonia entered, graceful.

"The door?" Lucius said.

"Yes, my son. Let us greet our guests." They all began to make their way to the atrium. With Clarinda tucked in bed for the night, they were ready for the evening.

Lucius' palms were sweating profusely, and he tried to dry them on a hidden part of his toga.

"Emrys. Carissa. It's good to see you both again. Welcome." Lucius had decided, since for the moment he was the man of the house, that he should greet them first. The slaves took their cloaks and Lucius extended his hand to Emrys who, he noticed, had a very powerful grip. "Please come in..." He turned to the apprentice. "Lady Carissa, welcome." The young woman bowed politely.

Alene noticed they seemed slightly uncomfortable. "Come my friends, let me introduce you. This is my mother, Antonia Metella."

"Thank you for having us into your home, Lady Metella. It is indeed an honour." Emrys bowed, his manners surprisingly good for an artisan, Antonia thought.

"The honour is mine. My children have raved about both of you, your work."

"And this is our friend, Ashur Mehrdad." The two artists looked at Ashur, Emrys smiling, Carissa nodding her head bashfully. Emrys extended a hand.

"*Warlike gift of the Gods*, I am pleased to meet you." Ashur was taken aback.

"Ah. I see you speak the ancient language."

"Only a little which I picked up in the east, on my travels." Emrys remembered the small bundle he had under his left arm. "Oh yes. This is for you, Lady Metella. A small token of our appreciation." Antonia accepted the bundle which was heavy, about a foot long and wrapped in soft linen decorated with small flowers. She unwrapped it carefully.

"By the sweet goddess, she's exquisite! I don't know what to say."

"A small sculpture of Venus that Carissa and I have been working on. We have tried a new technique of polishing marble. Does it please your eye?" No one answered immediately for they were all staring in admiration at the statue of the Goddess of Love, her hair down, body half covered. Her eyes portrayed a calm happiness with the world and she seemed to smile at some lovely thought.

"She's stunning, Emrys, Carissa. Truly a wonder, just like your other sculptures," Lucius said to break the quiet.

"Thank you, both." Antonia smiled and called for one of the slaves. "Cato, would you place this beautiful statue in the centre of the table?"

"Yes mistress, at once." He took the gift very carefully, cradling it as he went slowly to the triclinium.

"As it is Veneralia today, we shall dine in honour of Lady Venus so we can all admire her." Antonia spoke to everyone, suddenly very lively. "Come, let us move to the garden for some wine." Everyone followed, Emrys and Carissa admiring the frescoes and busts along the way as Alene and Antonia spoke. Lucius and Ashur came behind.

"Are you well, Ashur? You look a bit perplexed."

"I don't know why but I suddenly feel a little uncomfortable, bare."

"Maybe you're nervous too? Not to worry, I'll make sure everyone is included in the conversation."

"It's not that, Lucius. Oh never mind. This is going to be a splendid evening." Then the slaves opened the door once more.

"You go ahead to the garden, Ashur, I'll see who that is." Lucius moved quickly, but carefully so as not to set the folds of his toga in disarray. He always felt he had to walk more slowly when he wore it. When he came to the atrium, heart pounding, there was a single, tall man standing there.

Longus was middle-aged with loosely curled hair of reddish-brown; there was a slight twinkle in his eye and a friendly smile on his face. Lucius immediately recognized him from the banquet and stepped forward to greet him.

"Welcome, Gaius Longus." The man turned to meet Lucius.

"Tribune Metellus, good evening. I trust you are well?"

"Yes, very much so. I'm pleased you could come."

"I could not think of a better way to celebrate Veneralia than among good and beautiful people."

The poet at work. Wonderful! Lucius thought. *I hope that the Antoninii enjoy artists.*

"And here comes the Lady Venus herself." Longus turned to Alene who came down the corridor to greet him. He kissed her hand.

"Oh Longus, ever the charming flatterer. Welcome."

"I'm sorry I'm late my dear but the Lady Claudia wanted to hear some love poems on this day of days."

"I understand," she said. She knew that once the Lady Claudia had you seated in her home it was no easy task to escape.

Lucius was about to excuse himself to the garden when the door opened once again. This time the guests he had been so eager, so nervous to see, had arrived. Alene stepped forward at the same time as Lucius but stopped short. He had to be the one to greet them. Antonia came walking in just then as well, greeted Longus warmly and came to stand with her children.

Delphina stepped forward first, followed by Publius. Lucius wondered what to say. What could he say? All he would do was stand tall and welcome his guests. He took a deep breath.

"Publius Leander Antoninus and Lady Delphina Antonina, welcome to our home." Lucius smiled as naturally as he could manage, took Delphina's hand first, and bowed graciously before extending a friendly hand to Publius. "I am very pleased to meet you." He gripped tightly. Publius could tell the young man was nervous and so he tried to lighten things.

"Tribune Metellus, we are honoured to finally meet you in person. Our daughter has spoken very highly of you." He smiled warmly as did Lucius. He had a good feeling about both of Adara's parents. They seemed unpretentious and natural.

Delphina approached Alene and Antonia. "It is good to see you again, my dear." She took Alene's hands, then turned to Antonia. "And I am most pleased to finally meet you, Lady Metella." Antonia was truly softened by such a warm, un-Roman greeting.

"I too am pleased to meet you, Lady Antonina. Welcome to our home." Antonia turned to Publius who came toward her.

"Thank you indeed for your kind invitation." He took her hand and bowed. "Is the senator not within?" At this, Lucius and Alene stopped, but Antonia remained composed and uttered the reply she had practised a hundred times.

"No. I'm afraid my husband Quintus had to go to our estate in Etruria with our younger son to see to some things. He apologizes for his absence."

Publius, though surprised, replied comfortably. "No need to apologize, Lady Metella. I'm sure the Senator has many duties that keep him away. We shall meet him another time." Then, from behind Publius, came two younger women of about eighteen and sixteen. "Ah may I introduce our two younger daughters, Hadrea and Lavena."

What a beautiful family they are! thought Antonia.

Hadrea and Lavena came forward shyly. Hadrea had dark hair and wore a long red stola and Lavena had long blond curls that cascaded onto the shoulders of her deep blue stola. She obviously took after her father where Hadrea had her mother's dark complexion and stunning beauty.

"Ladies, I am pleased to meet you both finally." Lucius smiled to each of them. Their eyes sparkled as they studied their older sister's suitor up and down. Then from behind them came Adara, having given her cloak to the door slave. If Antonia had been struck by the beauty of the mother and two girls, she was absolutely overwhelmed by the magnificence of the young woman before her.

She made her way to greet Antonia.

Lucius thought she was radiant like a goddess in her elegant, white, gap-sleeved tunic with gold fastenings in the shape of delicate knots along the arms. She had a golden ribbon carefully wrapped around her, just below the breasts. Adara reached out for Antonia's hands, full of sincerity.

"Lady Metella, I am so happy to meet you. Thank you for having us."

Antonia was speechless. *Why do I feel like crying? I...I'm so happy,* she thought. Everyone's eyes were on her, expectant. "I too am very happy my dear. Come. Welcome to our home." Antonia bid everyone follow her as she led Adara and Delphina to the garden, followed by Alene and the two girls and Lucius and Publius.

As the two men walked, Publius spoke first. "So Tribune, how does it feel to be back in Rome?"

"To be honest sir, Rome has never seemed more beautiful to me."

"I believe I understand." As they passed the wall of the Metellus ancestors, Publius was struck by the reality in which he found himself. *Truly this is a family of greatness, of great men. Is he such a man?* He thought of this as they strolled, he in a pure white toga, the other in the toga of an equestrian.

When they arrived in the garden, slaves served honeyed wine to the guests amid the buzz of introductions. Nobody was excluded and everyone mingled happily. Delphina was thrilled to be among other artists and quickly found her place with Emrys, Carissa and Longus. Whilst Publius complimented Antonia on the beauty of the house, Alene, Hadrea, Lavena and Ashur spoke, the latter fielding questions about his travels. Lucius and Adara stood by and watched. Each had admitted to being nervous before.

"Are you still nervous, Lucius?" Her green eyes looked into his.

"Not anymore."

It had not been easy to arrange seating in the triclinium. Six couches with two guests each and not one, unimportant person. Antonia had always had a sense of the traditional when it came to dining and entertaining. The most honoured guests had to be seated on the central couches of the "U" shaped formation, closest to the hosts. That was certain; but conversation had to flow smoothly and interestingly without causing discomfort to anyone.

So, at the two head couches from left to right were Delphina and Publius, Lucius and Antonia. On the right of the room were Adara and Alene, Lavena and Hadrea. On the two left hand couches were Longus and Emrys, Carissa and Ashur who had insisted on an outside position near the door so as to allow everyone else to speak freely. This had seemed the best solution.

Once everyone had been seated and reclined, they were each given wine in blue glass goblets. The first courses were brought in, filling the room with a variety of wonderful smells. Lucius had wanted to sit next to Adara but he thought it would be more proper if he spoke with Publius and gave Antonia the chance to get to know Adara. He sat up to toast before the meal commenced. Everyone looked up.

"Before we begin, I would like to express my happiness and gratitude to you all for gracing our home with your presence." *Look around Lucius. Look at everyone!* he thought. Then he motioned to the image of the Goddess on the table, surrounded by flower petals and shimmering in the lamplight. "Let us drink to Venus Verticordia." He tipped some wine onto the floor for the Goddess before drinking. Everyone followed suit. "And to Apollo, our guardian. May they inspire and protect us all." Lucius sat back down and all were served.

Well spoken, respectful to the Gods and sincere. I have a good feeling about this young man, Publius thought.

Conversation flowed as Antonia intended and so she relaxed and enjoyed herself, conversing with new people around her. She even found herself laughing and as the meal progressed, thoughts of Quintus drifted away, releasing her for a short while.

For Lucius, it was hard at first to begin conversation; there was just too much going on with all the new guests, the food and of course Adara not five feet away, seemingly unreachable. He decided to ask Publius about life in Athens for a Roman, the crossing to Italy and whether he missed Rome at all. Publius answered willingly, relaxed.

"Well, I tell you, Tribune,"

"Please, call me 'Lucius'."

"Lucius," he continued, "Athens is unlike anywhere on this earth, indeed Greece itself is a wonder. When I was stationed there for the first time I didn't know what to expect, whether I would like it at all. But I soon fell in love with it." He took his wife's hand. Everyone else stopped to listen, Longus was itching to agree. "The weather, the culture, the ancient landscape, everything. I tell you, Emperor Hadrian knew what it was all about. His work in Athens, his favourite city, beautified it even more. The library is surpassed only by the one in Alexandria before that burned in Caesar's day. Then I met my own Greek goddess and I was forever bewitched, entangled in a soothing web of mystery, love and beauty. True, I'm a Roman and proud of it, but Greece is my home." The room was silent. To herself, Antonia thought it good her husband was not there; he would have been appalled at such a blatant expression of emotions – and from an Antoninus! Longus could no longer hold his breath especially after such poetry.

"I must say this truly is a momentous and inspiring gathering! We have love, beauty, art, warriors and praise of the most perfect place on earth. I shall be writing all night!" Everyone laughed. "And to dine with this perfect image of the Goddess before us. Truly Emrys and Carissa, you have outdone yourselves. She would inspire the lowliest poet to greatness."

"Very kind indeed," Emrys replied, "coming from an artist such as yourself."

The conversation shifted then, small pockets of discussion here and there. Lucius continued to speak with Publius and Longus about Greece, Lesbos and his brief time there while on campaign. Publius proved to be surprisingly easy going, yet strong in his views of the world. In a way Lucius found himself admiring qualities in Publius that he had found frustrating in his own father. From across the room, Delphina watched Lucius intently but not obviously; in her mind she tried to picture her daughter's life with the young man before her. The painting that developed in her mind was in every way perfect and she could see absolute happiness in her daughter's eyes and heart. How far the picture extended in time was not obvious and though this prospect was frightening, she knew that this was the man for Adara. Yes he was a soldier, not immune to certain dangers in his life but there were worse professions and besides, he would always be able to protect Adara, keep her safe.

Alene, Hadrea and Lavena talked about the latest fashions in Athens and Rome, the emergence of African styles and the newest colours. Hadrea spoke matter-of-factly while Lavena's eyes danced and smiled at every comment Alene made. Adara had told her that the two girls, especially Lavena, had come to look up to their sister's friend. Of course, Alene fully enjoyed their attention.

Adara and Antonia spoke freely, openly, their conversation uninterrupted by the serving of the main courses. Adara endeavoured to learn more about and understand this model Roman woman; she also wanted to help her free herself of the sadness she sensed in her, speak to her woman to woman. It seemed to work and as each posed questions, as each replied, they grew closer and more comfortable. A bond began to form between the two of them that evening.

The only awkwardness in the room came from the couch where Ashur and Carissa both sat upright, eating slowly and steadily without uttering a word. Carissa's head was bowed the entire time, her discomfort evident. She hadn't been used to such gatherings, despite the fame of her teacher's work, the many invitations he received. She usually stayed back to work in whatever workshop they were renting at the time; she had come now because of some sense of security and warmth she had felt from both Alene and Lucius. The source of her discomfort now however, was due to the presence of the dark foreigner next to her. For Ashur, it was no different. He hid his uneasiness more skilfully, not wanting to be rude, but silence can sometimes betray much more, despite a casual gaze and a steady drinking hand. Out of the corner of his eye Ashur noticed Carissa looking intently upon the wall painting across from them: the otherworldly scene, the animals, the dragon upon which her eyes rested as if the beast held some meaning for her. He decided to speak.

"A beautiful scene is it not?" Carissa jumped slightly, head down again as she replied.

"Yes. Yes it is." She sipped her wine, Ashur pressed on.

"Do you have dragons where you hail from, Lady Carissa?" The utterance of her name made the young artisan blush.

"I have heard only stories of such beasts in north-western Gaul, my home, but have met people who say they have seen them." Ashur turned to face her.

"You have? Really?"

"Yes, truly." Carissa's voice grew stronger as she looked at him. Ashur was intrigued by her short blond hair that slightly obscured her eyes, her delicate hands that bore a single cut from sculpting, even more so by her intense, lively grey eyes. She continued. "There is a story among my people that sometimes a child is born within which dwells a young, sleeping dragon. As the years pass, the child grows and so does the dragon. One day the two awaken together and often times a greatness is born within the man, or woman." She turned away again, shied by what she perceived as her sudden outburst. Ashur smiled.

"Would it surprise you to know that where I come from we have the same tradition?" She looked up at him, then back at the image on the wall but did not speak again. For the rest of the evening her thoughts were of the mysterious painting and the man next to her. As for Ashur, the image of this Celtic woman's eyes seemed burned into his mind.

Antonia was happy to see everyone enjoying the feast, eating their fair share, delighting in the store of Etrurian wine over discussions about art and travel and love, on the festival day of Venus Verticordia. She couldn't remember the last time there was so little talk of politics in her home and she thought to herself that the goddess in the middle of the table seemed pleased.

Over several well-watered cups, Lucius dazzled Publius, Emrys and the others with his descriptions of the deep desert and its austere, fiery beauty. As he spoke, Delphina watched her daughter listening, enrapt by the Roman's voice as though it were the sound of gentle notes plucked upon Apollo's lyre. She was impressed by the Metelli's reverence of the God of prophecy and music from whose sacred sanctuary she had come. It was not only a night of observation but one of pure enjoyment which was topped off by Longus who sweetened the night air with a recitation of his tale of *Daphnis and Chloe*.

It was well known that Longus had considerable insight into human affairs. He was famous for his sharp, pungent and fresh style that was both complex and elegant. So, when Alene rose and asked her friend to recite for them, the company moved to the torchlit garden where the poet from Lesbos did not disappoint. Adara laced her arm though Lucius' as they followed the party out. Couches had been arranged in a semi-circle formation to face Longus as he stood at the centre of the mosaic. The moon cast a soft light on the poet and his audience gave him their silent attention.

"When I was hunting in Lesbos, I saw in the grove of the Nymphs a spectacle, the most beauteous and pleasing of any I yet cast my eyes upon." As he began, the poet assumed an altogether different air, cloaking himself in the trappings of gentle reverie. His eyes closed as he remembered the scene and his breath was calm and steady as he heard the sounds, smelled the smells of his native island far away.

He spoke of a painting within a cave that told an ancient tale of love. Exposed babes, ewes, nymphs, shepherds, innocent youths, thieves and armed men, all were included in the mysterious painting that had so inspired him.

"This tale," he continued "is my votive offering to Love and to Pan and to the Nymphs...

...this will cure him that is sick, and rouse him that is in dumps; one that has loved will remember of it; one that has

310

not, it will instruct. For there was never any yet that wholly could escape love, and never shall there be any, never so long as beauty shall be, never so long as eyes can see."

His listeners sat awed by these opening lines, fully aware that they were about to hear something beyond beautiful. Longus proceeded with his tale of how the young boy, Daphnis, and the young girl, Chloe, were each in turn found by the goatherd, Lamo, and the shepherd, Dryas, in the cave of the Nymphs. The children who were two years apart in age, were said to be too beautiful to be of rustic blood. However, the two youths grew up happy and free in the idyllic, natural beauty of Lesbos. Fields and groves were their haunts as they cared for their goats and sheep.

The two of them lived a life of innocence in each other's company, never one without the other. One day Daphnis had an accident and was washing himself of dirt and blood. Chloe helped him and found that he was "of sweet and beautiful aspect." She praised him and from that moment on the seeds of their love grew. As he listened and dreamt, Adara at his side, her hand secretly gripping his, Lucius felt at times as though the tale were composed for them alone. His heart pounded when Daphnis was driven mad with the kiss Chloe gave him, his mind whirled when the rustic Philetas told the youths they were destined and that Love and Cupid were caring for them.

Longus' words struck his listeners with fear and anxiety as the island was invaded by Methymneans and Daphnis wounded. The love of Chloe and a kiss from her lips healed him. But the enemy returned in force, taking Chloe away, leaving Daphnis distraught. Relief came upon the audience with the appearance of the three Nymphs who reassured Daphnis that Chloe would return. When together again, the boy gave his thanks to Pan and Chloe to the Nymphs and each swore they would never live or die one without the other.

As he went on, the emotion on Longus' own face was visible; Alene, Lavena and Hadrea were teary-eyed, Antonia

311

wrung her hands. Adara could not get close enough to Lucius, the tale a sort of nourishment to the deep love they already felt. Time passed in the fields of Lesbos and many rich suitors approached the shepherd Dryas for Chloe's hand, but with the Nymphs on his side Daphnis found a purse of silver which he gave to Dryas. The local lord and lady were called to make the loving union official, and upon hearing Daphnis play sweet music on his pipe, it is revealed that the boy is their true son. Everyone listened to more misadventures and trials as Longus went on with his tale. But Love remains true to the young lovers, their destiny, and brings them together once more. Daphnis and Chloe are married in the countryside where they met, where they grew up and fell in love.

When Longus finished, there was a momentary silence as everyone returned to the world about them. They clapped, the women dried their tears, the men breathed deeply, recomposing themselves. Alene reached for a fresh cup of wine and went over to offer the poet a drink to quench his undoubted thirst.

"My friend, that was utter perfection. Thank you for treating us with such a beautiful tale." Longus smiled and bowed his head, drinking deeply. Then Delphina, who had listened to most of the story with eyes closed, savouring the words and images, rose.

"Longus you have warmed us all. I will dream of Greece, of the islands this night, and paint tomorrow." This pleased the poet greatly and Antonia and her guests rose to thank him personally. To one side of the garden, Lucius and Adara, beneath the gentle leaves of a jasmine bush, spoke in silent whispers for the first time that night.

"When shall I speak with your father? Do you think he'll approve, Adara?"

She looked up at him lovingly, her right hand upon his chest. "Oh, Lucius, you've won them over completely, but not nearly as much as you've won me." A happy tear rimmed her eyelid as she gazed up at the stars. "Is it possible that we could know such happiness? Would the Gods allow this?" Lucius detected utter joy and love in her questioning eyes but also a trace of fear. He understood. As a warrior he feared little if anything, but as a mortal man the thought of losing the love of the woman before him frightened him to the core of his being. But then he remembered, felt something.

"Adara, I too am afraid...but I'm also more sure than I've ever been of anything. I love you and nothing could ever keep me from you."

"And I love you, Lucius, more than in paintings, or poems or stories."

"The Gods are on our side, I feel it." She looked from Lucius to her father who spoke with the rest of the guests.

"Ask my father if you may speak with him tomorrow afternoon sometime, at our home on the Esquiline. Will that be too soon?"

"Not soon enough," Lucius replied, eyes alight. "I'll explain to him the situation with my father and that I'm to make arrangements in his stead." Just then Publius Antoninus came over to them.

"Pardon me, Adara, Lucius, but the hour is late and we must be leaving now."

"Yes, father. I'll just say goodbye to the others." Adara left the two men to talk while she thanked her hosts. Lucius looked to Publius who watched his daughter walk away. He was a very proud father.

"Sir, I was wondering if I might come by your home tomorrow to speak with you about an important matter. If you have the time, that is."

Publius knew what this 'matter' was, had tried to prepare himself for it. He put his hand on Lucius' shoulder. "Lucius Metellus." The name sounded good to him. "You're always welcome. Shall we say about the tenth hour of the day?"

"Perfect. I look forward to it."

"As do I. But now I must bid you a good night and thank you for the truly wonderful evening. I've enjoyed myself thoroughly."

In the atrium, after all the guests had been seen out, thanks given, the doors closed for the night, Lucius, Alene, Antonia and Ashur walked back down the corridor.

"Did you enjoy yourself, Ashur?" asked Antonia.

"Yes, truly, Lady Metella. A wonderful evening." Ashur struggled with a yawn he tried to hold back. "If you will excuse me, my friends, the world of dreams beckons. Thank you again."

"Good night, my friend," Lucius said. Once Ashur was gone, Lucius asked his mother what she thought of Adara and her family.

"I think they're lovely, Lucius. Really wonderful."

"You mean it mother?"

"Of course I do."

"And Adara? What do you think of her?"

"I've always liked her as your sister's friend but after seeing the two of you together I think she's even more lovely and kind than ever. You seem perfect for each other."

"I'm glad to hear you say that because I'm going to their house tomorrow to ask Publius for her hand."

Antonia's face lit up and Alene clapped her hands excitedly. "I am happy for you, son," Antonia said. "I'm sure it will all be fine." After bidding her children good night, Antonia retired to her rooms to write a letter to her husband before going to sleep, alone.

"Mother's really happy for you, Lucius," Alene said as she watched Antonia go up the stairs.

"I'm glad she is. Father is a completely other matter."

"Oh, who cares what he says? He's been so miserable for so long, so cold...this family needs a little warmth in it. You do what you want."

Lucius got up and went to sit next to Alene. Forget about him for now," he soothed. "Are you all right with all of this?" Her face was confused. "You know what I mean. I know that you've not met anyone yet and well...I want you to be happy, Alene."

Her face settled into a serene smile. "Lucius, don't you know how happy I am for you? You're going to marry my best friend. I saw it in my dreams and now it is coming true. I love you, Lucius. And I want you to be happy. Adara will make you happy, I'm certain."

Lucius hugged his sister warmly. "Thank you," he said, feeling safe with her there, the same safety he felt when he was a child and she would protect him, ease his worries with her kind words.

They stayed a little longer, looking up at the sky, enjoying the spring night and its freshness. His heart calm, Lucius kissed his sister on the cheek and went to bed to dream of love, of Adara, of the future. He awoke only once during the night, having heard a noise outside his small window and seen a faint glow of red light. He dismissed it and went back to sound, enjoyable sleep.

XXI

NUNTII

'Despatches'

The sea was sparkling as it slept, brilliant and blue beneath Helios' golden rays, awash with diamond-like flecks. A cloudless, perfect sky stood still between earth and stars and the only sounds were of dolphins playing, birds serenading, the gentle lapping of clear water on the edge of a pink and white-pebbled shoreline.

This was the shore of some remote island lost in time, as perfect a curve as that of the crescent moon. Lying upon time-worn rocks, a young man lay in peaceful slumber, safe, contented to pass the time thus. His skin was dark from the sun, his body smooth and muscled.

A warm breeze from an unknown place rustled his thick hair but he did not wake. Back and behind of the quiet shore where the ground rises up to the top of white cliffs is an area shaded by gentle olive and sweet-smelling pine. There sit three gods, sipping heavenly nectar from golden cups. The first plucks a cythera with silver strings, the music ringing out in melodic waves pleasing to the senses. Next to him lies a goddess of unimaginable beauty, quietly humming in unison as she twirls a purple flower between her slender fingers. The trees rain delicate leaves into her lap as offerings, she gazes up to the sky beyond and in her full hypnotic eyes, the stars are visible.

The third god leans his warlike body against a boulder, eyes closed in thought, arms crossed. Stuck deep into the ground at his side, a bright-bladed sword glistens in the sun and hums when the warm breeze licks it. Within his godly form, in his veins, fire flows in a mad rush. The cythera's music comes to a resonating halt echoed by the first god's voice.

"I know what is in your mind, brother. I won't allow it."

Fiery eyes open slowly as the third turns his muscled neck and speaks, his voice low and harsh. "What is it to you, Far-shooter? We each have our charges in the mortal realm. War must return to him, peace has become too comfortable."

Beauty turned to speak, her soft voice soothing the tension that threatened to build. "For too long has his life been awash with loneliness and uncertainty. Let him live now, for a while, bathed in sunlight and Love. He is over grateful." The warlike god rose and moved to the edge of the cliff to look down. In the water, dolphins dive once more and the birds among the cliffs cease their harmony. It is silent.

"He sacrifices to Love, and to you, God of the Silver Bow. But, to me? No, not once has he sacrificed or poured a libation to War, War who has given him victory and triumph in the field."

"You have hunted him several times and are upset that he has eluded you!" replied the Far-shooter rising and stringing his silver bow. "When he fights in battle, the very act of war is in your honour, not mine, or Love's." All three now stood at the cliff's edge, their white robes wavering. Love smiled caringly but War remained determined.

"He gives not a thought to me. This one needs a reminder, something to awaken his warlike senses, some pain in the midst of all his current joy, however minute."

"You cannot harm him!" protested Love. "I won't allow it. I have toiled too hard to bring the one to the other."

"He has lost the balance so crucial to mortal life, forgotten his duty. Something must be done."

"Very well, very well," the God of the Silver Bow interrupted the quarrelling Gods. "Be still. Do not wake him." He stepped forward, gazing out with the look of a worried father, the constellations whirling round in his eyes. He pulled forth a long-shafted arrow from a quiver that hung on a nearby branch and notched it upon his bow. "This shall decide. It will bring about loss, some pain. He is my charge, the task is mine.

317

Awareness of War will be reawakened while Love's work will be wholly preserved. Are we agreed?" He looked at the two gods who, though reluctant, agreed.

He drew the arrow back its full length and, his godly arm strong and steady, loosed it. In a streak of light, the arrow crested the far horizon and disappeared. Down on the beach the man stirred, his eyes squinting in the sun.

"Quickly!" said Love "We must away now. Day rises for mortals once more." The three gods then vanished on the warm breeze.

A ray of sunlight penetrated the small window in Lucius' cubicula to shine onto his face. He turned in his bed, the sound of birdsong from the garden reached his ears and he stretched lazily, feeling the momentary quiver of every muscle in his body. Then he remembered what he had to do that day and was suddenly very awake. He felt nervous and yet alive beyond reason as when one dreams a rejuvenating dream. He had to speak with his mother and Alene about what he might say to Publius. He had never negotiated a marriage before.

"But Lucius I don't know about that sort of thing," exclaimed Alene as he plied her with questions. Their mother looked on.

"My son, this is usually the duty of the father. In this case, well, I'm sorry but you are on your own."

"I understand. But there must be something I have to discuss." Antonia thought briefly of her own marriage contract for a few examples.

"People usually discuss the dowry of course, be it money, land or property. That's the most important. Then there's your income. Usually a father would want his daughter to be cared for properly, have a certain level of independence in case of divorce or death."

"Oh mother! How truly morbid and depressing," said Alene. "Lucius loves Adara and that's what should really matter. Not money or property."

"I know that, Alene. I am merely referring to my own experiences."

Lucius shook his head. "Don't worry. I'll...I'll just try to read Publius' feelings and go from there. Alene is right though, all that matters is that Adara and I can be together." Just then one of the slaves appeared at the edge of the garden, waiting until they spotted him.

"Yes, Cato, what is it?" asked Antonia. He stepped forward.

"Erm, a message for Master Lucius, Mistress. Just delivered at the door by an army courier." He handed the scroll to Lucius.

"Thank you, Cato."

"Master." He bowed.

It was a lengthy letter to him from Alerio. Seeing the name and handwriting brought a smile to his face as well as the grains of desert sand that fell into his lap, used to dry the ink on the papyrus. He began to read as Antonia and Alene continued to discuss what he should say to Publius.

The letter read:

Hail Tribune Lucius Metellus Anguis!

From your centurions and the men of your cohort.

Greetings!

My dear friend and comrade,

I trust that this letter finds you well and happy in Rome. It's been too long since we last parted in Carthage, on the docks, and so much has happened since that I feel it's time I wrote. Forgive my taking so long but things have been rather busy here. I had no idea how much you have to deal with commanding a full cohort. Your presence is sorely missed but I think you would be pleased at the way I've handled this lot. So much to say...I'm not quite sure where to begin.

By the time you receive this missive, the Triumph will probably be over. I hope it went well and that you managed to enjoy yourself. You deserve it after all you achieved in Africa.

The men have settled into life rather well in Numidia and have gained a large amount of respect within the III Augustan, legion of old farts that they are! As yet there is still no word at this end about any plans for our cohort. I suppose we'd better be prepared to settle in down here. Several of the men have taken wives in the neighbouring vici; the emperor's marriage laws are quite popular it seems. As for myself I am, as ever, still in search of the perfect Venus.

I have to admit that, though the weather is warm and the sun shines all the time, the desert is fast losing its appeal. Perhaps I should have taken up your offer to come to Rome with you. I'm tired of cleaning the sand out of every crack and orifice of my body.

I've been keeping the men in first-rate condition. Drills, drills and more drills. If we're needed to fight, we're definitely ready. I hope you haven't grown soft in Rome, my friend. Ha, ha. Never! If I know you, you're at the gymnasium every day. Maybe not...I know I'd find it difficult. Apart from drills, the men have been recruited for several building projects; a new road, a theatre and another bath house in Thamugadi. The change in routine is good for them, keeps them occupied.

The Legate and I have talked a great deal too; the old man really is interesting and I dare say, NICE! That is, if you stay on his good side, which I have. The men have been so well behaved that he's given the cohort leave to go to Thysdrus again, this time for the festival of Mars. Enjoyable though it may be, I'd rather be back in Rome with you, for even a day.

Lucius put the scroll down for a moment, wondering why Alerio sounded so dour. He had loved being a centurion, always drilling, looking after his men. What was going on? Lucius read on.

I suppose I can't wait any longer, having put this off long enough. Please sit my friend, if you are not.
Antanelis is dead.

Lucius' hand began to tremble as he read.

I'm sorry to be so blunt about it but there really is no way that I can think to say such a terrible thing. The words seem to just hang there in the air, out of spite. It happened about a month ago. I'm only telling you now because I haven't had the guts to do so earlier.
It was a sunny day in Februarius, not too cool. Garai, Maren and Antanelis decided to go out hunting for lions and jackals beyond the mountains south of the base. They left early in the morning for three days. According to Garai's report, Antanelis, while the others were finishing off a jackal they'd speared, spotted a lion in the brush, attracted by the smell of the blood. The lion was creeping up, ready to pounce when Antanelis saw it, He rode up in front of the others and launched his spear and grazed the lion's haunch.
The beast took off, thoroughly spooked and he chased after it. Before Garai and Maren knew what was happening, Antanelis was far off into the desert flats. They rode hard after him, following the tracks but were too late. When they came into view, it seemed to them that Antanelis' horse had stumbled at the gallop and broken its leg, throwing him onto some rocks. The lion, a giant of a male, then wheeled in a rage and came back at Antanelis who had dropped his extra spear where the horse had fallen. His sword had been tucked next to the saddle.
Lucius, the lion attacked him with full force and though he apparently delivered some heavy blows to the beast, it mauled him beyond recognition. I tremble as I write this…Garai and

321

Maren say that as they came riding up the lion fled. They caught Antanelis' last few breaths before he bled to death. The lion died about a mile away from blood loss. It had a broken leg and its throat was crushed where Antanelis had tried to choke it.

Lucius I swear I've never seen anything quite so horrible in all my life. I miss our young friend terribly and wish you were here. It has come as quite a shock to all of us. Rest assured that we gave him an honourable send-off. The whole legion turned out on the desert plain to sacrifice to Antanelis' shade and burn his remains. There was more than enough of his pay set aside for the burial fund and I ordered a magnificent tombstone to be made out of that golden African marble he liked so much. On it is a likeness of Antanelis wearing his corona, a desert palm and a lion. The inscription reads:

Here lies Antanelis Brennius Crispus, Centurion.
He defended Rome and his men,
Willingly. Faithfully.

I trust that you agree with this? Sometimes I think he was the best, the truest of all of us. I know this is probably the last thing you would want to do Lucius but his family should be notified. I've sent his personal effects along with this long letter so you can send them to his parents. I believe they live somewhere along the Via Flaminia near Foligno.

I'm sorry if this has brought you down Lucius. It does feel better to talk to you, even if it is only a letter. I've been spending some lonely, thoughtful evenings in my quarters reading the copy of Arrian you lent me on Alexander's campaigns. It's the only way I can take my mind off things. I trust that Ashur has found you? He saw me in Carthage and seemed quite distraught that you'd left. Perhaps he is a true friend after all. If so, keep him close Lucius.

And what of Argus? Have you two drifted apart so much? I hear from Garai that he's joined the Praetorians! I guess I have to promote two more men to centurion. However, I won't go into that now. After having unloaded all my thoughts on you I find myself at a loss for words. I suppose this letter is long enough. Don't worry. I'll write again and more frequently. If you have the time, let me know how you are and what might be happening for the cohort. Most importantly, my friend, take care of yourself and return to us safely. You are sorely missed.

May the Gods protect you.

Your friend and loyal centurion,

Alerio

Lucius was devastated. He went directly to his room where Cato had lain the package containing Antanelis' personal effects, his armour and his corona. For two hours, Lucius, the door bolted, went through the package wracked by feelings of sadness, anger and guilt. The only tears he shed for his youngest centurion fell within the four walls of his cubicula. He had saved Antanelis' life once before. Why had the Gods arranged that he wasn't there this time, to save his friend from an unthinkable end?

The day was to be one of extreme contrast; sadness and grief at the loss of a close friend, excitement and anticipation at an arrangement that would bind him to the only woman he would ever love. On the morning the man in love had awaken, so too had the warrior who had to face duty and death whether he liked it or not.

The tenth hour of the day was fast approaching, and Lucius, having made an offering to his lost friend in the Temple of Hercules in the Forum Boarium, made his way to the Esquiline hill and the house of Publius Leander Antoninus. He struggled hard to keep his mind on what was about to happen, that it was a happy occasion. The morning's letter rang frighteningly in his head and images of Antanelis' scarred face hovered before him. Lucius thought it fitting to make an offering at the Temple of Hercules because he was Antanelis' favourite god, but also because the two of them had fought and killed fierce lions; however, Hercules had been a half-god and Antanelis had not.

Lucius finally reached the crest of the Esquiline, nearing the blue doors of the house. He hadn't known what to wear so he decided on his other formal toga with the thin dark stripe. He was relieved not to have cut himself shaving that morning; his hand had been very unsteady.

The neighbourhood where Publius Leander had rented the domus for their stay in Rome was a quiet area; not as prestigious as the Palatine of course but highly desirable nonetheless. The only noise came from the nearby Baths of Trajan. The street was long and wider than most others, with the high walls of the houses running the length of the road, dotted with the occasional splash of coloured doors.

When the knock came at the door, Adara leapt from a seat where she had been reading in the garden and rushed around the peristyle as light on her feet as a forest nymph upon dewy grass. Her hair was still slightly wet from a visit to the baths earlier and she was dressed in a blue stola, a delicate necklace of golden sea horses about her neck. As a slave opened the door, Lucius appeared in the street, head down at first. When the slave spoke, he raised his head.

"Lucius Metellus here to see the master of the house." From where she stood behind a statue of Juno in the atrium, Adara knew immediately that something was wrong and her heart sank as a pebble to the bottom of the sea. Her greatest fear at that moment was that Lucius had changed his mind. She stepped out and went to him, not able to stand the pain of seeing the bereaved look upon his beautiful face.

"Lucius?" She moved toward him, her hands reaching out to hold his. "What's happened?" He took her hands in his, felt the absolute warmth and tenderness in them, looked up and found that at that moment there was no other place he would rather have been. He saw the fear in her eyes, realised he had to put her heart at ease; it was not the greeting either of them had expected.

"I'm sorry if I'm not myself today, Adara. This morning a despatch came from my centurion in Numidia."

"Yes? What did he say?" She tried to ignore the feelings of relief she felt in that instant and concentrate on Lucius.

"One of my junior centurions...my friend Antanelis...was killed last month in the desert. A lion killed him."

"The young man you saved in Parthia?" Adara remembered Lucius speaking fondly of him before.

"Yes, the same."

"Lucius, I'm so sorry." She took his face in her hands and kissed his forehead, ignoring the hovering slave in the corner. "You don't have to do this today, Lucius. Father will understand." She stood back looking at him for an answer. Lucius wondered at how beautiful she was; simply to behold her seemed to melt away the pain and anguish he had been feeling for half the day.

"Nothing, however terrible, could ever keep me from you, or prevent me from making our dream a reality. Adara, in the midst of death you make me feel alive. I will speak with your father." The young woman visibly relaxed and although she would have no qualms about postponing the marriage arrangements, her heart calmed once more in relief as she led Lucius to her father's study.

The room where Publius Leander Antoninus sat was rather bare with only a large table, four chairs and a wall with empty pigeon holes. The floor was decorated with a black and white geometric mosaic. It was quite Spartan as far as studies went but for rented accommodation it was clean and fresh. Publius was sitting at the table going through scrolls and papers by the light of a double-headed lamp that flickered from the breeze coming in the window that looked onto the garden. He had been up late, risen early, tried to work out what he believed to be a fair and suitable settlement pleasing to everyone involved.

Publius had often contemplated the thought of marrying off his eldest daughter but now that the time had come he was confronted with feelings of sadness, joy, apprehension and age. On top of a dowry for Adara he had to consider those of his other two girls. *Can she be that old already?* he wondered. But, to see the look of happiness on Adara's face made the task much more bearable than he had imagined. Determined to throw himself into the task wholeheartedly, Publius had been preparing ideas. A tray with wine, water, two cups and a plate of fruit and cheese had been set on the table. He waited and when the door opened, Adara led Lucius into the study. Publius rose from his chair and smiled broadly as he came around the table to greet Lucius. Try as he would to hide his sadness, Lucius' face revealed all and Publius' smile quickly faded to an expression of concern.

"Welcome Lucius, welcome. Please come in," he said, as cheerfully as he could, his hands outstretched in greeting.

"Thank you, Publius Leander." Adara's father looked at her for some hint as to what was going on.

"Do not worry, father. All is well between Lucius and I."

"I'm glad to hear it. Please sit down Lucius, have some wine."

"Thank you." Lucius accepted the cup and sat down, happy to be off his feet.

"I trust your family is well?"

"Oh yes, they are fine. Thank you."

"Father, Lucius has had some bad news from Africa about one of his men." Adara thought she should say something for Lucius so that neither he or Publius drowned in a pool of uncertainty and awkwardness.

"Oh, I see. Well if you would like to postpone, Lucius, I fully under-"

"Please no, not at all." Lucius mustered a smile, genuine as he looked at Adara who stood next to him. "I've been looking forward to this, really."

"Very well." Publius eased back into his chair. "Adara would you leave us for a while to talk? I will send for you after."

"Yes, father. Lucius. I'll be in the garden." She went out, closing the door gently behind her as the two watched her go.

Publius felt pity for the young man to have such a day marred by bad tidings. Perhaps he could do something? Say something to help? Lucius' father was away and he suspected, they were not on good terms.

"You know, Lucius, I was in the army too, a long time ago. If you would like to tell me about it I'm...well...Delphina tells me I am unsurpassed in the art of listening." Lucius looked up, warmed by this unexpected offer and an overwhelming urge to tell the man before him everything, though he barely knew him.

He spoke, Publius listened, digested every detail. He learned of the death of Lucius' friend, the pressures Lucius had experienced as a tribune. In that room Publius gained an insight into the man that was to be his son-in-law, an insight he had never expected to have. What might have seemed to some an average career as a young equestrian tribune was so much more. To have fought so hard to live up to a great name, to have climbed up the ranks so speedily at a young age and deal with the jealousies and prejudices that such successes brought. To have done all this and remained as true and strong as he was, to be a *good* man, was incredibly admirable. Publius could see what his daughter saw in him.

In turn Lucius was overwhelmed by the honest kindness of Adara's father and realised he was more at ease with him than he had ever felt with his own father. He wanted to tell him so, about his father, why he wasn't there, but Lucius knew that it would not be respectful, or honourable, to speak badly of his father to someone else no matter how hard the feelings.

327

Besides, Lucius knew that Publius was no fool, that he could see the reason for Quintus' absence and understood. He knew everything without a word being uttered on the subject.

A weight had been lifted and both men shared another cup of wine.

"To old friends and new!" Publius toasted.

"Old and new," Lucius repeated.

"Do you feel up to discussing this, Lucius?"

"More than ever. Though I must confess I haven't a clue what to discuss. All I know is that I love Adara and if you will allow it I would like to marry her. That is all I want."Publius smiled. "You have the full blessing of both Delphina and myself. However, I wouldn't dream of not giving you something for Adara's dowry. In some ways I am still very traditional. I admit that we are not an overly wealthy family, especially with three daughters to marry off, but I do have something in mind. I would like my daughter to have some measure of financial independence to which end I will provide her with two hundred thousand sestertii."

"I think that's a good idea. Unfortunately, I don't believe my inheritance will amount to much." Publius nodded understandingly. "But my tribune's salary should prove enough to give Adara a comfortable life."

"I agree. However, I would also like to give you another three-hundred-thousand sestertii to the two of you. No arguments!" He anticipated Lucius' generous protestation. "It is my duty as her father. I wish I could do more."

"You are already too generous, Publius."

"The Gods reward generosity, and what better time to be giving than the marriage of one's daughter? As for land, I'm afraid that I don't have much to offer you." Publius began to flip through some of the scrolls in front of him that he had been looking at that morning. "We live in Athens and as Delphina did not have a large dowry – ah...here it is." He unrolled a scroll and placed his cup on one curled end and a smoothed pebble on the other. "This is a plot of land that I acquired some years ago in a business transaction with a magistrate from Britannia. It's not much, but perhaps you would like to have a look. I really have no need for it."

"What is it?" asked Lucius, curiosity peaked. Publius turned it around for him to get a better look.

"I'm a little embarrassed to say I've never been there. Here are the surveyor's notes and sketches. They should be pretty accurate for the price he charged me." Lucius squinted as he looked over the descriptions of the land the main feature of which was a large earthwork in the centre. "Apparently it's an ancient hill-fort of the Durotriges or some Celtic tribe," he explained. "The surrounding land is perfect for farming, rich soil, though the climate is somewhat inhospitable." Lucius studied the plans carefully, having never seen anything like it.

"It certainly is an odd construction."

"Quite," Publius replied. " They say it was taken during the Claudian invasion of Britannia. At the moment, I have a few tenant farmers on the surrounding land and on the hill there are a couple of supply buildings and a stable that the army pays me to use. Oh! There's also a small temple for the locals."

"Fascinating. But I couldn't possibly accept it, really."

"Don't be silly, Lucius. I swear I have absolutely no need of it. Perhaps you and Adara can get some small income from it, some use?"

"Very kind."

"Think nothing of it. It's my pleasure." He poured more wine for them. "In return for Adara's hand however, there is one thing I would ask of you. Something very important to me." Lucius sat straight up, almost as if at attention.

"Name it," he said strongly.

"In return I would ask that you care for my daughter above all things, protect her and keep her safe in this sometimes violent world. Your duties may lead you very far away, into the unknown and I would feel better knowing she will be safe with you. I want to hear you say it."

Lucius could see that this meant a great deal to Publius, that he was exceedingly serious; he stood up, understanding of the father before him.

"I swear by Apollo that I will protect Adara with my life and would die before I let anything happen to her. You have my word." Publius relaxed. Lucius thought he spotted one of his hands trembling for a moment, the only sign of emotion in that moment when he agreed to give his daughter away.

"You don't know the comfort that gives me. Thank you. It's settled then!" Publius smacked the table with his hands. "Now, I think we should tell Adara the happy news, don't you? Let's go together."

The day had taken a wonderful turn and though part of Lucius' heart yet harboured a great sense of sadness and loss, another part of him rejoiced and was comforted by the ease with which his meeting with Publius had gone, what it all meant. When the two men came out into the sun-filled garden it was evident that there was to be a wedding. Adara, barely able to control her joy, threw her arms around Lucius, who despite the presence of her entire family, let himself be enveloped. She then went to where Publius stood with Delphina and hugged him tightly.

"Thank you father!" He held her head between his hands, as he always did when she was but a young starry-eyed child.

"You have our blessing my dear."

The mothers of the bride and groom-to-be were ecstatic and immediately set about organizing an engagement celebration. They had wanted to do it the very next day but Lucius had asked that they wait a week as he had to take care of something that could not wait; he had to ride up the Via Flaminia to bring news of Antanelis' death to his unsuspecting parents.

Everybody understood his need to do this and so while Lucius would make the journey with Ashur as his companion, Adara and their mothers would plan a celebration. Two days after Lucius' meeting with Publius, he and Ashur left Rome behind. Adara was strong and supportive and came to the house early to see him off. Lucius looked magnificent to her though he wore only simple travelling clothes. All his armour was slung carefully over his shoulder in a large satchel.

"Be safe, my love. No goodbyes."

"No goodbyes. Don't worry for me. I'll be back soon."

"Well, until then, hold this close to your heart." With those words, her hands on his chest, Adara leaned forward and kissed Lucius softly. The memory of their first embrace, the feel of her warm, full, soft lips upon his mouth eased the pain of the journey he was making and filled him with hope for their future together. They tore themselves from each other in that early morning light.

The streets were still quiet as the two men made their way through the Forum and past the Capitoline hill, its cluster of temples glinting in the first rays of morning light, to the northern part of the city. The Via Flaminia ran from the Capitol past the Ara Pacis Augustae and the large mausoleum of Augustus. The mausoleum itself had an air of peace about it, like soft clouds hovering around a mountaintop. Its circular design was simple, beautiful, with its crown of cypresses on a green earthen mound. Among the tall spire-like trees came the soft chattering of birds singing to the new day.

"Rome is beautiful at this time of the day," Ashur said as they walked toward the city gate. Lucius heard him but was too lost in thought to reply. The memory of Adara's kiss lingered on his lips and the thought of the journey occupied his mind. Ashur understood and waited for him to speak in his own time.

"We'll get the horses at the stables outside the gate," Lucius finally spoke. "I haven't been this way in years."

"What's the road like where we're headed?" Ashur was curious.

"Oh, the road is straight and passes over some small rolling hills. It won't be a difficult ride but we'll get a packhorse to carry our things anyway." They came to the stables, the high walls of Rome behind them now.

"Are we too early?" Ashur wondered as they looked around.

"Hello!" Lucius called, peering inside the stables where several horses turned to look at the curious newcomers. "Anyone here?"

"Yeah, yeah!" grumbled a bleary voice from a back room. "I'm coming, I'm coming." Out came a short man with a scraggly beard who had obviously just woken up. He rubbed his eyes and scratched his crotch as he approached the two travellers, squinting as his eyes adjusted to the increasing light. Lucius and Ashur held their breath as the smell of flatulence and sour wine emanating from the stableman assaulted their olfactory senses.

"We need horses, stableman," Lucius said in his tribune's voice. The man winced as though his ears hurt. "For a few days." The man was finally waking up.

"How many days is a few days?" He went over to a bucket of water, slurped some from a ladle, swirled it in his mouth and spat. "Well?"

"Five to seven days, depending on how long our journey takes. Three horses: two chargers and a packhorse." Ashur looked at the horses while Lucius talked. The man eyed the dark-skinned stranger uneasily.

"Tell your friend not to frighten the horses."

"How much? We have to get going and you're holding us up." Lucius was growing increasingly impatient.

"All right. Ah, let's see, that's…" He scratched his head and twisted up his features; so much thinking first thing in the morning was more than he could handle. "That'll be one eighty sestertii for the pack horse and, well, the chargers are more, let's say three hundred sestertii for both."

"Fine." Lucius opened his money pouch and counted out the correct amount. "But we choose the horses!" He dropped the coins into the man's dirty palm, his blackened teeth revealed in a greedy smile.

"Yes, fine, fine," he agreed, hypnotized by the shiny coinage, newly minted for the triumph. Lucius went over to Ashur who had already picked out the healthiest mounts.

"How do they look?"

"The chestnut packhorse will do for the packages and over there are a couple of Iberians. They're beautiful beasts, healthy, but what they're doing here I don't know."

"I heard that!" the stableman yelled from the back room where he was putting away his money.

Lucius smiled and hoisted a saddle off the wall. "Well, let's give them some fresh air. There's another saddle."

Once the horses were outside and the satchels strapped tightly onto the packhorse, they set out at a gentle trot down the road that stretched out over the low green hills to the north-east of the city. The air grew fresher and fresher as they rode on, with the sun growing warmer and brighter by the minute. It would be a two-day ride to get to where Antanelis' family lived, about ten miles past Foligno where they ran a large inn.

It was the first time since they had arrived in Rome that Lucius and Ashur were able to be alone as friends, unimpeded by the noisy hubbub of the city. The ride was a very pleasant one, much needed, and it gave Lucius a chance to relate to Ashur all his feelings about Adara and their forthcoming marriage. When he asked Ashur if he was enjoying Rome, he replied that he was more and more at ease and that he was impressed by several of the many people he had met thus far. One name in particular repeatedly escaped his usually discreet lips: Carissa.

Lucius tried not to be shocked, even amazed, whenever Ashur uttered her name in either a nervous, excited or impassioned manner. The cool desert warrior could not help himself and Lucius, as he listened, wondered whether Ashur, servant of Apollo, was permitted such an...earthly preoccupation as human affection. If he had believed before that he finally understood Ashur, who he was, he now found himself more perplexed by this new aspect of him that seemed to have sprung up from within like water from the heart of a stony mountain.

The day soon neared its end and on the northern route where the Via Flaminia diverged between Narni and Foligno, the two horsemen stopped at a small tavern for the night. It was clean and well-kept, and run by a young freedman and his wife.

With the horses taken care of in the back, the two men sat down to a meal of fresh stew and soft bread and cheese washed down with a pitcher of the owner's own wine.

"Do you think your father or Argus will attend your wedding?" Ashur asked as they ate. The question took Lucius by surprise but it was something that he had been thinking about.

"I don't think either of them will be there. Personally, I think it's disgraceful how Argus has just picked up and gone like that, without a farewell, after everything our family has done for him."

"Sometimes the urge to get on one's way is so strong and sudden that some men act without regard for anyone but themselves. I don't get along with Argus, I never have. But, I'm sure, Lucius, that he'll be thinking about you. If he knows that is. What of your father? Is Etruria very far from Rome?"

"Not very, no. Between us, I couldn't care less if he came or not. I know it is wrong to speak so ill of one's father but he's acted unforgivably." They were silent as they continued to eat. Then, Lucius pushed his plate away and leaned back in his chair. "I don't know what I'm going to say tomorrow, Ashur. How do I tell someone that their son, whom they haven't seen in years, is never coming home again? What will I say when they ask how he died?"

"I don't know, Anguis. Be mindful of their feelings, tell them slowly and with compassion. It won't be easy, for any of you, but Alerio is right to ask you to do this. It's the only way."

"I know."

"Antanelis was very dear to you, wasn't he?"

"Yes. He was more like a younger brother than little Quintus is."

Ashur nodded. "Your brother is young, Lucius. Perhaps he'll surprise you."

"I doubt it. He's father's little puppet now. Ach, who cares? Life's too precious to be bothered about such things."

"I agree with you there. Life is indeed precious." Ashur leaned back too, while Lucius drank. There seemed to be unspoken questions on Ashur's face but Lucius was too tired to ask; he thought of Antanelis and what he might say to his parents.

The inn was not busy, though it had been in the past weeks leading up to the triumph; the only other customers were a cloth merchant from Ariminum and another man travelling alone. The latter sat opposite Lucius and Ashur, a solitary drinker, while the merchant chatted with the innkeeper and his wife about the world in general.

The two friends had much on their minds and several times throughout the meal became silent again. Each understood the other and so when they had eaten their fill they thanked the innkeeper and retired. Lucius went to the room to sort out Antanelis' possessions to give to his parents and make sure his own armour was polished and presentable for the duty he had to perform. Ashur bid Lucius good night and went outside to clear his mind. The lone drinker watched them depart and went back to staring into the bottom of his cup.

How quiet and dark the world was outside of Rome. Ashur enjoyed the peace and solitude of the moment as he made his way to a fallen tree a few paces from the road. He sat down,

335

wrapped himself in his cloak and gazed up at the starlit canopy. It was cold. The images of Perseus, Cassiopeia and others twinkled brightly in their immortalized formations and the moon's light shone through a few thin scatterings of evening cloud as they passed. The silvery light reflected off the flagstones of the road, illuminating it for miles, a long smooth-scaled serpent winding its way over the countryside.

The past few months had been quite different for Ashur Mehrdad and, as he looked back, he thought that he would or should, be missing the desert and its beautiful simplicity, or even the sea where it met the Libyan sands. But he did not. These things were furthest from his mind. He did not want for soft, silky dunes, green oases or shady palms, nor visits to any of the sacred sanctuaries. No. What he, servant of Apollo missed, was Carissa. The humble artisan who was shy, not possessing of great beauty nor even much noticed by others; she had stirred his being unlike any other with a couple of glances, a few simple words. He spoke her name to himself, to the night, his breath showing in the cold air. Ashur was confused, unaccustomed to such feelings, and wondered what the God had planned for him, what He would think. Around him the world seemed so silent, the quiet broken only by the occasional night owl searching for prey, or a lone wolf calling out to its pack.

He stepped back onto the road and gazed back at the inn where only a few lamps were still alight. Lucius' room was dark. Then off to his right, in a group of trees came the harsh sound of a twig snapping. Alert once more, Ashur's eyes searched the shadows as his hand reached to find the handle of his curved dagger. He stood in the middle of the road, as still as a prowling leopard. He didn't speak but rather watched and waited and when the moment came he ran, fleet-footed, into the trees with feline speed. Several more twigs snapped with some hasty movements from nearby and as Ashur turned in that direction he was knocked from his feet, a stinging sensation across his face. As he fell back his dagger hand shot out instinctively making fleshy contact. A yell of pain pierced the air followed by a horse's hooves fleeing up the road, fading into the night.

Ashur got to his feet, put his hand to his face and felt an odd wetness from a gash across his cheek. He was surprised by the flow of blood. Expecting the wound to close and heal immediately as they usually did for him, he didn't worry until several minutes later when the wound was still open, fresh. He made his way to a small stream nearby and kneeled down beside it, straining to see his reflection in the water. He cupped his hands and dowsed his face, uttering a few words to Apollo in the ancient tongue. For a moment, he saw the reflection of someone behind him and felt the pain on his face dwindle to nothing, the wound appear to close and seal. But this time, as never before, he was left with a scar across his right cheek.

His fists clenched something in his tremulous sleep, his face was pained as he gazed across the water to that other place where memory resides. *Forward troops!* The sound of the voice blew in and out like a decisive wind, urging them on. *Form up and move on!* The air about Lucius and his comrades was dust-choked. He spun, looking for the source of the voice that almost certainly was the emperor, speeding by with his cavalry, a blur of silver and black. Lucius' heart pounded as he looked at Decimus, their centurion, dead in the sand. The bulging eyes stared back at him, still in the madness all about them.

A deafening war cry pierced the air above the screams of men. Parthian cataphracts charged toward them, cutting down Romans like sheaves of autumn wheat. *Form up!* Lucius heard himself yell. *Cavalry!* The men did their best to get things together in their confusion.

Antanelis! Lucius heard Alerio call out. Another three cataphracts charged the lone trooper where he stood above the bodies of four Parthians he had slain. Lucius could feel the shaft of the broken spear he had picked up as he ran to aid his young friend. He gripped the weapon and released it with all his skill so that it planted itself in the neck of the first enemy to reach Antanelis. The heavy, limp body fell from the horse into the young Roman's face, knocking his helmet from his head and himself to the ground. Lucius reached him and pulled him up; blood poured from Antanelis' forehead where the enemy's battle axe had gashed him, but he was alive. The yells of the Romans coming to their aid echoed in the clotted air as they fought back the other cataphracts. Screams, screams all around, and blood. But they were alive...

"Ahh!" Lucius roiled in the sweat-soaked sheets. His hands shook as he put them to his face, tried to remember where he was. Outside, the crowing of cocks and the heaving vocals of two donkeys in an adjacent field reminded him. He stretched and wiped the sweat from his brow before rising from the straw mattress. In a corner of the room were Antanelis' belongings. He remembered sorting them neatly the night before.

He went over to the window to look out over the mist-covered hills where clumps of cypresses rose out of the earth. Behind him, in the far corner of the room, Ashur lay fast asleep, curled up on his right side beneath his cloak, facing the wall. Surprised to see his companion still asleep, for he always rose early, Lucius dressed and went downstairs to see if he could get some bread, fruit and cheese from their hosts. A short while after, he returned to find Ashur sitting, gazing out the window at the road.

"Good! You're awake. Too much wine my friend?" Lucius placed the food on a nearby table. "I've brought you something to eat." Ashur said nothing. "Ashur? Are you sick?" Lucius put his hand on Ashur's shoulder. He turned slowly revealing the long, faint scar that ran from his chin to his ear. "What in Hades happened to you?"

Ashur hadn't wanted to tell but he could not hide what was fully apparent. "I was attacked last night when I was outside," he said, almost ashamed.

"By who? Where?"

"I don't know who. It was in the orchard next to the inn. A mounted man came out of the dark, took me by surprise. I too sunk my blade into him, perhaps his thigh, as he rode past."

"But why?"

"I don't know why he did! How should I know?" Lucius had never heard Ashur raise his voice before, in any way.

"No. I mean why do you have a scar, Ashur?" Lucius paused, uncertain how to phrase his thoughts. "You're not supposed to...well...I mean that that just isn't supposed to happen to you."

"I'm as confounded as you are." Ashur just could not bring himself to reveal what he was thinking; that perhaps Apollo had punished him for his thoughts of Carissa, the utterance of her name alone into the starlit night.

Lucius did not push things. The day was upon them and there was much to do. He left Ashur to his thoughts and his breakfast, washed and set about putting on his newly polished armour. He looked commanding, but in his heart he dreaded the first time that he would bring the news of the death of one of his men to an unknowing family.

It was another beautiful spring day, ideal for travelling as they made their way up the road past Foligno. The hills seemed to grow smaller in the long descent toward the sea. Most travellers were headed in the direction of Rome, the majority of them merchants. The stallion Lucius rode seemed to grow stronger and more spirited with every mile, happy to be out in the open and not locked away in a dank, smelly stable outside the walls of the city. For his part, Lucius enjoyed the distraction from what he would have to do shortly and occupied himself with controlling his mount, heading off the road at times to gallop on the soft grass. The horse showed its appreciation by obeying every command its rider gave. Lucius thought that perhaps the spirit of his dear Pegasus whispered gently to the stallion from the green fields beyond.

On the road, Ashur rode at a steady pace holding the reins of the pack horse who followed obediently, its tail swatting at hovering flies. As they came over a small rise in the road, the view opened onto a vast plain. The Via Flaminia stretched on into the distance and the horizon was broken only by the shapes of a few villas and clumps of trees. Directly ahead was the inn. They stopped.

"That's it up ahead," said Lucius.

"Are you ready for this?"

"It has to be done. They can't just find out about the death of their son by way of a cold letter dropped into their hands by some military messenger. They need to know what a good centurion he was. Do you want to come, or do you want to wait outside for me?"

"I think it best if you go alone, as the tribune."

"You're right." He lifted the bundle of Antanelis' things from the packhorse and hung them from the back of his saddle. "I may be a while."

"Take as long as is needed."

Lucius sighed. "I'll see you later."

Lucius spurred his stallion on down the road at a steady pace, the inn directly ahead and getting closer. *What should I say to them...how should I say it?* he thought as he rode, the inn's sign coming into view, singing gently in the breeze where it rocked on its iron rod.

The Inn of the Eagle's Head was larger than most roadside inns, well-kept and reasonably priced. The family Crispus had run it for several generations and as the years went by and the empire expanded, so did business. The Via Flaminia was one of the main arteries into Rome from Italy's east coast. The inn was made up of a large, two-story complex in the shape of a horseshoe in the middle of which was a pleasant garden. To the back were stables and other outbuildings where travellers' horses and slaves could spend the night while their masters slept in the comfort of the main building. At one corner of the inn was the tavern, well known for its hearty fare and good wine.

As Lucius came to a stop in front of the place, he remembered something Antanelis had once told him about the inn's name. Apparently it was called the Inn of the Eagle's Head because eagles were often seen high above the middle of the plain, soaring through the air until they spotted their prey on the vast openness below and dove as quick as lightning from the hand of Jupiter. There was even a temple built on the distant ridge overlooking the plain because of this phenomenon.

Lucius dismounted. As he did so, he looked up at the full, blue sky and saw them, two golden eagles, circling high above the road. As he walked up the path, leading his mount by the reins, he was sad because today he knew he would bring a dark pall of cloud into the lives of the Crispus family. He gave the stallion to a stable boy who offered to water the horse for him and, with the bundle in his hand, he went toward the inn's garden and the entrance to the tavern. Lucius felt as though he were in a trance of sorts and thought it was some protective frame of mind that had come upon him to allow his duty to be performed. The tribune stood tall, chest out beneath the gleaming cuirass, sword and dagger snug at his sides and his great crested helmet swaying atop his crown. A slight breeze blew his cloak to one side as he placed his hand upon the door and opened it.

The place was empty as it was still early in the day, except for a young girl who stood behind the main counter drying off several drinking cups. At the far end of the room, a man stood at a window gazing out before going back to his breakfast at a small table; he had a slight limp in his step and winced as he walked. Lucius moved towards the counter and placed the bundle carefully on a stool before addressing the girl. "Good day to you." The girl looked up from her drying and stepped back when confronted with the military uniform.

"Oh, erm…good day. How can I help you? Some food and wine?"

"No thank you," said Lucius softly so as not to alarm her. "Can you tell me if this is the inn run by Brennius Crispus?"

"Oh yes, of course! My uncle Sextus runs the inn."

"May I speak with him?"

"Oh yes," she repeated. "I'll go and fetch him for you." She ran into the back and Lucius waited. The room was now filling with sunlight, the darkness dissipating. Out of the corner of his eye he felt the man looking at him but decided it was nothing more than idle curiosity aroused by his uniform.

"Can I help you?" The voice came from behind Lucius. He turned back to the counter. Before him was a rather short man with greying blond hair on a round head with large, friendly but tired eyes.

"Sextus Brennius Crispus?" asked Lucius.

"Yes, that's me. How can I help you?"

"I am Tribune Lucius Metellus Anguis-" Before Lucius could finish his sentence, the man was around the corner of the counter.

"By all the Gods, it is an honour, Tribune!" he exclaimed as he grasped Lucius' forearm. "My son's told us all about you. Raving all the time he was! Drusilla!" he called to the girl. "Go and get your aunt for me. Tell her we have a very important visitor." The girl ran out and Sextus showed Lucius to a table on which he set a pitcher of wine and one of water with two cups. "Please sit, Tribune. Antanelis told us that if ever you passed by we should treat you like, well, dare I say the word, a 'king'." He laughed heartily, his whole chest shaking. "Aha! Vipsania, come and sit with us." Lucius stood as an elegant woman approached. "This is Tribune Metellus!"

"Tribune Metellus!" she echoed, folding her hands over her heart in a sign of thanks. "We are indeed happy to have you here with us. Antanelis told us everything about how you saved his life. We are grateful, truly."

Why do they have to be so nice? Such beautiful people, Lucius thought.

"Our son wrote to us that you were in Italy for the triumph but we never expected to see you." Sextus handed Lucius a cup of wine which he put back on the table. "We haven't had a letter from him in months! He must be very busy." The two parents looked at Lucius as though they were waiting for him to agree, for him to tell them that *Yes. Your son is indeed extremely busy defending the empire, winning glory for your family, for himself. He loves you and will be home sometime very soon. Then will you be able to hold him close and embrace him, tell him you are proud.* Such was the news they wanted, the news Lucius longed to give them; but they would never hear such words uttered, not for their ears, not concerning their son.

"Yes, he must be, quite busy," Vipsania reiterated. She and Sextus sat and looked up at Lucius who remained standing. He would find it easier to tell them standing up. They gazed at him, still smiling, waiting for him to say something.

"The reason I have come is..." He removed his helmet and placed it beneath his left arm. "I bring news of your son."

"Yes, yes," Sextus asked excitedly. "What news, Tribune?"

Lucius bowed his head, not able to look them in the eyes. "Antanelis has been killed."

He said it. It was done. The words hung there in the sombre air, still, motionless and painful. When he mustered the courage to look up again he was not met by the two kind, smiling faces of moments before but rather two deathly pale and fearful echoes of a father and mother. Vipsania buried her face in her hands and wept, shook, but Sextus Brennius Crispus simply stared at Lucius, his eyes smaller now, rimmed by watery shadows, tears that threatened to fall and never stop falling.

The tribune had covered them in a blanket of dark cloud. Sextus looked over at the bundle on the stool and realised that it did not contain the Tribune's belongings but those of his dead son. Finally, he spoke.

"Please, Tribune, tell me; how did my son die?" His hand shook as he asked the question. Vipsania looked up, her face sodden with tears.

Lucius proceeded to tell them about how Antanelis died. There was no way to make it sound less shocking without lying and so he recounted the report of the hunt, the lion, how he saved his friends and how he fought with all the power in his strong limbs. When Lucius finished, he went over to pick up the bundle and placed it on the table in front of the grieving parents. Sextus dried his eyes before accepting it.

"Do you know what the name 'Antanelis' means, Tribune? *Praiseworthy.* I am saddened beyond words to have lost him, but I always knew that when his end would come, it would be a heroic one. He did not disappoint."

Moved by the unbelievable poise displayed by Sextus, Lucius sat down and reached for the bag. He pulled gently on the lacing that sealed it, allowing the mouth to open wide. There on top was the corona that Antanelis had earned in battle.

"He was indeed worthy of praise. Antanelis was one of my best centurions and most loyal friends." Lucius had come to breaking point, no longer able to keep up a strong façade. Sextus placed a hand on his shoulder.

"He always spoke highly of you, Tribune. He loved you like a brother." Vipsania rose from her seat.

"We are ever grateful to you for saving his life."

Lucius' face twisted up in self-anger. "Saving his life? I was not there for him in Numidia, and now he is gone."

"But without your actions in Parthia our Antanelis would have been dead long ago. We would have missed out on years of letters, his promotion to centurion and *this*." Vipsania picked up the corona, running her fingers along it as though

she were running her hands along her son's hair. "I must
excuse myself however at this time. Forgive me. Though you
bring bad tidings I am happy to have finally met you,
Tribune." Lucius rose as she left to be alone. Sextus sat still,
staring at the bundle, deep in thought. Lucius felt he should go
and placed his helmet on his head.

"I should be going now. You and your wife must be left to
your grief and I do not wish to impose."

"Tribune, I'll accept no such words from you. We made a
promise to our son that you would always receive a welcome
in our home and that you shall have. It is an honour."

"I don't know what to say."

"Say nothing. Just accept our hospitality. If that is your
companion out in the courtyard he too is welcome." Sextus
gestured to Ashur who sat in the sun.

"You are too kind."

"Now if you will excuse me, I will see to my wife and then
return shortly to show you to your rooms."

"Please take your time," Lucius said as Sextus picked up
the bundle and went into the back room after his wife. The inn
was empty again, the only other customer, the one with the
limp, was gone too. Lucius went out to join Ashur and wait in
bewildered silence, to think about the day he had had thus far.

That night, Lucius had little sleep, his mind burdened with
emotion and heavy thoughts as he lay uncomfortably in bed.
Across the room, Ashur slept soundly. Sextus, despite the
punishing news Lucius had brought, had made sure to give
them the finest, cleanest room they had as well as a meal fit for
a Caesar. Every bite was filled with guilt and remorse in spite
of Ashur's reassurances that such feelings helped neither the
living nor the dead.

Only after retiring for the night did the family of Sextus
Brennius Crispus mourn the loss of a son, a brother, a cousin.
The sound of tearful wailing echoed through the corridors of
the inn to reach Lucius' ears and he wondered why the Gods

had taken the life of a good Roman such as Antanelis. In his heart it just didn't seem fair or right. He lay there all night, pondering that to the sounds of sadness penetrating the walls.

By the time the cock crew, Lucius had already dressed in his travelling clothes, strapped on his sword and dagger and packed up his armour. He woke Ashur who had slept soundly through the night as though not even there. The first rays of sunlight came in through the window to light his peaceful face and bring him back from whichever mysterious realm he had been to.

After breakfast, Ashur saw that the horses were prepared for the return journey while Lucius walked slowly to the edge of the road with Sextus. The tired man before him seemed to have aged overnight, the dark circles beneath his eyes now badges of loss and emptiness in his life.

"My wife apologizes for not seeing you off, Tribune, but she is far too distraught." He ran his hand through his hair slowly, blinking in the angling light.

"I understand," Lucius said as he looked up the road, the cobbles glistening with the remnants of morning dew. To the west, darkening clouds were rolling in to wet the hills in spring showers. Lucius peered into the distance, unknowingly letting out a sigh. He felt adrift in that moment, a warrior without a home or purpose. "Looks like the rains are coming." Sextus looked at a small mound of dirt nearby. On it, moving in two rows in opposite directions were hundreds of beetles carrying leaves twice their size. Sextus looked up at the sky, then down at the beetles again and noticed that they continued to work without hesitation.

"The rains won't pass this way," he said. "You should have dry travelling for at least half the day." He then turned to Lucius, his eyes concerned. "Tribune, there's something I must tell you. It confuses me somewhat but I feel I must tell you since Antanelis..." he paused, wiped away a tear, "...since my son thought it important enough to tell me."

346

Lucius, waited, stared at the old man, his shoulders weighed down by something. "What is it, Brennius Crispus?"

"You must understand that this must remain between the two of us."

"Of course." *What's all this about?*

Sextus looked around to make sure no one was near, then moved closer. "My son was troubled, Tribune, for he discovered certain 'elements' among the cohort. Antanelis, apart from the long letters to his family, wrote several to me alone in which he described conditions among some of your men; either details he believed would bore his mother or things he wanted only me to know of." He looked around again and led Lucius down the road a bit. "Antanelis didn't name anyone for fear of endangering his mother, myself and the rest of the familia. Imperial spies have been running rampant by order of Plautianus." The name made Lucius shiver for some reason. "They're reading letters sent from every corner of the Roman world." He then took Lucius by the arms, gazed up at him with a frightening intensity. "Tribune, my son claimed to have discovered certain bad feelings toward you in the ranks of your cohort." Lucius began to shake with rage but Sextus held him fast and continued. "Tribune, I don't know how much he discovered, how many were or are involved, but I do know that my son loved you and was no liar." Sextus waited for Lucius to speak, a moment for this news to sink in.

"My men are loyal!" Lucius protested aloud, his confusion overwhelming him.

"There is more," Sextus continued. "In his final letter to me Antanelis' tone was different, both secretive and fearful. He said that if anything happened to him...I should tell you everything, warn you. He didn't know or reveal exactly how high up this treachery reached, or what form it took, but it was enough to worry my brave son."

Lucius paced, staring at the road beneath his feet as he tried to clear his head. "But Antanelis was killed by a lion!" he said harshly.

"I know, I know." The man before Lucius crumbled, his eyes now stinging with hot tears that could not be wiped away. He mustered one last sentence. "You must promise me something, Tribune. If my son's death was more than what it appears to be, you must promise to avenge his death so that his shade does not drift alone, tormented in Hades. Make them suffer, Tribune, the way my boy did." For a moment, it was as though flames were kindled in the father's eyes, intense flames that shuddered and went out as quickly as they had been lit.

Lucius held the man's shaking hands. "Sextus, if I discover that anyone plotted against Antanelis and myself, they'll wish they'd never been born."

"Thank you."

At that moment, Ashur came up the path leading the two horses. The clouds had cleared for the time being but in the distance darkness seemed to be creeping in upon the world in waves. Lucius nodded to Ashur and they mounted up. Sextus approached Lucius and grasped his forearm.

"May the Gods protect you, Tribune."

"May they protect us all, Brennius Crispus. Farewell."

Lucius rode on in silence, Ashur behind, the darkening horizon ahead of them. He wondered who opposed him, who among the men he had fought and bled with could turn on him. He thought of this and only this for most of the day. He only came out of his thoughts when lightning struck not far off on a nearby hill. The rain was coming down cold and hard and Ashur, ahead now, yelled something incoherent back to Lucius as he pointed to an inn.

Rome was yet too distant, too long a road in the torrent. Cold and shaking, Lucius warmed himself with the one thought that could calm the raging sea he felt within: Adara. Warm and soft and beautiful, he heard her whisper in his ear as his horse plodded over the soaked earth, each step bringing him closer to Rome and his love.

XXII

FAMILIA METELLUS

'The Family Metellus'

To Quintus Metellus,
from his loving wife Antonia. Greetings.

My dear Quintus,

It has been a long while since you have sent word as to how you are fairing and what thoughts might possibly be playing on your troubled mind. So much has happened since you departed from our home, most of it joyful indeed. I wish you were here to share in the events with me. After all, you are my husband, I your wife, and as such is not my place by your side, here in Rome, at the head of our household and not tucked away in the hills of Etruria?

I pray nightly to Apollo for your return; that he might somehow reach the inner recesses of your heart and mind to successfully entreat you to return with our young son from this sad, self-imposed exile. You have been too long away and I am lonely for you, my husband. Yes, I know I should not speak so expressly but Venus has breathed honeyed music into the air of Rome and I find it inescapable and refreshing. Without you though, I fear I am susceptible to fits of sadness; I long for the years of our youth when we revelled in each other's presence. You would write to me much more then...

However, this letter is not about me but rather of Lucius. Yes! Our son *Lucius Metellus Anguis*. No matter how much you convince yourself otherwise he is still our brave son. It is of Lucius that I write and his newfound happiness with Adara Antonina of Athens. As you were not here I have given my blessing to the two of them. Her family is well known and *respected, Publius Leander Antoninus and Delphina his wife being very kind and generous people whom I find most agreeable.*

I wish I knew what thoughts were plaguing your mind at this moment, husband. But as you are absent I have made the decision as I see fit. Lucius and Adara will be wed on the Nones of Quinctilis at the Temple of Apollo on the Palatine hill. I have already spoken with the priests there and they will be prepared. It is still to be decided what sacrifice they will make.

I had thought it would be our daughter who would marry first, but the Gods have a plan in mind and so we must bow to their wishes. Quintus, I do hope that you will come for this happy occasion if not sooner. Already people are speaking of the union between our families. You really should be here, in Rome.

Before I go, husband, there is one more thing I wish to say, something that I have heard whispered in the Forum. There are some who are suspicious of your absence and who doubt the reasons for it. I need not say that much is known by certain parties who cannot be fooled, no matter how innocent the matter.

For now, know that I love you and miss you and would that you were here where you belong. Think on what I have said husband and come back soon.

Your loving, dutiful wife,

Antonia Metella

"The messenger awaits your reply, master. He is on the front path." The house slave waited nervously, twiddling his fingers behind his back, his head hung low; the master had been in an interminably foul mood and was prone to beating the servants in his frustration.

"Send him away! There is no reply."

"Yes, Master." The slave ran hastily out of the door to tell the messenger who was standing in the hard falling rain beneath a black sky.

Quintus Metellus crumpled the message in his hand and threw it on top of a brazier that burned in the upper loggia of the family villa. He walked over to the railing, his icy eyes looked down to the courtyard where the slave was sending the messenger away. Wearily, the rider mounted his horse and set off down the path and the road that led east to join the Via Cassia and then back to Rome.

He remained there for some time, staring out over the Etrurian hills where black and charcoal storm clouds weaved their way in and out of the higher peaks. He felt old, and weak and useless and it angered him more than anything that he was helpless to change his situation, the incessant drifting in which he found himself. Or was he helpless? As he looked out over the villa lands, drenched with Spring rain, he thought, as he had for months, about ways in which he could possibly salvage what remained of his honour, his dignitas.

The Metellus villa was a medium sized estate in the green Etrurian hills located mid-way between the Via Cassia to the east and the Via Aemilia Scauri to the west along the coast. Both roads were long-time remnants of Rome's Republican age and it was along them that generations of Metelli had journeyed between Rome and their Etrurian homeland. The minor road, on which the villa lands were located, ran east-west to link the ancient highways.

Quintus had always been proud of his inheritance of the estate; a typical villa rustica of the old order. The main house was made up of a large, two-storied U-shape. On the first floor were several cubicula, sitting rooms, a study, a triclinium, kitchen and small estate office and lavatory; on the upper floor were two larger cubicula, another sitting room and a covered loggia. At the north-eastern corner of the house was a private bath house with tepidarium, caldarium and frigidarium, fed from a natural spring that flowed down from the hills. Quintus had always prided himself on this display of engineering on the part of his ancestors which kept the bath waters constantly refreshed and flowing. North-west of the small plateau on which the two main buildings were constructed, with their garden and towering cypresses, were the prized vineyards of the estate and the wine stores located in an adjacent, rectangular storehouse. To the East and South of the plateau were the olive groves and apple and plum orchards. Along the soft-flowing stream that fronted the land were grazing pastures for several head of cattle as well as goats. Horses were housed in the stables to the immediate south of the main house, beneath the plateau, along with quarters for the estate slaves.

Quintus Metellus clung to this idyllic image all of his life like a Phoenician merchant with his hands wrapped tightly about a purse of sestertii. It was his refuge in his youth, and later his sanctuary in times of political upheaval. Now, it was his prison in times of domestic crisis and discontent.

The tall, wooded hills rose high above the estate, shielding it from the outside world like masses of sleeping Titans none would dare to approach. Crowning them was an ever-present reminder of Rome's past as well as that of the Metellus family. On one of the far peaks, seemingly above the low rain clouds, was a solemn tomb, a remnant of when the Etruscan ancestors of the Metelli were as indomitable as the wind and rain. Beyond the trees, atop a large grassy mound, stood three giant cypresses to mark the resting place of fallen warriors. In that place, their presence was still thick in the air, as much as any element of nature; silent, sleeping watchers of the new world under Rome.

Quintus Metellus spent much of his time wandering the lands he had loved so much, but which now grew more and more detestable to him. Every olive tasted rotten, every sip of wine increasingly sour, soporific. Much of the time he would sit in his study perusing old scrolls or family documents, losing himself in a time when the Metelli were one of the foremost families of the Republic. It had always been his wish to be the one to raise his family from the ashes of the past, to be reborn like a phoenix from the flames. If only, he believed, he had never been born into the ridiculous cognomen of 'Anguis'. *Caecilius Metellus*: the illustrious name of so many Metelli before him earned much more respect in the past than that silly name meaning 'Dragon', invented by some superstitious ancestor belonging to a supposedly ancient line of warriors. *What stupidity!* he thought.

Although Quintus Metellus believed that he was descended from the infamous Caecilius Metellus line, his father (as mad as he was) insisted that they were directly descended from the Anguis line. At the birth of Quintus' first son, the then proud grandfather, Avus Metellus, was relentless in his insistence that the child be given the "true" cognomen of their line. He said that in a dream sent from the Gods themselves he was told that the child must be called Metellus Anguis and if not he, the grandfather, would die a horrible death. Bowing to such pressure and guilt, Quintus named his son Lucius Metellus Anguis. A month later, Avus Metellus died anyway, but he died happy.

When yet another son was born to Antonia and Quintus, there was no hesitation; he was named after what Quintus believed to be the true line to which they belonged and was called Quintus Caecilius Metellus. Metellus pater firmly held that because the family was so very ancient in its origins, there had been confusion for some time as to the true lineage. He made himself the one to clear all the confusion away with the birth of his second son. The blood of the Metellus forbears ran as purely in his veins as life did in the land of his ancestors, the land on which he stood; it flowed in every handful of rich soil, every strong tree root around him. However, the dream he had once believed in so desperately was slipping further and

353

further away, disappearing into the mists of time as he wallowed away the days, years, in self-pity and self-loathing.

In the midst of Metellus pater's lamentations for the shades of his dwindling dreams and hopes was young Quintus Caecilius Metellus, utterly alone. At a time when all young children are meant to be happy with the approach of a new summer, playing outside and splashing in fresh streams, young Quintus wandered the grounds with only himself to talk to. Not even the slaves would amuse him as they used to for fear of angering their master. Even Numa, the estate steward, and his wife did not approach young Quintus for fear of their master; the times when the joyous couple would entertain him with hilarious tales of gossip from the surrounding estates were now vanished. Instead, Numa and his wife drifted through the corridors and rooms of the villa hunched and quiet, withdrawn into their own, safe world.

Occasionally a question to the gods he believed dwelt at the top of the mountain would fall from his pursed lips. *Why did my brother ever have to return?* he would ask. *Why does father hate me so and mother ignore me?* He would stare up at the mountain, waiting for answers that would never come on the wind or be revealed in the flights of soaring eagles or scavenging crows. Such responses were given to Lucius alone. *Why?*

Young Quintus was a stranger to everyone. So much expectation without the attention needed to enrich, encourage; he was left to his own thoughts and doubts with tutors who could not have cared less. Lucius had Diodorus and he, he had an endless line of favour seeking men who would quickly move on to another pupil belonging to one of the richer families of Rome. When a tutor eventually decided to leave, it always ended up being young Quintus' fault in some way.

At least in Etruria, on the family estate, there were no tutors to scold him or ignore him. He was free to do as he wished, to roam the fields and hillsides near the ancient tombs at the top where he tried to converse with the Gods. He wouldn't approach the very peak for fear of angering them, but would watch from a distance, quiet. If he was good, they would say *You are a very good young man, Quintus Caecilius*, or some other words of comfort.

In the mornings and evenings, the kitchen slave would prepare food for him which he would eat alone in the triclinium whilst his father chose to eat in his study or the covered loggia in contemplative, unapproachable silence. The only words he would hear from his father in the evening were "Have you read your scrolls today? Keep at it, my son." However, he didn't feel like a son of any kind but rather a burden. So passed the days, slowly and lazily, uneventful as usual. That is until another messenger appeared on the road up to the villa early one morning. The messenger rode a black stallion and was dressed all in black giving him the semblance of a shadow, faceless. The only noticeable items on him were the bronze fittings on the scabbards of a short sword and dagger.

Quintus Metellus pater watched from where he ate in the loggia, observing the visitor with a suspicious eye before recognition dawned on him. He raised a finger to call the slave over to him, said that the visitor was to be brought directly to him without delay. The slave hurried to do his bidding.

Down in the courtyard, the black-cloaked figure had dismounted, leaving his horse to stand obediently. Young Quintus peered at him from behind a pillar. He noticed the man was tall and strong-looking but limped when he followed the slave into the house. Curious and having nothing better to do, he went inside to see if he could find out who the man was and what he wanted with his father.

Quintus Metellus did not rise when the messenger approached him but remained in his chair, indignant, as he ate from a bowl of figs.

Unperturbed by this, the messenger took another chair from nearby and sat himself down, his face not humble or gracious but arrogant and determined. After helping himself to some wine from a small flagon on the table, he spoke.

"Quintus Metellus *Anguis*," he emphasised the Anguis. "I've come with a message from my superior."

"Is it so important that you've come all the way out here to disturb my breakfast and drink my wine?"

"Tut, tut, Senator." The man clicked his tongue as if teasing a child. "I thought that the Metelli were renown for their hospitality."

"Tell me what it is you've come to tell me, by Hades, and leave!" Quintus leaned forward staring in anger at the man, his disrespect.

The man popped an entire fig into his mouth and spoke. "My superior says that he will be here to visit you personally on a matter of great importance to you and your family. You have no choice in the matter." Now the man was serious indeed, the sarcasm distinctly lacking from his voice. "He is already on his way here and says you are to meet with him at the final hour of daylight somewhere outside of the villa."

Quintus smiled smugly. "And where, may I ask, does your so-called *superior* expect me to meet him?"

The man smiled and pointed to the north. "Up there."

Quintus heaved an accidental sigh of exasperation and the man laughed slightly.

"It seems like a long trek for a man of your years, Senator. Perhaps you should use one of those fine stallions you have down in the pasture to carry you."

"You go too far, Praetorian," Quintus growled.

"Ha, ha," he laughed before shaking his hands clean and rising to leave. "He'll be expecting you. Be prompt." The man turned and made his way to the stairs that led down to the ground floor. Quintus noticed his limp as he went, wanted to make some insult toward him for his arrogance, but said nothing. His dignity lay in tatters on the floor at his feet.

An hour later, when he passed young Quintus on the stairs as he was going up to the loggia, he said: "Have you read any of your scrolls today? Get to it!" That was all.

The day had passed languidly for Quintus, his mind caught up in a web of distrust and uncertainty about the purpose of this visit. He sat staring out at the land below, the clouds. Every now and then he would look to his right where an amphora clepsydra counted the hours of daylight that remained; with the slow release of small drops of water the stick indicating the time dropped minutely, frustratingly. When the eleventh hour of daylight began to approach Quintus asked that a horse be brought to him immediately from the stables, that he was going for a ride and none were to come after him for any reason. The threat of a severe beating ensured the slaves' compliance. Wearing a thick, brown cloak over a tunic and riding leggings, he mounted the horse with the help of the stableman and set off along the path that went uphill from behind the villa complex at the north end of the vineyard. Tucked into his belt was a long dagger he had decided he should have, just in case.

It had been many, many years since Quintus had gone up the hill, been in the steep, thick woods of the south-facing slope. The path was overgrown with all manner of weeds and bracken, the path occasionally blocked by a fallen tree. The smell of wild garlic was pungent in the air and caused his eyes to water. Then his horse started at the sound of a cracking twig and he reigned in to listen. Nothing. Not a sound except the wind in the leaves and the squawking of a raven somewhere in the forest. He moved on and soon the top became visible as the trees thinned and opened up onto the perfect slope of the large grassy mound topped by giant cypresses. He paused at the edge of the trees and looked about; even for the most irreligious Roman this place held something unknown, an uneasiness.

"Right on time, Senator!" the voice came from the stone-lined entrance to the tomb, from the shadows.

"What's the meaning of this? Why in the name of Jupiter did you come out here when you could have written?" Quintus glared at the blackness within, awaited a response.

"We'll talk inside. Follow me." Black moved within black as a shadow turned to go into the depths of the damp place, toward a slight glow at its heart.

"This is ridiculous!" said Quintus as he made his way in, careful not to surprise any snakes or scorpions that slept in the shadows.

Darkness was beginning to fall, the sky reddened as young Quintus' small legs carried him over tree limb and rock. He had never gone so far up the hill before, had been too afraid. But, something pushed him on, working his will against the fear that grew more and more within him. *The gods up there will be angry with me if I go any closer* he thought, but closer he went until the trees ended and his legs stopped. He felt like going back down the hill, regretting his sacrilege to the place, but the curiosity was so intense that it overcame fear, respect for gods or the thought of his father's wrath. Cautiously, he crept toward the monument, never taking his eyes off the entrance, so dark, so dark. Part of him wished he hadn't overheard his father's conversation with the messenger that day, not knowing was easier, less confusing.

The voices inside rose to inaudible shouts, startling him with their unearthly echoes. Young Quintus jumped aside of the entrance, afraid of being spotted but no one came out. His heart heaving, he entered the blackness of the corridor, his eyes on the dim light too far ahead.

The tomb complex was large, with many chambers revolving around a large, central room. Each chamber housed the burned remains of up to twenty-four warriors and their families in large bronze barrels or clay urns, some of which had cracked or fallen with the rumblings far, far below the earth. There were four entrances to the tomb, each one facing a different direction, north, south, east, west; the gods of the winds could come and go as they pleased. When the winds did arrive with a particular fury, the corridors leading to the chambers rang out in deathly tones hearkening the dead to the presence of trespassers, driving the unwelcome away.

Quintus shifted uneasily in the light of the two torches. Tired and angry, he demanded to know at once the purpose of such a visit.

"Because, Quintus Anguis," the man said. "I have a message from *my* superior and it does not bode well for you!" His back to Quintus, he removed his cloak and threw it on a stone slab where several bones lay disturbed.

"Turn around and face me like a man, without hiding behind that fancy uniform! Argus!"

In the dark of one of the antechambers, young Quintus shuddered at the name but remained silent.

Argus wheeled quickly to face Quintus, the sweat on his brow glistening in the faint light, his eyes fearsome. "I don't have to answer to you, *old man*! For your recommendation I said I would keep you apprised of what was happening in Rome, in your own house, that's all! I owe you nothing more. My allegiance is to Plautianus."

"Hmmph!" Quintus spat. "Praetorian spy eh? So that's what you've become? Another tool for an upstart."

Argus sat down, arrogant once more, unmoved, cold. "You should mind what you say, Senator. I have my own network of spies and they're everywhere. I know what has been going on with yourself and your family and it's killing you because you are dying to know every last detail. You need me! The truth is, I don't need *you* anymore." In the long silence that followed, Quintus paced a few times and then sat, Argus' hateful eyes upon him the whole time, a smirk on his face. Then Argus spoke. "All right. I'll tell you a few last things that I haven't told you in my letters just so that I can see the stupid look on your old, tired face."

Quintus' face shook with rage, the colour rose to his ears. He wanted to kill the creature before him but more than that he wanted to know what was happening in Rome.

"As you know, Lucius is going to marry that Antonina girl, I don't remember her name. What you don't know is that Lucius, your son, has come to the attention of certain imperials and they are watching him closely."

"I have no son by that name!" Quintus interrupted stubbornly.

"At any rate," Argus continued, thoroughly enjoying the telling, "The Antonina girl is a snob along with her idiot parents. I've had their place watched for some time along with yours. In fact one night I went myself to see what was happening. I watched Lucius go to sleep with a stupid grin on his face...actually he almost saw me but I managed to get away quickly."

"Spy indeed!" said Quintus disdainfully. "You couldn't sneak up on a tree."

"You're right, it's much easier to sneak up on your wife and daughters. Oh calm yourself! You should be more concerned with what I have to say next. Once again your brilliant son has gotten you into trouble with a comment he made at the banquet to the entire Imperial family."

Quintus sighed, preparing for the worst; *Another stain on the Metellus name,* he thought.

"In his attempt to make excuses for the absence of you and your wife he let it be known that you intentionally lied in order to avoid the emperor's triumph and banquet, or rather you had your son lie for you."

"I never gave any such instructions!"

"I know," said Argus laughing. "But that's what they think. And now you're under suspicion. All of Rome knows it." Quintus held his head in his hands in despair and frustration. "However, Plautianus has the emperor's ear, as I have

Plautianus'.'" His head rose, fearful of what Argus would say next. "Plautianus has an offer for you."

Has it really come to this? he wondered. *Bowing down to the most ruthless man in Rome, a cur from Africa province who connived and murdered his way into the emperor's favour, a man whose spies are spread all over the empire. And all because of my idiot son!* "What does your superior have to say, Argus?"

"Plautianus says that he will eliminate any suspicion of deceit regarding yourself and your family in the eyes of the emperor. He says that he will make sure you and your family are given high honours in Rome, in the Senate, once again."

"And what, may I ask, does he expect in return?"

"My superior insists that you return to Rome, to your family, to your back bench in the Senate and that you attend the wedding of your, erm, *son*." To be ordered about thus was over much to bear, but what choice did he have? To refuse meant the loss of all the family owned, exile, perhaps even death in one form or another. "There is one more thing," Argus added, almost gleeful. "You must also inform on Lucius and the rest of the family to make sure they do not rise too quickly, too eagerly; you will inform Plautianus of everything through me." Argus leaned back against the wall, pleased with himself and what he had done to the man before him. He waited for a response.

Quintus turned all of this over in his mind and at first was angry, full of rage, then scared. But all of these feelings eventually gave way to new determination. One skill at which his ancestors had been quite adept was knowing the ins and outs of the political sphere, using situations and people as a means to an end, an ultimate end. For him, as was now clear, that end was the rebirth of the Caecilius Metellus family name, his name and his true son's name, young Quintus Caecilius Metellus. *I shall use this fool before me, as well as Plautianus,* he thought to himself. *They will help me unknowingly and I shall have what I want.* Argus did not receive the reaction he had expected, hoped for - a broken man weeping before him, grabbing at his feet, begging for his help.

"Agreed." That was all Quintus said, his face emotionless and cold. At the same moment, down the dark, lonely corridor, in a corner of a dark tomb, the tears flowed from young Quintus' eyes, not wanting to believe the horrors he was witness to at that moment.

"Agreed? Is that all you have to say? That's your only comment in return for being asked to betray your family?"

"I know who my true family is. Do you, Argus? You always were a *bastard*!" Now it was Quintus who smirked, full knowing that his words had cut deeply and painfully, even through a skin as thick and hardened as Argus'.

"How about I cut your throat right now, old man?" Argus drew his sword, raised it to Quintus's head.

"Tut, tut, little Argus," said Quintus as though speaking to a baby. "Put your little sword away, Praetorian. How long do you think your master would let you live if you killed an informant as important as myself? Hmm? Not long! Your guts would be flowing down the Tiber before the next day's breakfast."

Argus lowered his sword. He would not have thought twice about striking any other man down then and there. This time, however, he found his hand unwilling to move for fear of Plautianus, but also for fear of retribution; to be a parricide was to damn oneself and no matter how much one refused to believe in the Gods, Nemesis always lay in wait.

"My mother told me all about you and though I was still a little brat I understood what she had said, *father…*"

By Hades! He knows. Inside Quintus panicked as the memory of a certain freedwoman came rushing back. Events he had convinced himself never happened, that he had managed to keep hidden from all…from all except Argus. Perhaps his mother had told him in the hopes that it would help him.

362

"So, as it turns out, I too am a Metellus. I wonder how this news would go over in the Forum? Your chances of rising to prominence would surely be gone."

"You're not my bastard!"

"Oh, but I am your bastard, brought into this life by my bitch of a mother." The slap was so fast that Argus had little time to react and received the blow full on the cheek. He held his arm, showing more will than ever he had.

"I should have sold you to the vilest Numidian slave trader in the markets when I had the chance, Argus."

"Yes, well you didn't and now I'm here and *you* work for *me*! That is unless you want everyone to know the truth about Senator Quintus Metellus *Anguis*?" Quintus knew that Argus wouldn't kill him but he had no doubt that he would reveal this harmful secret. He had everything to gain in being revealed as a Metellus and Quintus had everything to lose.

"Agreed," was all he said again. "It appears Argus that we have a deal. I will return to Rome to inform on the family and in return you will whisper sweet nothings into the ears of Plautianus."

"Yes." Argus gathered up his cloak, dusty from the pile of bones, ready to leave.

"Done. Now get off my land!"

Argus turned down another dark corridor, lit now by moonlight, turned and said "Tut tut *father*, the Metelli are listening. It's my land too. Ha, ha..." his laughter disappeared into the night and, Quintus hoped, back to Rome.

Quintus stayed only a short time longer before gathering his senses for the ride back to the villa. The forest was not the safest place at night and he would have to rely on his horse to follow the path he hoped it would remember.

On the top of the hill, young Quintus was left alone in the dark, unwilling to move, incredulous at what had transpired, what he had heard. Luckily his father didn't care enough to check in on him when he arrived back at the villa. He couldn't bring himself to leave the chamber of the tomb for it was too dark and he was too terrified. And so, crying to himself and shivering in the tomb of his ancestors, young Quintus Caecilius Metellus stayed the entire night with his nightmares, the howling gods of the four winds and the dead.

XXIII

LUDI APOLLINARES

'The Games of Apollo'

There was a sweetness in the air, a feeling of life that could only exist with the gentle melding of Spring into Summer and the thought of long, bright, hot days. Cicadas sang lazily in the tops of trees, the shade of bushes, their melodic complaints sounding from sun-up to sundown. Life in Rome went on mainly in the morning and the evening as many businesses closed for a time beneath the sun's full height.

The city dozed and the Forum was calm, the markets still, the Senate adjourned until the evening session. All was peace and quiet at midday except, that is, in the home of Publius Leander Antoninus. From morning to night the house was abuzz with the hasty preparations of a marriage.

Having extended his family's stay in view of these unforeseen circumstances, and having no work but that which he had left behind in Athens with his assistant and staff, Publius Leander was left to his own devices in a home with four women rushing about in an endless dance. He often wondered from what secret spring their energy flowed, for while he dozed the day away in the peristyle garden one or another of them would come running up to him with questions such as: "Father, do you like this colour?" or "Publius, shall we invite so and so? We don't want to insult anyone." To which he would answer "Yes, yes, it's lovely," or "Invite whom you wish as long as I'm there too." Often times his attempts at humour would go wholly unnoticed.

Sitting the days away in the garden or visiting the baths, Publius Leander frequently found himself thinking about his future son-in-law; he had not known Lucius long but already he felt a sort of fatherly worry for the young man. He could see that, despite the great joy he enjoyed, Lucius was pressed by worries that no doubt were related to the news he had received from his centurion. Publius also longed for some decent male conversation, for variety's sake, because when he was with all of the women of both houses the conversation more times than not would turn to wedding arrangements.

In the face of this organizational chaos, Publius' mind drifted back to the unusual heaviness that was so apparent in Lucius; indeed every member of the Metellus and Antoninus family wondered what exactly was going on behind all the smiles, all the excitement of the wedding. No one worried more than the future bride; she had been busy with planning and knew that perhaps she had neglected her husband-to-be, the feelings that so obviously pained him. When planning was finished for the day she would sit in her cubicula by the light of half a dozen lamps and write as if she were speaking to him where he slept on the other side of the city. She hoped that some god would hear her and pass on her affections and her thoughts to the man she had fallen so helplessly in love with.

When they did have occasion to speak alone, Lucius had told Adara that it was the first time he had been the bearer of such news, Death's messenger as it were. Adara was quick to comfort him of this thought, saying that it was the Gods' plan, that Antanelis' parents might have had such news by means of a much colder messenger. Lucius wanted to tell her what Antanelis' father had told him his son wrote about in his letters, what was happening among the men, his men, but he couldn't. Not now. The day of their wedding was at hand and nothing would spoil the occasion, not war, not duty, not death.

"We need to stop sir, my leg's killing me!"

"You're such an idiot, Sabinus! I swear it would have been less trouble bringing a woman along. You can't do anything right."

The two men led their horses off the road to a nearby stream and dismounted, the one with the bad leg biting his tongue, trying not to answer Argus' comments. *Who does he think he is?* he thought. As he went to the stream to rinse the fresh blood away and change the bandages on his thigh, Argus sat down on a felled tree, disgusted by his womanly companion. He drank from his wineskin.

"It's your own fault, you know."

"What is?" said Sabinus, cringing as the water penetrated the wound.

"That you're wounded. I ask you to do one simple thing, and you're the one who gets hurt."

"I told you, that man doesn't move like a man! He's as fast as a fury. The Gods must be helping him."

"He's as much a man as any other. And I thought I told you to keep your superstitions to yourself! Had I been there, he'd be dead and Lucius alone on the road. Now they're alert and we have to be extra careful, all because you screwed up."

"Me? Where were *you*?" Argus didn't like being questioned by one of his spies and rose to stand over the wounded man.

"Are you questioning me? Hmm! I was in Rome getting instructions from Plautianus and if you talk to me again like that I'll flog you until your skin falls off. Understood?"

"Understood Argus, sir."

Argus went back to the tree and sat again. Over and over in his mind he had gone through what he perceived as a grand scheme to bring down the Metelli by using Quintus Metellus himself. He owed Quintus and he wanted to make him squirm now in the knowledge that he knew everything and would betray him in an instant. He felt he had gotten the better of the old man the night before last and grinned with cold pleasure. It was only a matter of time before Plautianus helped him bring down his true prey. In the meantime, his prey's allies had to be eliminated. His campaign of elimination was already underway; one victim had already fallen and that had been covered up nicely. He would wait to see if the others would come over to his cause. For now, this last failed attempt concerned him. He couldn't fail again.

The Praetorian prefect had taken a liking to Argus the moment he saw him in the camp in Rome. When Argus first entered the Guard, he had been brutal on the field. He was one of the strongest fighters and one against whom many of the more senior troops had tested themselves in training. Not many of them left the field without some remembrance upon their bodies: a broken arm, a scar across the face or a flattened nose. There was even one man who left the parade ground unconscious; he didn't come back.

Eventually one of the Praetorian centurions went to Plautianus to complain about this new recruit who had been brutalizing their own men.

"He's a strong son of a bitch, sir, an absolute beast! But we're losing men every time he goes onto the parade ground. There's got to be a better place for him, one where we can channel his aggression in our favour?"

Plautianus listened to this report, intrigued, his curiosity peaked.

"Yes, it would be a shame to have to slit his throat on the field just to eliminate the rumblings in the ranks. I just might have a use for him. Send him to me in the morning and I'll have a chat with this monster."

"Yes, sir!" The centurion saluted and went out pleased at the prospect of being rid of such a nuisance.

And so, one morning, Argus found himself face to face with Plautianus, Praetorian Prefect, in his office inside the Praetorian camp. He stood stock still, wondered what in Hades was going on as he looked around the room, at Plautianus' back, turned to him from the moment he entered.

"Your commanders tell me that I should make an example of you by slitting your filthy throat..." Still he did not turn, let Argus ponder the thought for a few moments. Then he spun, his dark eyes fixed, piercing and cold as ice and Argus knew that this man had no feeling or compunction at all when it came to taking a life. For the first time in his life he was awed and afraid.

"What do you have to say to that? Anything?"

"I have always done my duty, sir."

"Duty? Is that what you call it, incapacitating your fellow Praetorians?" He stepped up to Argus, so tall he looked down on him.

"No, sir."

"What then?"

"My duty is to you, the emperor, to Rome. It's to point out the weaknesses in the elite of the military."

"Did these *weaknesses* challenge you?"

"Not all of them, sir."

"No?"

"I felt the need to take out some frustration."

"On your fellows, my guard?"

"Yes, sir. They were weak."

Plautianus paced the floor of his office, circling Argus, scratching his chin. "Well. It appears to me trooper that you don't work well with others and if you had to take to the field with your fellows you wouldn't do any good...so...I'm going to use you elsewhere."

"May I ask where, sir?"

"Everywhere."

"I don't understand. Everywhere?"

"That's what I said! Are you deaf?"

"No, sir!"

"I'm making you one of my spies." Argus was truly taken aback by this development. *A spy! Why?* "You will report to me and only me. You will be my eyes and ears, *everywhere*! And you will work alone, apart from a few underlings whom you will be able to choose yourself, provided I approve them afterward. Do you understand?"

"Yes...yes, sir! But why me?"

"Because monster, you're friendless, cold-blooded and heartless and it seems you don't have any qualms about gutting anyone. You've got what it takes to be a Praetorian spy." Argus wanted to smile at this, laugh, but couldn't bring himself to. He nodded.

"Yes, sir…"

"Oh, and one more thing!" continued Plautianus, standing directly in front of Argus. "If you ever cross me, or fail to inform me, or question my orders…I'll kill you myself and let your carcass float down the Tiber to the sea. Got it? If you please me, you'll go far, monster."

"Yes, sir!"

Plautianus slapped him on the back. "Good! Now, sit. I have an assignment for you." Argus sat and accepted, hesitantly, a cup of wine from his new superior. "Let's have a talk about your foster family, the Metelli."

Argus often thought of that first meeting with Plautianus and the promise of reward. He would get what he had always thought he deserved. He was better than Lucius and he wanted all of Rome to know it. To reach the top, he needed to please Plautianus and only Plautianus, for he was the true power in Rome, not Severus, or Caracalla, and certainly not Geta. No, Plautianus was the one who would rise, and Argus with him.

"Are you finished fucking around with your leg yet Sabinus?"

"Yes, sir."

"Good. Let's go. I want to reach Rome the day after tomorrow and I want you to kill that desert turd without failing. I have other work to do." With that the two riders set off again down the Via Cassia toward Rome and the business at hand.

Later that day, two more travellers set out along the Via Aemilia Scauri and the coastal route that joined the Via Aurelia to Rome. They travelled in a large wagon and were followed by three more that carried several slaves, amphorae of Etrurian wine and olive oil, baskets of fruit and pots of olives. It should have been a happy time, the air fresh and the world out of doors alive with fragrance and colour and Summer song.

For the two travellers it should indeed have been a joyful voyage, especially after so long in seclusion, after so long away from Rome; to return with laden wagons for a wedding should indeed have been joyful but, it was not. Quintus Metellus pater rode sternly, hands gripped tightly around the reigns while young Quintus Caecilius Metellus sat silent, still, unnaturally serious. Not a word was spoken by either; the father didn't care to talk to his son and the son begrudged his father the deep, dark secret he was now unknowingly, unwillingly privy to.

The ancient gods at the top of the mountain had cast him back down into a world in turmoil, a life and family that he no longer recognized. Caring, as he once had, would now be difficult. How could he smile at his father or his mother; hatred for the one and sadness for the other. The mountain gods were punishing him for intruding on their sacred soil and though the winds had hounded him furiously all that night in the tomb, he had remained. Ever since that dreadful night, young Quintus had taken to making silent prayers to the winds, begging for forgiveness, or casting wild flowers into the air as offerings. He hoped vainly that they would reverse his misfortune, that he would wake the next day and all of the anger and sadness would have been but a dream. However, it was not to be; the sun still rose and set and each time the pain and anguish were still there, ever hurtful.

He looked up at his father as they rode, felt a hatred he had not felt before. He wanted to stab him but he had no knife, push him off of the wagon's edge to plummet down the cliffs to the sea below, but he had not the strength. At the same time Quintus pater thought to himself how wonderfully young Quintus had been behaving, how still and obedient. *I am proud of him* he thought, but never said as much.

371

The Metellus domus was in a flutter, Antonia and Alene, the slaves and even little Clarinda all engaged in a sort of pre-wedding ritual that would set the head of any observer spinning. When Lucius and Ashur had returned from their journey they were swept into the doorway of the home as if sucked into some otherworldly vortex that only a priest of Jupiter could discern. It had not stopped since.

The updates Lucius received regularly from his mother and sister about the plans of his own wedding were more complicated than any battle strategy he had had to deal with in the field. The marriage was taking place on the Nones of Quinctilis, a week hence. He would approach in the vanguard up the steps of the Temple of Apollo. His flanks would be covered by the guests and musicians. The bride and her family would bring up the rear. The priests of Apollo would rendezvous with him at the appointed time. A truly remarkable campaign, expertly devised and thought out.

"Sounds fantastic!" said Lucius, when Antonia and Alene had finished, his head reeling.

"Is there anyone in particular you would like to invite Lucius?" asked Alene hurriedly. "I've already talked with Adara and she's given me a list."

"Uhm… Hmm." Until now, it hadn't really occurred to Lucius that there would even be any guests. All he had known was that he wanted to marry Adara as soon as possible, unknowing of the logistics of such a timetable. "I hadn't really thought about it Alene."

"What? Mother, he hasn't even thought about it!"

"Oh, Lucius!" cried Antonia from across the garden. He had blundered, forgotten.

Quickly Lucius, recover yourself, think of something, he thought.

"Oh yes! Now I remember. Umm. Invite Emrys and Carissa and Longus."

"Already done," Alene said curtly, twirling her stylus in her hand.

"Umm. Invite Senator Cassius Dio." That was all he could think of as most of his friends were in Africa.

"That's it? Oh, Lucius. By Vesta's pure white robes! Only one?" An utterly confused Lucius scratched his head. He felt as though he were back under Diodorus' tutelage; he had been asked a simple question to which he did not know the answer and he felt his ears and neck growing hotter and hotter beneath the gaze of his tutor. "What about the Imperial guests?"

"Imperial guests! Are you completely mad, Alene?"

"She's right, Lucius!" came Antonia's voice as she approached. "It is customary to extend the invitation if you are either of Equestrian or Patrician class to the emperor and his family, even though they probably won't come."

"By Apollo's silver bow! I'll be too nervous to perform the sacrifice!"

"For love of Venus, Lucius. You've faced down howling barbarians in the thick of battle, men dying all around you, and you're afraid of a few guests at your back?" Alene now tapped her stylus tensely on her wax tablet, lips pursed, eyes piercing. Lucius noticed that she resembled a strict Vestal matron with her hair tied up as it was in a tight bun.

"You win! Invite them all, the emperor, Julia Domna and her sisters, Caracalla, Geta, the rest of the Senate if you like. It doesn't matter anyway since as you say they won't attend."

"Exactly." Alene was already jotting the names down.

The days before the wedding, one saw the masters and servants of both households flowing in and out of doors, flying about on this errand or giving that message; from sun-up they were tossed about, bobbing around as waves in the sea during a tempest. However, the chaos in which the Metelli and Antoninii now found themselves would settle, the storm recede, and at the end of it all there would be such peace and happiness that they all found the task worth every drop of sweat, every pounding headache.

Invitations went out hurriedly, orders were placed with flower vendors in the various forum markets and Emrys was even able to help in finding an artist to make the rings in time for the ceremony. Quinctilis was always a busy time of the year in Rome, not because of weddings, triumphs or other occasions. Rome was jubilant, its pulse quick with the approach of the much anticipated Ludi Apollinares, the games dedicated to Apollo.

Not since the emperor's triumph had the city streets swelled so, the inns overflowed, the fora gone without sleep. It was a beautiful summer and what better time, thought Lucius and Adara's mothers, to celebrate a marriage of two wonderfully fated youths. As soon as the wedding had been decided upon, Antonia had gone directly to the Temple of Apollo on the Palatine to see the head priest there, whom she had known for many years. Every time she mounted the steps leading up to one of Rome's oldest temples, he was there to greet her, always bowing respectfully, though it was not something asked or expected of any priest.

When she had mentioned to the priest that her son was to be wed and that they wanted to hold the wedding in the temple, a place that had always been welcoming to them, he was so happy that she thought he would cry for joy. He was getting on in years, so old his age was unknown, and he wanted to witness at least one more joyous event in that place. He explained that this year the celebrations for the Games of Apollo would take place in the other temple on the far side of the Theatre of Marcellus. He and his other priests would be happy to hold the ceremony on the Palatine; he even went so far as to offer the open space in front of the temple for the wedding feast; the omens were good, the weather would be fair for the whole of Quinctilis. Antonia accepted excitedly, made her offering and went to tell the rest of the family.

Between decisions pertaining to the wedding, his time with Adara and fittings for a ring and a new toga, Lucius also busied himself with training again and further writing to Alerio in Africa for updates on the men and the situation there. He had been away for too long, neglected his duties. He enjoyed his leisure time however and in any case, time with Adara was now his priority; at least as much as was possible. But, he knew that the heavenly sojourn in which he found himself would soon, as must, come to an end. This thought returned to him again and again but he fought it off, tucked it away in the back of his mind, at least until after the wedding.

As he frequented the gymnasium and the baths, he thought, nonetheless, that there was no harm in being prepared, strong and ready for whatever lay ahead. Ashur too went with him to the baths to help Lucius train but he spent most of his time wandering the streets of Rome in thought or in the Temple of Apollo in silent prayer, for what nobody knew, except Ashur and Phoebus Apollo himself.

Three days before the wedding, days in which Lucius and Adara were not permitted to see one another, Publius came to the Metellus household to find Lucius and Ashur.

"My house is wild with women!" the older man roared as he sat down with Lucius and Ashur in the garden. "Ten years ago I wouldn't have minded so much but now…now with your mother and sister, Lucius, and my wife and daughters organizing this flower and that food, I felt as useless as a cup of sea water in the desert. They actually kicked me out!" He laughed exhaustedly. Lucius and Ashur smiled at each other.

"Publius Leander," said Ashur, an idea dawning on him as he looked at the two men before him. "It is a warm summer's evening, the sun will be up for long yet and my friend here is to wed your lovely daughter. Why don't we take him out and celebrate and speak as men in friendship? It seems to me you could use some respite." This suggestion, to Lucius' mind, was quite unlike Ashur.

"That's a great idea, Ashur!" Lucius clapped his hands.

"Thank the Gods you two were here! Let's go." Publius Leander jumped up with new-found energy and waited in the atrium while Lucius and Ashur collected their things, money, a thin cloak and a small dagger each. The city was joyful but even in times of joy the streets of Rome held certain danger, especially at night.

The three men walked to the Forum Boarium where a great crowd was gathered to watch some acrobats perform. This was a common sight during the Games of Apollo when every open space in the city was filled with spectators and performers from all reaches of the empire. They turned right down the thoroughfare that ran from the forum toward the Theatre of Marcellus, walking in comfortable silence as they went, taking in the scene. Each had his own thoughts to which he yielded as they turned right once more below the cliff of the Capitoline Hill, Rome's spiritual capital.

Atop the Capitoline, the temples of Jupiter and the Gods of Rome shone in the light as the final auspices were read for the day's end. Out of the Temple of Jupiter Optimus Maximus came the hooded figure of a woman who was met by several attendants. Julia Domna, clad in a stola of brown, gold and Tyrian purple with her head veiled in the eastern fashion, walked with a commanding presence that drew everyone's eyes. Among the attendants waiting for her as she descended the great marble stairs leading from the Capitol, were several of the usual philosophers, historians, rhetoricians and scientists, hangers-on seeking the empress' ear for a moment or two, her favour and her patronage. Her reputation for surrounding herself with learned men was known through all of the Roman world. As she walked back to the Palatine, they spoke, and she answered, and so it was every day.

Beneath this scene of pious worship and shameless favour-seeking display, at the bottom of the Capitoline cliff, the artists of Rome indulged themselves in pre-performance drinking and gambling. The theatres of Rome were packed to capacity every night during the Ludi Apollinares and as Apollo was also the god of art and music, the occasion for artistic displays was even more sanctified.

On a narrow street, along the cliff base and built up against the rock, were no less than a dozen taverns, all of them busy, all of them smelling of wine. Some were louder than others, taken over entirely by troupes of actors and musicians, while some were filled with patrons who were there to sup before the entertainment. Lucius wondered if it was a bad idea bringing his future father-in-law to such a raucous neighbourhood, but then his fears were allayed when Publius expressed how good it was to be in deep with all of the artists, the excitement. Having married a Greek painter, he was used to such scenes and enjoyed an atmosphere he had not experienced since leaving Athens.

Ashur led them to a smaller but well-kept tavern at the end of the street, called the Taverna Macedonica. The outside was decorated with Ionic columns covered with grape vines, two torches on either side of the large wooden doors. There were many people inside from the sound of things, but nowhere near the deafening roar that came from the other taverns. Pleased with the choice Ashur had made, Publius Leander, feeling like a youth again, entered first and upon setting foot inside he burst into a verse of Catullus.

"Boy server of old Falernian,
Pour me out more pungent cups
As toastmistress Postumia rules,
Who's drunker than the drunken grape.
Pure water, find your level elsewhere.
You ruin wine. Shift to the sober.
Here is unmixed Thyonian!"

Great applause greeted Publius' magnificent entrance from all corners of the tavern accompanied by cheers of "Io! Io!"

All this as Lucius and Ashur stood still at the door, mouths agape.

"Ashur," Lucius whispered, "my father-in-law is a Bacchite!" Ashur laughed.

The Greek proprietor came up to his three new guests, men he hadn't seen before, and led them inside with a broad smile; he was very pleased by the magnificent entrance. There was a vacant table at the back of the tavern and so they ploughed their way through the crowd of theatre-goers and artists, many of them patting Publius on the back as they went. The atmosphere was definitely more lax than a palace banquet.

"Are you the proprietor of this grand place?" Publius asked as they sat.

"Yes indeed, citizen. Philemon is my name and I've run this taverna for many years. You'll find that I serve the *best* of everything." The man waved his hands in dramatic fashion, emphasizing his bold statement.

"Well then, Philemon, bring us a crater of your best Thyonian and several of whichever delectables you deem fit. We're drinking to my future son and his silent friend, two warriors in need of quenching."

"I shall bring you the very best of everything." Philemon bowed and went into the kitchens. Publius leaned back against the wall and heaved a great sigh. Lucius and Ashur still stared at him.

"Ha, ha, ha!" Publius boomed. "I believe I've shocked the two of you. Forgive me but living in Athens for so long I have lost some of my Romanness."

"We're not shocked Publius Leander, just surprised. My own father would never have dreamed of voicing himself so. It's a welcome change."

"Well, I wouldn't worry about it much. Had I stayed in Rome instead of going to Greece I would have retained all of the staunch conservatism that comes with being from an old Roman family." Philemon returned with a massive crater of wine decorated with theatre masks and Dionysian scenes of revelry. A serving girl followed with three cups and then a young man with two trays, one with cheeses and sweet meats, the other with honeyed pastries. "Ah! Wonderful. Thank you, Philemon."

"I hope you enjoy, masters." With that, the proprietor went into the centre of the tavern to join in a song that someone had started.

"To the marriage of you and my daughter, Lucius." Publius held up his cup to Lucius and Ashur who did the same. "I feel that Fortuna has smiled on our entire family in giving me a good son...and of course new friends." He nodded to Ashur. They all drank, savoured the taste of the wine as they relaxed into their seats and their conversation. After a while, it became clear that Publius had been in need of some male bonding and conversation, a chance to speak freely with his own sex and the young man to whom his daughter, his first-born, would be joined. The reality that Adara would be leaving his household, the fold of his protective fatherly arms, had sunk in the week before.

"You know, Lucius," he began in a philosophical mood. "Being married to a woman who truly loves you and admires you is a blessing that Venus grants very few mortals. I believe that you two are so blessed."

"I know we are, Publius."

"Good, because there's nothing better in all this world than the unconditional love of a beautiful woman. I know that Adara bears such a love for you. I am so blessed in my own marriage and I can tell you it's worth cherishing and protecting at all costs."

"I couldn't agree more." Lucius smiled affectionately to the gentle man before him, realised how special he was, that he had indeed undergone a profound transformation in his life and all because of the woman he had married.

Throughout this truly moving conversation, Ashur listened, a strange feeling of exclusion and loneliness creeping into his heart, a heart that had lain in shadow for a long, long time. He thought of Carissa. He had not spoken to her since that first night and yet she had been with him ever since. He had seen her, many times when his walks would inevitably lead him past the workshop, from a silent, unintrusive distance. A part of him hoped that she thought of him as he watched her. But, how was it possible that she, a beautiful, gentle creature from the northern reaches, could ever feel for him, a dark-skinned warrior who had lived many lives alone, in the solitude that only a true servant of Apollo experienced?

In the past weeks, he had gone everyday to the Temple of Apollo to offer and meditate, wait for an answer from the Far Shooter himself. He had only ever served the God, ever without a feeling of doubt, or a longing for something more. In his guilt, Ashur prayed for an answer, some guidance, but none came. His penance was to be unknowing, awash in uncertainty. Yet he still longed to look upon her, the quiet artist with the timid, bright eyes as deep as the sea.

"I know you haven't received any orders yet, Lucius," Ashur heard Publius saying once more, his thoughts broken, "so I was thinking that you and Adara might want to escape the city for a time after your wedding."

"That sounds like a good idea, Publius, but I haven't a clue where to go. My father is at the villa in Etruria and-"

"No, no. Not Etruria. Somewhere south. I have a client who has a villa by the sea, in Cumae. He's offered it to us during the month of Quinctilis. The man is in Rome for the month and so the villa lies empty."

"Well, I don't have any orders as yet – I don't see why not as long as Adara wants to."

"She does. She wanted me to make the offer to you."

"Perfect. More wine?"

"Of course. Philemon! More wine!" Publius called out before popping a pastry into his mouth.

By the time the three men had finished drinking, the tavern had emptied, most of the patrons having gone to the theatre for the performance. Only a few people remained as Philemon and his staff busied themselves with cleaning for the post-performance crowd. Not having risen for some hours, Lucius, Ashur and Publius' legs were slightly unsteady until the fresh, sweet-smelling night air of summer revived them.

"The moon is full tonight," said Ashur as he gazed up.

"A perfect night for a walk."

"I agree, Publius. Ashur and I will walk you back to the Esquiline. We'll go through the Forum Romanum."

Rome was unsleeping at night, especially during any festival or games. The streets were thronging with revellers, young and old, rich and poor. There were certainly areas that were unsafe, where gangs of hungry youths went in search of a fight or an easy target. The Subura was to be avoided, most definitely; the narrow alleyways flanked by multi-storey tenement buildings provided the perfect spot for an ambush. One did not go there unless it was completely necessary.

As they walked around the front of the Capitoline to the Forum, Publius felt quite safe flanked by his two young escorts. No one came near them as they passed through the streets although many stared at Ashur. The moon was so big and bright that torches along the streets were not needed and as they came into the Forum, in front of the temple of Mars Ultor, the Curia and the Arch of Septimius Severus, the flagstones of the Via Sacra were so lit up that it seemed to be daylight.

Groups of people stood about singing, conversing and looking about beneath the ivory-like marble of the monuments. The flame burned as ever in front of the Temple of the Divine Julius and the sounds of ritual chants emanated from the open roof of the House of the Vestal Virgins as offerings were made to the goddess beneath the fullness of the moon. In front of the Temple of Castor and Pollux a giant tripod had been set up for the duration of the Ludi; pungent smoke rolled and billowed from the top, a thing alive, mingling with the world around it, blue in the moonlight. The sacred incense would burn continuously, cared for by one of the priests of Apollo.

The games in the Colosseum had ended before the sun had gone down for yet another night, the crowds dissipated from its arches and benches. The torches in every arch of the structure were still lit however, so that the perimeter of the amphitheatre flickered with hints of orange.

A large crowd was gathered on the north side of the Colosseum, angry shouting could be heard. "It doesn't look as though they're going to leave anytime soon," said Lucius. "We'd better go around the other way, near the Temple of the Divine Claudius. It seems much quieter." Just then, some people in the crowd noticed the three men standing there and started jeering at them.

"I think you're right, Lucius," said Publius. "Let's avoid any problems. Ashur?" Ashur simply nodded warily as he looked around and then up at the moon. They began to round the Colosseum, passing one of the main entrances with the walls of the temple precinct of the Divine Claudius coming into view. The walls were fronted by thick trees from which floated the sound of owls hooting. Then the hooting stopped and wings fluttered wildly. Ashur stopped, raised his hand. Lucius held Publius' arm and they listened.

"What is it, Ashur?" Lucius whispered.

"It's too quiet," he replied, his feline senses alerted to something. "All the yelling has stopped." They looked around, Publius was confused, his heart pounding in his breast.

"Lucius, some of the torches in four of the arches of the Colosseum are out," said Publius, his mouth dry, his voice hoarse. He wished they had not drunk so much. Lucius heard Ashur's dagger unsheathe beneath his cloak and did likewise. Then the footsteps, in front and behind, to the sides as well.

"Publius, get between Ashur and myself," said Lucius as the silhouettes of six men appeared out of the shadows – three from the trees of the temple complex and three from the arches of the Colosseum. At a glance Ashur and Lucius noticed the glint of daggers in two hands and cudgels in the other four, though they could also have had daggers at their belts. Lucius and Ashur rotated, Publius in the middle, giving each other a chance to see all around.

"Ashur, daggers first."

"Understood, Anguis." Ashur then noticed one of the men with a dagger had a limp. He was staying back from the others for the moment but needed watching.

The six men attacked, their assault all the more difficult to see because of the dark clothes they wore. The footsteps quickened in Lucius' ears and he charged at one of the men to their rear, Publius behind him. The second and third ran to help the thug.

Lucius' dagger had flown through the darkness as he ran and struck the attacker in the chest so that he fell immediately. Lucius kept running to rip his dagger free and pick up the cudgel his victim had dropped. No one at his back, he turned on the other two who came at him simultaneously. He wheeled his cloak at one to slow him down and parried a blow with the cudgel from the other attacker whose lower stomach met Lucius' blade. The third was running for Lucius once more before he was up but Publius scrambled to Lucius' aid and ran into the assailant from the side, knocking him off balance. On his feet again, Lucius ran as fast as his feet would carry him and pulverized the man's face with the cudgel, setting him screaming in agony.

"Publius! Up against the wall!" Lucius yelled as he went to help Ashur who had already killed one thug and was struggling with a second, massive beast. The animal swung his extra-long cudgel in a violent frenzy as he tried to crush Ashur. But Ashur was too fast, moving in and out like an angry serpent to dip his curved dagger into the man's body several times, slowing him more and more until he fell immobilized. Ashur then turned to the man with the limp who stood off to the side, dagger outstretched in a shaking hand. The cold of the moon in the desert was reflected in Ashur's piercing eyes and the man saw only his end as he came closer and closer.

Just then Lucius remembered that there had been four darkened arches in the Colosseum, one on the second storey. He ran hard as he could.

"Ashur, look out!" The snap of a bowstring echoed over the street and Lucius dove to knock Ashur from his feet so that they rolled for several paces before getting up again. Another arrow ricocheted off the stone slabs. Meanwhile a stranger had come running along the wall, out of breath and wielding one of the fallen cudgels. He struck the sixth man, the leader, from behind.

"Ahhhh!" the man with the limp yelled as the newcomer landed a clumsy blow on the side of his head. The man went down several feet from the walls of the Colosseum just as Lucius and Ashur came running back.

"Numonius?" Lucius yelled as he held his blade to the fallen man's neck, kicking his dagger out of the way.

"Later!" he replied, his voice trembling.

"I know him!" said Ashur, grabbing the attacker by the hair. "He's the one who attacked me along the Via Flaminia. Who are you?"

"Piss off *peregrinus*!" he replied, blood leaking from the corner of his mouth. Ashur then dug his hand into the man's left thigh. "Ahhhhhh!" he yelled in pain.

"I remember you! How is your wound? Not yet healed?" He turned his fingers inside the man's festering wound causing him to scream in pain again. Ashur was emitting an anger quite unlike himself, or so it seemed to Lucius as he looked above and around for any other signs of danger.

"All right, enough! Just stop, I beg you." The man wept slightly, the pain in his leg too much to bear. "I was sent by-" An arrow came whizzing through the air to plunge into the man's chest, killing him instantly. Footsteps faded quickly into the shadows above their heads and were gone.

"Arrrrrgh!" Ashur yelled in frustration and pounded the dead body with his fist.

"Come, Ashur, let's get Publius to safety. Numonius, come with us. The Vigiles and the Guard will be along soon. Quickly!" He pulled Ashur to his feet and, his arm around his shaken father-in-law, they fled with Numonius up a street alongside the Ludus Magnus toward the Esquiline Hill and out of danger.

Back at the house, Publius was taken inside, exhausted and afraid after the attack. Lucius felt guilt-ridden that the evening should have ended thus and kept asking the door slave to see that his master was unhurt. It had been many, many years since Publius had been in any sort of violent situation and the shock of it had quite unnerved him. Delphina came to the door with Antonia and Alene to see that Lucius, Ashur and the other fellow were all right.

"Please come in, Lucius," Delphina insisted, but Lucius did not want to bring on any bad luck by seeing Adara too soon.

"Really, Lucius it will be fine," Antonia pleaded.

"We'll be safe mother, Delphina."

"Mother?" came Adara's voice from within the house. "Tell him I shall keep to my rooms the entire time he is here. As long as he is safe."

"Well, Lucius?" asked Delphina.

"Very well. Can Numonius here enter as well?"

"Of course, of course. Come inside, all of you."

Adara went to her rooms and closed the door as the three men were ushered inside. Slaves took their dirty cloaks and brought basins of warm rosewater to wash the dirt and blood from themselves.

"Numonius. How did you know where we were, that we needed help?" Numonius looked up, eyes still wide with fright.

"I was out in front of the Temple of Venus and Rome this morning when I saw a group of scruffy looking fellows gathered just below me on the steps. I didn't pay them much attention – they weren't religious types if you know what I mean – but I heard your name mentioned a couple times along with some talk about payments of some kind and got to worrying. They hung around for most of the day and so I watched them. After dark, they started a scuffle on the north side of the Colosseum and then took off leaving others to fight it out...not long after I heard yelling near the Temple of Claudius and that's when I ran and found you there."

"Did you recognise any of them?" asked Lucius.

"No. None of them. Not my usual customers. These sorts stick to their slums to harass old men and little girls."

"Well, I'm glad you came when you did." Lucius patted him on the back after drying his hands. "Where's Ashur?"

"I think he's in the garden looking after that older fellow we brought back."

"Why don't you go and join them Numonius, and get some food. I'll be along shortly."

"Thank you." Numonius went to join the others and meet those he didn't know. He was warmly welcomed. Down one of the corridors, Lucius found himself outside the door to Adara's cubicula. He knocked lightly.

"Lucius? Is that you?" Her voice trembled slightly.

"Yes, it's me, Adara," he reassured as he pressed his face to the painted door.

"Are you hurt?" He thought he could hear her crying.

"No, my love. I'm fine. Don't worry." The door creaked open slightly and one of her slender arms reached out for him to grasp. He kissed her hand and she squeezed his firmly not wanting to let go.

"Thank Apollo, you're safe. Stay in the house tonight. Don't leave."

"I will." He put her hand to his face. "I'll sleep outside your door all night."

"Then I shall sleep inside the door, right next to you."

Despite the coaxing of the rest of the family, Lucius and Adara both slept on the floor, either side of the door that night, never once seeing each other but safe in the comfort of knowing the other was there and safe.

"Did he say anything?"

"Who, sir?"

"Don't play dumb with me monster! That idiot Sabinus, that's who!" Plautianus was red with rage, despite his dark complexion.

"No, sir. I killed him before he said anything."

"Good." The Praetorian prefect scratched his closely shorn head of hair. "Did you at least use a bunch of Suburan nobodies in the assault?"

"Yes, all of them lived near the tenement I'm staying in at the moment."

Plautianus nodded. "Good. Come with me." Before Argus could say anything else, he was out the door and on the Via Praetoria of the Castra Praetoria. They walked for a while, men either avoiding Plautianus' gaze or saluting without thought. Finally, they came to a small brick building without windows. Argus had not seen this place before. A guard opened the door and in they went.

It was dark, very dark, except for a single brazier with several irons sticking out.

"You know, Argus, you're a tough son of a bitch. Very useful. But you're going to cause me great inconvenience some day."

"How do you mean, sir?" Argus was worried now by the tone in Plautianus' voice.

"I told you to *watch* Lucius Metellus, not kill him."

"I was trying to kill his companion, Ashur."

"Yes, well. That man is always about the city on his own, visiting the temples, walking by the workshop of that sculptor the emperor likes so much. You could just as easily take care of him when he's on his own and not with Metellus or any others for that matter."

"Yes, sir."

"You disobeyed your orders and have risked my reputation and my standing in the process."

"Yes, sir." Argus noticed four burly men step forward to surround him, one from each corner.

"I hate being disobeyed!" Plautianus' shrill voice struck an unknown fear into Argus. Then the four men grabbed him and, struggle though he tried, he was helpless against them as they chained his hands above his head. "I won't kill you Argus. But, you won't disobey an order again. I guarantee it." With that, Plautianus went over to the brazier and pulled out an iron flail, the strands of wire red-hot.

Argus wasn't sure how many times he was struck, for he lost consciousness after a while. The last thing he remembered was the sound of the flail sizzling through the air and into his skin, Plautianus rejoicing in his little game, and the trickle-turned-flood of blood he felt pouring out of the lashings.

"Leave him there overnight to think about it!" Plautianus said to the henchmen when he had administered the fiftieth lash. "In the morning, wake him up and send him to the surgeon. He needs to be able to work." He threw the flail at Argus' feet, his body hanging loose and bloody, and went out. No one heard Argus' cries as he was whipped, no one cared about the sobbing that emanated from within those four walls during the night.

Lucius awoke very stiff on the marble floor in front of Adara's cubicula after a surprisingly peaceful slumber. When his eyes opened, Publius was standing above him, looking much better.

"Come, Lucius. I have food and wine for us in the garden." He helped Lucius up and they went to join the others. Once they were around the corner, Delphina went in to see Adara and take her some food.

It was a quiet breakfast but one in which there hovered a sense of serene relief that everyone was well. Eventually the conversation turned to wedding preparations.

"Numonius. While you're here," began Alene, "I'd like to place an order for a small calf for the marital sacrifice." Numonius smiled, happy to change his thoughts back to work and so joined in the discussion.

When everyone had eaten, the Metelli, Ashur and Numonius left the Antoninii to their plans and sought their way home again, along with a couple of bodyguards Publius had insisted on calling for. They took a longer route behind the Baths of Trajan, went down into the Forum Romanum and from there to the Forum Boarium and their home nearby. When they arrived at the house, they found several carts outside and slaves busily unloading masses of supplies. It was still early and carts were permitted in the streets for a short while longer.

"But who is-," began Antonia but she was interrupted.

"Mama! Mama!" Out came young Quintus, running to embrace his mother as he had not done in a long while.

"Young Quintus?" Antonia felt like weeping. However, as the stern figure of a man appeared in the doorway, arms crossed, Lucius felt a tightness in his chest and an anger rise. Quintus Metellus pater was home.

XXIV

LAETITIA

'Joy'

The day before the Nones of Quinctilis, the city surged with life. Cheers emanated from every theatre, arena, and forum, and the scent of perfumed offerings to Apollo laced the air. Rome revelled and delighted itself in the games put on by the praetor to entertain the masses. Every citizen enjoyed time off from daily work; men met in the taverns to discuss the world and throw dice, women met in the markets and gardens of Rome to trade pieces of juicy gossip and joke about their dice-throwing men.

For some however, the need for gossip or gaming was distinctly lacking, their hearts filled with anticipation for the following day when two youths would be joined eternally. The houses of Antoninus and Metellus were awash in joy, their hearts drenched and their cups full. The only shadows that had threatened to cast a gloom on the Nones were the attack two days earlier and the return of a seemingly different Quintus Metellus pater to the domus. Not even these events had blunted Lucius' resolve the he would wed Adara on their terms in the temple of his ancestors' patron god. True, he had been gripped by some inner rage the moment he had seen his father appear in the doorway. Luckily, after some soothing words from Alene, Lucius had realised that nothing, not even a disapproving father, could mar the happiness he and Adara would share in a marriage blessed by the Gods themselves. The Gods had brought them together and only They could set them apart.

Antonia had not been sure how to receive her husband's return but she had hidden her discomfort like a true matron and went directly to Quintus to embrace him, ignoring the slight tremor she had felt upon touching him. She was pleased however to see that her errant husband was civil to their eldest son and daughter. Clarinda had received a mere nod though and Ashur was all but ignored. Still, things went better than she had feared.

The day after his return, Quintus had allowed himself to be persuaded to go to the house of Publius Leander and Delphina so that he could meet them and his future daughter-in-law, although he would never call her that. Publius had known that relations between Lucius and his father were not good, and so he did his utmost to welcome a man whom he had inwardly met with some trepidation. The meeting had gone outwardly well, but afterward the Antoninii could not help but feel a measure of regret for Antonia whom they had grown to love. Quintus had behaved well enough, but he had obviously been happy when they left the house, had felt somewhat disgusted at the artistic nature of the mother and how she had cuckolded a man of good Roman stock.

The day before the wedding, at midday, when all of Rome was indoors for an afternoon rest, Ashur had gone out for his daily visit to the temple and a walk through the streets. This was his favourite time to be out in Rome, a city he had grown to love for its beauty and hate for its politics. Inevitably his feet, which had carried him down countless roads, led him to the edge of the Tiber where he followed the shoreline to the warehouse district near the Forum Boarium. At the far end of the rows of docks and storage buildings, he came to the small building outside of which were masses of slabs of marble of all colours. Perched atop his usual spot, a large flat piece of pink marble baked in sunlight, Ashur gazed at her between the maze of stacks and rows of multi-hued stone.

He watched Carissa work, entranced by her lithe hands and their movement as they caressed and chiselled and polished two large statues. He watched her eyes, so dedicated to the one task she undertook. Her short blond hair, the colour of golden wheat, swayed with each tilt of her head. Then Emrys appeared next to her, his strong sculptor's hands holding something, Ashur couldn't make it out; there were several brilliant flashes of light, words uttered in some Celtic tongue and then, before the smoke cleared, the statues were covered in silks flecked with gold.

Ashur's curiosity was peaked, he wanted to go in and speak with her, find out what they were doing, for it was something that not even he had seen before. But he could not disturb her for fear she would shed the creative light that surrounded her in that moment; the only time Carissa seemed completely at ease and confident, was when she was working, creating. It was in that state that Ashur liked to watch her most.

There were times when he thought she caught a glimpse of him but neither Emrys nor Carissa ever came out to see who was there. And so Ashur was content to sit and watch, to fill his day thus engaged. Indeed, of late there was a great deal weighing upon his mind not the least of which was the fact that the following day his dearest friend was to be wed in the Temple of Apollo. It was because of the great import of this union, the joyfulness of the occasion, that Ashur was troubled. As he sat, he remembered the attack several nights before, a well-organized and potentially fatal attack, an event that had opened the inner gates of his strength to anger and rage. He had not given in to such emotions before and it worried him deeply. Ever since he first met Lucius in the desert at night, similar incidents had occurred, only before he had been more than able to handle himself, control his emotions.

A dark shadow seemed to follow his friend everywhere he went, threatening to throw down the happiness he so deserved. And what of Ashur Mehrdad's role in all of this? Apollo had made him Lucius' protector, that much was clear, but what else? In the distant past, Ashur's role had always been obvious, his duty up to a certain point in time definite, but not this time, not now. Apollo had been vague with his servant of late, at times silent. Ashur feared that it might have been because his thoughts had drifted to the young woman within the building across from him.

These thoughts and more spun within the lone warrior's mind, foremost among them was to make sure that Lucius and Adara's wedding day went exactly as intended. He pounded the marble with his fist, then sighed. He felt unbalanced and caught unawares. When he was near to Carissa however, when he looked upon her, the rage dissipated and he felt himself again.

"Ashur?" the soft voice came from behind him, highlighted by a hint of surprise. "Wha…what are you doing here?"

He turned quickly, knowing instantly who it was and wondering how he would explain himself. Embarrassment also was something new to him and he flushed guiltily.

"Lady Carissa…I…"

"Please…just Carissa," she said smiling, her head down.

"Carissa." It felt good to say her name. "I was walking along the river and saw you working and…"

"It does me good to see you Ashur." She blurted the words out uncomfortably but they were as music to his ears. Her eyes lifted, flickers of reflected sun off of the river lighting them. "Will you sit with me for a while as I rest?" she asked.

"As long as you wish," he replied.

From the door to the workshop, Emrys spotted his apprentice and Ashur sitting side by side and smiled to himself despite a slight sadness welling up. He gazed at them momentarily, decided not to say anything, and went back inside to work.

That same day, as the sun began its descent to the west and a soft haze began to weave its way into the city streets from the cooling countryside, the Empress Julia Domna lay reclined on a purple, ivory-footed couch in the uppermost room at the south-eastern corner of the new palace. Always calm, collected, she read casually through a scroll that had been presented to her by one of her favoured Greeks, Lucius Flavius

Philostratus. It was part of a work she had commissioned from him about the life of the Cappadocian-Greek philosopher, Apollonius of Tyana, an ascetic who travelled from place to place teaching and who claimed to have miraculous powers such as the ability to fly and foretell the future.

The text thus far pleased her and she made a mental note to reward Philostratus well. Other commissions were already forming in her mind. As she read, her eyes would occasionally stray over the top of the page to the world outside; in the distance, the Via Appia stretched out over the countryside, marble shrines to great Romans of the past dotting the way alongside it. Julia Domna's eyes gazed farther still, as if travelling a great distance to the land of her birth. A short strand fell from the side of her tightly-bound hair and she brushed it aside just as she brushed aside the longing in her heart.

Syria seemed worlds away, so different from Rome where she was recognized as the most powerful woman in the empire, the Roman *Augusta*…and yet, she too had enemies. They were everywhere and so she was ever wary of anyone who came into her presence. For three years she had been losing power and influence over the emperor, her husband, to Plautianus and his lackeys who had spies in every inch of the empire from the palace and Senate to the brothels of Alexandria. She needed allies, desperately. She stood, straightened her robe and walked onto the balcony. Her dark eyes took in the waning sun and she said a silent prayer to her eastern sun god, Elagabalus, for whom her father had been a priest and who had been the patron of her family for a long, long time.

A knock echoed on the door of her room and a guard entered. "Augusta?" the man addressed her steadily.

"Yes. What is it?" she replied without turning.

"Your son, Caesar Marcus Aurelius Antoninus, is here to see you with your sister, Lady Julia Maesa."

"Send them in," she answered, curious as to the purpose of their visit, what news they brought. Fortunately her son Caracalla and her sister were loyal to her and so she did not fear their presence. As she stood there in the rays of sunlight, their footsteps came closer, as did their laughing voices. Caracalla and his aunt Julia had always gotten along well and he was very protective of her. Some even whispered that they were *very* close, but that was only hearsay.

"Mother?" came Caracalla's harsh voice. "You've been in here all day."

"Are you ill, Sister?" asked Julia Maesa as the empress turned to face them.

"No. Just thoughtful, nothing more." She went back to her couch to get more comfortable, and motioned to her son and sister to sit on the couches opposite. "I assume you have news of some sort." Caracalla looked at his aunt, she looked at him. "Both of you are as subtle as elephants. Now tell me, what is it today?"

Julia Maesa put her hands in front of her face as if wanting to keep any words from escaping her mouth. The empress looked at her; her sister resembled her in some ways, the same hair, stature, but she was different in many other ways, more beautiful, her features finer and more delicate. Julia Domna loved her dearly but could not help being comforted by the fact that she was empress and her sister was not.

"Oh I'll just say it!" her son blurted out, unafraid of her or her reaction. "It seems that bastard Plautianus has been spreading rumours about you being promiscuous and even hinted that we are involved incestuously!" Caracalla jumped up, suddenly furious. "I'll kill him! I swear by Mars and Baal! Put him in the arena with me and I'll finish it all right now!"

"Sit yourself down, my son," Julia Domna said calmly, as her heart screamed out with rage inside. "Control your temper and think. These are ridiculous lies and anybody who believes them is a fool."

"Nevertheless sister, people will believe these lies and it will harm you even more." Julia Maesa put her hand on her sister's shoulder.

"That is exactly what they are intended to do. Luckily my husband is smarter than that. Has he said anything about the rumours?"

"I asked father if he would punish those responsible and all he said was 'The mob is fickle, my son. We must learn to ignore these absurdities and whispers.' That's it. He doesn't believe it but he has no intention of doing anything since the lies appear to originate with the nobodies of Rome. Plautianus covers his tracks well."

"He does indeed." The empress' features hardened. "But, one day we'll have him, and by Elagabalus we'll crush him into dust." Caracalla smiled wickedly at the thought. "What else have your spies found out?"

"Hmm. Not much except that there was an assassination attempt on Tribune Lucius Metellus Anguis the other night."

"That is already known to me, Caracalla."

"Yes, but did you also know that Plautianus was behind it?"

The empress was silent, pensive. She had only met the young tribune once in passing, heard her husband mention him briefly with regards to an incident in Africa province. Apart from that she knew little else except that he was rumoured to be a good commander and loyal to the emperor, despite his father's Republican leanings.

"He is to be wed to Adara Antonina of Athens tomorrow in the temple of Palatine Apollo," added Julia Maesa.

"Yes I know. My clerk received the usual invitation not long ago." The empress paused yet again, her son watching her and knowing that she was thinking of something devious. "Sister, would you leave my son and I to discuss some things alone? I know that political ramblings sometime bore you to tears." They didn't bore her, but Julia Maesa knew better than to object.

"Of course. I was just about to take my leave and go to the baths." She rose gracefully, nodded to her sister and then went over to Caracalla and kissed him on the lips before leaving.

"Until later, matertera," he said to his aunt.

"I do hope, my son, that there is no truth to the rumours about you and your aunt either," Julia Domna said after her sister had left.

"Oh mother please, I'm a married man."

"Yes well, I don't know how honest a man being married to Plautianus' daughter has made you."

Caracalla laughed at the irony of it all. "So, Mother? What's this plan that I see forming in your head?"

"You won't like it but I must insist that you go along with it."

"What is it?" He was already growing impatient.

"My son, even though you and your brother Geta are both 'Caesar' and I am 'Augusta', Plautianus yet holds the reins of power and stands closest to your father's ear."

"Don't remind me."

"You know it's true. You also know that we need as many allies as we can get, especially from the upper ranks of the military and the old Roman families." She let him think about her words for a few moments, then seemingly changed the topic. "Tomorrow we will attend the wedding of Lucius Metellus and Adara Antonina and wish them well."

"Why in Hades would I want to do that?" he almost shouted. "He's pathetic."

"Because, my son, Lucius Metellus Anguis has become a silent hero...and I want him on our side." She stared at Caracalla the way she had ever since he was a child; it was a look that said *I mean what I say and you shall not defy me!* "It is apparent that the young tribune has, albeit unknowingly, made himself an enemy of Plautianus and any enemy of Plautianus is a possible ally of ours."

"You can't be serious. He's out for himself and therefore a threat to us, as are any others like him." Caracalla threw back his long military-style cloak and poured himself some wine.

"I am quite serious," she replied matter-of-factly. "My sources tell me that he is one of the few 'honest Romans' left in this world, faithful to his family and the memory of his ancestors, despite the strained relationship between him and his father."

"There's another concern of ours. The father. Quintus Metellus is a die-hard republican and has no love for my father, or either of us for that matter."

"He's not a problem. The son is stronger, he's the one we want. Nevertheless, I shall have my people keep a close watch on the senator."

"Fine, fine. So, since you seem so adamant about Lucius Metellus, what is it you want to do?" Caracalla slouched back, fed up with giving in to his mother's wishes.

"For the moment, I want him and his family protected from Plautianus' thugs...and I want you to be civil, almost friendly, to Metellus and his new wife."

"That sounds easy enough." An evil smile crossed his lips, as though he entertained some grim thought.

"I said civil, not lecherous," his mother warned.

"Me, mother?" he said, feigning shock.

"Yes, you. Nothing can make a man have a change of heart or allegiance so much as another posing a threat to his wife. We will be civil, and friendly, win the tribune over to our side without him knowing it."

"Agreed," he answered grudgingly.

"Good." Julia Domna reclined again, more relaxed in the knowledge that she had her son's obedience, for now. "Tomorrow we shall go to the Temple of Apollo and wish the young couple and their families well."

"Yes, yes," the son said to his mother as he rose to leave. "Whatever you say mother. But things better turn out the way you believe they will."

"If they do not, you will slit his Equestrian throat in the Temple of Baal."

Caracalla left, relishing that final possibility, and the empress went back out onto the balcony to view the final rays of the setting sun.

The eve of the Nones proved strange, an uneasiness lingered in the air. The wind had howled all night and there was a deathly silence in streets that should have been busy. Lucius turned in his bed, wondered what was happening outside, whether the day would be fair or dour. However, when morning came, the day dawned bright and clear and the air itself smelled sweetly, as though after a storm. The sun's rays burst through Lucius' small window to lighten his heart and wake him for the most important of days. He had the entire morning to prepare: to bathe, shave and dress himself in the new toga he had ordered.

In the courtyard, Alene, Antonia, young Quintus and Clarinda all sat waiting for Lucius for the morning meal. Even Quintus pater deigned to come out of his study to eat with everyone. Throughout the meal, Lucius wondered what Adara was doing, how she had slept and how she felt in that exact moment. Was she nervous? Excited? He couldn't wait to see her, to hold her hand in the Temple of Apollo as they were wed. It would not be long now, three hours until the ceremony. With all that had happened, Lucius felt that he had waited a lifetime and more for that day, and now it was time.

As Lucius and the rest of the Metelli came up the stairs and into the open area in front of the temple, the voices of a crowd of guests met their ears. There was applause for the tribune. He looked resplendent and strong, an ideal Roman in his pure white toga with a thin purple stripe around the edge. He looked around and nodded greetings to many that he recognised, Numonius, Emrys and Carissa, Senator Dio, Longus, the Lady Claudia and her frail husband, other senators and some friends of Alene's. Other citizens who had been passing by and heard the commotion stopped to watch and ask others who the young man with the bright eyes was. Inevitably many passers-by stayed to watch, eager for the arrival of the bride; it was a rare occasion to see a wedding ceremony performed at a temple such as this, most being performed in the atrium of the bride's house. But, as was whispered among the spectators, the priests had made an exception for the Metelli. Some even said that the omens had demanded the ceremony take place there. No one was sure but everyone talked about it.

Lucius went half way up the temple steps and turned to watch and wait, Ashur only a few paces behind him. The wait was not a long one, for beneath the bright sunlight and a blue sky the arrival of the bride and her family was heralded by an explosion of music in the distance. Horns rang out, flutes whistled and lyres resonated as the party arrived from the left of the temple to step onto the white marble of the square. They halted, the bride not yet visible for all the musicians. The augur walked at the front. Everyone was silent and the music slowed as the white-bearded man moved into the centre of the square and looked up at the sky above the temple. He gazed for what seemed like ages and then he pointed; far above in the heavens, almost out of sight, soared what looked like two eagles circling, their cries barely audible.

All gazed up in amazement, all were still, for this couple seemed blessed, their union approved by Jupiter himself.

"Mother, do you see them?" Alene whispered.

"Yes, child. Yes." A tear trickled down Antonia's cheek.

The augur nodded to the bridal procession and the music burst out once more as they moved onto the square. The musicians moved to the far side of the temple stairs and a collective gasp filled the space like a hushed wind in summer pines as Adara Antonina came into view.

She wore the flammeum, a long flame-coloured mantle the edge of which covered half of her face so that only her eyes, as brilliant as emeralds, were revealed. This special mantle was originally worn by the Flaminica Dialis, the wife of the priest

400

of Jupiter, and therefore came to represent constancy of the most sacred kind. Only one whose intentions were true wore the flammeum.

Lucius watched in awe as Adara turned at the bottom of the stairs, her eyes resting lovingly on him. Her long, deep black curls were dressed in a special manner, tied with purple vittae, woollen ribbons, and twisted and bound about her head. Beneath her mantle, Adara wore the tunica recta of a bride, a specially woven, straight tunic that was fastened beneath the breasts with ribbons in a Herculean knot that only the new husband could undo.

Finally, Adara reached the top of the stairs and Lucius smiled. He felt a familiar cool breeze caress the back of his neck as he took her hand in his and went into the temple, followed by their families, the musicians and the rest of the guests. The music was reduced now to the soft sounding of only one horn, one flute and one lyre so as to allow all assembled to hear the chants of the priests of Apollo as they presented the couple to the God and his muses.

Inside the temple, a torch hung from every column leading to the main altar and on either side frankincense burned in two enormous tripods, blue-grey smoke writhing and dancing into the air and blanketing all present. Antonia wept joyfully seeing her son at that altar once more, after so many years. Alene smiled gratefully as she looked up at the statue of Palatine Apollo. Delphina and Publius watched their daughter with love and pride, thankful to the Gods for giving her to them. Quintus Metellus pater watched absently, remembering the time long ago when Lucius was met by the eagle and how that had scared and angered him. Never had the Gods seen fit to bless him as they had his son. How history repeated itself, and how he was overshadowed by his own offspring!

Everyone watched and listened as Lucius and Adara turned to face each other and make their promises.

"Adara," he began. "Before Apollo and the rest of the Gods that look over us and protect us, I, Lucius Metellus Anguis, swear by my ancestors, by the life that flows in my veins, that I will honour and protect you forever. I will remain at your side and nothing shall ever part us. In life, in death, in the hereafter, I am yours." Adara's eyes watered briefly and beneath her mantle she smiled a joyful smile that would have lit the entire temple were it uncovered. Then she took his hands and said:

"Lucius, I thank Apollo and the rest of the Gods who have brought you to me, again. Before these people, beneath the blue sky and the constant sun, I swear by my life and all that I am that I shall ever be faithful in my love for you and the well from which my love flows will never fail. The light in my heart will never fade, for you are my life now and evermore."

The two looked into each other's eyes and knew the truth of what they had said, felt the breath of life and love enter them and fill their hearts. Ashur, who stood behind them thought to himself that Apollo looked pleased with the union and he stepped forward with the rings. In the palm of his aged, dark hand glowed two golden rings in the form of two intertwined dragons, a brilliant red jewel where their heads met.

Lucius took the smaller of the two rings and placed it on Adara's second finger, and she then placed the other on his second finger. Since the birth of Rome and beyond, this had been the tradition when rings were exchanged in marriage as the second finger was believed to be directly attached to the heart. The priest then ritually clasped their hands together, a union never to be broken.

After a few moments, another priest came over to them and handed a long curved dagger to Lucius. Numonius entered from the side with a young calf of purest white. Lucius approached the altar onto which the calf was lifted, whining. This was not a task Lucius relished and Adara watched him nervously. As he made to draw the dagger across the calf's neck, a sudden fury came into its eyes and one of its hooves caught Lucius in the nose, causing him to bleed slightly.

Numonius moved to the altar to help Lucius restrain the calf but the priest held him back subtly. It was for Lucius to do.

The calf would not stop flailing and people began to whisper at Lucius' back. Then Adara appeared at his side and her outstretched arm caressed the calf's cheek and neck and to the amazement of all, it calmed immediately. She continued stroking it softly, her eyes meeting the calf's, almost singing it silently to peaceful slumber. Lucius then put the dagger to its neck once more and drew it deeply through the soft flesh without so much as a tremble from the beast that was giving its life in sacrifice. The blood poured slowly out onto the altar top and Lucius and Adara gazed up at Apollo offering their silent thanks.

Before turning, Lucius wiped his nose of his own blood so that those present would not see it, that he had been bloodied by the calf on the altar. That done, the newly joined couple turned to face everyone for the first time as man and wife and the priest proclaimed their union. They walked the length of the temple toward the light of day as the great bronze doors were swung open to let them out into the world.

As Lucius and Adara moved outside onto the steps of the Temple of Apollo they were met with roaring cheers from the great crowd of citizens and servants that had gathered. Word had spread of the marriage of the Tribune Metellus and the striking Adara Antonina and many had gathered to look upon them for themselves, admire them. The interior of the square was set up with tables loaded with flowers and garlands for the wedding banquet and the musicians struck up once more. They descended the stairs and were congratulated and embraced by their families and friends. Then to one side, the crowd parted and Lucius looked to see Julia Domna and her son, Caesar Caracalla, standing there.

"These cheers are not for us my son. We must congratulate the couple and give our blessing," the empress whispered.

They moved to face Lucius and Adara who came graciously toward them, bowing. Caracalla spoke first.

"Tribune Metellus and Lady Antonina," he proclaimed exaggeratedly, speaking more to the crowd assembled. "I congratulate you both on your union! You are an example of true Romanness."

"Thank you, Sire!" replied Lucius, noticing that Caracalla looked more at Adara and the crowd than him. "You are most kind and august to grace us with your presence."

"You are most kind to have extended an invitation," began the empress. "May all the Gods bless your union as we do, and may joy spring eternally for us all."

"Augusta, we are grateful for your heartening words and will remember them always," Adara said, her mouth hidden behind her mantle.

"I hope so, my dear," the empress replied.

Lucius and Adara felt uncomfortable indeed by this odd display of warmth and were at a loss of what to say next. Then a commotion started on the other side of the square where a tall dark figure stepped out, followed by several Praetorians. The man stood next to and spoke some words with Quintus Metellus.

"Good day, Senator, is it not?"

"Prefect? What are you doing here?" Quintus asked.

"Plautianus, the bastard!" murmured Caracalla through clenched teeth.

"Well my son," said Julia Domna flatly. "The father is ensnared; that is why we must secure the son."

Quintus felt ill at ease, angry that Plautianus should confront him like that in front of all his family and fellow citizens. People would talk. They always did. Plautianus gripped Quintus' arm, hidden by the folds of their togas.

"I trust you have not forgotten our agreement, Senator."

"I have not, but I don't see why you should-"

"Don't be a fool," Plautianus said quietly. "I know what you have to do. And, do it with a smile. If you aren't smiling on the day of your son's wedding then people will get suspicious and we can't have that, can we?"

"No, indeed," Quintus said gravely. He could feel Antonia's eyes on him from afar.

"Very well. Now, enjoy the day and be mindful of anything untoward. Remember, I'm having you watched." With that, Plautianus pointed to a far corner of the square where a tall cloaked figure stood smirking in shadow. "You know Argus, don't you? Of course you do." Plautianus laughed and moved on casually to greet the other guests and members of the family.

From the top of the stairs, Ashur had spotted Argus who had been staring directly at him, so much so that Ashur felt something choking him. Hatred could do that. But when Ashur stared back at Argus, he had disappeared around a corner and didn't come back. Meanwhile, in the middle of the square Lucius and Adara had introduced their family to the empress. Caracalla eyed Plautianus hatefully; Lucius could almost feel the hate flowing between the two men as he stood between them but nothing eluded the empress' senses and she noticed Lucius' discomfort with the situation. She decided to put an end to it.

"Again, Tribune, congratulations to you both. We must be going now. We only wanted to wish you well."

"Thank you again, Augusta. I am at your service," he said. He did not know why.

"I hope so, indeed." She turned to leave, Caracalla following behind her. Plautianus then departed the way that he had come and the wedding celebration was left to begin.

The newly wed couple was seated at the central table and servants bustled to and fro all afternoon with bottomless jugs of wine and cornucopic platters of food. Everyone feasted well into the evening to the sounds of music and laughter and as night fell, torches were lit in the square, the light of which reflected off of the temple façade.

Early on, Emrys and Carissa rose to say goodbye to Lucius and Adara because, they said, they had some work to do. The couple thanked them wholeheartedly for their presence and bid them good evening. Ashur watched from his table as Carissa went away with Emrys but before disappearing she turned and smiled to him and he was happy. For the most part, the banquet was a gathering filled with love and joy and the closeness of family and friends. Even Quintus Metellus pater pushed out a smile or two, though nobody knew why he had changed his ways so suddenly. When everyone had had their fill of food and drunk too much wine, the entire party decided to escort Lucius and Adara through the streets to the house on the Esquiline where they would stay that night before going to Cumae the following day. Delphina and Publius had decided to let the couple stay there for that night, in peace and privacy. In the Metellus household, rooms had been prepared for them.

When the party reached the Esquiline, goodnights were made and Lucius and Adara were finally left to go indoors together, to remember the day and all that had transpired as though it were a warm comforting dream. The house had been lit with lamps in every corner, and a table had been laid out with wine, more food and fresh fruit. Inside the door, the atrium walls reflected the lamplight, casting the couple's dancing shadows onto the walls.

Lucius turned to his wife and gently pulled aside the mantle where it hid her face to reveal her full, soft lips. She smiled, unbelieving that the day had finally come to pass and kissed him.

"Alene said we should go to the garden right away...before *anything* else," Adara said mischievously.

"Then we'd better go!" Lucius swept her up in his arms effortlessly, laughing as he carried her down the corridor.

When they arrived in the garden, they found two large objects covered in beautiful silks decorated with gold flickers that shone in the moonlight. There was a note at the base of one of them and Lucius picked it up.

"What does it say?" Adara asked eagerly.

"It says..."

Dearest Lucius and Adara,

From all of those who love you and hold you dear.
Never has an artist had two such beautiful subjects.
These reflect the light and love which you
represent to us. May you always be together and
love as only few are permitted.
The Gods bless you both.

Your family and friends.

"Well? Shall we uncover them?"

"After you," he said, unable to stop smiling as Adara pulled away one of the silks.

"Oh, Lucius...it's you!" They both stood in amazement and gazed upon the marble statue of Lucius. It felt as though there were a third person with them. "I can't believe it." Adara went over to it, looked back at Lucius and then at the statue again. "I've never seen anything like this." She ran her hand along one of the muscular arms, up to the shoulder and the cheek. "I feel your eyes gazing at me through the statue!" Lucius was silent as he looked upon himself, clad in full armour, greaves, dragon-emblazoned breastplate, sword and helmet beneath the left arm as always. The eyes were like his, exactly.

"It seems that Emrys and Carissa used some kind of glass or gems to get the colour of my eyes. They're too real!" Then he went over to the other silk, looked at Adara, then pulled it to the ground.

"By the Gods!" he exclaimed, falling to his knees and looking in astonishment from the statue to his wife and back. "I must be dreaming." The likeness of Adara was even more

407

life-like than that of Lucius. Dressed as a goddess, a simple robe hugged her beautiful shape. Smooth, slender arms reached slightly outward as though bidding the admirer to a loving embrace. Long curls of beautiful hair cascaded down her shoulders to the middle of her back. The mouth smiled warmly and the eyes...the gems in the eyes gleamed and looked into Lucius'. They both stepped back, their eyes fixed on the statues. Each wondered how Emrys and Carissa had managed such a feat of...magic? For that is the only word that they could think of to describe such masterful creations. Life had been breathed into the marble and the statues carried a life of their own.

"This is the most wonderful day of my entire life," Adara said to Lucius, her prepossessing eyes looking up at her husband full of love.

"It has been for me as well, my love. You've made me the happiest man in the entire world."

"I love you, Lucius Metellus Anguis." She reached up to put her olive arms around his neck, to bring his lips to hers for a heated embrace.

Hand in hand, they walked from the garden to a cubiculum on the second floor that had been prepared especially for them on their wedding night. Through air filled with sweet incense, they followed the lamps to a doorway wreathed with fresh garlands and opened the door. The room looked out over the edge of the Esquiline to the countryside in the distance. Moon and starlight flooded in through the window, revealing the rose petals scattered all about their feet. On the large bed were sprinkled blue lotus flowers, their scent strong, sweetly pungent.

Adara went over to the window, breathed deeply, slightly nervous, and turned to face Lucius who stood admiring her from the other side of the room. A fire burned within both of them, each longing for the other with every beat of their hearts, every heavy breath. Outlined by silver moonlight, Adara let her flammeum fall to the floor, revealing the knot beneath her full breasts that bound her in the tunica recta. She smiled as Lucius walked around to her and kissed her neck where it was bared, quickening her heartbeat. It was time for him to undo the Herculean knot that had been so skilfully tied. The golden band that bound the white tunic was wrapped around her three times and he could not find the ends of the knot. Then he spotted a minuscule edge of fabric sticking out and pulled on it. It gave way smoothly, unravelling as though a coiled serpent. The tunic loosened and slid slowly down her body to reveal the wife to her husband.

In her nakedness, Adara shone like the goddess Lucius believed her to be, silhouetted in the otherworldly light that crept in through the window. She swept her hair back to reveal her shoulders above her breasts. Her tall, slender body was perfect, disarming.

As she stood there, her longing overcame her and she stepped to Lucius to unfold the toga wrapped about him. Every one of her movements seemed slow and hypnotic to him, as though time was theirs and only theirs to do with as they pleased. Left only in his tunic, Lucius pulled it above his head. The strength and beauty of her husband was disclosed to Adara in that moment as she looked upon the naked man before her. His muscles, arms, legs, chest and back were solid and refined, flawless. And yet she thought, this was the body of a warrior, and she traced the many scars upon him with loving fingers and kissed each of them, finishing with the painful wound on his thigh. How was it that with so many scars he was still perfect and pure to her? She wondered at this for a moment and knew that she loved him more than anything, that it would always be so. She placed her hand on his chest, feeling his heart and he did the same, caressing her breast as he did so. Their hearts pounded together as he drew her close to him, their bodies pressed, alive and burning with loving desire.

Lucius then picked Adara up and laid her on the lotus-strewn bed to caress and kiss every inch of her beauty, wanting to memorize every detail for himself. The night was spent in a blissful eternity in which each pleasured the other in unconditional love and caring. Man and woman, husband and wife, were brought to full life and awakening, and in their lovemaking, Lucius and Adara felt a familiarity, a power and peace that could never be described in words or song.

When finally they lay down to loving slumber, they held each other closely, immune to all the ills and sorrows that might seek to mar such joy and beauty in the world. Untouchable, they lay there in the light of the waxing moon and slept.

In the courtyard below, the lamps had burned their length and the smell of jasmine and dew pervaded the garden where the two lively statues stood. And it seemed to Love and the God of the Silver Bow, as they looked down from airy cliffs, that a fire was kindled in the eyes of the marble likenesses of their charges. They wondered at this, and knew that they had done well, for in that house lay two mortals whose fates were entwined for all time.

XXV

CUMAE

"In times of joy and peace, it is often the fault of mortals to allow their minds to stray, to think of other times when they should be delighting in the present of their lives. By no means should the world without be forgotten, however, fleeting moments of calm in a raging sea should be savoured. You should stand up and look with both eyes, feel the light of the sun with your heart and smell the sweetness of the air around you with your soul. For unfortunately, times such as these seem only to last momentarily and before you know it, the sea rages once more."

Diodorus gave these words to Lucius in parting, not long before he died. The young student had not quite understood what he meant at the time, so keen was he for adventure and excitement, but the words remained with him always.

When Lucius awoke the morning after his and Adara's wedding, Diodorus' words never rang more true nor made more sense than they did in that moment. He turned in bed to look at his wife, blanketed as she was in the golden light of a summer morning, and decided that he would always be aware of and grateful for the time they had together. Until then, he had always said he was, first and foremost, a tribune of Rome. That had changed. His duty as a tribune was still very important to him but it would always be secondary to his role as husband.

"Good morning mariti," Adara said as her eyes opened and her hand reached out for Lucius' cheek. She had not stopped smiling all night, even in her sleep. She liked calling him her husband and he liked hearing it.

"Good morning to you, marita. Did you sleep well?" he asked as he drew her to him.

"The Gods themselves do not sleep so well as I have." She edged her head comfortably into the crook of his neck. Outside, the sounds of birdsong were everywhere, and a gentle summer breeze wafted into the room, ruffling the window silks like the sails of an Egyptian Nile barge.

"I suppose we ought to go down soon. They're probably waiting to see us before we go."

"Just a few more moments of rest, Lucius... I love waking up with you."

"It's perfect, I agree."

"How are we getting to Cumae anyway? What did my father say?"

"He said he's hired a wagon for the journey, a special one apparently."

"Wonderful. I'm so excited! I've never been to Cumae and the villa is supposed to be quite beautiful." Lucius sat up on the edge of the bed to look out of the window, and she leaned herself against his back, her hair falling gently over the front of his shoulders. He could feel the heat from her naked body on his back and sighed.

"I'm sure the villa is idyllic but not so much as you." And with that he turned and took her up in his arms, kissed her and made love to her again before they rose for their journey. The morning was just too perfect to end.

When the newly wed couple finally emerged from their room, Lucius in a new white and blue tunic and Adara with a stunning saffron stola with gold fastenings, they found both of their families down in the garden talking and admiring Emrys and Carissa's work. Everyone was so taken by the statues that they hardly noticed the two of them come out of the peristyle. Everyone seemed so happy and engaged, that is all save Quintus Metellus pater who sat alone eating figs and keeping to himself and young Quintus who was wandering around the courtyard muttering something. He noticed Lucius and Adara first and went over to them, his head down.

"Quintus," Lucius called. "Come say good morning to your new sister." The young man raised his head and managed a polite but shy smile.

"Good morning, lady," he squeaked. Adara bent down to look him in the eyes and put her hands on his shoulders.

"Now Quintus, if we are to be sister and brother there is one thing I must insist on." Young Quintus pulled away slightly. *Not another one to chide me along with all the others!* he thought. Adara smiled. "You must call me Adara." That was all. Quintus' face changed immediately and he became a little boy once more.

"I can do that!" he said excitedly. "Adara!"

"Good!" she encouraged.

"Adara!" he repeated before looking at his older brother. "Lucius-"

"I know you know my name, little brother," Lucius interrupted.

"No! I... Of course I know your name, you big grunt. I just wanted to tell you something that-"

"Well? What is it, Quintus?"

"Nothing. Never mind...congratulations on your marriage. I like Adara. She's really nice to me."

"To me too, brother," Lucius said absently. "Me too." He watched his wife walk around the garden, go straight to Metellus pater to try and warm his mood. She succeeded in bringing a quarter smile to his face with a plate of more figs. When Lucius turned to speak to his brother again, he found him gone. Seeing Lucius admire his new wife so much was too painful for young Quintus because it reminded him of his own parents and the terrible secret he was now privy to. Everything in fact, reminded him of that secret.

"Good morning, Lucius!" Alene came skipping over to him like a little girl and kissed his cheek. "*Sleep* well?"

"What's gotten into you? You're all full of mischief it seems." He prodded her side as he stole a few grapes from the bunch she was holding.

"I'm just happy for you, and for myself as I now have three new sisters whom I adore, two of which are in admiration of my sense of fashion and hang off every one of my words."

"Even I admit you have great taste, Alene."

"Of course you do!" she joked. " So while you steal my best friend away from me and go to sun yourselves in Cumae, Hadrea, Lavena and I are going shopping.

"Gods help us!" Lucius exclaimed. "You're going to cause quite a sensation in the markets." Lucius put his arm around his sister as they looked at everyone gathered around Adara.

"Are you happy?" she asked, more serious. Once again the older sister.

"More than I ever thought possible, Alene. The Gods have smiled on me again."

"My heart rejoices for you both." Lucius noticed she was indeed very, very happy for them but he couldn't help but think of her own happiness. He wished she could know even the smallest measure of what he was feeling. "Now spring brings back unfrozen warmth, Now the sky's equinoctial fury is hushed by Zephyr's welcome airs." She spouted the words like a gently weeping fountain.

"What are you saying, Alene? Sounds like Ovid again," he called to her as she walked toward Adara.

"No!" she turned smiling. "It's Catullus!"

After they had spoken to everyone and thanked them for the gift of the statues, Emrys and Carissa for making them, family and friends toasted the couple's happiness and good fortune before they departed. In the atrium, Publius Antoninus was speaking with a messenger that had come to inform Lucius that there was a special gift from the empress.

"What is it, Publius?" Lucius asked.

"Apparently the empress has sent a special escort to accompany you to Cumae."

"That's...kind of her I suppose. But why would she do us such an honour?"

"Politics, Tribune. Politics." Quintus Metellus pater spoke for the first time to his son that morning. "It would not be wise to deny the empress' gift."

"On the contrary, father, I've no intention of refusing. I accept it happily. Anything to make the journey safer and more pleasant for Adara."

"Are you both ready?" asked Antonia as she and Delphina came up.

"Yes. The servants are loading our chests onto the wagon now," Adara answered.

They said goodbye to everyone and went out to the wagon which was loaded up with cushions, shaded by a yellow silk awning. There were bowls of fruit and some bread and wine for the long journey. Around the wagon were a dozen armed guards on horseback and four slaves who would walk alongside the wagon if the couple should need anything.

Before getting in after his wife, Lucius nodded to Ashur in farewell. They had decided that Ashur would remain behind to watch over everyone while he was away. His friend had been somewhat hesitant but knew better than to impose on their escape. Indeed, the truth was that he wanted to stay.

"Tribune? Shall we go?" asked the neat but stocky driver.

"Ready when you are, my good man!" The cart lurched forward, with six cavalry troopers in the front and six in the rear at a respectable distance so as not to crowd the tribune and his new wife. They waved to their family and friends until they turned a corner and then settled into the comfortable cushions for a pleasant journey under the summer sun. Before long, they were headed to the coast road and the walls of Rome were but a dot in the distance.

By the time they had reached the coast and the winding Via Domitiana, the world around them seemed to have faded away into the sea's haze. The only sounds that reached their ears, apart from each other's voices, were the sounds of waves on the rocky shoreline and of sea birds nestled in among the rocky outcroppings.

There were a few grumblings among the men of their escort; guarding some pampered tribune and his wife on a picnic parade to Cumae was less than desirable. For some of the men however, a summer ride out in the fresh sea breeze was a cushy assignment compared to guarding the entrances to the Palatine in the sweaty streets of Rome. Each guard simply put up with it and enjoyed it as best he could while the four slaves walking on one side of the wagon joked about as they skipped along in the tall grasses that flanked the road.

After a second restful night at a roadside inn in which the proprietors wished the young couple health and happiness and gave them some food for the road, the party set out once more on the final day of travel. Lucius and Adara were as relaxed as ever, ready to settle into the villa for their getaway.

Cumae. Diodorus had taught Lucius about the oracles of the world of which this was one of the most important. So, when Adara asked Lucius what he knew about it, he searched his memory for what he did know about the mysterious place. He decided to start where his tutor had told him to start from whenever in doubt: the beginning.

"Diodorus used to say," Lucius began "that Cumae was the home of the prophetess called the Sibyl. She was very beautiful and was once loved by Apollo who promised her any gift if she would take him as a lover. She accepted, and as her gift she asked for as many years of life as there were grains of dust in a pile of floor sweepings."

"That's odd," Adara said, imagining how many years that could possibly have been.

"But, the Sibyl forgot to ask for perpetual beauty as part of her gift and so as the ages passed, she slowly shrivelled up without dying. A long time later, when some children found their way into the cave and asked her what she wanted, she replied that she wanted to die."

"How sad..." The two of them thought about that for a moment. "But why is the Sibyl so important to Rome, Lucius?"

"Well, for a start, when Aeneas journeyed here after the Trojan War it was the Sibyl who told him how to pluck the golden bough that would give him entrance into the Underworld. She then went with him on that fearful journey. Years later, during the infancy of Rome, she offered nine books of prophecies to the Roman king Tarquinius Superbus. He refused because her price was too high. Then she burnt three books and offered the rest at the same price. He refused. So, she burnt another three and sold the last three books to the king for the same price. The books were supposed to prophesy the destiny of Rome. During the Republic, the books were kept in the Temple of Capitoline Jupiter and were consulted in times of crisis but they burned in a fire and were lost."

"I wonder what they said... Do you suppose they survive in secret or that copies were made?"

"I seem to remember something my tutor said about a new collection of the books being compiled with copies that had been made. The Emperor Augustus had the new books transferred to the Temple of Apollo on the Palatine." He paused. "I had forgotten about that. Then again, only the priest of Apollo consults them; so much is hidden from the peoples' eyes...who knows what they say anymore."

"One day I'll take you to the oracle at Delphi."

"You've been? Ashur has told me something about it."

"Oh, yes. Well, that's where mother is from. Oh, you should see it, Lucius! The sun beats down upon the mountainside so intensely you feel as though Apollo is constantly watching you. Far below, the massive trees of the sacred olive groves shimmer like a sea of green and silver, whispering up the mountain in and out of the treasuries, up to the Temple of Apollo, the theatre and the stadium. Even after so many ages, there are still people who line the paths to hear riddles from the Pythia."

"I want to see the world with you, my love." Lucius held her close as a cool breeze came off of the sea blowing back the thick strands of her hair.

"Oh, we will, we will." She paused for a moment, a childlike excitement in her eyes. "Lucius, do you think that there's still a Sibyl in Cumae? I'd like to go and see." Upon hearing this, the slaves walking next to the wagon made some sort of superstitious gesture of protection and distanced themselves. Lucius did not notice.

"I don't think there's been a Sybil there for years but we can go and look if you like."

"Oh, yes. I'm very curious after what you've told me about it. Did Diodorus tell you anything else about the place?" Lucius thought about it for a moment, nothing coming to mind, until he remembered one thing he had said to Lucius.

"Actually there was one thing he told me but not necessarily about the place itself."

"Oh?"

"He said that one day I should go there myself and be still."

"Be still?"

"Yes...usually he was a lot more specific in what he told me."

"Well, it looks as though you are going to do what he said you should do."

"So it seems." His thoughts drifted to his old tutor, his kindness and how nothing he ever told Lucius seemed false or senseless.

"You miss him, don't you?" Adara could spot the hint of sad remembrance in her husband's eyes.

"Yes." Lucius held her close again. "I would have liked for him to have met you."

The wagon moved on at a quick pace now that the land along the coast was flattening out, avoiding the sparse volcanic rock formations along the shoreline. The air seemed to grow suddenly still, silent. As Lucius and Adara sat up to be able to see the surroundings, the first thing that attracted their eyes was the imposing shape of Mount Vesuvius in the distance, towering over the world below. Clouds hovered around its peak and its slopes, though green in places, looked angrily creased like the lines on the face of an old, embittered man.

Once they ripped their gaze away from the mountain, they noticed the smoky haze from Neapolis to the east, and to the south of their position, on a volcanic peninsula jutting out into the bay, lay Cumae. Immediately the eye travelled past the small town to the acropolis encircled by smoke and mystery. Atop the acropolis of Cumae stood a few temples: on the eastern and lower summit stood the Temple of Apollo and on the higher, western summit was erected the Temple of Olympian Zeus. These temples, Lucius remembered, were built by the ancient Greeks who had settled the area when Rome was but a collection of mean dwellings. The age of the place, of the land was tangible, thick in the air, making Lucius and Adara feel both curiously excited and anxious.

"We're turning off of the road now, Tribune." The driver of the wagon said suddenly, breaking the stillness.

"We are?" asked Lucius, realizing he did not know where exactly they were going. "We're not going to town?"

"No, sir. The villa is on the coast down this road."

"Oh. All right." Lucius raised an eyebrow as he looked to Adara who shrugged. Instinctively, he felt for the handle of his sword which he had tucked under the cushions beside himself.

"As soon as we reach the water, Tribune, we'll get you and the lady onto the boat so you can go on ahead. Your belongings will follow."

"Did you say boat?" This was too much.

"Yes, Tribune. The villa can only be approached from the sea." The man drove on through a grove of orange trees.

"Well," acknowledged Adara, "there it is."

The villa was indeed accessible only from the water. As rich Romans had flocked to Cumae, Baiae and Neapolis in increasing numbers to build luxurious villas as retreats from the noise of Rome, the search for more secluded pieces of land had grown voracious. The villa to which they were headed was no exception. It stood high above the sandy shoreline on a rock with steep sides. As the boat was rowed a short distance from the dock where they had arrived with the wagon, they rounded a corner to find another smaller jetty next to a private beach. A small stairway carved out of the rock led up to the top. This was the only entrance.

They disembarked with two of the guards while the boat was rowed back to get the slaves and their belongings. The guards went up the stairs first; their orders from the empress were to see the couple safely inside and give the steward her instructions insisting that they be taken care of as befits a favoured tribune and his wife.

The villa was of an irregular shape, necessarily so because of the shape of the rock on which it was built. Every attempt had been made to use as much space as possible in order to fit as many luxuries as possible. Once the stairs reached the top there was a small platform before two large, thick wooden doors painted a deep, rich red. There was a small covered atrium which led directly to an open garden filled with beautiful statuary surrounding an ornate fountain depicting Leto, mother of Apollo and Artemis, beneath a magnificent palm tree. Around the edges of the garden was a peristyle, the columns of which were embraced by full-blooming yellow jasmine.

On the north of the house, away from the sea, were the kitchens, food stores and a water cistern. To the west was a small bath house and then a long wide room that was actually a triclinium with ten couches; the people who owned this villa were wont to have large dinner parties. Off of the dining room was a large outdoor garden with groomed pathways and a large oval bathing pool in the centre where an ornate mosaic of scenes from Odysseus' travels shimmered beneath the clear water. At each corner of the square garden stood a large cypress tree.

This was a house that centred on the outdoors, the sea. In fact all of the windows faced the water. Lastly, along the southern corridor of the villa were the cubicula; five small rooms and one very large one with marble arches that led onto a private loggia half-shaded by grape vines and pink and white bougainvillaea. Once inside, Lucius realised how ingenious the construction was as none of it was visible from either of the three landward sides. Only from the sea was part of it visible.

Upon arrival at the doors, they were met by the steward of the house, an older man in his fifties with curly blond-dyed hair and pale blue eyes. He was slender, of medium height and neatly dressed in a long white tunic with blue, wave-like borders. At first he was taken aback by the guards who knocked on the door and pushed their way through, but relaxed once they handed him the letter from the empress. At least he knew he was not in any sort of trouble. His guests were more important than he had thought and so he immediately got to work.

"Welcome, welcome Tribune Metellus, Lady, welcome!" He spread his arms wide, gesturing them into the house. "My name is Cassius and I am the steward here and your humble servant for the duration of your stay." He snapped his fingers and a small slave girl brought in a tray with two glasses of cold sanguine orange juice.

"Thank you, Cassius," Adara returned the greeting. "You have a beautiful home here."

"Thank you, my lady." He was very proud of how well he kept the place running, how utterly clean. He whispered something to the slaves who were arriving with the baggage and then led Lucius and Adara on a tour of the villa after the guards had finished inspecting every room.

After having shown them around, he led them to their rooms where the slaves had already set out their belongings and thrown open the shutters onto the loggia.

"This is beautiful!" gasped Adara.

"Isn't it?" said Cassius proudly. "You will find that no one will disturb you here, I promise you. And if you wish to go to town at all, let me know and I shall arrange for some bodyguards to accompany you. The master has some nearby that he trusts and uses regularly." Just then, the head guard appeared in the doorway.

"Tribune?" he called. Lucius went over to him while Cassius led Adara out beneath the loggia and pulled down some grapes from her to taste.

"Yes? Is everything all right, Drusus?" Lucius had been wondering why they were being so thorough.

"Yes, Tribune. Everything checks out."

"Good. But why all the secrecy and protection?"

"Don't know, sir. All I know is that the empress ordered me and my men to see you here safely, make sure there was nothing suspicious and leave you to it." Lucius thought briefly of the attack near the Colosseum before the wedding and was grateful for the extra protection, especially since Ashur was back in Rome.

"Well, we're grateful, Drusus. Our thanks."

"No trouble at all, Tribune. If you need anything, my men and I will be staying in town. Otherwise, we'll return in a weeks' time for your journey home."

"Sounds good," Lucius said as Drusus saluted him and left with his two men. He watched the fellow go; he seemed a good man, trustworthy. Lucius then joined Adara outside as Cassius pointed out the magnificent view.

That evening, after having refreshed themselves in the small ornate baths, Lucius and Adara dined on a magnificent feast in the triclinium. The doors to the garden had been opened, allowing them to enjoy the final rays of red sunshine before

422

the sun sank. Along the garden paths, braziers had been set alight, the smoke wafting and whirling around the cypress trees.

As they were alone, they sat nestled together on one of the larger couches while they ate; the two cooking slaves the empress had sent along had prepared an exquisite array of seafoods with fragrant herb sauces. There were also tender sweetmeats, regional cheeses, fruits, stuffed olives and other dainty treats. A large crater of rich Sicilian wine had been placed near them with crafted blue glass cups. When they had neared the end of their meal, unable to eat any more, Cassius appeared discreetly.

"Tribune, Lady? Was everything to your satisfaction?"

"Oh yes, Cassius, quite," Adara said, her voice soft and relaxed.

"Everything was delicious." Lucius helped Adara off of the plush couch.

"Wonderful." Cassius smiled, was relieved. "Now, you may wander about the gardens if you wish. I have set out a table for you with warm, spiced wine next to a couch. Your cloaks have been placed on the couch in case the evening chill is too much. The Gods seem to have lit all the stars this night and they are quite beautiful."

"That sounds lovely." Adara nodded her thanks and took her husband by the hand, leading him out through the opened doors and into the fire-lit garden. The air smelled like sweet clove, most likely the incense in the braziers, and in the pool, the lively images from the mosaic bottom reflected the dim light. The farther they got from the villa, the brighter the stars became until they reached the far wall overlooking the sea below and they looked up. "By Jupiter," said a stunned Adara, "it's been some time since I've seen so many stars. The Gods must be pleased."

Lucius was listening to her but not looking up for he couldn't stop staring at his beautiful wife and how the myriad stars above shone in her bright green eyes. From behind them, a bright crescent moon lit her hair with silver streaks. How was it that the moon's light hypnotized him so? Combined with Adara's beauty, this was increased tenfold. She could feel his loving gaze on her and enjoyed the warm, safe feeling it brought to her heart, her body. She gave him a little elbow in the ribs.

"Not inclined to look at stars are we?"

"The brightest star in all the heavens has come down to me. Why look up when I can simply turn my head to the right?" He did look up to the sky however, and acknowledged that he too had not seen such a sky for a long while, since Africa.

They poured two cups of spiced wine and settled back on the couch, covered by their cloaks, to look up at the sky. They had been so busy for so long, always around other people, it was odd to be alone now, quiet. For some time Adara had wanted to ask her husband some things; the strange and sometimes dangerous events that surrounded Lucius had not gone unnoticed. She wondered what went through his mind when he would gaze up at the moon, what sort of commander he was and whether his men loved him. She also feared for him.

"Lucius, my love?" She wanted to know now, everything.

"Yes?"

"Until now I've not spoken of the strange events that have surrounded you, the attacks, our escort here. But I'd like to know what you're thinking, I want to know that you'll be safe."

He thought about this for a moment. She had a right to know what he knew, though even that was little, not enough to put one's mind at ease.

"For a long time now I've felt as though some dark force has been shadowing me wherever I go. There have been several attempts on my life but for what reason I can't say; in Africa there were a couple and then in Rome before our wedding."

"But who would want to hurt you?"

"I don't know. I do know that the attacks have been different. In Rome it was planned, certainly, but in Africa they were as shades come out of the darkness. I can't explain anymore than that, I simply don't know. I feel that Ashur was sent to protect me or guide me along the way and I know that I have the favour of Apollo and Venus for which I am eternally grateful." He stroked her cheek lightly. "As for the escort here, I suppose the empress heard about the attack in Rome and wanted to see to our safety. She probably wants to safeguard a future use for us."

"That much is obvious, but what?"

"Not sure. I'm a soldier not a politician. The little confrontation at our wedding banquet between the empress, Caracalla and Plautianus may have something to do with it, it may not."

"I don't trust any of them, Lucius. We should be careful."

"Yes, but we too need allies it seems. I'll just go on doing what I do best, leading my men." He realised as soon as he said this that it brought into their minds the thought that he would be called back to duty and danger someday soon.

"Let's not talk of that for now my love. This time is ours."

"You're right."

"One last thing though. Your name."

"My name?"

"Anguis. I know that you've told me it belongs to a more obscure line of the Metelli, that it was adopted by some ancestor your father chooses to forget."

"Yes, I remember telling you."

"Did you ever think that so many of the mysteries surrounding you may be linked with that part of you? I've heard Ashur call you *Dragon* with great reverence in his voice. Why?"

"Ashur believes that certain people through time have been blessed with something special, a power or a connection to something greater, that they have all born the name of *Anguis,* or a word for dragon in one form or another. I don't know what to make of that. Ashur speaks in riddles. Sometimes I think I've just ended up with the name of some distant ancestor, nothing more."

"I think you're wrong," she said absolutely. "You're special, and I don't say that because I'm connected to you by an infinity of love. You're meant for greatness. All I want is to be by your side, to protect you and love you as I can." Lucius was silent again, staring up at the sky.

"Did you know there is a dragon in the heavens?"

"Really? Where?"

"There." He pointed. "You see that line of stars? That's it. Diodorus used to show it to me all the time. He said I shouldn't forget it." There were many things that Diodorus had said which were now becoming unusually clear to Lucius.

"I think Diodorus knew much more than history, philosophy and science. He was schooling you for greatness." Adara looked up at the starry sky and tried to envision their future.

The two of them lay there for some time, having told Cassius that they didn't need anything else for the night and that he could retire. The servants were all fast asleep in their quarters at the back of the house. The world was still and riddled with magic as Lucius and Adara made love beneath their cloaks, the stars, moon, and the sea beyond, their only witnesses. A soft, cool, all embracing breath came on the winds to protect them as Venus looked on from the firmament, pleased to dewy tears while several stars shot across the heavens loosed fast from Apollo's bow. In a quiet, ancient cave along the shoreline, a light was kindled.

When the golden-hued dawn arrived, it was bright, fresh and melodic. Minuscule birds sang as they flit wildly in and out of the garden trees and sunned themselves on top of the loggia where warming rays penetrated the vines and flowers that opened for the new day. There was no rush to arise, and so time stood still for a while, content to dress in the lush greens

426

and brilliant yellows of summer, scent itself in the blue mist of the heated sea.

As the two lovers lay there entwined amid the twisted Egyptian sheets, they each wished that every day of their entire lives could be as a summer morning by the sea. The pink marble of the columns around their room seemed to warm the very air and mood.

"What would you like to do today?" Lucius whispered into Adara's ear as they looked outside.

"When was the last time you sunned yourself by the sea and swam?"

"I can't even remember." He realised it must have been years.

"Then that's what I would like to do. I've grown too pale for my liking." She held up her arm to look at it, how her olive skin had turned to a pale, golden brown. Lucius laughed.

"You know, proper *Roman* ladies prefer to have a white complexion."

"Well, then I guess it's a good thing that you married someone more Greek than Roman."

"It is indeed." How he loved her olive skin.

Once they had eaten a light breakfast, Lucius informed Cassius that they were going down to the villa's private beach and that they wished not to be disturbed. The steward assured them that no one would intrude, that the boat was there and none would be returning. Cassius also informed Lucius that he had set out a silk awning with more food on the beach in case the sun became too intense. He was a good man. When Lucius asked him how long he had been working in the house, he said that he had been there for thirty years, and that he had stayed even after earning his freedom ten years before. He loved his work, the place, that much.

The sun was an hour or so from its midday height and had been out long enough for it to be very hot, for the sand on the beach to be soft and dry. It seemed that Cassius had even had one of the slaves groom the beach, clear away any trace of seaweed or pebbles. Everything they needed was there for them, and so, when they arrived, both Lucius and Adara were filled with a childlike excitement that comes with a visit to the seaside. The memories of outings gone by, of playful frolicking long ago, came in waves as the smell of seawater filled their nostrils and the sound of gentle lapping flooded their ears.

The sea was clear and calm, a harmonious blend of crystal and turquoise, the Gods' own mirror. For several feet out, the bottom was a soft sand that eventually gave way to black and grey pebbles among which colourful fish darted, reflecting the filtered light. Without wasting any time, Adara shed her white stola, leaving it beneath the awning, and walked naked to the shore, a feeling of freedom as the sun beat down on every part of her body. She turned to face Lucius who had removed his tunic and motioned for him to come to her as she backed into the embracing water.

"Are you coming?" She winked.

Lucius thought that she seemed completely at ease in the sea, a mermaid returned home. A part of him had a sudden fear that she would swim away, that he should make his way in also so as not to lose her. Adara watched as her husband waded out to her, his powerful shoulders bobbing on the surface of the water. The scars on his body immersed in the salt sea seemed to hiss as they were wetted. The brown of his eyes lightened with the seawater as he came toward her. They swam for some time then went back onto the beach to lay in the sun.

All day they did this: swim then lie in the sun. When the time came for them to go back up to the villa, they stood up and put on their clothes. Down the shoreline, in the distance they spotted smoke from the temples on Cumae's acropolis.

"Shall we go explore tomorrow? I'm curious." Adara's adventurous side was becoming more and more apparent.

"I think we should. I can't stop staring over there whenever I have the chance."

They departed early the following morning, at the break of dawn, so as to allow enough time to look around and be back at the villa before nightfall. The world was quiet; the trees were hushed and the sea lay still, asleep. Lucius and Adara had worn cloaks for the morning chill, his gladius hung beneath, at his side. When they approached the moorings on the other side, the bodyguards, groggy and not a little churlish, were awaiting them with a horse-drawn wagon. There were six of them, all former gladiators, well-armed and well-muscled.

"Is all this really necessary?" Adara asked Lucius as she pulled her hood over her head and covered half her face with a part of her silk veil. She didn't like the look of this bunch.

"Cassius has his orders. He said they were a good bunch of men. It's just a little early for them is all." He stood up upon reaching the dock and helped her out. One of the bodyguards came forward while the others stood where they were.

"Tribune?" The man was short, dark and stalky. He spoke with power and authority but seemed respectful of his clients. It was probably, Lucius thought, his business. "My name's Lycus. Cassius informed me that you need an escort to and from Cumae today."

"Yes, Lycus." Lucius felt better about the situation with this man in charge.

"You'll have to excuse the lads, Tribune. They're not used to such early mornings but I assure you they're ready for action in an instant."

"Glad to hear it, Lycus." He helped Adara up into the wagon and followed while Lycus took the reigns and the others spread out around the wagon.

"So," began Lycus after a while, "are you going to shop in the town? Visiting friends?"

"Actually we wanted to see the Sybil's cave," Adara said cheerfully. Lycus' head whipped around quickly.

"Brrrrr! Why would you want to do a thing like that? Begging your pardon."

"Curiosity more than anything," she replied, surprised by his reaction.

"Me, I don't go near the place. Haunted they say."

"You and your men can wait outside the gates for us if you wish." Lucius was surprised by the fear he heard in this gladiator's voice.

"Aye...that we'll do," he said, relieved, as the wagon lolled on through the trees and onto the coastal road of the peninsula.

Cumae was an ancient settlement established by the Greeks long before the rise of Rome, and the acropolis there was the only fortified town for many miles; one hundred yards from the sandy seashore, it rose two hundred and seventy feet or so above the water. The only approach to it was from the southeast; it was steep on all other sides. The rock was riddled with caves, three levels with many branches where it was said many unwary travellers had been lost. To the north of the acropolis was the old town, to the south the newer Roman buildings including an amphitheatre. Always visible however, always looming heavily above the town were the temples of Olympian Zeus and of Apollo; somewhere beneath them, in the dark corridors of rock, was the Sibyl's cave.

The wagon squeezed through the narrow streets of the old town. A haze from the sea had blown up the pathways to give a dim view of the surroundings. Lycus and his men grew visibly edgy but this was due to their dislike of the place which they approached. In the sky above, the sun was making its daily attempt to break through the morning haze.

Lycus and his men halted. "Well," he said, "there's the way up." He pointed to an aged arch covered in ivy. "Shouldn't be anyone there at this time. If you need us just shout." He regretted saying that in case they did need him and he actually had to go inside.

"Thank you, Lycus. We won't be long." Lucius and Adara turned to go through the arch and up the stairs.

When they finally reached the top, the sun appeared brighter, and to their surprise, the precinct was extremely well-kept. A few priests hovered around the temples of Zeus and Apollo but they kept to themselves. They could see for miles in every direction but they could not see the town below but for the haze.

They walked around for a time, visited the temple of Zeus first. It had been well taken care of. They were impressed by the shear mass of its Doric columns. From that high summit they looked across the acropolis plateau to the lower summit where the temple of Apollo stood. It was smaller than the one on the Palatine, older too.

"Do you have the oil?" Lucius asked when they reached the altar that stood in front of the temple.

"Yes, here it is. Do you want to do it?" Adara held out the pale blue glass bottle.

"Let's both pour the libation."

As they held the bottle together, they poured part of the oil onto the altar so that it mingled with the remnants of blood from offerings made by the priests.

"Mighty Apollo, we honour You. Bless us and keep us under your protection." They bowed their heads.

"Great far-shooting God. Accept our offering," Adara added.

"By Zeus! What are you doing?" A voice startled them from behind. Lucius instinctively reached for the handle of his sword beneath his cloak. "This altar is for the priests' offerings alone!" The man who confronted them was old, white-haired and wrinkly. "Who are you that you come to this revered place?"

Lucius stepped forward. "I am Tribune Lucius Metellus Anguis and this is my wife, Lady Adara Antonina Metella. We have come from Rome and wish to pay our respects to the great god Apollo. I am sorry if we have troubled you." The man studied them intently, said nothing and turned to go back to the other priests. Lucius could see that when he joined his fellow priests again he seemed to be saying something as he pointed toward Lucius and Adara.

"Maybe we should move along," Adara cautioned.

"Probably right. What's that over there?" He had spotted a temple of the same size on an even lower summit surrounded by trees.

"It looks like another temple. Let's have a quick look." They made their way down the marble path to this third temple. It was much less ornate than the other two and had a simple image of a woman on the pediment, seated beneath a god.

"This must be a temple to the Sibyl herself."

"You're right. Here." Adara held out the remaining oil. "We should make an offering to her as well. You can do it this time."

Lucius took the bottle and went over to a small altar set in the middle of the stairs of the temple. He knew not what to say however, poured the remaining oil into the carved bowl on top. As he backed up, into the dark shade of some trees, he spotted a staircase going down the side of the rock.

"Where do you suppose those lead to?" Adara suddenly clung to her husband, a chill coming over her.

"Something tells me we should go and find out," Lucius said.

They both knew that they might not ever return to Cumae, that they had been drawn to that place despite the anxiety they felt. The white-robed priest that had confronted them watched from behind the trunk of a tree as they made their way down the short flight of stairs. First, they passed a crypt, then went down another flight of stairs until they stood before what looked like a long corridor carved out of the stone.

A raven suddenly fluttered and cawed in a nearby cypress tree and a heavy breeze came rushing out of the entrance, stinging their senses.

"Whoa! What a stench! The air smells old and stale within. If you want Adara, you can stay here."

"Lucius Metellus! By now you must know that wherever you go, I go! I'm not leaving your side." She went over to a brazier next to the entrance that contained several torches, took one and went back to his side. Lucius quietly drew his sword.

"Just in case," he said as they went in, their hearts pounding in unison.

The corridor was long and narrow, its walls sloped inwardly to form a square peak at the top. The smell was a convoluted mixture of mould, vapid incense and decay. Though their torch burned brightly, Lucius and Adara could see only a few feet in front. The eerie corridor seemed to swallow up any invading light. So many wisdom seekers had tread this dark path before, for hundreds of years and yet now, it seemed deserted. Their steps echoed as they went on slowly, hesitantly.

"I wonder if Aeneas walked down this very corridor long ago." Lucius' blade shed sharp reflections onto the walls as the torchlight flickered along its edge. Both of them were glad for the other's company; neither of them would have wanted to go in alone. Then, when they believed the corridor would go on ceaselessly, the path opened up and led into a large vaulted room. The walls dripped with age, were painted with glistening greens and blacks. Adara held out the torch, scouring the edges of the room. They were alone at least.

"This must be the Sibyl's inner chamber." She pointed to an arched alcove with benches carved into the rock. "See Lucius? She must have come out of another tunnel through there and prophesied to people on those benches."

"You're right. This is where she stood." He walked into the alcove and turned. "They say that the Sibyl told her prophecies in an ecstatic state…that she was possessed by Apollo himself." He shivered.

"Let's sit for a moment before leaving, Lucius. We know which way to go. See? There's the entrance." At the end of the corridor down which they had ventured they could see a little light from the outside world.

The stone benches were cold and they pulled their cloaks close about themselves. Lucius sheathed his sword.

"I guess there isn't a Sibyl here anymore," he said, looking up and around and then at Adara.

Suddenly, a loud ringing sound penetrated his ears, like to the reverberation of metal struck on metal. He could see Adara's lips moving, knew she was talking, but he couldn't hear her. His heart quickened. *I feel dizzy!* he wanted to say but didn't know if she heard him. Panic bruised her beautiful face and then the world spun, went black.

In the darkness a beautiful woman came out of the shadows. Her hair was golden, her eyes grey. She approached, her mouth open as if to speak but no sound emerged from her lips. Closer and closer she came, then stopped, her eyes alight. Then a sound, a voice to pierce the depths of Hades; *AHHHHHHHHHHHHHH!* With this the young woman melted into oblivion leaving behind a decrepit old crone. Her hair was thin, oily, her body wrinkled and filthy, draped in rags. In her eyes burned a fire that would have brought a gorgon to its knees. The screaming stopped…then,

Beloved of Apollo…
Love! Blood! A sea of plots!
He bites at your heels…ravenous!
The Avenger is a harsh judge.
Keep her close. Empress. *Your empress!*

The crone's features twisted into an unnatural knot of pain, the fire in her eyes died, then rekindled as her head jerked back.

Sands and Forests.
South and North.
Where does your home lie?
Where does your heart lie?
Where does your sword lie?
Loyalty! Listen to the immortal!

Again she stopped, slumped over where she stood, a hunched old hag. Then a painful, tortuous yell, *Ooooooooooarrrhgg!*

Bravery and Wisdom.
Eagles and Dragons.
Horses beneath.
They will come to you as thunder!
All scales...and death.
Use them...know them.
Upon the grassy mound.........

Metellussssssssssss.......

The fire died and the crone disappeared into the shadows. The hateful voice faded with a hiss and gave way to the ringing, metal upon metal, once again.

"Lucius! Lucius!" the voice cried out, sobbing and shaken. Fearful. "Come back to me, my love! Apollo help him! Venus!" Adara's voice rang as though in an endless void. Closer, nearer, within reach. Then his eyes opened, his mouth moved without sound, gasping. He lay upon the cold floor, in a huddle, his face wet with his wife's pleading tears and his own sweat. He was colder than he had ever been before, even with her cloak around him.

"Lucius…you're safe now." The torch which she had thrown aside was almost burnt out, its final embers glowing in and out. "Hear me, Lucius. Hear my voice." He turned his head, shivering.

"A..Ad..Adara? Take…me…from this place." The words took great effort. Adara took his sword and put it over her shoulder to lessen the weight upon him. With all of the strength she possessed, she hoisted him to his feet, his arm around her and began the long walk down the corridor, toward the light.

When Adara finally reached the outdoors with Lucius, she collapsed with the tremendous strain and they both lay still for a time upon the ground, under the watchful eye of the raven.

Lucius opened his eyes, awoken by the feel of a moist cloth wiping his face. "Adara." He reached over to her, where she lay next to him, her eyes closed.

"She'll be fine," a voice said from behind him. It was the priest who had met them before going in. "You are both quite well."

"Lucius?" Adara's eyes opened and she threw her arms about her husband, squeezing tightly, reassuring herself he was real.

"What happened, Adara?" The priest helped them to their feet.

"I don't know. You collapsed to the floor…I thought you were dying." She began to remember again and began to shake and sob. He held her close, put her cloak around her scratched shoulders and took his sword back.

"She comes to people in different ways, in many forms, guided by the God of Prophecy himself," said the priest, observing the young couple.

"What are you saying, old man?" Lucius was in no mood for courtesy. "That the Sibyl did this? Why in Hades should she care about me?"

"Ah, Tribune Metellus. That is a question only you can answer, not I."

Adara stepped toward the priest. "I didn't feel the good graces of Apollo in that place!" She pointed to the entrance.

"My dear, the Sibyl prophesies both good and evil with the help of Apollo. She speaks in riddles, it is up to you to decipher what you have been told. Remember what was revealed to you." Lucius rubbed his eyes, tired and rimmed with black circles like crescent moons. The priest went toward the stairs. "Come, let me show you the way out." They followed him silently up the stairs and through the pathways of the acropolis until they reached the stairs that led to where the bodyguards were waiting.

The ride back to the villa was long and quiet. Neither of them knew what to make of the experience, both were afraid, confused. Lycus and his men didn't know what to make of Lucius and Adara and their haggard appearance. They had been gone for most of the day, in *that* place.

When they arrived at the dock where the boat slaves were waiting for them, night was already darkening the sky. Lucius thanked Lycus and gave him a pouch of denarii to buy wine for him and his men. Lycus bade them farewell and hurried off with his companions.

Relieved to see them returned safely, Cassius busied the slaves with preparing a soothing meal for his guests while they bathed. They soaked their tired bodies and oiled each other's scrapes and bruises with rosemary oil. In the caldarium they held one another as they warmed themselves in the steaming waters, melting away the fearful chill. Lucius didn't talk about what he remembered, not yet. He wanted to write down what he could before anything else. For the moment he was by far more concerned with Adara who was still shaky. She was not herself, then again neither was he.

"I'm here for you Lucius, always," she finally said, her shaking coming to an end.

"And I'll never leave your side. We'll figure this out together."

"Yes," she assured. "No matter what."

The following morning, the sun shone brightly once again, summer's brilliant glow creeping softly into the room where they slept soundly, exhausted from the previous day. They awoke surprisingly rested and refreshed and though they had much on their minds, Lucius and Adara found all the comfort that was needed in each other. Worries seemed to melt away with the slightest touch or loving whisper.

When he was ready, Lucius jotted down all that he could remember about what happened, what was said to him in the cave, on a wax tablet he had set aside. As they lay on the sandy shore again, naked and warmed by the sun, he told Adara what he remembered. Her strength of character, which he loved so dearly, shone through anew as she listened. Together they talked of what it might mean.

"Clearly, I was being warned," Lucius decided. *"Empress? Keep her close?"* he repeated the words.

"I suppose it means you should heed what the empress says." Adara was sceptical but could think of no other meaning.

"Riddles, riddles and more riddles. What does this all mean? *Forests and Sands...They will come like thunder?* Who? Ach! I've had enough of this!" he threw the wax tablet down into the sand. "All I want is to live with you in peace and love."

"That's my wish too...but it may not always be possible, Lucius. You're a military tribune." She hung her head.

"Don't think of that now, my love. Let's enjoy *this*, being together for so long as it lasts."

The next day, after blissful hours by the sea, they readied themselves for a special meal; Cassius had ordered all manner of meats and fish prepared fresh, vintage Falernian wine, pomegranate seeds with rich cheeses and other exotic fruits. There were even some musicians that he had brought in to play light, hypnotic music to soothe them. It was exactly what was needed.

When dinner was over, Adara clapped her hands and a slave came in with a bundle of sea-blue cloth. He laid it on the cleared table before her and left.

"What's this?" Lucius asked, eyeing the slender bundle.

"I have something for you." She picked it up and handed it to him. "It's a wedding present I had made for you." She smiled. "I was waiting for the right time to give it to you."

"Adara, you shouldn't have!" He kissed her cheek lovingly.

"Well, go on! Open it." She couldn't wait.

Lucius sat up on the couch, the bundle on his lap. It was heavy. Slowly, he pulled back the blue cloth until a brilliant gold pommel was revealed; on the end were the heads of two gods, Apollo and Venus, and around the edges were lively scenes of ancient warriors with fluttering crests and war chariots. Then a wood and silver handle appeared before an intricately carved golden hilt, formed by the heads of two dragons. Beneath the dragons, the gold spilled onto the base of the blade to form the head of a warrior surrounded with laurel leaves.

"By the Gods, Adara! It...it's magnificent. His hands moved with careful reverence as he slid the remaining cloth away. The scabbard was skilfully made too, in hardened black bull's hide, studded with golden moons and suns down the centre, with similar images also along the shoulder strap.

Adara watched her husband as he stood up, moved to the centre of the room where there was more space, and unsheathed the sword. The blade seemed to intone a heavenly note, in and out like waves upon the sea. The metal was stronger and more brilliant than any he had seen before, the balance perfect. He swung it with dextrous speed, the movements deadly and artistic at the same time. He held it up to look at it again; the blade was longer than a gladius and slightly wider near the point, aiding the balance when swung. It would be especially deadly from horseback with the extra reach.

"Do you like it?" she asked.

"I love it..." his voice was a whisper. "Where did you get this?"

"I had it made in Rome. Emrys recommended someone, even helped the craftsman make it."

"He's outdone himself again." He was still looking at the blade, the haunting images. "Did he design the scenes?"

"No. I did." He looked at her curiously, remembering having seen such a sword a long time ago. "I dreamt of it," she continued, "a long time ago, before we met." She went over to him.

The desert! Now he remembered where he had seen it. The night grey-eyed Apollo had come to him. Lucius smiled, remembered what the god had told him about the sword, his destiny.

"What's wrong, Lucius? You're not saying anything."

"Nothing's wrong. Everything is right." He sheathed the sword. "I've married the right woman. You are my heart, my life." He placed the sword on the couch and kissed her.

"So...you like it?"

"Oh yes. Thank you." He realised that he didn't have a wedding gift for her! He had been so preoccupied with the wedding, the attack and other matters that – wait!

"I don't have a gift for you Adara, but-"

"Oh Lucius, you're my gift from the Gods. I don't need anything else."

"Nevertheless, I want to give you something." He reached into his tunic and pulled out a small cloth. "Here. One of these is yours."

"Lucius! Not the eagle feathers! The Gods have granted those to you, a great omen and gift."

"The Gods have granted me you! Thanks to you my life has a meaning I could never have guessed at. Here..." Lucius took up the sword once more and cut the cloth into two equal pieces, barely touching the blade. "Keep it with you so that our thoughts can travel to each other on their wings."

They walked outside to gaze at the night sky as they had every night since arriving. Each time they looked up, new wonders met their eyes and the moon grew fuller and brighter. They still had four more days to their stay, days they planned to enjoy, remember, savour.

Two days before they were scheduled to depart, early in the morning, Cassius interrupted them for the first time since they arrived. He was breathing heavily and sweating. Lucius rose from the bed, put on a robe and left Adara in rapturous sleep to go out of the room into the garden to see what it was Cassius wanted.

"Please, please forgive me, Tribune," he said almost begging, he felt so badly for disturbing them.

"Calm down, Cassius. What is it?"

"Not half an hour ago Drusus, the bodyguard who accompanied you and your lady here, came back with one of the servants on the boat with an urgent message for you. Here it is!" He handed the sealed scroll to Lucius who took it hesitantly. He recognised the Imperial insignia. Lucius breathed deeply, afraid of what this meant.

"Thank you, Cassius. I think I would like to read this alone if you'll excuse me."

"In your own time, Tribune, please. If I can do anything else, anything-"

"My thanks." Lucius went quietly back into the room, not wanting to disturb Adara. He stepped across the cold marble floor and past the bed to go outside but paused to look at her nestled happily, safely, amongst the linen sheets. Her sun-darkened skin was as soft and smooth as oil and her black hair shone with the brightness of much time in the sea. He grasped the scroll tightly in his fist and went outside to read it.

Half an hour later, Adara awoke full of warmth and love. When her eyes opened she saw her husband standing outside in the morning sun beneath the flowering bougainvillaea. Small petals of red and white were strewn about his feet and his crown was lit by a ray of light. If she didn't know who he was, she would have thought him a god come to visit her with the light of dawn.

"Thank you, Gods..." she sighed. "What?" Adara then noticed the crumpled scroll at Lucius feet. "Please no..." Tears threatened to well in her eyes and Lucius turned as if knowing she was in pain. He walked over to her, his eyes red with emotion. He sat on the bed, his arm about her as she buried her face in his chest.

"I've been recalled to duty..." His hands shook, his head throbbed.

"When?"

"This afternoon. The empress has sent our bodyguards with a ship that will take us back to Ostia and from there back to Rome." There was more but he didn't want to tell her. How does one ever break the heart of a woman one loves beyond all things, would risk all dangers for; let alone a woman to whom one has recently been wed? She would have to know.

"What more is there, Lucius? Please tell me."

"I...I have to go back..." The words were as lead, heavy and burdensome.

"Back where?"

"To Numidia." Adara made not a sound but as she listened to the beating of Lucius' heart, he felt streams of saddened tears burning down his skin.

They lay there for some time before rising, not wanting their time alone by the sea to end, trying vainly to waylay their inevitable departure.

When Lucius informed Cassius that they had to leave, he too was upset as he had grown quite fond of the two of them. He had the slaves pack their belongings and prepare food for them for the journey, and left Lucius and Adara to enjoy what little time they had left there, wandering the garden together in silence.

As they stood at the wall, looking out at the sea, Adara spoke.

"I'm going with you, you know," she stated determinedly. "I can't be without you Lucius, not now."

He smiled, kissed her forehead. How he loved her. But, even he knew that it would not be possible, there would be too many dangers still. He could not risk her life, not until he discovered what had happened to Antanelis, dealt with the traitors in his cohort. She didn't need to know this now though, not yet.

At that moment, far out to sea, beneath the blazing sun, a sail appeared, the Imperial insignia upon it. Lucius moved to the wall to see the speedy trireme turn toward them. The ship had come.

"Is that them?" She gripped his hand.

"Yes," he sighed. "I feel like Odysseus watching the ships of Agamemnon and Menelaus approach Ithaca to take me away to Troy, away from Penelope."

"Except, Penelope stayed behind. I'm going with you."

He wished that were true.

XXVI

TRISTITIA

'Sadness'

The journey back to Rome was long, tiresome and cramped. Lucius and Adara were not the only passengers on the ship; others who had been recalled to Rome were there also. While Drusus and his men spent most of the time on deck, quarters were given to the tribune and his wife. Small but cosy, they spent most of their time in there, resting and talking, or on deck gazing out to sea. They hoped it was all an unpleasant dream, that they were actually back in Cumae.

There was not a large military force on board the ship, just enough men to run things smoothly on the journey to Ostia. Once they made port, Drusus accompanied Lucius and Adara aboard a barge that would take them up the Tiber to the city. As he watched the water ripple, the Tiber's swampy shoreline slip by, Lucius wondered what he would do. Obviously, he had to go, it was his duty, the emperor's command that all military tribunes in Rome should accompany him to Africa. It was supposed to be an honour but he could not help thinking that the sojourn was at and end, so much more for him because of what he might have to leave behind. The empress, Caracalla and Geta were also going, as well as almost the entire Praetorian guard, including Plautianus. Lucius remembered what the Sibyl had said: *Keep her close. Empress. Your Empress!* At least that would be possible. But to what end? He didn't know.

The orders were to accompany the Imperial family to Leptis Magna for various public displays etceteras, etceteras, and then he was to sail back to Carthage; from there he would strike out for Lambaesis. He wanted Adara to come with him, be at his side, but a shadow lingered in the back of his mind, a fear. *It just isn't possible, not yet. Perhaps later,* he kept thinking, turning the brilliant gold wedding ring he now wore, worried about how he would tell her, who would look after her. Of course she had lived peacefully before they had met, been safe, but now it was different. He wanted to be the one who protected her from harm.

Finally, he decided that if he could not be there to protect Adara, to see to her safety, she would have the next best thing: Ashur. Perhaps Ashur would remain with her?

"There it is," Adara came up beside him at the prow of the barge. "Rome." She thread her arm through his. "I'll miss it here while we're away. This is where we met after all."

"I know." He sighed. "This will probably be the most difficult departure from Rome I'll ever have to make."

"Oh, look! There are Alene and Ashur, over there!" The two of them stood on the crowded quay at the front of a sea of heads and litters, awaiting the passengers arriving from Ostia. Alene waived frantically while Ashur stood still and smiled, happy to see his friend returned safely. When they disembarked, they greeted each other warmly and went directly to the Metellus domus.

"How did you know we were coming?" Adara asked Alene as they walked.

"It's been the talk of Rome, this trip the emperor is making to Africa. People are saying that many public and military officials have been recalled to make the trip as well."

"Yes but how did you know when *we* would arrive?" Lucius found it odd but he was happy to see them nevertheless.

"The empress sent a messenger to tell us when you would be arriving," Alene answered.

"That's odd," murmured Lucius to Ashur walking next to him.

"Odd indeed." Ashur looked around, alert. "Is there anything Julia Domna doesn't know?"

When they arrived back at the house they found the entire family waiting for them, eager to see the couple and settle down to a wonderful feast that Antonia had had the slaves prepare. His mother seemed to look differently on him now, slightly more removed. Perhaps, Lucius thought, she was giving him more space now that he had a wife. His father was quiet, though oddly pleasant; no doubt Lucius' departure had eased his stubborn mind.

Publius and Delphina embraced the two of them fondly. They had worry written all over their faces despite a brave effort at jollity. They knew what it all meant, Lucius' recall to duties. Their daughter would be taken from them, to somewhere far away, a frontier. Hadrea and Lavena still clung to Alene, with whom they had become close. Clarinda sat, playing with a new toy, completely oblivious to all that was going on around her, including young Quintus who sat next to her, eyeing his father hatefully. Inwardly, the young boy imagined a thousand different ways he could make his father suffer for what he had done, for the secret he had kept from them. The dark emotions inside his small frame had begun to fester.

As they ate, no one breached the subject of when Lucius and Adara had to leave and when they might see them again. A great cloud hung above Ashur's head as he too wondered about his role in all of this. He would naturally have to go back to Africa with Lucius, he wanted to. But, he also wanted to stay with Carissa who, to him, was more beautiful than all the stars in the sky, or the silvery pearls in the sea. He had spent much time with her while Lucius was away, talking of magical places, tales from their own lands. Much of the time however, they would sit in comfortable silence, content to feel the other's presence.

Of everybody there however, Lucius noticed Alene's sad countenance and realised she would be left alone…again. The awkward lack of conversation was finally broken by Publius. "Well my friends, I believe that our Roman holiday will soon be coming to an unfortunate end. Delphina and I must return to Athens as I have business to attend to. City affairs will not wait." He trembled slightly in his hand, almost spilling wine. "Our time here has been a true gift from the Gods..." He looked at Adara and Lucius proudly. "...who could ask for anything more beautiful or inspiring than this! A new and astounding family! To all of us, I say!" He raised his glass. "May our paths never stray far from each other's."

Adara looked at her father, thought that he had aged a great deal in the past weeks since before the wedding. Every person there had their own thoughts and worries, as do all mortals, whether about the piece of wood that had fallen off of a toy, as in Clarinda's case, or about having to leave behind all those whom he loved, as it was for Lucius. An odd concoction of sadness and joy hovered gloomily in the flickering light of the braziers like an uneasy sky before a storm.

Of all of them, the one who was happiest was Quintus Metellus; soon his *son* would be gone as well as his tiresome new family. He would be able to acquaint young Quintus with the steps he should take to gaining a public career now that there were no more distractions. He would also have his house to himself again.

When the meal had finished and people began to yawn, the children asleep on the couches where they lay, they all decided to yield to exhaustion for the night. Publius, Delphina, Hadrea and Lavena went with their escort back to the Esquiline, leaving Lucius and Adara behind.

That night, before going to sleep with his wife, Lucius lit the lamps in their room, burned some incense and knelt to pray to Apollo. He closed his eyes and bowed his head. *Lord. I'm so confused by what is happening. I don't know what to expect. I don't understand what the Sibyl meant in her message. Were the words yours, mighty Apollo? If so, enlighten me as to their meaning so that I do not disappoint you; you, who have been with me for so long. Help me to face the coming months with honour and strength. I pray that I have made the right decision to leave my wife behind, to go on alone. Light the way for me if you will.*

In the doorway, Adara stood silently, wondering what was going through Lucius' mind as he knelt. When he finished, she entered the room and led him to the bed where they huddled together beneath the thin sheets. They held each other close and gave in to the passions that a man and wife enjoy with freedom.

After some time, sheened in summer sweat and married bliss, they lay together watching the lamps burn down. In a corner of the room, his armour hung on a wooden stand where the emblazoned dragon on his cuirass reflected the light, flapped its wings. His imminent departure came back to mind. It was time to tell her.

"Adara?" he whispered. She felt his heart beat quicken. How she loved to listen to it.

"Yes, my love?" she answered, running her finger along the scar on his thigh.

"I...I..." He just couldn't get the words out. She saw his downcast face and held it between her warm hands, stared into his eyes and tilted her head slightly to the left the way she always did.

"It's all right, Lucius. Tell me what's wrong." She was beautiful in every way to him. He loved how she tilted her head like that when looking intently at him.

"I must...go alone, to Africa."

Those horrible words wavered sharply, painfully. She yet held his face, her hands trembling ever so slightly. Her eyes glossed over like saddened moonlit pools, still and soft. But she did not cry. Adara straightened her neck and pulled the sheet about her naked body.

"But...we've just been married," her voice wavered. "You can't, Lucius. You can't leave me! Remember what we said about never leaving each other's side, always being there?"

"I know, I know, my love. Don't you think all of those things have gone through my mind a hundred times since I received my orders? It feels as though this world we've only just discovered, full of all that is pure and unblemished, is crumbling into memory." He tried to turn his head away, it being too painful to look into her eyes and see the hurt she was feeling. She held him fast, held him in her eyes.

"If you know all this, feel it, then why do you wish to go on alone?"

"I don't wish it! Know that. I swore that I'd never endanger you, ever. There's too much uncertainty, too much unexplained." For the first time, Adara saw real fear and worry in Lucius' eyes.

"Tell me, Lucius, everything you haven't told me about what happened out there." Of course Adara knew about Sabratha, everybody knew that. What she did not know about, at least not in great detail, were the attacks in dark alleyways, daggers out of the shadows, possible treachery within his own ranks and how far it had spread; not even Lucius knew the latter. He had to find out on his own.

So, over the next several hours Lucius talked, Adara listened, pushing her own growing fears to the back of her mind, hidden. She tried desperately not to be angry or disappointed with him but Lucius could see that she was. Her anxieties also ran to his interactions with the Imperial family. *What do they want of him?* she wondered. *They always want something!* Only in Rome had she become pessimistic about the world, about people. Funny, considering that only in Rome had she also developed a true understanding of hope, faith and of course, love.

After listening to Lucius' reasons and having held back the tears that flowed in and out like mournful waves, she conceded to her husband's wishes. He only wanted to keep her safe because he loved her beyond all the mysteries of the world.

"I'll agree only on one condition." He could see that she meant business. Adara breathed calmly and stared into Lucius' eyes. "I'll remain behind *only* if I'm allowed to join you in Numidia once you've figured things out and dealt with any dangers there. I don't like it but I'll do it because I don't want to be a burden to you."

"Adara, you could never be a burden-"

"Just answer, my love." She hated talking like that to him but she knew she had to. She could feel her resolve crumbling.

"Of course I agree. The less time we're apart the better. You know I feel the same as you."

"Good."

"Will you return to Athens with your parents and sisters?" Lucius asked as she leaned back against his body.

"Yes. There are some things I would like to gather before I come to join you. Besides, I don't know if they're quite ready to be parted from me. Did you see how sad they were?"

"Yes, I did. I'm also worried about Alene. She seems so withdrawn lately."

Adara thought about that for a moment. "You know, Lucius, I could ask Alene if she'd like to come with me, to Greece."

"That's perfect!"

"And we won't long for friends either. Mother told me tonight that Carissa and Emrys will be travelling to Athens with them. Something about work they have to finish there." When Lucius heard this he thought of Ashur. Tomorrow he would ask him to accompany Adara to Greece as her guard. He knew Ashur would refuse but perhaps with Carissa going as well he would reconsider.

Lucius rose from the bed and went over to the window. The moon was nearing its fullness again, shrouding the city in a silvery haze. A part of him regretted the decision he had made to leave her behind, but he knew it was safer that way. He wanted to be sure about things.

"I miss you already. I feel so, alone." He hung his head. Adara knew exactly what he meant. She felt the same.

450

"You'll never be alone, Lucius. Never. Not while I live. Apollo will carry our words and thoughts to each other across the sky on a golden arrow. And you'll know I'm thinking of you, whispering to you." She rose and put her arms about his shoulders. "Besides, you're not gone yet, not for a few days. Let's take advantage of the time we have, Lucius. Like Diodorus said."

"You're right." He turned and led her back to bed. "Let's sleep." They lay again beneath the sheets, Lucius holding her closely as she curled up in front of him. He tried to remember her sweet smell, her hair in his face as he fell asleep. That memory would get him through many lonely nights to come.

When she was sure that he slept, far away enough not to hear, she let her tears fall for some time, unable to bear the thought of him going away to some far corner of the empire, alone, without her.

The following day when they told Alene what they planned to do and asked whether she would like to go to Athens she was at once shocked, confused and excited. Lucius explained to her his reasons for going alone and she agreed that it would be dangerous for Adara but she worried greatly for him, especially when he told her he planned to ask Ashur to go with them.

Hadrea and Lavena were both youthfully aquiver when they discovered Alene was going with them; Publius and Delphina too were happy about Alene and silently pleased about having their eldest daughter for a time longer. Alene thought that perhaps Antonia would be too lonely without her, but Antonia put her mind at ease, told her that since her father and younger brother were back in the house, she would not be lonely. Clarinda too was proving to be more helpful and social as she grew older.

It was settled then, Alene would go to Greece. For Lucius, Ashur proved much more difficult to convince. When he returned from his daily walk to see Carissa at the workshops,

Lucius met him in the atrium and asked if he had a few minutes to talk in the garden.

"Of course, my friend, lead the way!" Ashur seemed so lively after his visits to the workshop.

The house was empty with Quintus back in the Senate, Antonia and the girls out shopping and young Quintus with his new tutor. In the garden, the jasmine was in full bloom, its small white flowers rustled by the warm summer breeze that blew throughout the house. Lucius poured watered wine for both of them and they sat on their own couches. Lucius noticed that Ashur had begun to wear Roman fashions more and more; today he wore a blue and crimson tunic with a pair of sandals. He had even tried shaving but said he felt naked without his small beard. Lucius laughed.

"Lucius, my friend, say what it is you have to say." Ashur knew him better than most, how to read his behaviour. Carissa kept drifting into his thoughts, even as he sat there with Lucius.

"I'm not taking Adara with me to Africa, not until I figure out what's happening with my men and what happened to Antanelis. It's too dangerous and I don't want to put her in harm's way. You, more than anyone, Ashur, know what I'm up against out there."

"Yes. I see what you mean." Ashur rubbed his chin where he usually rubbed his beard. "How did she take the news?"

"Well enough. She tried to be brave but I could tell that it was torturing her inside...me too. But..."

"But you have to be sure that all is well before she joins you?"

"Exactly."

"I agree with your decision though I know it must be excruciating. She's a wonderful, blessed woman, Lucius. Apollo is generous to you." Ashur thought then of his patron god, fighting guilt once more.

"In your friendship too, he's been generous beyond all things, Ashur." Lucius didn't know if he had ever truly told him how much he meant to him, how grateful he was for him saving his life, guiding him. "There is something I would ask of you. You've been by my side for so long now. But, at the moment, I need for you to leave me, Ashur." The words didn't come out quite right, sounded insulting.

"What do you mean, Lucius?" Ashur had not been expecting this.

"That sounded wrong. Forgive me. What I mean is that while I'm in Africa, I would be most grateful to you, honoured, if you would watch over Adara for me, keep her safe."

"I see." He was quiet for a few moments, serious. "I don't know if I can do that."

"Of course you can! For me, please. I couldn't bear it if anything happened to her."

"But you're sending her away from yourself, Lucius."

"Only to keep her safe so that we may be together again."

Ashur looked up at the sun, thought of the desert and how he would have liked to see it again. He thought of the dangers that might await his friend. It intensified as he looked at it. The god would not forgive him for leaving Lucius. Or was it what He intended?

"I can't. I can't leave your side."

Lucius shook his head and drank some wine. Then he remembered Carissa. He needed to mention her.

"Ashur, Alene is also going to Greece with Adara, she'll need your protection too."

"I understand your worries my friend but-"

"And Carissa." The mere mention of her name stopped Ashur's words, like a knife in his chest.

"Carissa?" He seemed to sing her name.

"Yes. She and Emrys are going with the Antoninii to Athens."

"She did not tell me this…"

"Perhaps she didn't want to upset you so that you could enjoy your time together before going your separate ways?"

"Yes, perhaps. She is selfless that way." He stood up and paced the garden, distraught. "Oh Lucius Metellus Anguis, you trouble me. I am not used to being weak."

"It's not weakness, my friend, it's love." Lucius put his hand on Ashur's shoulder, smiling.

"Love? Lucius, I'm not supposed to love, not permitted." He looked up at the sun again, Apollo in one of his many guises. The summer sun seemed angry.

"If I've learned anything these past months, Ashur, it's that love should be nurtured wherever it takes root in this world full of politics, war and death. The Gods themselves often love mortals!"

"Please Lucius, no blasphemy."

"It isn't blasphemy, Ashur, it's truth! And what could be truer than love? I've seen how you've been acting ever since that first dinner with Carissa, how happy you've been. It's not a gift you should throw away lightly."

"Neither is our friendship."

"You'll never cease to be my friend. Anyway, it's only for a short time."

Ashur thought about this, how tempting it was, how utterly right it seemed that he should stay with Carissa. He also thought about how wrong it seemed that he should leave Lucius. Then again, Lucius wanted him to leave, and for a good reason. He would have to reflect in the temple, and speak with Carissa to make sure it is what she wanted.

"I will tell you in a few days, Lucius, what my answer will be. I have to think about this. It isn't every day that one's world spins uncontrollably."

"No. But, some whirlwinds are worth it."

Shortly after, the ladies returned from their shopping and Ashur took his leave to be alone with his thoughts, meditate upon the reasons and repercussions of such a decision.

When they had a quiet moment Antonia sat down next to her eldest son in the garden; they had not talked for some time.

She looked about, as though to capture the feeling of life that her home had experienced since his return. She looked at her own hands, cupped in her lap. "You seem so grown up to me, Lucius. The Gods steal time from us so quickly."

"I know how you feel."

Antonia took her son's hand and stroked it gently, like she did when he was a child and he had cut himself. There were more scars on his hands than she ever thought possible. "Lucius, I'm worried about you." She continued to stare at their hands. "Your decision to go to Africa alone...it worries me."

"I can take care of myself."

"Can you? I suppose you can. But that's beside the point. I'm worried about the reasons *why* you're going alone. I know that you haven't told me everything about what happened to you in Africa and Numidia, probably because you think I could not handle hearing it. No. Don't speak. Let me finish. If I were to ask you to tell me everything I'm sure that, out of love for me, you would exclude a great deal. And that's fine. I, on the other hand cannot withhold my fears and feelings. It pains me too much."

"What is it, mother?" Lucius turned to face her on the marble bench.

"Several nights ago, I had a dream. I know you believe that the Gods show us things in our dreams. You've always been inclined to my way of thinking. In my dream, the moon was but a sliver in the blackest of skies, shiny, like a curved blade. Crows squawked all night outside my window. I saw you...surrounded by dark, faceless shapes. You were yelling out for someone but no one heard your calls. The ground shook beneath your feet and the sand swallowed you up to your chest as you strained to stay up." Lucius realised he must have looked afraid in that moment, as he did when he used to wake up screaming in the night after a nightmare. "The shadows around you burned away however by the appearance of a brilliant light. It hurt my eyes to look but I forced myself

455

to see. You were reaching out but no hand grasped yours. I thought the sand would swallow you up, take you, but it didn't. Instead, you remained stuck, helpless." Antonia released his hands and looked him over. "I woke up then."

"It was just a dream, mother," he tried to ease her mind.

"No. You know as well as I it was not *just* a dream. There's no such thing. It was a warning."

"About what?" He could guess but he wanted to hear what she thought it was.

"It was a warning that you are going into darkness, the light of the moon will leave you for a time. You will be alone." Antonia knelt in front of Lucius and clasped his knees. She did not care if Quintus saw her. "My son, please be careful wherever you go; be wary of strangers, of lonesome roads and of peaceful nights when the moon is hiding."

"Mother." Lucius pulled her to her feet and hugged her. "I know what you're saying. At least I think I do; dreams are so cryptic. Believe me, I'd stay if I could. But I can't. I have to go; not just because I have my orders, but because I've made a promise to find out who killed one of my closest friends." Antonia closed her eyes and leaned against him. She did not know if he had heard what she had told him.

Lucius had heard her, her warnings. The fact was however, that it did not change things. He knew what he had to do, hoped that he was not underestimating the situation. In training they had always been told never to underestimate an enemy; but what happened when one did not know who the enemy was? He could not tell her about his own fears though, he did not want to. Those were for him to deal with.

"The empress has been seeing to my safety, mother. Perhaps she'll continue?"

"She's a politician, Lucius."

"She's shown me some kindness." The Sibyl's words echoed in his mind. "Besides, before long, I'll be back with my men." He realised that that was not the most comforting thought.

"I know all this." She backed up slightly. "I suppose that wherever you are, whomever you are with, I will worry for you." Antonia smiled. "It's my duty as your mother."

"I'll be fine."

Later, Lucius decided that since his mother was so upset, he would leave the statues of himself and Adara with her for safekeeping, until they had a home of their own. The statues were so lifelike, so perfect, they would keep her company on lonely days when her husband was out and the children asleep. She could speak to them and they would appear to talk back. Antonia accepted the charge willingly.

Four days flowed by as swiftly and as unnoticed as a drop of water in a gurgling stream. For everybody travelling, preparations had been made, packing finished. For those staying behind, they prepared themselves for the sense of loss that comes with saying goodbye to loved ones after a lengthy visit. For a father who despised his son, the day could not have come swiftly enough. In his study, Quintus Metellus pater, greeted his son with cool civility, asked what his plans were. Lucius looked upon this man with disdain. He had tried in the past to regain some form of relationship, but to no avail. His coldness toward the new family members, Lucius' wife, his own wife, was both appalling and embarrassing. He would not miss him and the feeling was mutual.

"Try not to humiliate yourself, our family, or me this time, would you? You've done enough already."

Lucius fumed, but restrained himself. "Father." he stood up. "I've only ever honoured our ancestors and our family. It's you who dishonour all of us." Quintus turned with fire in his eyes but Lucius was not a boy any more. He was tall, imposing, confident and free to speak his mind. "You can spit whatever poisons you see fit at me, insult me. I don't care anymore. Fortune favours me."

"In what? You ignorant cur! In what?" He shouted so violently that spittle dripped out of the corner of his mouth.

"In that I'm as far from being like you as possible."
Quintus shook with rage. He wanted to kill the boy before him
but he couldn't. Something stayed his hand, he felt as cold as
stone, frozen. Lucius turned, went to the door of the study and
turned. "Farewell, father. May the Gods care for you. I'll not
write this time."

Lucius walked out of the room, his blood racing. Never
could he be a parricide, but neither could he ever allow
someone so mean-spirited to walk all over his familia as his
father did.

The barge was leaving toward the middle of a foggy, creeping
morning, to carry its passengers to Ostia where the ships
awaited their cargo to sail to Leptis Magna. Adara's family
had come to see Lucius off. They were all leaving the
following day, set to travel the Via Appia to Brundisium where
they would board a ship bound for Corinth; from there they
would travel to Athens.

It was a solemn gathering in the Metellus household,
especially since everyone had heard Lucius and his father
arguing. Luckily, Quintus had decided to remain in his study
until everybody had gone. Adara had helped Lucius pack all of
his belongings so that all there was in his cubicula was an
empty bed. Packing had been quiet with an occasional touch or
kiss to ease the increasing hurt. He had decided to wear his full
armour, polished to a blinding shine, and Adara had insisted on
helping him to put it all on; any reason to be able to look at
him closely, to touch him before he left. Her hands moved in a
loving, slow and ritualistic manner over his body as she
dressed him, and when every strap was secure, every buckle
fastened, she draped his newly washed crimson cloak over his
shoulders and fastened it with the red and blue enamelled
brooch. She stepped back to look at her husband.

"You're so beautiful to me. I'm going to miss looking at
you." Her eyes closed slowly and he went to hold her.

"It won't be long, my love. I promise."

"Yes. Please promise me. Every day I'm apart from you is unbearable. And write to me, whenever you get the chance. I need to know you are safe."

"I will," he reassured. "This will never leave my hand either." He held up his hand with the golden ring of intertwined dragons. Adara held up hers also and threw her arms around him, gripped him tightly. There was a knock at the door.

"Come in," Lucius said.

"Forgive the intrusion, Master." It was one of the slaves who spoke, followed by another. "The mistress asked us to come and see if you would like for us to take your trunks away."

"Yes. They're ready now."

The two slaves shuffled into the room to carry away one trunk and then the other. Once they had taken the second, Adara handed Lucius his crested helm.

"The final touch, here." He took it.

"Not quite the final touch. There's one more item." He reached for the long blue bundle on the bed. "This sword isn't leaving my side."

"Keep it close. It will protect you."

"I will." He slung the sword over his shoulder and kissed her. "Shall we?"

"Yes. We'd better go. Everybody's waiting." Lucius helped her put on her deep blue, floor-length cloak to keep her warm in the morning gloom down by the river. They did not want to leave that room.

The family had gathered in the atrium, and stood in orderly, almost military rows. Lucius went over to young Quintus and Clarinda, knelt down and hugged each of them. Clarinda shied away slightly, his armour scared her. Young Quintus stood tall, looked at Lucius as if he were ready to burst.

"Quintus? You all right? Don't worry. Hopefully I'll see you again soon." He knew it wasn't true but wanted to make him feel better.

"Lucius, I...I wish I could go with you and leave this place." The words were totally unexpected. No one knew what was going through the boy's mind, the hateful thoughts, the agony of a dark secret that had haunted his dreams of late. He had always thought Lucius a terrible son for not getting on with their father, but now he understood what sort of man their father really was and he despised him, understood Lucius all the more.

"Who knows, Quintus, maybe someday you'll join me in the Legions."

"Goodbye, Lucius. Be safe, look out for, for..." He ran away then as he heard the door to his father's study open and then hurried footsteps toward the garden. Lucius watched his brother run then turned to the others.

"Publius, Delphina. Thank you, for everything." He kissed them each like a son does his parents.

"Watch yourself, my boy," said Publius. "We'll look after her for you."

"Come back to us safely, Lucius."

"I will, Delphina. Thank you." Then Lucius turned to his mother. "Mama," he said lovingly and kissed her cheek. "I shall miss you."

"And I you, my son. This is the second time I've had to see you leave. I hope it will not be for as long this time. May the Gods protect and look over you."

"They will, mama, they always do. Don't worry about me. I'll be fine and I'll even write to you, often."

"I would like that." She shook slightly as she held him close, almost rocking him as if he were a young boy again.

By the door, Ashur, Alene and Adara waited to walk Lucius down to the docks. That morning, Ashur had informed Lucius that he would indeed go with Adara and the rest to Greece but that he would come at a moment's notice should

Lucius have need of him. He had spent some time in the Temple of Apollo and though he had received no answer, he felt he had made the right decision, especially when he saw the joy on Carissa's face when he told her he was coming.

As they stepped out onto the street and the door closed behind them, the sound of Antonia's sobbing reached their ears. She had held it long enough for them to leave but was overcome. Publius and Delphina comforted her.

The docks were packed high with cargo that was being loaded onto numerous barges, along with a multitude of passengers, Praetorian soldiers, servants and family members. Lucius recognised several faces from the palace banquet, greeted people as they passed through the crowd to a space between crates along the water.

The fog was even thicker along the river which flowed by with a glassy reflection. Horns blew signalling that the passenger barges were being readied to leave. The servants had found which barge Lucius was on and loaded his two trunks. The time had passed far too swiftly and now it was time to go. He turned to Alene first.

"Will you be all right?" he asked, holding her hand and looking at her sweet face which he remembered so dearly. Strands of her long wheat-golden hair stuck out of the hood of her cloak.

"Yes. I just can't believe...you're leaving so soon. I don't know when I'll see you again."

"Sister...there's ever a place in my heart for you. I'll miss you more than ever." He looked at Adara, then back to Alene. "Thank you, Alene, for bringing us together." He embraced her, kissed both her cheeks.

"Bye Lucius. I'll pray to Apollo for you." She tried to smile, then stepped aside to give Ashur a chance to say what he wanted to say.

"Far-shooting Apollo will be watching you, guiding you."

"Thank you for this, Ashur. It means a lot to me." The two warriors clasped forearms tightly in friendship. "I'll see you again."

"A pride of lions couldn't keep me from it. Give my greetings to Alerio and speak my name out over the desert sands for me."

"I will."

Ashur's dark face still looked creased with worry over his decision. He hugged Lucius and whispered in his ear. "Stay watchful."

Lucius nodded determinedly. "Farewell my friend." Then Ashur and Alene stepped away to give Adara and Lucius some privacy, knowing how difficult this moment was for them. The horns rang out again to call passengers.

"You'd better get going, my love." He had never seen her so sad. "I feel so alone, Lucius, my blood has run cold."

"Mine too. Now it comes to it, I don't think I can leave." He hugged her closely trying not to hurt her against his armour. She didn't care, she squeezed with all of her strength.

"But you must go."

"Yes. I must." She tilted her head again to the left as he held her smooth face. "I'll be with you at every moment, here." He put his hand over her heart and her eyes closed to remember his touch.

"I'll pray to Venus and Apollo for your safety and for the moment when we'll be together again."

"Adara...keep Ashur close, for my peace of mind." She nodded.

"And you do what you have to do, my love, so that we see each other again soon. I need you."

"And I need you." They kissed longingly, both trying to embed the sensation in their hearts and minds, something to visit when alone with their thoughts. "When the stars are bright about the moon, look up and know that I'm looking too."

"Every night, my love. Every night." She hugged him again as the horn broke through the fog a final time.

"Tribune? We must set out!" The voice of a soldier called to Lucius.

"Goodbye, my love." He turned to leave, then came back to kiss his wife one last time, her lips salty with tears.

As they watched Lucius make his way through the fog to the gangplank and onto the barge, his armour glistened even then. He stood at the edge of the barge, his right hand raised in farewell as he watched his wife come to the edge of the river, her hand on her lips.

"Goodbye, Lucius. I love you," she whispered into the fog to the shining warrior, the horsehair crest of his helmet cutting through the thick air until he was beyond her sight.

"I love you," Lucius said, willing his words to her ear. "Venus and Apollo protect her for me, keep her safe…"

EPILOGUS

Atop the ivory cliffs of a crescent isle, the song of heavenly birds faded to nothing, the rustling limbs of their olive perches now limp in the frightful cold. Nor did dolphins frolic in the light-flecked seas beyond the pink and white beach; rough waves of blood now suffocated the shore with gore and sadness.

"It will make him stronger," War said, fire in his eyes.

"Or it will break him." The Far Shooter stared out, still. War grinned and was gone. Dark skies roiled overhead.

In the distance, the lone ship fought against the sea's anger, a bobbing plaything emanating hollow screams. The Far Shooter crossed his arms, his heavenly head hung sombrely as the sound of red waves crashing below heightened.

"Would that the sound of my cythera could drown out my brother's rage and make him see."

"It may yet."

The God of the Silver Bow felt Love's warm touch upon his brawny shoulders and turned to look into her starry eyes.

"How many heroes have we seen sail into the void of time, into danger?"

"Many…" Her voice was a sad whisper.

"And how many have actually returned from such journeys?" He stepped to the cliff's edge, above the crimson beach, and watched as the ship was swallowed by blackness.

Love had no answer, only a tear for the truth he spoke. She stepped closer to thread her golden arm through his. In that place removed from time, Love spoke without speaking.

You have brought mortals back safely from both fresh-flowered meadows and fields of slaughter. Men who were Hades-bound have returned sane and unscathed to the world at our sandalled feet. Wisdom, Creativity and Light have flourished by your hand. Love passed her hand over his face, then whispered into his ear. "Do not forget those heroes who *have* returned. Your altars are overflowing with offerings. Honour your children as they honour you. *Fight for them.*"

Love's lissom voice stilled the waves for a heartbeat and the Far Shooter looked to the heavens, the stars' whirling. He looked to Love again.

"Will you help me?"

She smiled. "Need you ask?"

They turned away from the bloody sea, the cliff, and passed beneath the olive tree. As they went, white-robed and shining, Love laid a supple hand upon one of the tree's sad limbs. The leaves shuddered and greened and new fruit came forth.

She smiled, and in that timeless space, a heavenly bird sounded its music.

Thank you for reading!

Did you enjoy *Children of Apollo*? Here is what you can do next.

If you enjoyed this adventure with Lucius Metellus Anguis, and if you have a minute to spare, please post a short review on the web page where you purchased the book.

Reviews are a wonderful way for new readers to find this series of books and your help in spreading the word is greatly appreciated.

The story continues in *Killing the Hydra*, and the next Eagles and Dragons novel will be coming soon, so be sure to sign-up for e-mail updates at:

https://eaglesanddragonspublishing.com/newsletter-join-the-legions/

Newsletter subscribers get a FREE BOOK, and first access to new releases, special offers, and much more!

To read more about the history, people and places featured in this book, check out *The World of Children of Apollo* blog series on the Eagles and Dragons Publishing website.

Become a Patron of Eagles and Dragons Publishing!

If you enjoy the books that Eagles and Dragons Publishing puts out, our blogs about history, mythology, and archaeology, our video tours of historic sites and more, then you should consider becoming an official patron.

We love our regular visitors to the website, and of course our wonderful newsletter subscribers, but we want to offer more to our 'super fans', those readers and history-lovers who enjoy everything we do and create.

You can become a patron for as little as $1 per month. For your support, you will also get loads of fantastic rewards as tokens of our appreciation.

If you are interested, just visit the website below to go to the Eagles and Dragons Publishing Patreon page to watch the introductory video and check out the patronage levels and exciting rewards.

https://www.patreon.com/EaglesandDragonsPublishing

Join us for an exciting future as we bring the past to life!

AUTHOR'S NOTE

The early third century A.D. is an extremely fascinating period in the history of ancient Rome. It is also a period that is often overlooked by most historical novelists.

By the early third century, the Roman Empire was vastly different than it had been. In the wake of the death of Commodus, the Praetorians had taken over and put the imperial throne up for auction. In the ensuing civil war between Clodius Albinus, Pescenius Niger and Septimius Severus, the latter came out the victor.

In A.D. 197, Septimius Severus became undisputed emperor and so began to cleanse the Senate of his rivals' past supporters in a round of proscriptions that echoed the severity of Sulla. Because the Praetorians had proved so powerful and problematic since the death of Commodus, Severus quickly set about replacing them with 15,000 troops from his own, fiercely loyal Danubian legions. Praetorians had better equipment and much more pay. If there was one thing Severus was good at, it was maintaining the favour of his troops. Under Severus, the empire was at its greatest extent, stretching from Britannia to North Africa, and from the Pillars of Hercules to the former Parthian Empire which he finally defeated.

Severus made many reforms to the army, shifting troops about and changing the laws so that soldiers could marry and live with their wives. He democratized the army, making it possible for common troops to rise to equestrian status. More posts also became open to Equites. Severus tolerated the Senate but with a ready force of thirty thousand men in Italy alone, including the Praetorian Guard and the II Parthica stationed at Alba, he had a firm hold on Italy and the capital. The army and the loyalty of the troops gave him real power, despite his ailing health.

This was however, not only an age for the army but also a time when the empire was changing socially. The Syrian empress, Julia Domna, was one of the most powerful, intelligent women in Roman history and had gathered scholars from around the world to produce works on any number of subjects. Some of the greatest minds of the age came to discuss and debate with the empress. The empress' sister, Julia Maesa, was no less intelligent and politically astute. The 'Syrian women', as they were known, made great headway as far as the role of women is concerned.

Severus himself was born in Leptis Magna, the great city of Africa Proconsularis. Under Severus' rule, the Provinces gained more status compared to Rome and Italy, especially Africa, Syria and the Danube frontier.

The main primary sources for this period are Cassius Dio and Herodian. Though Herodian is entertaining, I have opted more for Dio for much of the story and some hints about the character of Severus, his family and the emperor's kinsman, Gaius Fulvius Plautianus who ushered his own reign of terror as sole prefect of the Praetorian Guard. Though Dio and Herodian both lived through the historical events that take place in *Children of Apollo*, Dio is generally seen as the more reliable source between the two. Herodian, it seems, held minor civil servant positions and though unbiased at times in his writing, he would not have had the access to the Imperial court that Dio would have had as a senator and consul.

In a way, there is more to inform the period by way of archaeological remains. Rome of course is blanketed with remains, from the Arch of Septimius Severus in front of the Curia building in the Forum Romanun, to the remains of the Severan palace complex on the Palatine Hill overlooking the Circus Maximus. One can, even now, take in a concert at the massive Baths of Caracalla. The Shapwick coin hoard at the Taunton Museum in Somerset, England, provided an amazing opportunity to look closely at the faces of Septimius Severus and his family.

Much of *Children of Apollo* takes place in North Africa and for anyone who enjoys travelling I would highly recommend a safari of Roman archaeological ruins in what is now Tunisia.

The amphitheatre at ancient Thysdrus (modern El Jem), the cities of Thugga and Thuburbo Majus are all accessible and more or less devoid of tourists. In these places, intricate mosaics and intact streets are open to the sky. And then there is the desert. The Sahara is truly a place unlike any other and has remained the same since the days of Carthage and Rome.

The historic personages in *Children of Apollo* have been portrayed as accurately as possible and many of the events described are true to history. The major changes that Severus made to the army, the shifting of units and commands, allowed me to take some liberties when it came to Lucius' career; normally an Equestrian citizen would not start out in the ranks and move from legionary to centurion to tribune. Such a person would more likely begin a career as a tribune or hold some other administrative post. This was however, a time of flux in the army and how it was organized so I have used that to my advantage. In the interests of story and conflict, I decided to make Lucius' career goals more militaristic so as to balance his father's senatorial and political goals.

Also in the interest of story, I have taken some liberties when it comes to Lucius and Adara's wedding. Normally, a Roman wedding was more understated, performed in the atrium of a household. However, as I wanted to illustrate Lucius' family's special, ancient connection with the Temple of Apollo on the Palatine, I decided to hold the wedding there, an exception made by the temple priests for a favourite of Apollo's.

Lucius Metellus Anguis is, of course, a fictional character. The Metelli were indeed one of the foremost families of the Roman Republic and I often found myself wondering why one stopped reading about them during the days of the empire. What happened to the Metelli who had once been so powerful? Thus, I decided that Lucius' branch of that once-great Roman family should still remain but rather in a poorer state of existence. It is a fictional branch of the Metelli which, of course, allowed for some of the more fantastical elements. The cognomen of 'Anguis' refers the ancient worm, the serpent, the python or the dragon. 'Anguis' is another name for the constellation in the night sky also known as the Draco. In mythology, Apollo slew the great Python at Delphi where his oracle was then established. In the ancient world, the 'anguis' or 'drakon' was a symbol of power and prophecy.

When it comes to the religious beliefs of ancient Greece and Rome, the array of gods and goddesses, each with their accompanying rites, is rich indeed. People believed in the Gods, believed that the Gods influenced every aspect of their lives. Indeed, there was a god or goddess for almost every aspect of life. Soldiers were especially superstitious and held strongly to their beliefs. Emperor Severus and Julia Domna were noted for their fervent belief in the art of astrology and consulted regularly with the imperial astrologer on all matters. The Roman Empire was a true mosaic of faiths and belief systems at the time, with most people - slave or free - holding their own rituals to whichever god or gods they chose to worship.

Lucius Metellus Anguis returns in the second book of the *Eagles and Dragons* series, *Killing the Hydra*.

For more discussion on the period, loads of photos, some maps, and *The World of Children of Apollo* blog series, go to www.eaglesanddragonspublishing.com.

Adam Alexander Haviaras
March, 2013
Toronto, Ontario

GLOSSARY

aedes – a temple; sometimes a room

aedituus – a keeper of a temple

aestivus – relating to summer; a summer camp or pasture

agora – Greek word for the central gathering place of a city or settlement

ala – an auxiliary cavalry unit

amita – an aunt

amphitheatre – an oval or round arena where people enjoyed gladiatorial combat and other spectacles

anguis – a dragon, serpent or hydra; also used to refer to the 'Draco' constellation

angusticlavius – 'narrow stripe' on a tunic; Lucius Metellus Anguis is a *tribunus angusticlavius*

apodyterium – the changing room of a bath house

aquila – a legion's eagle standard which was made of gold during the Empire

aquilifer – senior standard bearer in a Roman legion who carried the legion's eagle

ara – an altar

armilla – an arm band that served as a military decoration

augur – a priest who observes natural occurrences to determine if omens are good or bad; a soothsayer

aureus – a Roman gold coin; worth twenty-five silver *denarii* auriga – a charioteer

ballista – an ancient missile-firing weapon that fired either heavy 'bolts' or rocks

bireme – a galley with two banks of oars on either side

bracae – knee or full-length breeches originally worn by barbarians but adopted by the Romans

caldarium – the 'hot' room of a bath house; from the Latin *calidus*

caligae – military shoes or boots with or without hobnail soles

cardo – a hinge-point or central, north-south thoroughfare in a fort or settlement, the *cardo maximus*

castrum – a Roman fort

cataphract – a heavy cavalryman; both horse and rider were armoured

cena- the principal, afternoon meal of the Romans

chiton – a long woollen tunic of Greek fashion

chryselephantine – ancient Greek sculptural medium using gold and ivory; used for cult statues

civica – relating to 'civic'; the civic crown was awarded to one who saved a Roman citizen in war

civitas – a settlement or commonwealth; an administrative centre in tribal areas of the empire clepsydra – a water clock

cognomen – the surname of a Roman which distinguished the branch of a gens

collegia – an association or guild; e.g. *collegium pontificum* means 'college of priests'

colonia – a colony; also used for a farm or estate

consul – an honorary position in the Empire; during the Republic they presided over the Senate

contubernium – a military unit of ten men within a century who shared a tent

contus – a long cavalry spear

cornicen – the horn blower in a legion

cornu – a curved military horn

cornucopia – the horn of plenty

corona – a crown; often used as a military decoration

cubiculum – a bedchamber

curule – refers to the chair upon which Roman magistrates would sit (e.g. *curule aedile*)

decumanus – refers to the tenth; the *decumanus maximus* ran east to west in a Roman fort or city

denarius – A Roman silver coin; worth one hundred brass *sestertii*

dignitas – a Roman's worth, honour and reputation

domus – a home or house

draco – a military standard in the shape of a dragon's head first used by Sarmatians and adopted by Rome

draconarius – a military standard bearer who held the draco

eques – a horseman or rider

equites – cavalry; of the order of knights in ancient Rome

fabrica – a workshop

fabula – an untrue or mythical story; a play or drama

familia – a Roman's household, including slaves

flammeum – a flame-coloured bridal veil

forum – an open square or marketplace; also a place of public business (e.g. the *Forum Romanum*)

fossa – a ditch or trench; a part of defensive earthworks

frigidarium – the 'cold room' of a bath house; a cold plunge pool

funeraticia – from *funereus* for funeral; the *collegia funeraticia* assured all received decent burial

garum – a fish sauce that was very popular in the Roman world

gladius – a Roman short sword

gorgon – a terrifying visage of a woman with snakes for hair; also known as Medusa greaves – armoured shin and knee guards worn by high-ranking officers

groma – a surveying instrument; used for accurately marking out towns, marching camps and forts etc.

hasta – a spear or javelin

horreum – a granary

hydraulis – a water organ

hypocaust – area beneath a floor in a home or bath house that is heated by a furnace

imperator – a commander or leader; commander-in-chief

insula – a block of flats leased to the poor

intervallum – the space between two palisades

itinere – a road or itinerary; the journey

lanista – a gladiator trainer

lemure – a ghost

libellus – a little book or diary

lituus – the curved staff or wand of an augur; also a cavalry trumpet

lorica – body armour; can be made of mail, scales or metal strips; can also refer to a cuirass

lustratio – a ritual purification, usually involving a sacrifice manica – handcuffs; also refers to the long sleeves of a tunic

marita - wife

maritus - husband

matertera – a maternal aunt

maximus – meaning great or 'of greatness'

missum – used as a call for mercy by the crowd for a gladiator who had fought bravely

murmillo – a heavily armed gladiator with a helmet, shield and sword

nomen – the gens of a family (as opposed to *cognomen* which was the specific branch of a wider gens)

nones – the fifth day of every month in the Roman calendar

novendialis – refers to the ninth day

nutrix – a wet-nurse or foster mother

nymphaeum – a pool, fountain or other monument dedicated to the nymphs

officium – an official employment; also a sense of duty or respect

onager – a powerful catapult used by the Romans; named after a wild ass because of its kick optio – the officer beneath a centurion; second-in-command within a century

palaestra – the open space of a gymnasium where wrestling, boxing and other such events were practiced

palliatus – indicating someone clad in a pallium

pancration – a no-holds-barred sport that combined wrestling and boxing

parentalis – of parents or ancestors; (e.g. *Parentalia* was a festival in honour of the dead)

parma – a small, round shield often used by light-armed troops; also referred to as *parmula*

pater – a father

pax – peace; a state of peace as opposed to war

peregrinus – a strange or foreign person or thing

peristylum – a peristyle; a colonnade around a building; can be inside or outside of a building or home

phalerae – decorative medals or discs worn by centurions or other officers on the chest

pilum – a heavy javelin used by Roman legionaries

plebeius – of the plebeian class or the people

pontifex – a Roman high priest

popa – a junior priest or temple servant

primus pilus – the senior centurion of a legion who commanded the first cohort

pronaos – the porch or entrance to a building such as a temple

protome – an adornment on a work of art, usually a frontal view of an animal

pteruges – protective leather straps used on armour; often a leather skirt for officers

pugio – a dagger

quadriga – a four-horse chariot

quinqueremis – a ship with five banks of oars

retiarius – a gladiator who fights with a net and trident

rosemarinus – the herb rosemary

rusticus – of the country; e.g. a *villa rustica* was a country villa

sacrum – sacred or holy; e.g. the *via sacra* or 'sacred way'

schola – a place of learning and learned discussion

scutum – the large, rectangular, curved shield of a legionary

secutor – a gladiator armed with a sword and shield; often pitted against a *retiarius*

sestertius – a Roman silver coin worth a quarter *denarius*

sica – a type of dagger

signum – a military standard or banner

signifer – a military standard bearer

spatha – an auxiliary trooper's long sword; normally used by cavalry because of its longer reach

spina – the ornamented, central median in stadiums such as the Circus Maximus in Rome

stadium – a measure of length approximately 607 feet; also refers to a race course

stibium – *antimony*, which was used for dyeing eyebrows by women in the ancient world

stoa – a columned, public walkway or portico for public use; often used by merchants to sell their wares

stola – a long outer garment worn by Roman women

strigilis – a curved scraper used at the baths to remove oil and grime from the skin

taberna – an inn or tavern

tabula – a Roman board game similar to backgammon; also a writing-tablet for keeping records

tepidarium – the 'warm room' of a bath house

tessera – a piece of mosaic paving; a die for playing; also a small wooden plaque

testudo – a tortoise formation created by troops' interlocking shields

thraex – a gladiator in Thracian armour

titulus – a title of honour or honourable designation

torques – also 'torc'; a neck band worn by Celtic peoples and adopted by Rome as a military decoration

trepidatio – trepidation, anxiety or alarm

tribunus – a senior officer in an imperial legion; there were six per legion, each commanding a cohort

triclinium – a dining room

tunica – a sleeved garment worn by both men and women

ustrinum – the site of a funeral pyre

vallum – an earthen wall or rampart with a palisade

veterinarius – a veterinary surgeon in the Roman army

vexillarius – a Roman standard bearer who carried the *vexillum* for each unit

vexillum – a standard carried in each unit of the Roman army

vicus – a settlement of civilians living outside a Roman fort

vigiles – Roman firemen; literally 'watchmen'

vitis – the twisted 'vinerod' of a Roman centurion; a centurion's emblem of office

vittae – a ribbon or band

ACKNOWLEDGMENTS

As with any novel, especially a debut, there are a great many people who deserve my sincere thanks for all the help and support they have given me over the years.

Firstly, my parents Stefanos and Jeanette, for without them my love of history and story would not have come to full fruition had they not encouraged it from a young age. They read until my young lids closed to dream, and made all manner of books accessible to me. Thank you.

The late poet, Leila Pepper, friend and kindred spirit gave me critical advice and encouragement at the early stages of writing *Children of Apollo*. Her words and enthusiasm kept me going and pushed me to experiment with the craft. Would that this true daughter of the Muses were here to see the finished product. Thank you, *Danny*, wherever you are…

Mr. Geoffrey Ashe of Glastonbury, England. Though unaware of the help you provided, I thank you for your inspiring work and encouraging words at a time of academic crisis. Sincere thanks also go to Steve Michalicka for his helpful and encouraging feedback in a last round of test reading.

Much gratitude to Constantinos Podotas who created an amazing book trailer and whose guru marketing advice has proved most helpful to this indie author.

I am by no stretch of the imagination a Latin scholar or linguist and so I have had to rely heavily on a few people for help navigating the forest that is Latin tense and declension etc. My thanks to Tom and Eleftheria Crouch for revising my poor Latin and providing much needed input. I am very grateful. Needless to say, any errors that remain are entirely my own.

Thanks must also be extended to Kostis Diassitis of Athens for all his advice on military history and tactics, as well as his additional revisions of my Latin grammar. Long conversations into the night, accompanied by numerous glasses of ouzo helped to make history even more fun. Giassou levendi!

I am forever indebted to my good friend and reviewer, artist and historian, Maria Carmen Brunello who managed to smile with sincere excitement when I handed her a first draft printout of the manuscript that could have crushed a small dog. Her input, editing skills and enthusiasm were essential. Gracias!

Very sincere thanks to a few more folks, especially, Andrew Fenwick of Dundee, Scotland, fellow historian, Roman re-enactor and expert on all things ancient and medieval. Thanks for the long conversations and the tips on Roman battle commands. Your memory is impressively druidic, your friendship invaluable.

To Kevin Blair from Washington State, all my thanks for being my travel buddy and daring the Sahara with me all those years ago. It was one of the greatest adventures; from visiting the cities of Roman North Africa, to angry haggling in the bazaars, to dealing with aggressive, riffle-wielding Berber horsemen. Never a dull moment. Don't eat the soup.

My close friend, Janik Lamontagne, deserves many thanks for being there at the end of the writing. Thanks for letting us crash in your house when we came back to Canada from England with a load of suitcases and no plan. All those visits to the coffee house certainly helped to ease the culture shock of our return. Merci, mon ami.

To my darling girls, Alexandra and Athena, thank you for always making me smile. Your childish enthusiasm is perfectly contagious. I promise to keep the bedtime stories exciting and happy ever after.

Finally, the greatest debt imaginable goes to my wife, Angelina. Without her unwavering faith, encouragement and no-nonsense editing I would not have come very far. Every writer should be so blessed.

Adam Alexander Haviaras
March, 2013
Toronto, Ontario

ABOUT THE AUTHOR

Adam Alexander Haviaras is a writer and historian who has studied ancient and medieval history and archaeology in Canada and the United Kingdom. He currently resides in Toronto with his wife and children. *Children of Apollo* is his first novel.

Other works by Adam Alexander Haviaras:

The Eagles and Dragons series

A Dragon among the Eagles (Prequel)

Children of Apollo (Book I)

Killing the Hydra (Book II)

Warriors of Epona (Book III)

Isle of the Blessed (Book IV)

The Stolen Throne (Book V)

The Carpathian Interlude Series

Immortui (Part I)

Lykoi (Part II)

Thanatos (Part III)

The Mythologia Series

Chariot of the Son

Heart of Fire: A Novel of the Ancient Olympics

Saturnalia: A Tale of Wickedness and Redemption in Ancient Rome

Titles in the Historia Non-fiction Series

Historia I: Celtic Literary Archetypes in *The Mabinogion*: A Study of the Ancient Tale of *Pwyll, Lord of Dyved*

Historia II: Arthurian Romance and the Knightly Ideal: A study of Medieval Romantic Literature and its Effect upon Warrior Culture in Europe

Historia III: *Y Gododdin*: The Last Stand of Three Hundred Britons - Understanding People and Events during Britain's Heroic Age

Historia IV: Camelot: The Historical, Archaeological and Toponymic Considerations for South Cadbury Castle as King Arthur's Capital

STAY CONNECTED

To connect with Adam and learn more about the ancient world visit www.eaglesanddragonspublishing.com

Sign up for the Eagles and Dragons Publishing Newsletter at www.eaglesanddragonspublishing.com/newsletter-join-the-legions/ to receive a FREE BOOK, first access to new releases and posts on ancient history, special offers, and much more!

Readers can also connect with Adam on Twitter @AdamHaviaras and Instagram @ adam_haviaras.

On Facebook you can 'Like' the Eagles and Dragons page to get regular updates on new historical fiction and fantasy from Eagles and Dragons Publishing.

90545009R10297

Made in the USA
San Bernardino, CA
13 October 2018